KNIGHTS WITHOUT ARMOR

KNIGHTS WITHOUT ARMOR

A Practical Guide for Men in Quest of Masculine Soul

AARON R. KIPNIS, Ph.D.
Foreword by Robert A. Johnson

JEREMY P. TARCHER, INC.
Los Angeles

Library of Congress Cataloging-in-Publication Data

Kipnis, Aaron R.
　Knights without armor: a practical guide for men in quest of masculine soul/
Aaron R. Kipnis; foreword by Robert A. Johnson.—1st ed.
　　p.　　cm.
　Includes bibliographical references
　ISBN 0-87477-658-9: $19.95
　1. Men—Psychology. 2. Masculinity (Psychology) I. Title.
HQ1090.K57　1991　　　　　　　　　　　　　　　　　　　91-14820
305.31—dc20　　　　　　　　　　　　　　　　　　　　　　　　CIP

Copyright © 1991 by Aaron R. Kipnis

All rights reserved. No part of this work may be reproduced or transmitted in any form by any means, electronic or mechanical, including photocopying and recording, or by any information storage or retrieval system, except as may be expressly permitted by the 1976 Copyright Act or in writing by the publisher. Requests for such permissions should be addressed to:

Jeremy P. Tarcher, Inc.
5858 Wilshire Blvd., Suite 200
Los Angeles, CA 90036

Distributed by St. Martin's Press, New York

Manufactured in the United States of America
10　9　8　7　6　5　4　3　2　1

First Edition

For my Father:
Tough and tender
Foolish and wise
From city boy to mountain man
May the trout ever leap gladly for your hook

Contents

Introduction … 1

Part I. The Problem with Men … 9

1. The Heroic Male … 11

A Few Nights Out with the Guys 12
The Knights Lay Down Their Armor 15
The Hero's Folly 18
Male Oppression and Inequality: Making Hardened Men out of Sensitive Boys 20
Nature's Double Standard: Biological Differences between Men and Women 23
A Foot in the Balls, and Other Boyhood Games 25
Creating Killers in High School 28
Dying for Dollars 31
The First Task of Men: To Admit That We Have Been Wounded 33

2. The Wounded Male … 35

The Social-Services Gap: You Can't Afford to Stumble, You've Got No Place to Fall 36
Staying Alive: How Men Neglect Their Health 38
The Wounded Body: Men's Inadequate Medical Care 42
The Wounded Penis 43
Fathers Change Diapers, Too 45
The Inequities of Divorce 48
False Allegations of Child Abuse 50
The Wound of the Exiled Father 53
Abortion is Also a Man's Issue 55
Violence Against Men 56
The Second Task of Men: To Begin Healing One Another through Examining Our Wounds 58

3. Angry Women and Feminized Men — 61

Turning Away from the Goddess 62
Are Men Really to Blame for Everything? 64
The Male-Bashing Media 68
Friction between Women and Men at Work 70
The Real War between the Sexes Is Violent, Abusive, and Deadly 74
Feminized Men 77
Separation from the Feminine: A Step toward Mutual Balance 80
The Last Angry Men 83
The Third Task of Men: To Rebuild Self-Esteem on Deep Masculine Foundations 84

Part II. Reclaiming the Masculine Soul — 87

4. Authentic Masculinity and the New Male Manifesto — 89

Authentic Men Who Have Inspired Us 92
The New Male Manifesto 93
Shaping a New Image 96
Radical Masculinity 97
Heroic, Feminized, and Authentic Masculinity (Chart) 99
The New Renaissance Man 102
The Fourth Task of Men: To Break Out of Old Stereotypes and Claim Our Diversity 103

5. Beyond Patriarchy and Matriarchy: Our Ancient Roots in the Earth — 105

The Roots of Patriarchy 107
Authentic Masculinity and the Gaia Hypothesis 108
Earth Mother, Stone Father: Ancient Traces of Earth-Based Masculinity 112
A Brief Chronology of the Rise and Fall of Earth-Based Masculinity 114
The Destruction of the Earth Father Cults 116
The Taming of the Ancient Wild Bull-Man 119
I Seem to Be an Us 122
The Fifth Task of Men: To Reclaim the Ancient, Sacred Images of Masculinity 124

6. The Forgotten and Forbidden Sacred Images of Men — 125

The Lost Fathers of the Earth 126
Moon Fathers 129
Returning to the Earth 130
Wild Gods of Deep, Fluid Feeling 131

Shiva, the Wild, Dancing God 134
Gods of Laughter and Sacred Play 136
Playful Coyote and Other Sly Rogues 139
The Trickster as Outlaw, Peacemaker, and Jester 141
The Nature God of Shameless Masculine Sensuality 146
The Sixth Task of Men: To Apply the Myths of
   Masculine Soul to Our Daily Lives 150

Part III. Revisioning Masculinity: Men's New Roles in a Changing World 153

7. *The Nurtured Son and the Initiated Young Man* 155

Our Fathers, Our Children, Our Selves 157
Zeus: The Uninitiated Sky Father 158
The Grounded Father 159
To Become a Man 162
Initiation and the Masculine Soul 165
A Boy Needs a Tribe and Elder Males 168
Hamlet: The Uninitiated Male 170
Problems with the Uninitiated Male 172
The Seventh Task of Men: To Rediscover Male Initiation
   and Heal the Wounds between Fathers and Sons 174

8. *Love, Work, and Dreams* 177

The Five F's and Other Sexual Initiations 178
Women Gracefully Drop Their Handkerchiefs As Men Stumble
   Trying to Pick Them Up 180
Men Who Give Too Much: The Male Side of Codependence 182
The Way It Was 185
You *Can* Teach Old Knights New Tricks 187
Pan Sexuality versus Eros Sexuality 189
Right Livelihood: Practical and Sacred Dreams 190
The Zen of Work 192
Hunting: The Traditional Work of Men 195
Hunting in the Twenty-First Century 198
The Eighth Task of Men: To Love and Work
   in Ways That Heal Our Lives 199

9. *The Elder Male: A Nonrenewable Resource* 201

There Are No Old Heroes—Only Wise or Foolish Old Men 203
Our Grandfathers 206

The Y Chromosome: Men's Genetic Resonance
with the Ancients 210
Plumbing the Depths of the Masculine Soul 212
Facing the Faceless God 214
Death, the Rapist 217
The Death of the Hero: Communing with the Deep 219
Spiraling Down into the Center of Our Lives 221
The Ninth Task of Men: To Restore a Connection with Our Ancestors and
Come to Terms with Our Mortality 223

Part IV: Rebuilding the Community and the World 225

10. *Meetings with Ordinary Men* 227

Building a Men's Lodge 229
Now that We're All Here, What Do We Say? What Should We Do? 231
Sharing Power in a Men's Group 234
Breaking the Spell 236
Bang the Drum and Raise a Joyful Noise 238
Dancing the Dream Awake in the World 242
Healing the Ancient Wounds between Men and Women 244
The Tenth Task of Men: To Build Male Community
and Begin Healing the Wounds between the Sexes 247

11. *Toward a New Male Psychology* 249

The Great Mother and Lost Father in Psychology 251
Nurture over Nature: Is Society to Blame? 254
Are Our Schools Deficient in Masculine Soul? 257
Nature over Nurture: Is Biology to Blame? 260
The Secret Language of Men 262
Men in Psychotherapy 265
Sexism toward Male Clients 269
Are Men Really More Deviant Than Women? 273
Where Do We Go from Here? 276
The Eleventh Task of Men: To Develop a
Masculine-Affirming Psychology 277

Conclusion 279

The Final Task of Men: To Continue Reawakening
the Masculine Soul 280

Men's Resources 283

Notes 285

Acknowledgments

First and foremost, I want to thank Alan Rinzler, my editor. He brought a potent male perspective to this book grounded in his experience as a man, a father of five, and a psychotherapist on the front lines of urban community mental health. With precision and thoughtfulness, he patiently guided both me and this book through numerous revisions. In the spirt of a true male mentor he brought an elegant synthesis of fierce confrontation and gentle encouragement to every step of the process.

Connie Zweig, my chief editor, has seen deeply into the core of this book from its inception. Also fierce and kind, she has been an inspired book mother, like a lioness both protecting and reprimanding her cub. Her understanding of depth psychology, combined with her enlightened feminist perspective, has brought balance to the work.

Jeremy P. Tarcher, my publisher, has taken a very personal interest in the manuscript and been actively engaged as it developed. It took courage to publish a book about men in an industry that has historically been geared toward the female reader. For that, and for all his support for me as a writer, I am indebted.

My agent, Katinka Matson of John Brockman Associates, made it possible for me to stay focused on the writing of this book by consistently taking excellent care of all the business details.

I am grateful to the poet Robert Bly for his compassion and vision. He inspired portions of this book and pointed the way into the evocative wilderness of masculine soul. Also, over the last fifteen years, the archetypal psychologist James Hillman has been another hermeneutic guide teaching me a new way of psychological thinking. This has been valuable and transformative. Warren Farrell raised my consciousness about male oppression. This has been liberating.

The faculty and students of Pacifica Graduate Institute have provided invaluable guidance and support, as well as a forum for many spirited debates on this material. In particular, Dr. Diane

Skafte and Dr. Charles Asher have read portions of the manuscript and helped me integrate my new ideas about male psychology into the existing field of psychological theory.

Dr. David Thompson has done an amazing and thorough job of fact checking and compiling statistical research for the book. This was a frustrating and painstaking task in a society that keeps many records on women's issues, but few concerning men's. Fredric Hayward of Men's Rights, Inc., and Tom Williamson from the National Coalition of Free Men also made valuable contributions to the research effort.

Elizabeth Hingston has continually presented the conscious woman's perspective on this work, grounded in her experience as a mythologist, ceremonialist, and leader of women's groups. Through her many readings of earlier drafts, she has attempted to keep me honest. She and our eleven-year-old daughter, Noelani, have kept alive the love and play in our relationship. Without their alliance, their understanding about my long hours locked in my study, and their unconditional support, I don't know how I could have faced the solitary discipline of writing this book.

Most of all, I owe an incalculable debt to the hundreds of men, of all ages and segments of our culture, who have courageously, sincerely, and honestly shared their inner lives with me. I am also grateful to the small, pioneering group of writers on men's issues whose works are referenced in the text.

Finally, to the men of the new knights of the round table: I remain awed, honored, and delighted by the depth of honesty and breadth of adventure you have shared with me. I am grateful for the healing and inspiration that have come out of our work together. Thank you for your willingness to share our experiences with the readers of this book. May you always have love, money, health, soul, and the time to enjoy them.

Foreword

The knights of ancient times were heavily armored from head to toe. These men in steel were invincible in battle—until the crossbow was invented. This new technology, introduced in the late medieval times, gave arrows the force to penetrate even the thickest armor. The armored knight quickly became a thing of the past as men realized that they could no longer remain safe behind their impervious coverings. However, the knightly ideals of chivalry and masculine honor, and the spiritual quest for the Holy Grail persisted for centuries.

Today, men doing battle in the marketplace have donned a new sort of armor. Many powerful men have constructed a heroic personality that is hard, inflexible and, like the armor of old, heavy to drag around. It is difficult to feel much pleasure or joy in life when one is burdened with a self-image that says: in order to be a man you must be tough and cool as steel. In today's society, however, men are discovering, like their medieval counterparts, that they are no longer impervious to the armor-piercing arrows slung by people who have lost connection to their souls.

Environmental degradation and our myriad social crises touch everyone. Even the socially elite are not protected from the hole in the ozone, global warming, and the rising levels of violence in our culture. We are all vulnerable; yet many of us are afraid to acknowledge that vulnerability. Many men today are like Hamlet, of whom I wrote in my latest book, *Transformation: Understanding the Three Levels of Masculine Consciousness*. These men are immobilized and unable to take decisive action to help heal the wounds of the world.

Men are beginning to realize that in order to face the challenges ahead, they must find a way to remove the armor that immobilizes them. This armor makes it difficult to feel much and also renders men unable to tend their own wounds, which are festering beneath their hardened exteriors. In order to remain powerful without their armor, men must find a new way of being in the world. They must cultivate a new self-image that accurately reflects what it truly means to be a man, which is the quest undertaken by those whose lives are examined in this book.

The men who speak in *Knights Without Armor* are facing the same dilemma shared by many modern men. They have climbed the ladder of success only to find that it was set up against the wrong wall. Many men who cannot bear the mute suffering of alienation attempt to take refuge in drugs, alcohol, workaholism, and sex-obsessions characteristic of immature masculinity. Through the course of this book, however, these new knights of the round table learn to meet the challenges of life by rising to a new level of consciousness and deepening their awareness of the inner aspects of the masculine soul. These men aid one another in claiming their capacity for authentic, mature masculinity and recovering from the wounds of their past addictive behaviors. They candidly speak about their pain and inspire one another to discover new ways of thinking and living that can bring greater happiness into their lives.

The myth of the lone hero, who conquers all through the force of his will, is no longer the image that inspires the modern man in search of his soul. And the idealized feminine—whether wife, mother, lover, goddess, or inner woman—is no longer seen as the sole source of nurturance, healing and wholeness for man. A new myth for a new time emerges in this book, bringing a new dimension to the spiritual quest undertaken by the knights of other ages. The image that becomes apparent from the dialogues of these new knights is of a soulful, life-generating, sensitive, and joyful man who is also potent, fierce, and powerful in the world. Through cultivating male friends who risk revealing who they really are behind their iron masks, these men break out of the isolation that plagues so many contemporary men.

This group of men learns how to create a safe container that supports their innate, masculine capacity for healing. They build a forum for celebrating one another's successes, expressing their grief over losses, and voicing appreciation to one another for who they authentically are. These men discover a much more exciting quest ahead of them, a quest which knows no limit, a quest which does not lead merely to the mid-life query of despair: "Is this all there is?"

Building upon all of the work that has come before, Aaron Kipnis represents a new generation of male psychologists who have gone beyond the patriarchal formulation of the nineteenth century and the feminist revisions of the twentieth century. He lays the foundations for a new male psychology that is more applicable to the challenges of a new millennium. His revisioning of male myths and intriguing perspectives on archetypal psychology have opened a new door into the male psyche.

Knights Without Armor weds ancient myths of masculinity to the subjective experience of modern men and the objective perspectives of hundreds of studies from various scientific fields. What emerges is a fresh vision and new understanding of men that points the way for a new male psychology and spirituality.

The book presents a rich adventure of self-discovery for the male reader who will undoubtedly hear many of his own issues expressed by the male voices in this book. Women readers will gain new insights into the inner lives of men, deepen their understanding of the forces that shape the men in their lives, and learn how to support men's changes in a changing world. This knowledge will be helpful in improving relations between men and women.

I hope you enjoy the book. I feel confident that it will be inspiring to both men and women on their own particular quests for soul.

ROBERT A. JOHNSON
May 1991

Introduction

This is a book for men and the women who care about them. It has developed from my work with male clients and my dialogues with thousands of men over the last two decades. I've tried to take a hard look at the cultural illusions that underlie many of our dysfunctional beliefs about the basic nature of masculinity. I've also tried to present a new vision that is more life-supporting for men and applicable to the challenges presented by a new millennium.

In this task I have been encouraged and nourished by many men in the equal-rights, recovery, and mythopoetic wings of the men's movement. I have also been blessed with the support of many visionary women who are attempting to work with men in alliance.

FEELING GOOD AGAIN ABOUT BEING MALE

This work attempts to bring compassionate understanding to men. Men who feel that something is wrong with their role in the social order, who feel angry, frustrated, or confused about what it means to be a man today, who feel trapped or disappointed and wish for more happiness and fulfillment in their lives, who feel hopeful and long for more wild magic, love, and beauty—these men will find solidarity with the multitude of male voices that are raised in the following pages.

A number of clear themes have emerged from the men's groups I have participated in over the years. It is obvious that there are significant problems with the dominant cultural model of masculinity as it is currently imagined. Many men report that they feel alienated, alone, remote from the world, disconnected from their families and the community at large. They report that they have few—especially few male—friends and confidants. Underlying the numbness, anger, and frustration many men experience is a well of grief that is often difficult to touch and express, yet floods the inner life or drowns the outer world of relationships. Alcoholism, drug abuse, workaholism, obsessive sexuality, numb complacency, and other dysfunctional behaviors are increasing in reaction to the underlying pain and discomfort many men experience.

For most men, admitting that we have problems betrays our masculine self-image as problem solvers. A ruined career, broken marriage, heart attack, car accident, work injury, or other serious loss is often the shock that brings a man face-to-face with his real limitations. By then, it is often, sadly, too late. Most men are caught in a painful double bind that prevents them from seeking help from other men because it is humiliating for them even to admit they need help.

That is why I have written this book. It provides an opportunity for us to think about these issues together in the privacy of the written page. If at the end of this reading you want to connect to a world of men who are aiding one another during the radical transformation of our culture, that opportunity will be there. You are not alone.

A NOTE TO FEMALE READERS

This book is also for women who want to understand what men are like inside, how they really are different from women, and what their struggles are at this time in the evolution of Western culture. I hope women who want to improve relationships with the men in their lives and hold a vision of a society with genuine gender equality and partnership will find insight here into the dynamics that separate the sexes and continue to wound them. I think women who continue to view themselves as victims of male dominance, who blame men, and who are invested in the belief that men are vastly more privileged than they are will have their perspective significantly challenged.

Some women have expressed fear that the creation of a forum for men's issues, such as the emerging men's movement, will somehow take away from their own political and cultural liberation. That certainly is not the intention of this book. Rather, I have attempted to produce a work that is not reactionary or oppositional to women, yet at the same time unapologetically addresses the significant gender-specific issues that men face today. I have also attempted to avoid the trap, which has been shadowing gender politics over the last few decades, of becoming polarized, strident, other-blaming, or victimized—all of which are counterproductive to the ultimate balance and partnership that most of us seek.

Men are not encouraged to speak out with their feelings. It is the measured, even response and commentary of Henry Kissinger, John Sununu, George Bush, or Ted Koppel—not the impassioned presentation of Jesse Jackson—that is the vogue of male expression today. Yet women have successfully found a forum—through numerous books, articles, and organizations such as NOW—for voicing their anger and their grief. Part of our work as men has been to find access to those feelings as well, even at the risk of our efforts being perceived as threatening to women or uncool to other men.

The line between self-empowerment and honest confrontation on one hand and self-indulgence and covert shaming on the other is razor thin indeed. If I have crossed that line in places and deepened wounds, that was not my intention. Today men must walk along that sharpened edge to tell the truth of our experience. We cannot reveal the whole truth without acknowledging that many of us have, at various times, felt victimized, scapegoated, manipulated, dominated, or abused by women.

Early feminist writers had to confront numerous patriarchal beliefs about the limited abilities of women held by both women and men. Similarly, new male writing and research will bring us into direct confrontation with patriarchal myths about the abilities and rights of men. They will challenge matriarchal myths regarding the essential nature of men and masculinity as well.

I hope that this book will improve relationships between men and women, but, unlike so many popular psychology books today, that is not its primary focus. My belief is that positive change is more likely in a non-goal-directed atmosphere of uncompromising love, honest confrontation, and unconditional support. If a man who is in relationship with a woman starts to feel better about himself, his relationship with her will automatically improve.

ABOUT THE AUTHOR

I bring an eclectic past to my current work in psychology. In addition to a twenty-year background in humanistic, transpersonal, and depth psychology, I draw from my experience as a home and boat builder, feature-film set artist, performing artist, events producer, and creator of a successful holistic health center.

After completing graduate work in psychology at Sonoma State University in California, I continued training and research at several private graduate institutes that specialize in different psychological approaches. My private practice with clients is oriented toward archetypal, post-Jungian psychology. I have also taught meditation internationally and have led numerous groups in dreamwork, gestalt, gender issues, and wilderness experience, teaching in high schools, universities, and human-potential centers.

Currently I make my home in western Sonoma County, California, where I'm rebuilding a house and tending a bountiful garden with my companion, Liz, and our daughter, Noelani. When not working with individual clients or teaching, I devote my time to a number of men's groups, both as a man pursuing my own personal recovery and as a facilitator supporting other men in this work. Liz and I are codirectors of the Pangaea Institute for Gender Studies, which hosts men's and women's groups, encouraging dialogue and gender-reconciliation work. I am also an associate of the Redwood Men's Center and an editor of the *Redwood Men's Center Re-Source*. Recently, I have been a guest lecturer on gender issues at a number of universities and institutes that are training new clinicians in psychology.

My interest in men's work began about twenty years ago. During my undergraduate training in psychology I worked full-time, for two years, as a counselor and director of wilderness programs at a residential treatment center for disturbed and delinquent adolescent boys. Many of these boys lacked fathers. Consequently I did extensive research into rites of passage and other initiations into manhood as an alternative therapeutic methodology. This led to some rewarding experiences with the boys, both in the wilderness and in the home.

I began to believe that one of the things that was making us dysfunctional as a culture was that we had lost an essential connection to nature and a living body of myth that could support a healthy society. I continued working with ritual, ceremony, dreams, and wilderness experiences with adults. Much of my work in the arts, as I gravitated in and out of the field of psychology over the years, also had to do with community-based ritual.

Indian-style sweat lodges, vision quests, encounter groups, and wilderness experiences—often involving work with separate groups of women and men who were then brought together—revealed deep wounds within us all. In an attempt to gain deeper insight, I withdrew for several years and lived as a monk, studying with yogis in monasteries in India, the Swiss mountains, and

Germany. I returned to the United States and continued studies with elder men of the Native American church and with other men and women involved in earth-based religions. I was in search of personal healing and in quest of techniques for collective healing that were not clearly emerging from my studies in psychology.

I often found it a challenge to hold the paradox between the inward, subtle experiences of a spiritual seeker and the outward, rough-and-tumble world of working with men on construction sites and in performing-arts productions, which I returned to from time to time in order to make a living. Academia did not often value what I experienced as the simple, vital, honest, and frequently playful experience of physical work alongside unpretentious men. Unfortunately, during the course of this hard-driving lifestyle, alcohol abuse crept into my life.

Its gift was that recovery then became the focus of my personal work with men. I began to realize that the spiritual journey is essentially a collective one, in contradistinction to the solo quests I had undertaken in the past. As my attention returned to professional psychology and I continued to meet with other men, we became more concerned with building healthy inner lives together than with creating more *things* in the world.

In recent years, a number of men have begun to seek new visions and alternatives to the old ones offered by the traditional culture and the newer ones offered by women. Men in my groups were always looking for writings that related specifically to men's issues. Although there were thousands of books for women, there was little available for us. I decided in 1986 to begin writing this book for men in the hope of lending some shape and support to the new visions for men that seemed to be emerging. One of these new visions is concerned with recovering the masculine soul.

MEN IN QUEST OF THE MASCULINE SOUL

In the first section of this book, "The Problem with Men," we will explore the many ways in which men are oppressed and wounded by virtue of the traditional heroic male sex-role model and we will examine the source of our wounds. We will retrace the ways we have lost our connection to a rich depth of feeling and aliveness within us—the masculine soul.

Specific issues concerning the psycho-social development and cultural oppression of gay men and cultural or racial minorities are, for the most part, not separately addressed in this book. There are many other texts and articles that do just that. In many cases, I have focused on less obvious aspects of male oppression in an attempt to bring the whole subject into a wider arena. This broader view holds the assumption that what oppresses any man, by virtue of his gender, affects us all. The inimical aspects of the socialization of men in this culture touch every man. The sanctions against those who diverge from rigid definitions of the dominant culture's expectations for men wound us all *to varying degrees* regardless of our sexual, cultural, economic, or racial affiliation.

This work is distinct from the movement over the last few decades that has encouraged men to become more feminine, to get in touch with their feminine side. Nor does it, in the style of male antifeminist backlash literature, hark back to an anachronistic, dominating, and heroic model of masculinity. Rather, a third view emerges.

In the second section of this book, "Reclaiming the Masculine Soul," we will take a journey in a different direction—in quest of a new image for male psychology. In an attempt to understand the cultural and psychological beliefs and imaginal structures that give rise to the sociological phenomena cited in the first section, we will descend into the ancient, sacred mythologies of diverse civilizations. The experiences of modern men will be contrasted with ancient and cross-cultural images. Contemporary ideas in archetypal psychology about deep or authentic masculinity that emerge from these mythic structures embedded in the male psyche also will be considered. These new templates, through which we will view men's lives, may be more in balance with nature and with the political, economic, and social needs of women than the older dominating or recently feminized ideals for men. Simultaneously, these images support the life-affirming, soulful, creative, vital, and nurturing capacities of men. An affirming view toward many misunderstood aspects of masculinity will be elaborated.

The third section of this book, "Revisioning Masculinity," will offer some possible solutions and avenues of approach to many current problems that are specific to men. Child-rearing, adolescent initiation, work, love, marriage, individuation, mentorship, old age, and dying will be viewed through an image of masculinity that embraces sensitivity to feelings, grace, gentleness, creativity, and responsibility, without abandoning traditional masculine values of courage, strength, irreverence, perseverance, wildness, and potency. This section also attempts to support an increased appreciation for the healthy and necessary function that the father provides in the psychological development of his sons and daughters, the risk that overinvolved mothers present for boys, and the neglected role of elders.

The fourth section, "Rebuilding the Community and the World," will discuss the pros and cons of the various wings of the men's movement and provide some practical information for starting and continuing to develop your own men's group. We will explore some routes along which the ancient wounds between the sexes may begin to heal, in the spirit of a gender reconciliation that is empowering and ennobling to both men and women. New approaches to traditional psychology will be suggested, which are more suitable to working with men than much of what is being offered by today's educators and mental-health professionals.

At the end of each chapter I name specific tasks men need to undertake in order to change, heal themselves, and adapt to a rapidly shifting social reality. And at the conclusion of this book you will find a list of resources for men who want more information or opportunities to connect with other men who are working with all these issues. My address is also listed in case you wish to communicate to me your feelings about this book or to share the experiences of your own quest for masculine soul. I hope this book will aid you on that quest.

PART I

The Problem with Men

CHAPTER 1

The Heroic Male

Every hero becomes a bore at last.
    Emerson

Something is stirring in the hearts of men. We're beginning to come up hard against many painful limitations in our traditional role models. We are beginning to seek new images of masculinity that support us in a return to feeling, aliveness, and a connection to nature, our bodies, our children, women, and other men.

Is this a men's movement? Many of us have heard something about one. But what it is and what it does remain a mystery for most men. What is clear, however, is that there is a phenomenon sweeping the nation. Men everywhere are beginning to reexamine their lives from new perspectives.

I've been talking to thousands of men over the last several years and attending dozens of conferences. Many of us are beginning to question much of what we have been taught about what it means to be a man. The conventional notion that men are somehow more privileged than women is starting to look like a bad joke. Many of us are struggling with the rapid pace of change in our society, while attempting to heal wounds incurred in pursuit of some masculine ideal that often has little to do with how we really feel or experience ourselves as men. There's a lot of pain being expressed in men's private gatherings.

We're angry and confused about the double standards we encounter in many arenas, the reverse sexism and rigid gender-role expectations. Many of us are isolated, and uncertain about how to break out of old male stereotypes. Some are simply numb. We lack elders, positive role models, or leaders with vision. In the past we have often turned to women for solutions, which can create different sorts of problems such as dependency and isolation from other men.

If there is a men's movement, it's a movement within our hearts and minds. For the most part we are still stumbling in the dark. Some of us are finding one another in the darkness, forming small groups, and starting to help one another find a better way. This is one beginning of a hopeful search for new options and new ways of being in the world.

A FEW NIGHTS OUT WITH THE GUYS

My men's group started out as a poker game. We didn't set out to be a men's group per se. We came together, initially, with an intention to support one another in our recovery from alcohol and drug abuse. We were a group of men in our forties and early fifties who had met one another through mutual friends and through our associations with several different recovery groups. Although we all held those groups in positive regard, we also felt the need for a smaller, more focused, and more private group.

At first we couldn't seem to talk to each other about our specific issues as men. Yet this must have been one of the unconscious reasons we set up a meeting that didn't include women. We could agree, however, to have a weekly card game at which no intoxicants would be used, and in between bad jokes and tales of exploits from days gone by, we began to discuss our problems with substance abuse.

As the weeks progressed, we played less and talked more. Eventually we put the cards away and just talked, often deep into the night. We were seven men, sitting around a circular table. For the next three years we spent four to six hours together every week, sharing our hopes, dreams, failures, fears, and insights into one another's predicaments as men in a rapidly changing world.

In the beginning the major question on the table was how to live our lives free from the debilitating effects of alcohol and other drugs. So for the first few months we talked a lot about our addictions. Rodger, for example, was a married dentist with two small children and two older children from a former marriage who lived with their mother. He told us, "My current wife threatened to leave me unless I stopped drinking. I stopped, but she continues to have her evening half bottle of wine." Weekend bingeing on cocaine also had been a problem for him and at one point almost cost him his career. He had been clean and sober for almost two years now, but was still having difficulty with recurring bouts of all-consuming anger—often provoked by seemingly trivial issues.

Other men in our group had issues running the gamut from chronic long-term alcoholism to recreational substance abuse. In my own case, I had become a social drinker who finally realized that not a single day had passed in five years during which I had not used some form of intoxicant. It just crept up on me as my life became increasingly stressful and demanding.

This behavior seemed inconsistent with my professional life in psychology. I felt hypocritical with clients and students, who were often struggling with similar issues. I also experienced several financial, social, and romantic disasters that would undoubtedly not have occurred if I had been coping with my stress in a healthier manner. I no longer knew for certain if I could get through life without alcohol, even though during the fifteen years prior to drinking I had practiced meditation daily and not touched a drop.

Because we all still felt tempted to drink at social gatherings, this group helped us avoid the feeling of social isolation that many men experience when they decide to adopt a healthier lifestyle. More importantly, we began to give each other support in dealing with the aftereffects of a stressful day at work or a rough incident in one of our relationships. We also celebrated one another's successes, as when one of us would discover a creative way to deal with an old emotional problem. Meanwhile, the world around us was more likely to applaud our more tangible creations as the measure of a man's success.

We would be considered, for the most part, fairly successful men. We numbered one multimillionaire, three middle-class men with property or investments, two working-class men with good skills and training, and one professional artist with a lot of class. We were mostly in good health—especially for a bunch of former drunks and abusers—and were generally above the average in formal education, with three advanced degrees between us. Although we had had varying degrees of difficulties in our relationships, we also had had a number of long-term successes. Why, we began to wonder, with all our apparent advantages, had we resorted to substance abuse in order to cope with the stress of our lives?

As time went on and we got more recovery under our belts, our attention focused less on the issue of sobriety and more on our paradoxical experiences as men in general. For example, we had all been told since childhood that we were better off than women, yet we found ourselves continually at risk for a wide range of serious problems. Consequently, we became curious about the reasons we had started engaging in self-destructive behaviors.

With the absence of drugs and alcohol in our lives, feelings, some of which had been buried for decades, began to surface for all of us. With this return there often came a growing awareness of loss, accompanied by grief about failures in our past.

Ben, for example, is a building contractor who has created some of the more beautiful and interesting homes in our area. As our group developed, he began reassessing his life, which, up until then, had been mostly about long hours of hard work. He had been recently divorced and was involved in a bitter custody dispute. One night he said, "I am beginning to think that quitting the booze is the easy part of getting my life back on track; the real challenge is learning how to deal with all the feelings and memories that are starting to come up now that I'm not constantly drowning them out."

Carl, another member of our group, is a computer analyst with one of the country's larger telecommunications corporations. He's happily married and has a five-year-old daughter, yet he's been depressed for several years. He hates his work and feels trapped. After several job changes, he cannot seem to make any transition that makes him feel more fulfilled. He realized one night that "if I had half the money I've put into remodeling our house over the last three years, I could take a year off to regroup, redesign my life, and start all over. But with all the bills piling up now, shit, I can't even take a whole weekend off anymore."

Jack, our oldest member, is the fifty-four-year-old CEO of a midsize corporation that he built from the ground up after creating and selling several other small businesses. Twice married and divorced, he has three adult children and two teenaged ex-stepchildren to whom he still feels deeply connected. He was tangled up in an exciting but ultimately unsatisfying relationship with a much younger woman. He, like Ben, had spent the bulk of the last thirty-odd years working ten-hour days, six days a week, supporting family and ex-family with hardly a thought about what he really wanted to do with his own life. He was beginning to ask that question for the first time since he was a child.

"Whenever I encountered an obstacle in life," Jack noted one night, "I just rolled right over it like a Sherman tank. I left a wake of resentful employees and bitter women behind me, but I didn't really care. I had to make the tough calls. I was the responsible one. And I was a huge success as a result—a success at making money, but a failure in my marriages and as a father. I sacrificed most of the dreams of my youth. Now I'm almost friendless, with the exception of this small group of men and a few people who knew me before my scramble up the ladder. Looking back on my life, I realize it was really the small moments—a trip to the Southwest, horseback riding with my sons—that stand out as the most significant, rich, and memorable events of my life."

Because of our excesses we had all lost income, damaged our physical and mental health, damaged relationships with wives, friends, and children, and certainly crashed more than our fair share of cars. We began to realize that the *underlying* behavioral patterns that led to abuse in the first place were much more dangerous, destructive, and difficult to change. We also began to believe that these patterns affect the lives of all men in our culture, regardless of whether they are manifested in substance abuse or other types of self-destructive behaviors such as sex or work obsessions, addiction to excitement or other risky business. We saw, in time, that our substance abuse was actually only a superficial problem. So what was the *real* problem?

THE KNIGHTS LAY DOWN THEIR ARMOR

The answer: every one of us had attempted to live his life as some type of masculine hero. We had all, in various ways, attempted to extend ourselves beyond the natural limits of our bodies, hearts, and minds in an attempt to achieve some ideal of manhood and productivity. In fact, we had been indoctrinated, from a variety of sources, to believe that this heroic ideal was our sole role and purpose as men.

There is a certain beauty and romantic sense of great destiny that comes through surrendering to the image—or archetype—of the Hero. For a time we may feel powerful and invulnerable. But there is also a heavy price to pay: alienation, isolation, stress-induced physical or mental illness, injury, and an early death—to name a few consequences. As our work together progressed, our catalogue of pseudoheroic self-destructive behaviors eventually expanded to include the following.

Codependence. For men this means habitually taking care of women's needs at the expense of our own; automatically considering them before thinking of ourselves. For example, when doing his taxes in the last year of his marriage, Jack noticed that "even though I made over one hundred thousand dollars, I only spent eighteen hundred dollars on myself. Every other cent went into the house, the kids, and my wife. Whenever I wanted something just for me, I felt guilty. But I never thought twice about spending almost ten thousand dollars for my wife's psychotherapy." Underlying such behavior is often a belief that we cannot be loved by a woman just for who we are. We may then turn into *men who give too much,* believing that we are loved only for what we can provide. This can lead to:

Workaholism. This involves an obsessive overachieving beyond the need for creating what Erich Fromm calls "a pleasant sufficiency of the means to life." My tendency, in recent years, had been to continually overcommit my energy to various projects, which at times left me exhausted and isolated from my friends and family. Consequently, I never seemed to have time to pursue many simpler interests in life, which in the past had made my life more rich, meaningful, and enjoyable. Overwork is also a way of burying fears, covering up emptiness, and avoiding anxieties about relationship issues. Workaholism often leads to:

Numbness. This includes loss of emotional and even physical sensitivity. Carl commented, "When I came home from work I didn't even want to talk to my family anymore. I headed for the icebox for a beer and the den for the tube. For chrissakes, I love my wife and adore my little girl. What the hell happened to me that turned me into a dynamo at work and a zombie at home?" Numbness slowly creeps up on many of us. It can lead to:

Addiction to excitement. To counter the numbness, to be able to feel, we take on habits that provide stimulation and intensity, including unnecessarily stirring up conflicts in our relationships. Rodger told us, "I got into the habit of trying to shave a little time off my commute to the office. It was my little rebellious game of me against the world. I would push it a little more every day. I finally got a ticket for going eighty miles an hour in a thirty-five zone on a back road near my house. Then I received another one four days later. I had to stop or lose my license. Good thing, too. I might have eventually killed someone." He had already had two single-car accidents in the last five years.

"At home," Rodger continued, "I notice that I sometimes start arguments with my wife over little things, just to raise the level of intensity in our relationship. It's as if peaceful coexistence between us is just too boring. Yet, actually, I really hate it when we fight. It's hard to stop, though. It's like a compulsion." A related type of behavior is:

Sex addiction. Sometimes men become dominated by various sexual obsessions and romantic fantasies, and often sacrifice relationships that are more supportive and nurturing. For example, Brad is a single parent of two adolescent boys. He told us, "When I don't have a woman in my life, any woman, then I feel like shit . . . restless, you know, anxious. I keep thinking that if I can just get that one, that special foxy one, in bed, then I'll feel satisfied. But I never do. I'm often sorry in the morning to wake up and see who's there. I had a great steady lady but screwed it up with all my running around. It's gotten me into some pretty desperate situations at times. I'm surprised some irate guy hasn't come through my door with a shotgun yet."

Ultimately, we began to believe that what all these manifestations of heroic masculinity express is:

Loss of soul. Men frequently feel disconnected from an authentic spiritual source of aliveness within us. Soul is that mysterious quality that animates dead matter and makes it alive. When we lose our soul, we no longer feel fully alive or completely connected to life itself. So the work at hand for all of us became rediscovering our souls, plumbing the depths of our feelings, reclaiming our capacity for joy and pleasure, reawakening our creativity, and finding peace of mind.

Recovery became the work of *uncovery*. We helped one another to uncover, identify, understand, and become aware of dysfunctional patterns from the past. Instead of simply being a determined group of men united by a quest for sobriety, we became an audacious, experimental, and adventurous band embarking on a novel expedition—rediscovering what it really means to be a man in America today.

We began to develop a metaphor for the masculine gender role that had encouraged us to act like an invulnerable hero or self-sacrificing martyr: it was an old suit of armor. It was heavy, rusty, hot, and stuffy. It was a hand-me-down that didn't fit too well, being made for a smaller generation. And it was inflexible: wearing it made it impossible to swim, dance, leap, or even make love very well. We didn't choose it, but we wore it because we thought that was our duty.

The armored knights of yore rode off in quest of the Holy Grail, gold, and glory. We were more in search of a grail within—the masculine soul. And as new knights of the round (poker) table we devised a number of tasks that we felt might lead us toward this goal.

The first was to admit that underneath the armor were untended wounds. Secondly, through revealing the full extent of these wounds to one another we began to heal them. Thirdly, while regularly meeting separately from women, we began to rebuild our self-esteem on deep, masculine foundations. Our fourth task was to break out of old stereotypes and learn to enjoy our multiplicity and diversity. Next, we attempted to recover some of the ancient forgotten and forbidden sacred images of men. As a sixth task, we sought to learn what these mythologies from other cultures had to offer our lives as contemporary Western men.

Our seventh task was to rediscover male initiation and begin to heal the wounds between fathers and sons. We then attempted, as an eighth task, to develop some new insights into our traditional adult roles as lovers, workers, hunters, and preservers of the earth. Our ninth task was to reconnect to the cultural wealth of our ancestors and elders and to face our own mortality. Building male community and beginning to heal the wounds between men and women was our tenth undertaking. As an eleventh task we reexamined education and psychology from our new perspectives on authentic masculinity. And as a final task, we continue to pursue our own healing and quest for masculine soul and to reach out to other men who are on a similar quest. Each chapter of this book focuses on one of these tasks.

THE HERO'S FOLLY

One of the primary techniques we used early on in our group was to risk letting down our pretenses about how cool, decisive, in control, and invulnerable we were. Instead, we tried to tell the whole truth of our experience. That truth included our fears, weakness, grief, anger, shame, confusion, illusions, hope, love, and eventually our spirituality and magic as well. Admitting to weakness is not an easy thing for heroes to do. Unfortunately, most men have to hit the wall first. Had we met each other in the past, we might have presented ourselves in a more hip, more restrained, and glib manner, never getting to know who we really were and missing the deep friendships that emerged between us as a result of our honesty.

Jim was one of the first to let down his guard. An intermittently successful sculptor, he had been unable to maintain lasting relationships with women and was ambivalent about an affair he was having with a married woman. Although he was living out his *sacred dream* through his artwork, he was beginning to feel that his *practical dream* for a stable home life was slipping away—forever beyond his reach. "Lots of women want to date me," he said, "but when it comes down to a long-term relationship, the fact that my money comes only once in a while is hard for most of them to handle. When it comes right down to it, when I'm not busy butchering wood and stone—like when I'm just hanging around at home—I feel, well, uh, just very cold and alone. I often wish I could just call someone up and cry,—'Help!'" We reminded him that he had our phone numbers and encouraged him to call us anytime.

To better understand how my group's experience compared with those of other men, I began to host and attend other groups for men from a variety of backgrounds. What began to emerge was a picture of a culture that carried some deeply rooted notions about the nature of masculinity, which were at best unhealthy and at worst highly destructive to men's lives and the lives of everyone around them.

Although many cultures have very different ideals concerning masculinity, in our culture the hero is one of the more prominent figures. We all grew up on John Wayne, whose basic image was that of a loner who defeats the bad guys against impossible odds and saves the lady in distress. This image was reinforced during our young adult years by Clint Eastwood and Charles Bronson, and is perpetuated in the current generation by Arnold Schwarzenegger as Conan/Terminator, Sylvester Stallone as Rocky/Rambo, and billionaires like Donald Trump, the business hero who was recently named the most admired man among college undergraduates.

The entrepreneur, the lone financier/magnate, has become a prominent heroic ideal in our culture. Jack, our group's business hero, got wounded in the process of trying to maintain this role. Our cinema heroes, after getting shot repeatedly during their conquests, would react with a mere wince: "Why, shucks, it's only a scratch." Could Jack do any less? It wasn't until he had almost bled his life to death that he took notice: "Hey, I'm shot—

I'm isolated, exhausted, divorced from myself and from the wild dreams I once had for my life." Many men do not notice this woundedness until they find themselves in a hospital bed after a heart attack. The heroic self-image appears to cause difficulties for all men, regardless of whether, as in our case, it drives them into substance abuse, or into the myriad other forms of self-destruction and self-denial most men engage in to keep up the pretense of invulnerability.

Where did we get the oppressive idea that we aren't supposed to feel or express pain? It starts early. Very early, in most of our lives. Jack summed it up one night: "I started working part-time in high school and drinking beers every night to come down from the day. I just kept it up for the next thirty-five years. I'm now beginning to realize that some part of me went numb back then and has been numb ever since, until now. All I ever wanted to be as a kid was a musician and to travel around the world. How did I lose sight of that dream for so long?"

Jack had asked a profound question. So we began to discuss various aspects of life that made us feel oppressed as men.

MALE OPPRESSION AND INEQUALITY: MAKING HARDENED MEN OUT OF SENSITIVE BOYS

If we look underneath the strong-man persona, much oppression becomes apparent in almost every arena of a man's life. When I try to talk about this issue publicly, women often say, "What male oppression? Everyone knows that men have *all* the privileges." And some men agree. They inevitably feel some discomfort around seeing themselves as subjects of oppression, since it runs counter to the dominant Western worldview of masculinity. Our predominant male self-image is tough, strong, optimistic, cool, and superior.

As we compared notes in our group, however, we began to uncover shared patterns of conditioning that we experienced during the process of becoming men, conditioning that seemed to drive us into various forms of risky business. In fact, the deliberate toughening up of boys generally begins immediately after birth. In his book *Touching: The Human Significance of the Skin*, Ashley Montagu cites a number of studies that indicate that infant boys in America receive fewer demonstrative acts of affection from their mothers than infant girls and are touched less. He concluded that this is one of the reasons men are "more uptight about tactuality [touching]" than women. Boys are also more likely to be held facing outward, toward the world and other people. Girls are held inward, toward the security, warmth, and comfort of the parent.

In America today there appears to be an attitude that boys do not need or deserve the same degree of nurturance, safety, intimacy, love, and support to which girls are entitled. Boys are weaned earlier than girls and thus are deprived of the natural tranquilizers and the immune-system support of mother's milk—not to mention the soothing comfort of the breast. Coincidentally, boys tend to lag about four to six weeks behind girls in their development. They crawl, sit, and speak later and tend to cry more during infancy.

Young girls are encouraged to stay near the mother, restricted, nurtured, and protected, while same-aged boys are generally encouraged, even pushed, to become more independent, to play with objects that distract them from the mother, and to move away at greater distances. Girl toddlers are more likely to get a positive response when crying for help than boys, who play away from home earlier and are more likely to be permitted to play with sharp objects that can cause injury. When a child complains of a minor injury, parents are quicker to comfort girls than boys.

Boys are *pushed* into assertive, aggressive, and nondependent behavior. They are also more restricted, especially by the father, to traditionally heroic, male-gender-specific toys. For example, a girl may be allowed to play with a truck or a G.I. Joe, but a boy is likely to get disapproval for playing with a girl doll or a dish set. Since boys are considered by most people to be emotionally tougher than girls, they are more typically reprimanded in front of the whole class for misbehavior by teachers, whereas girls are more likely to be taken aside and spoken to more softly.

Some feminist writers have commented that these types of gender disparities in child care cause girls to become overly dependent. This is true. However, there is an equal downside for boys: they become independent to the point of isolation. They are trained to disconnect from those very feelings that make life rich. Stereotypical, rigid role expectations for either gender can be equally damaging to full personality development.

As boys, we are actively engaged in the process of becoming men. But we're not exactly sure what that means. We certainly don't want to do anything that might make us seem unmanly or like girls. To become *unmen* is to essentially risk nonexistence; there are no other viable options presented to us. So as we grow up we are always alert for clues about what is manly. Throughout our development and education we are encouraged to repress pain. This attitude is continually reinforced during our adult lives. If we cry out in pain, we'll be labeled a sissy, wimp, or whiner and risk being shamed for appearing unmasculine.

Boys learn that girls are permitted to have feelings. But we also learn that it makes our peers, parents, and other adult authorities uneasy if *we* express our feelings. *Feelings are not masculine.* Most male children are repeatedly told, "Don't be a baby. Don't cry when you are hurt. Don't whine. Be a big boy now and wipe those tears away; big boys don't cry." Every one of us in the group had many such memories. *Men should suffer alone and in silence!* It's like an ancient, evil spell that hangs over us.

This desensitivity training continues as we grow older and begin to leave the familiar field of the mother to enter the more distant world of men. In their adolescent games, boys learn that they are expected not to show pain, not to flinch when startled, not to back down from a fight or show fear in the face of real or imagined danger, injury, or pain. Football and other contact sports give the message to the adolescent male, who has already learned that he must forgo pleasure and endure pain to be a man, that he must perform in a heroic manner to win intimacy and success—that is, the affection of an attractive young woman and the acceptance or recognition of powerful older men.

Although we are introduced to the arts and sciences, we do not get a lot of strokes, for the most part, for pursuing those interests. The entire school, including a squad of the most attractive girls, will not turn out to watch a boy build a Tesla coil from old car parts, recite original poetry, give a creative dance performance, or present a dramatic reading from *Hamlet*. They will, however, turn out to watch him make a touchdown.

Boys who emphasize artistic or intellectual pursuits are often labeled geeks, nerds, wimps, sissies, losers, creeps, and fags, or are dismissed as too sensitive. These epithets are almost exclusively reserved for boys and are just as likely to be delivered by scorning, mocking girls as by the more heroic-acting boys. One can decline to take an elective class in the arts with no shame, but boys are required and coerced into taking physical education, with its requisite, potentially brutalizing component of contact sports. Young women are not forced into contact competition with one another, yet are conditioned to believe that they should not give love, attention, and intimacy to a man who has not demonstrated his heroic abilities.

This conditioning betrays our innate sensitivity as children. It is not surprising, therefore, to note that young boys are admitted to mental hospitals and juvenile institutions about seven times more frequently than girls of similar age and socioeconomic background. It is easy to see how boys with this type of training might grow into domineering, insensitive men. It also makes many men covertly angry. Covertly, because this is how we are trained to carry our anger. Being cool is a primary role model for men: keep your cool, cool down, cool out, take it like a man, hold your mud, chill out, keep it all together, stiff upper lip, grin and bear it, don't get mad, don't blow it, keep your shirt on, back off, don't get uptight, hang loose.

These admonitions are part of the whole complex of subtle and not-so-subtle directions that lead men not to express their experiences of strong emotions other than the expansive, positive ones associated with winning and triumph. If a man is angry, it is seen as a shameful exposure of his inability to be the victor. This perspective holds that if he were powerful enough to win, he would be a cool and self-assured James Bondish character, who does not get angry, just even. The dominant male ethic perceives both tears and anger as expressions of failure.

Often our anger is just the cap on a deep well of grief. Rodger recalled that when he was nine years old, his father died unexpectedly of a heart attack. When he started to weep uncontrollably at the funeral, his grandmother told him, "Stand up straight and stop that sniveling. You're the man of the family and now is the time to start acting like one." The night Rodger shared that story with us, he gave up a chunk of his numbness and just wept—completing the grieving process for his father that had been interrupted almost forty years ago. His frequent, irrational attacks of rage began to cease thereafter.

NATURE'S DOUBLE STANDARD: BIOLOGICAL DIFFERENCES BETWEEN MEN AND WOMEN

We also began to wonder why, as we were growing up, the men in our group experienced a double standard concerning what was expected of us as compared with what was expected of women and girls. We were always told that we were stronger and tougher and therefore expected to take on more heroic, risky, and difficult tasks. Brad said, "I remember feeling a little disturbed when I found out that girls' restrooms had cots in them. I can't tell you how many times in my life I wished I could have laid down somewhere for a few minutes during a stressful day."

The fact is, we're actually not so tough. In reality, men are often not as strong or as biologically advantaged as women, much less superior to them, as we've all been told. For example, male embryos suffer a much higher rate of mortality due to spontaneous abortion. The rate of male infant mortality after birth is also higher. From a physiological perspective, nature seems to make more genetic errors in the production of human males. Unlike the biblical story of Eve being formed from Adam's rib, the male fetus evolves out of a female prototype, and thus must go through greater biological differentiation than the female fetus. Consequently, boys are much more likely to suffer from a variety of birth defects. Boys are more prone to schizophrenia, which is increasingly becoming understood as a genetically predisposed brain disorder. They also suffer a higher incidence of mental retardation. All told, there are about two hundred genetic diseases that affect only boys, including the most severe forms of muscular dystrophy and hemophilia.

Boys are twice as likely as girls to suffer from autism and six times as likely to be diagnosed as having hyperkinesis. Boys stutter more and have significantly more learning and speech disabilities than girls. Dyslexia, one of the more serious learning disorders, is found in at least four times as many boys as girls. Some researchers indicate that the ratio may be as high as nine to one.

These neurological problems may not be due simply to genetics. Tactile stimulation is an important factor in stimulating the growth of nerve tissues and their protective coatings. Since the neural pathways of the brain are still being formed during the first sixteen months, the dramatic difference in verbal dexterity between girls and boys may be related to the manner in which the infants are introduced to language and the degree of nurturance and stimulation they receive. Boys are touched less frequently by their mothers than girls, and they are talked to less, and for shorter durations.

Girls are also more likely to be spoken to by their mothers in language that is age-appropriate—that is, consistent with their level of neurological and cognitive development—whereas boys tend to receive more complex communications, which may tend to put a strain on their development. Girls are spoken to more often than boys. They also have their own speech repeated or mirrored back to them by the mother more often than boys. Not surprisingly, girls talk earlier than boys and speak with longer chains of words as well. Is it any wonder many adult men often have a reputation for being silent types? And these studies point to only a few of the many biological, structural, and social inequalities men start out with in life.

A FOOT IN THE BALLS AND OTHER BOYHOOD GAMES

Girls arrive at puberty one and one half to two years earlier than boys and also experience a growth spurt that makes them taller and heavier than the average eleven-to-fourteen-year-old boy. Adolescent girls also continue to demonstrate superior verbal skills—as anyone who's had to share a phone with one can easily confirm. When the adolescent boy comes into his sexuality, he often realizes that the girls his age are somehow more cognizant of the nature of this mystery. He feels his inferiority—his inability to match them in their mastery of sexual power. Thus he may turn to developing his growing sense of physical strength as a compensation for the emotional, sexual, and verbal immaturity he senses, often believing that the display of some manner of physical prowess, beyond the capacity of a girl, is his only possible access to equal power.

Although the psycho-social development of many gay men may take a different turn at this stage of adolescence, the pressures to conform to the dominant, heroic male image are no less of an imperative for him than for his heterosexual counterpart. In some cases, gay adolescents who lack support for coming out may feel even greater pressure to *power-up* in order to assuage any doubts they or others may feel about their masculinity.

Girl-slasher movies, like those featuring the character of Freddy Kruger, have become increasingly popular among adolescent boys—the target audience for these films. I believe these films vividly express the unconscious underlying anger, fear, and frustration many young men develop during their early exposure to girls' advanced sexual development.

By late adolescence these different so-called advantages have become finely honed, as young women begin to use their sexual power and young men attempt to parlay their physical strength. "You've got to be a football hero to go out with the beautiful girls" the old songs goes. Young men will carry these polarized notions of gender with them throughout their lives—the woman dependent on the man for strength, and the man dependent on the woman for nurturance and a connection to beauty, emotion, sensuality, and mystery.

A few year ago, I was doing research on the campus of Sonoma State University, in northern California. The dorms were empty for the summer break, so the university had rented out the student housing facility, along with its surrounding playing fields, to a nationwide football camp for middle-school boys. As I watched the boys moving around the campus that week I was struck by the clumsiness of their gait, their awkward and graceless movements. Then I realized that many of the boys were limping from injuries. I saw several bruised faces and bloody noses. There were even a few on the sidelines with more serious injuries that kept them out of play.

My observations are consistent with studies that showed, as long as thirteen years ago, that almost one-third of all high school and college football players receive serious injuries. That figure is now up to 36 percent for any given year of play. This translates to approximately 331,000 boys injured every year, with about 14,000 actually requiring surgery. At least twelve boys *died* from injuries in 1989 alone. On almost any given day you can turn to the sports section of your local paper and see that a significant number of the stories are devoted to the status of various team members who have received injuries.

The general ambiance in the dining hall that summer week was boisterous yet joyless. I wondered why the men apparently did not see how they were wrecking these boys' bodies in the name of athletic excellence. The longtime athletic trainer Jack Rockwell hopes that someday softer protective gear may become available to protect these boys, yet laments that "then the pop will be gone from the sport." The trainer Byron Craighead agrees that "the fans like the hitting in football. So do the coaches, who love to hear the pop. But it's the trainer who hears that other terrible sound—the break."

A friend of mine who managed the dorms that summer told me, "The buildings were practically destroyed in just three weeks. Doors were kicked in, sheetrock punched full of holes, and even toilets ripped out." Many of these boys were in pain and, apparently, full of rage as well. Football is touted as teaching team building, cooperation between men, and athletic ideals. The metaphors of football are often used in the corporate world and in the world of politics to enforce the idea of the individual working for the benefit of the team, for a share of the glory of the whole, no matter how much personal sacrifice is involved. Athletic excellence that enhances the strength, agility, and beauty of the human body is an ideal I think most of us support. When we examine the training football provides, however, it's clear that it does not actually promote that ideal.

As a finish carpenter, Brad has been on and off construction sites for twenty-five years. Ironically, he received the most serious injury of his life on the football playing field. His spinal disks were compressed and cracked. Even though his back wasn't injured enough to keep him out of military service, it still goes out on him. His back pain became one of the major issues involved in his drinking. He has increasing disability, for which he is uncompensated, and has less ability to work as he gets older, despite corrective surgeries. He once said, showing us a huge jagged scar on his leg, that by contrast "this shrapnel wound I got in 'Nam was minor."

Just prior to dropping dead at thirty-eight, the superstar athlete John Matuszak wrote in his autobiography, "Overdoing it helped me at times; in part, I believe it's why I own a pair of Super Bowl rings. But on balance, it did me much more harm than good. I still don't know what the hell I was trying to prove, but I could never do anything in moderation." He was taught by his coaches, his colleagues, and his culture that the only way to be a man was to continually push beyond his limits. He was allowed, by a number of doctors, to take massive doses of painkillers. All this abuse eventually killed him.

Today the abuse of steroids by high-school athletes is reaching major proportions. Young men attempt to bulk up and increase strength at any cost, even though this hero-building drug of champions puts their health, future Olympic and professional sports careers, and even their lives at risk. U.S. attorney Phillip Halpren, of San Diego, has called steroids "a 250-million-to-400-million-dollar-a-year industry, with 2 million users around the country, including 500,000 teenagers." Student athletes are following the example set by professional athletes, who are under such extreme pressure to perform that they are willing to risk heart disease, unnatural hair growth or loss, kidney disease, liver cancer, stunted bone growth, atrophied testicles, and even steroid-induced psychosis and death—all for that extra burst of speed or endurace.

This phenomenon is one of many distorted echoes from men's ancient preurban history. In tribal hunter societies, the blood of a sacrificial animal—often a bull in neolithic times—was drunk to transfer the power, or *mana,* of the animal to the man before a hunt, or prior to entering battle. Today drugs play a similar role.

The all-pro Atlanta Falcons lineman Bill Fralic was quoted in the press as saying that "steroid madness" is pervasive and that he estimates that 75 percent of active linemen use steroids. In the same article, Steve Courson, a former Pittsburgh Steeler and Tampa Bay Buccaneer, called himself a "man possessed" when he used steroids and reported that doctors have given him five years to live due to a damaged heart. He said, "Every athlete pursues a dream, and sometimes that dream can become distorted. Taking steroids is the biggest regret of my life." In the summer of 1990, even Mr. Universe was arrested for smuggling five thousand doses of steroids into the United States.

We cheer the sports hero who, after being clobbered and smashed on the playing field, gets up and plays even though he is hurt. Little is said about those who do not recover and are maimed for life. Pressure to play while they're hurt is also a major contributor to drug abuse among professional athletes as they attempt to numb the pain. This epidemic problem reflects the broader state of the entire speeded-up culture, in which almost every man is *playing hurt,* to some degree.

As a spectator sport with a vast, mostly male audience, football may make up for the emptiness and boredom many men feel in their modern lives and also provide an opportunity for them to feel closer to one another, united by a common interest. The audience's repressed aggressions and frustrations may become vicariously expressed and released as men watch their gladiators battling on the field.

Ironically, older men often look back on their sports-team experiences or their experiences as soldiers—another time when they faced the limits of their endurance together—as the time in their lives when they felt a sense of purpose, membership, and belonging with other men.

CREATING KILLERS IN HIGH SCHOOL

The social toleration for the destruction of men's bodies is not limited to the popularity of destructive sports such as football, hockey, boxing, daredevil stunts, rodeo, and auto racing. A majority of men still believe, from their conditioning, that it is their duty alone to go into battle in wars. Jim recalls a comment from his high-school gym teacher, who reprimanded him for cutting class by saying, "Son, this class is mighty important. This training you get here is gonna give you an edge on them gooks in Vietnam."

Boys are told they must be prepared to be mutilated or die in order to protect women and children and the ideologies of the nation. Much of the conditioning adolescent boys receive is the perfect preparation for molding a playful, life-affirming boy into a complacent soldier, unquestioning cannon fodder, a killing machine—a real man.

Carl took ROTC in high school, where he told us he learned that the most important things in life were "to shoot straight, dress sharp, and keep a stiff upper lip, a stiff back, and a stiff cock."

Induction or threat of induction into the military is the coup de grace in the process of desensitization of young men. They learn that pain must be repressed and that they must perform heroically in order to receive love and affection; they also learn to die—like a hero or the self-sacrificing martyr Christ—for society's benefit. They must also be prepared to kill in order to please a distant father in Washington and are faced with prison if they refuse to do so in time of war.

My generation of men endured the Vietnam War, in which over fifty-eight thousand American men and eight American women died. The men were drafted to fight a war in which, for the most part, they did not believe. This is one of the many areas in which male oppression and inequality are completely taken for granted.

The value placed on men's lives as compared with women's is greatly depreciated in our culture. As we discussed the Vietnam War one night in the group, we couldn't help but wonder what would have happened if, every night on the news, America had watched thousands of healthy, robust, attractive adolescent women in their prime being blown to bits on the battlefield and stuffed into body bags for shipment home. Would the war have lasted as long as it did? Would more mothers and fathers have come out against the war and supported their children's resistance? Would their boyfriends have wept, cheered, and praised them for their heroism, or would they have been furious and outraged, and joined the forces against the war?

Jim told us, "At a protest once I was beaten up by three marines and spat upon by an older woman who called me a coward for refusing to go to Vietnam and fight. The wounds from the beating healed long ago, but that woman's spit has been very difficult to wipe off my memory. Even so, I still feel that resisting the war was the most courageous thing I have done in my life."

Some of those who did risk their lives to uphold the beliefs of their nation also report being spat upon when they returned home. Many were shunned and rejected by the women left behind and by the heroic fathers they failed. They were feared as having become brutal or unstable, unsafe, flawed, and tainted; they failed to win the war and perpetuate the heroic myth. This experience was not limited to disabled veterans, whose issues were so brilliantly depicted in the film *Born on the Fourth of July*. It affected many men on both sides of the conflict.

In our group we have two vets and three men who actively resisted the war, now finding their solidarity as men by supporting one another in recovery. We mostly blame the demented fathers who started the war in the first place. Yet it's still hard for many men to understand why they were found unworthy of a woman's love for having served their country in the manner dictated by their government.

I know of several women therapists who won't accept these men as clients. Some have told me that they just cannot face the horror of the stories these vets need to tell and retell. They're also afraid of the veterans' intensity and what they perceive as their potential for violence. The survivors of this war are still trying to heal one another in what may be the only way possible: man to man. At a recent gathering of more than one hundred male therapists who work with men, we performed a small ceremony to honor the continuing grief this issue carries for many of us, more than fifteen years after the end of the war. We simply wailed aloud for a few minutes. Those who could, wept.

One veteran told me later that it was the first time in twenty years anyone had publicly acknowledged or honored his pain. More than one hundred thousand veterans of the Vietnam War have committed suicide since the end of the war, almost twice the number actually killed in battle. This suicide rate is significantly higher than that for the general population. Twenty-five percent of men in prison, including 50 percent of the inmates in one prison in Detroit, are veterans of Vietnam, as well as 30 percent of the homeless men on the streets. We have pitifully failed these men as a society and as a culture. Perhaps we will do a better job with the soldiers of this generation who return from battle in the Middle East.

What, after all, is equality? War may finally end when society begins to hold the security and lives of men to be as sacred as those of women.

DYING FOR DOLLARS

If men survive their adolescent acts of bravado, sports abuse, ritual sacrifice in war, and their greater predisposition toward adolescent suicide, they grow up and enter the work force. Here, too, they tend to become injured, disabled by stress-related disease, and killed to a much greater extent than women.

Warren Farrell is a men's advocate who was formerly an active feminist on the board of NOW. In his excellent book *Why Men Are the Way They Are,* he explores the socialization process men receive while growing up as "success objects." This objectification of men as performers—or *succesexuality,* as I call it—has the same dehumanizing consequences for men as the objectification of women as sex objects has for women.

Francis Baumli, the editor of a potent anthology on men's issues, *Men Freeing Men,* believes that "many men who are defined as successful by society resemble machines . . . that function impressively for a while. But like powerful engines, racing at high speed without any oil, they will soon burn out." Men also are encouraged by their heroic and self-sacrificing role models to engage in the most dangerous and high-stress professions without complaint or any sign of weakness or fear.

I worked in the feature-film industry for about three years. On many low-budget shoots, the director would ask our crew to do something completely impossible with the time, money, and materials we had available. However, we all wanted to succeed in the business and knew we wouldn't get very far by saying, "Gee, it seems a little unrealistic for you to ask us to build a model of a nuclear submarine in four days with only papier-mâché, some old plywood, and a few cans of paint." We could say only one thing: "No problem!"

So we would stay up for four nights in a row, using a variety of high-octane fuels to stay awake, crashing occasionally for a few hours on the set or in the prop truck. We would beg, borrow, or even steal whatever was needed to build the set. Sure enough, the camera crew would arrive four days later and there would be a submarine, an art-deco living room, a nightclub, or whatever else was wanted—ready and waiting. We were geniuses, we were heroes, we were great—and we were burned out, exhausted, drugged drunks who would usually plunge into deep depressions after each wrap, until the next job.

It was an exciting and wonderful life in many ways. Yet, like many fast-track occupations, it destroyed families and our physical and mental health. For this reason, the contemporary fast-paced workplace, based on the heroic performance model, is becoming the realm of increasingly younger men and women who are still willing to sacrifice the overall quality of their lives for glory and economic success.

Men frequently destroy their health through obsessive overwork, attempting to provide for their families. According to an analysis by Warren Farrell, even in this age of equality men are still responsible for approximately 75 percent of the financial support for the average American family. Consequently, the overachieving business hero is applauded for his performance. There is usually little compassion, however, for the man who crashes and burns. He is seen as not tough enough, especially by other men who may be repressing the fear that "there but for the grace of God go I."

"If you can't take the heat, stay out of the kitchen" is the slogan of the competitive workplace. Where is the voice of reason, which says, "Hey, the kitchen is on fire and we are all going to burn"? Until recently, 90 percent of all peptic ulcers were found in men, as well as significantly higher rates of heart disease. This gender disparity is rapidly changing as more and more women begin to face the life-threatening stresses of the fast-track American workplace. Even so, men still die of work-related injuries approximately twenty to one over women.

By virtue of their physical ability to lift heavier loads, men are expected to expose their bodies to greater danger, abuse, and strain. Consequently, they suffer many more hernias, other weight-load-induced muscle strains, and disabling injuries.

The most dangerous professions are ones that have traditionally been filled by men and which modern women, despite their demands for economic parity, have been reluctant to enter. A San Francisco Bay–area labor-relations attorney recently observed that the reverse discrimination many men are now experiencing, due to affirmative-action quotas keeping them out of many of the more desirable professions, is creating a situation in which many men have no other choices but to seek more dangerous work.

The highest mortality rates in the nation are found among timber cutters, who are 95 percent male; insulation workers, power-line workers, garbage collectors, and miners, who are all about 85 percent male; and farmers, who are 79 percent male. Of course these men, and men in general, also have a much higher rate of serious injury and disability than women do. On many of the hazardous construction sites and high-rigging jobs I have worked over the years, I have often witnessed men shunning available protective gear as unmanly. Many of us took unnecessary, even daredevil risks on the job. It makes work more exciting, but it also creates a higher incidence of injury and death.

While I was writing this chapter, a roofer fell off the second-story roof of our clinic, breaking his pelvis and hip. Every one of the workers up there was male, while most of the therapists and social workers in the air-conditioned offices below were female. This is actually one of the reasons I returned to the practice of psychology after years of rousting about on various projects: beyond my life-long desire to be of direct service to others, I wanted a profession for the second half of my life that was not so hard on my body. Many men are not fortunate enough to have this choice.

At one gathering I attended with Robert Bly, James Hillman, Doug Von Koss, and Michael Meade, several thousand red strips of cloth were passed out to the six hundred men present. We tied them over various past wounds to our bodies and then walked past one another bearing witness to the damage that years of work, war, and recklessness had laid upon us. The conference leaders vastly underestimated the number of cloths needed for that task. Even so, it was quite dramatic for us to see one another thus revealed. Some men were practically covered with red.

Are men really more privileged than women when their life expectancy is as much as nine years less than women's? Until the age of twenty-five, there are slightly more men in the population than women. This proportion then starts to reverse itself, until by age sixty there are one hundred fifteen women for every hundred men, one hundred fifty to one hundred by age seventy-five, and more than two women for every man by the age of eighty-five.

THE FIRST TASK OF MEN:
TO ADMIT THAT WE HAVE BEEN WOUNDED

As we men of the round table continued our talks, we began to realize that our feeling of having been wounded along the way was not just what some might view as wimping out on our parts.

Despite our apparent advantages and privileges as men, there appeared to be good reasons for our underlying feelings of inequality with women.

Ben told us one night that in his entire life he had heard his father, an eminent scientist, complain only once: "Two nights before his death, lying in the bed, he turned his head away from me and wept, realizing for the first time in his life the true extent of his powerlessness." This is not an unusual story about men; it's no wonder that it took us a while to admit to one another that we had all suffered a great deal of pain.

We had been trained to live a lie. I still find it a little embarrassing to report all this material since it violates a basic social contract against men acknowledging their pain. I fear a reader's commenting, "Methinks thou dost protest too much!" Even so, I believe that the first step toward recovery is the naming and exposure of our old, festering wounds. How else can we heal the shame that comes from bearing them in silence? The consequences of trying to live up to the role model of the invincible hero or silently suffering martyr are more significant than the repression of our individual pains. Our society as a whole suffers a great deal from the unhealed scars of its wounded men.

If, as many psychologists believe, rage erupts as a reaction to the deep-rooted pain many men carry, then the increase of violence in our culture may be related to the degree of unreconciled grief many of us experience today. The alienation, loneliness, isolation, shame, substance abuse, distrust of women, and emotional numbness associated with the heroic model of masculinity may be both symptom and cause of the breakdown in the social fabric.

The Hero is one-sided and one-dimensional. Perhaps we needed this archetype more in a world at war with nature and other nations. Now the time for peace and healing is upon us— time to welcome home the hero, attend to his wounds, and then help him create a more cooperative world between men, women, and nature.

Admitting that we have been wounded was our first task. Through revealing the full extent of these wounds, we felt we could then begin to heal them. This was the second task we faced.

CHAPTER 2

The Wounded Male

*Man was made for Joy & Woe
and when this we rightly know
thro' the World we safely go
Joy & Woe are woven fine
a clothing for the Soul divine.*
  William Blake

Many men feel alienated today because their inner experience, which is often secretly painful, is not reflected in a society that keeps telling them they are the more privileged gender. Fortunately, men are beginning to reexamine their lives and talk about their experiences with one another. The naming of specific wounds in men's groups, such as our new knights of the round table, helps to lessen one of the most ubiquitous problems for men in our culture—isolation.

Men have a lot of resistance to identifying themselves as victims. Many feel secretly ashamed; it's not heroic to be a victim. Yet, becoming aware of how unconscious we have been of the ways in which we were wounded is an important first step toward growing out of the dysfunctional behaviors generated in reaction to that victimization. Through developing awareness about the repressed shame many of us carry, we can cease being victims once and for all.

Shame occurs in many men who feel they have failed to live up to the heroic ideal. In contrast, guilt is what healthy people feel in response to what they have *done* wrong; it creates an impetus to rectify misdeeds. Shame, however, is what we feel when experiencing ourselves as somehow *being* wrong. It's immobilizing and destroys self-esteem. Much pathology, including a lot of male violence, arises in an attempt to assuage or repress this feeling. Shame, unlike guilt, is dehumanizing. It may be inherited and intergenerational. It may be caused by early trauma or maintained by a lifestyle, relationship, or social context that systematically erodes our feelings of worth, self-respect, and dignity.

Some of the material in this chapter is controversial because it exposes misinformation, disseminated over the last few decades, that has fueled false judgments about the ontological character of men. The shame-inducing wounds of isolation, sex discrimination, poverty, divorce, child-custody disputes, physical, sexual, and emotional abuse, abortion, unequal opportunity, and gender-role rigidity are issues for both women *and* men. My intention is not to vilify or condemn women. Yet much of the information in this chapter is contrasted against the parallel condition of women, who in some cases actually appear to be *less* at risk than men—a view contrary to many current cultural beliefs.

Men face many double standards. We don't get the same cultural and institutional support that women do when dealing with a number of important personal, social, and legal isses. This reality alone can be shame inducing, giving men the impression that for some reason their lives are not as valuable as women's. This becomes, as we shall see, a sort of salt in the wound.

THE SOCIAL-SERVICES GAP: YOU CAN'T AFFORD TO STUMBLE, YOU'VE GOT NO PLACE TO FALL

One of the reasons we formed our men's group was that we were unable to find any other context for support in our recovery. Anonymous public meetings or expensive private therapy, while of value, do little to help build real community—something many men need the most.

One of the dangerous social attitudes that come with the hero myth is that men don't need the same level of community support that women do in terms of health care, health maintenance, preventive-care education, psychological counseling, parenting education, social-welfare assistance, and advocacy against discrimination. Because men supposedly earn more money than women, many people assume that their needs are disproportionately less than those of women. The reality is that a very small minority of men hold a disproportionately large amount of the wealth in this country. When these men are excluded from the statistical mean, it appears that the economic plight of the average man is, essentially, not so different from that of the average woman in this country.

There is a great deal written about the feminization of poverty these days. But we usually fail to hear about the over 10 million men—a record number—who are also now below the poverty line in America. They account for almost 40 percent of the nation's poor, with single men representing the fastest-growing group of impoverished citizens during the last decade.

The health of single men is generally poorer than that of married men or women in general. But single men who find themselves financially disabled or unable to work, or who are reluctant to disregard whatever degree of hazard or degradation they may be exposed to in low-skilled, high-risk labor, do not receive the same support, concern, and protection from society as single women or mothers with children. More women are covered by private health insurance than men, and government insurance programs such as Medicaid cover twice as many women as men.

Now that there are increasing numbers of women and children on the streets, society is finally becoming alarmed about homelessness. Just as AIDS did not get much attention as long as it was primarily confined to unmarried homosexual men, homelessness also elicited significantly less social concern until it began to affect more women and children. Today, for example, approximately 50 percent of the federal funding for AIDS care is spent on women and children, who represent less than 10 percent of the victims. The author of a book on pediatric AIDS states that the head of the National Academy of Sciences' commission on research admits that there has "always been a huge strain of homophobia about AIDS in Washington. Their motto is 'Women and children first.'"

A recent lawsuit against Contra Costa County, California, exposes a similar attitude toward homeless men. The suit was brought in an attempt to change a county policy that prohibits single homeless men from receiving free emergency shelter at motels, a resource available to all other classes of the economically disadvantaged. As many as one-third of these men are Vietnam veterans who have been in need of social services for many years. Many other counties continue to practice this sort of discrimination unchallenged.

One of our group members, Brad, is a single parent who has frequently been less than a paycheck away from losing his apartment. He told us that past attempts to get public assistance have been frustrating: "The county social worker actually laughed at me when I asked her to try and get some money out of my working ex-wife, who has not contributed anything to the support of my sons since she left seven years ago."

On the other hand, women in distress are more likely to find support from all quarters. Bulletin boards and self-help publications advertise dozens of support groups, educational and cultural activities, counseling, and other opportunities exclusively for women.

At our local county mental-health-care facility there is a group for women with low self-esteem, a general women's group, a group for women who were recently divorced, a group for women who are adult children of alcoholics, a group for women who are survivors of childhood incest, a group for low-functioning women, one mixed-gender group, and one group for low-functioning men that has three members and is the only group for men.

In some areas of the country, men's centers are beginning to develop. Even so, at our new facility, the Redwood Men's Center, which offers therapy and health services, we frequently hear men tell us that they've previously been unable to connect with any service or group *directly* concerned with men's issues. And this is in northern California, where the men's movement is as active as any other place in the country. By contrast, in our area there are several dozen groups, clinics, and service centers that are strictly for women, many of which offer special reduced rates, supported by public and private grants.

The women's movement has mobilized community resources for women and children. Men, on the other hand, have done a pretty poor job of supporting one another. We've been socialized since birth to think of women as the weaker sex, who need protection and support from us. However, there's some doubt about which gender can rightly claim that dubious title.

STAYING ALIVE:
HOW MEN NEGLECT THEIR HEALTH

Many of us often don't learn a lot about caring for and maintaining ourselves in our early years. Carl noted, "At school I was advised to take auto shop, not health and hygiene." Outside of a few progressive areas of the nation, very little support is found for promoting the general physical and mental health of men, other than admonitions to exercise and eat right so that we can live longer and keep on working.

This is our fault as men. We have not done a very good job of taking care of one another. Even many so-called changing men in the men's movement are more concerned with women's issues than the wounds of men.

Women seek regular dental care and see physicians for regular checkups more often than men. They are also more likely to get professional help for health problems at earlier stages of development than men, who often wait for problems to become more serious and debilitating before seeking help. Women also enter psychotherapy, asking for help with emotional problems, to a much greater degree than men. They have been trained since childhood to take better personal care of themselves and the people they love.

Some men are just beginning to take better care of themselves and each other. For example, in our group we take turns cooking a meal for all the other members. This ensures that we all get at least one good home-cooked meal a week. Men are often overly dependent upon women to provide this type of care. But one of the ways to heal the wound of dependency is to learn how to care for ourselves. Yes, it's true that many of the world's great chefs are male, but they are a minority of men. As Rodger noted, "When I was single I survived on tuna straight out of the can, Campbell's soup, and sandwiches."

Our cooking skills have all expanded. My partner, Liz, has commented that this is one of the many indirect benefits she has received from my men's work. Putting on a great spread with healthy ingredients is a way we demonstrate our affection for one another and also receive a lot of appreciation. We even exchange recipes. One evening, we focused on ways to lower our intake of cholesterol, having discovered that half of us had seriously elevated cholesterol levels.

Part of the desensitizing process that men go through in their training to become masculine prevents them from seeking necessary health care or getting the rest and diet necessary to promote good health. Heroes can eat anything, it seems, especially fat-laden, junk-type foods. Some men actually think it's effeminate to be selective about their diet. George Bush extolls the virtues of potentially carcinogenic fried pork rinds, while shunning broccoli—which, like quiche, is not suitable food for *real* men.

Men also encourage one another to drink excessively and indulge in other overconsumptions as an expression of their heroic masculinity. Men suffer alcoholism and drug-abuse rates about four times higher than those of women. This ratio has been changing, however, as more women become subjected to the same stresses of working in the dysfunctional economic system that men have been confronting since the inception of the industrial revolution.

If a man *is* sensitive to the needs of his body and emotions, he will not be acknowledged by his culture as manly. Yet if he doesn't respond to his pain, he may die an early death or seek refuge in drugs, alcohol, obsessive sexual relations, workaholism, or violent acting out. Men are incarcerated—most frequently for crimes committed under the influence of drugs or alcohol—at a rate of almost twenty to one over women. Alcoholism and drug abuse are diseases exacerbated by the health-neglecting, toxic male role model in our culture. Most of these abuses and the criminal behaviors related to them are essentially an unconscious form of social protest against a cultural ethic that systematically degrades and damages men's bodies and souls.

Suicide rates are about four times higher for men than women. Men's rates increase with age and have steadily increased overall during the last two decades, while women's rates, which decline after age forty-five, have remained relatively stable overall. In many cases, men lose their capacity for spontaneity, joyful self-expression, and pleasure as time goes on. When men do attempt to transform their lifestyles, however, they often encounter many resistances and obstacles to change.

For example, the columnist David Grimes described an article written for the *Los Angeles Times Magazine* by the aerobics teacher Susan Littwin as "highly offensive and insulting." Ms. Littwin had written that aerobics classes are a "woman's domain" in which men are "annoying, unwelcome intruders." She complained about "half-naked" middle-aged men who are "out of step with the music and perspire too heavily." She summed up her stance by saying, "I'm highly annoyed by men in aerobics classes because, in my experience, men—with the exception of professional athletes and the Chippendales dancers—are not good at aerobics. Their movements are too big, too lumbering, too uncoordinated."

I was surprised to find Ms. Littwin's ideas picked up in subsequent weeks by the *San Francisco Chronicle* and the *Seattle Times,* which published extensive articles in which she further stated:

> Physically, women have better control and coordination. We can remember steps, keep the beat. Perhaps it is a matter of sex hormones. . . . They [men] probably shouldn't take es-

trogen but it might occur to them to emulate us . . . to strive for grace, rhythm, and control instead of sticking to the male ethos. . . . They might also dress like women. Men feel funny about wearing tights but a man in shorts spread-eagled on a mat is no sight for strangers.

This critical, condescending attitude toward men is also evidenced by the numerous health clubs that do not admit men. For Women Only, a major club in Los Angeles, proudly proclaims on a huge billboard, "We Have No Men's Room." This seems to represent an unbalanced approach to gender equality. Private men's clubs are frequently sued for discrimination because women feel excluded from the deal making that may go on there. Perhaps women don't consider access to health maintenance and access to economic-power shmoozing as equally important. I suspect, though, that if *they* were dying nine years earlier than men, women would be addressing the issue.

Recently, members of San Francisco's seventy-five-year-old, all-female Metropolitan Club, a social and athletic club, filed a lawsuit asking a judge for a permanent injunction against admitting men. A spokeswoman for this group of highly educated, privileged, wealthy, and powerful women is quoted as stating that "no amount of money can compensate them [the members]. . . . Once a male is admitted as a full member, all will be lost." Two months later, students at Mills College, across San Francisco Bay, echoed this sentiment by protesting their administration's decision to integrate the all-women's school, appearing on the national news with the slogan "Better dead than coed."

Coed health clubs, on the other hand, also present special problems for men. Through sexually provocative ads they activate and reinforce a man's performance anxieties and other heroic compulsions around women. This may actually keep away the very men who need exercise the most: those who don't already fit the "Chippendales dancers" esthetic for male beauty and fitness.

The physical activities most popular with men today are competitive sports like racquetball and basketball, or solitary exercises like working out with machines and weights. It's not surprising that jogging, which is primarily a solo sport, has become one of the most popular forms of exercise with men. Men's goals regarding exercise and leisure-time activities are generally to prolong life, eliminate stress, and increase energy and stamina, primarily so they can work harder and longer. Little is encouraged that reduces pain or increases the flexibility, grace, and comfort of the body, and rarely do most adult males play for the simple pleasure of it.

THE WOUNDED BODY: MEN'S INADEQUATE MEDICAL CARE

The lack of health-care information for men is indicative of the ways men's lives are held to be of lesser worth than women's by our society. Many successful programs alert women to the dangers of cervical and breast cancer and encourage regular checkups, sometimes at publicly funded clinics devoted to just that purpose. Many health plans have a provision for women's gynecological and breast checkups. But they don't have the same provisions for preventive medicine regarding male-specific disorders. Gynecologists are considered to be primary-care specialists. Yet urologists, who guard the health of male plumbing, are classed as surgical subspecialists. The subtle implication of this classification system is that women's generative organs require preventive checkups, whereas men's need attention only when they require surgical remedies.

There's a long-standing, widespread campaign to educate women about how to perform self-examinations for breast cancer. Women's breasts are generally considered beautiful; thus the depiction of such an exam in an ad on a bus, or even on the cover of *Time* magazine, is generally acceptable. The male body, however, doesn't rate the same sort of idealization, value, or care. Males are almost never taught how to do a self-exam for testicular cancer, a disease for which men are at risk from late adolescence through the age of forty. This sort of exam should be done once a month. But I can't remember the last time I saw an ad or health brochure showing a man how to examine his testicles for this disease.

The lack of education concerning prostate disease is even more serious and deadly. *One in eleven men can expect to develop prostate cancer* sometime in his life. It will kill thirty thousand American men this year—a number that is steadily growing. This is the most frequently occurring cancer in men next to lung cancer and approximates the incidence of breast cancer in women. Approximately one hundred thousand new cases are reported in the United States every year. This slow-growing cancer responds extremely well to early treatment. But many men die painfully and unnecessarily of this disease because they are afraid to seek treatment until it's too late.

One of the early symptoms of prostate disease is restricted flow of urine. Other symptoms are change in frequency of urination or pain in the prostate region or perineum. Even though these early warning signs may persist for a long time, my interviews with urologists indicate that men often delay treatment until their bladders become completely plugged up and they're in extreme pain. Men also may wait until there is concurrent loss of sexual function, thereby receiving their first exam when the disease is already in an advanced stage. Many doctors say that the prostate digital exam is the test most frequently avoided or overlooked in a general health exam. Women, however, are usually vigorously encouraged to get regular gynecological exams.

Rectal cancer is also prevalent among men and suffers from the same lack of early detection. Many physicians themselves won't submit to an examination until there is significant, prolonged bleeding. We have a lot of anxiety about bending over and having someone look up our ass. It isn't very cool. But then again, neither is slow, painful disintegration and death.

Every man over the age of forty should get a prostate examination at least once every three years; men over fifty should go every year. Only one in six do, even when they have health insurance or money is not the issue. This heroic "Shucks, it's only a scratch" attitude is typical for many other health-related issues for men.

THE WOUNDED PENIS

Inhibitions around male-specific health-care issues are not surprising since at every stage of a man's development there is negative imprinting about the phallic aspect of maleness. Men are often taught that there is something wrong, nasty, or even evil about the penis. Often a little of it is cut off just after we're born. Sixty percent of the baby boys in this culture are still circumcised.

Men who have been circumcised as adults report that their sensitivity and capacity for experiencing sexual pleasure are dramatically reduced following circumcision. They describe the postcircumcision sexual experience as feeling like "wearing a glove" or "only being able to see in black and white." Most of us who were circumcised as infants will never know to what enhanced degree we might have been able to enjoy sexual relations. However, urologists assure me that for men's long-term health, this practice has more benefits than losses.

We discover our penises at a pretty early age. After all, there it is, just hanging out, right there within easy grasp. Like everything else in a small child's realm, it is subject to intense investigation and curiosity. We also quickly discover that it feels pretty good to mess around with it. Boys exhibit an erection within twenty-four hours of birth, and it is believed that they may even have erections while within the womb.

But boys' infantile sexuality is often disturbing to their mothers. The message that often comes from this first woman in our lives is clear: the penis is a bad thing. We are usually told not to let anyone else see it. As time goes on, we eventually begin to realize that there is something sort of shameful about the whole thing. We experience early on that the rest of our body is touched differently than our genitals when we are being washed or dressed. Chances are we were scolded or prevented from touching ourselves as infants and as children.

We may have been forbidden to touch ourselves under the threat of dire consequences, ranging from getting hair or warts on our hands to burning in hell. We may even have been punished for engaging in an activity that felt perfectly normal to us and that harmed no one. According to some child psychologists, in addition to providing "pleasure and self-solace for infants and young children," masturbation also is a means by which an adolescent "may learn to master a seemingly uncontrollable body."

Jim remembered, "When I was eleven my mom walked in on me when I was jacking off in my bedroom. She made a big deal about it. She could have just walked back out of the room, you know. But no, she just had to say something. Then she brought it up again at dinner in front of Dad and my fourteen-year-old sister. I felt ashamed for years after that."

Men also often believe that any failure of the penis to perform as expected somehow reflects on their wholeness as a man. Men have a lot of shame about prostate disease and genital distress in general because these problems completely shatter the hero myth. Superman may have a cock of steel that can go all night, but real men are subject to a host of problems.

Urologists tell me that men express much greater fear about necessary surgery in this area than women. They also display more concern about voluntary vasectomy than women do concerning a tubal ligation, which is essentially a more serious operation. We often believe that one of the major reasons we're loved by a woman is because of our cock's ability to perform. So there is a lot at risk if it stops getting hard. Maybe it is just easier to die of cancer than to face those fears. The unheroic cock is simply human. It ebbs and flows in its performance abilities from time to time and according to each situation.

Impotence is an extremely loaded and sexist word. It needs to be eliminated from our professional language, as have been terms to describe women's sexuality, like *frigidity* and *nymphomania*. Herb Goldberg advises that this problem of unresponsiveness, which I now prefer to call *diminished erotic response,* is often the "body's wisdom" in reaction to a lack of intimacy with a partner.

It is not a *male* problem, to be treated in isolation. In nonmedical cases, the ideal therapy for DER is sex counseling for both partners. Learning from other men that it is okay, even appropriate at times, to be nonresponsive also helps decrease the shame of feeling that this problem somehow reduces our manliness. It happens to all of us at times, especially under the influence of alcohol.

In most cases, diminished erotic response is a *relationship* problem. In other cases, DER accompanies some disorder like prostate disease or diabetes. In many cases early detection and a little nonsurgical treatment help. In others, there are a host of surgical options that are worth exploring. According to the Male Sexual Dysfunctional Institute, in Chicago, this problem now affects as many as 20 million men in America; previous studies put the figure about 25 percent lower. Although this potentially psychologically devastating phenomenon can be ameliorated in a majority of cases, *less than 5 percent of men actually seek help.* In a recent survey of men, almost 75 percent of the respondents said they were unaware that there was anything at all that could be done about it.

The popular magazines are full of articles regarding women's G spots, techniques for enhancing their capacity for multiple orgasms, and other promotions for ever more fulfilling sex. Yet we see little that even attempts to educate men about the very basics of their own sexual functioning.

FATHERS CHANGE DIAPERS, TOO

Although we cannot give birth or nurse infants, men are no less equipped to nurture, love, educate, and care for children. Yet another of the cultural illusions that perpetuate the oppression of men is that women are better parents than men. Feminism has taught us that biological predisposition does not regulate our capacity for achievement in areas that are not limited by obvious biological constraint, such as smaller stature in women or lack of breasts in men. But commercials for diapers, children's foods, toys, and other juvenile consumer items continue to depict mothers as the only parents who diaper, feed, and entertain the children. This is contrary and inimical to the widespread trend in this country for men to increasingly assume these roles.

Beatle John Lennon was frustrated in the last few years of his life by public response to his staying home to raise his infant son, Sean, while his wife, Yoko, managed their business. When asked what he was doing, he would often reply, "I've been baking bread and looking after the baby," to which others would say, according to Lennon, "Yes, but what else have you been doing? What secret projects are going on in the basement?" His reply would be, "Are you kidding? Bread and babies, as every housewife knows, is a full-time job. After I make the loaves, I feel like I have conquered something."

He felt that "the reason kids are so crazy is nobody can face the responsibility of bringing them up." He was upset that people would not accept and even condemned him for no longer feeling interested in being a rock-and-roll hero, a role he felt more comfortable playing in his twenties and thirties. Very few people could conceive that being a full-time father was the most meaningful activity he could engage in during midlife.

Only recently have fathers been permitted in the delivery room. Now that they feel more welcome by doctors, they are showing up in ever-increasing numbers. Male nurses, however, still report widespread discrimination by senior female nurses, keeping them out of obstetrics. Some women have a tendency to act like members of an old-girl network, as if the birth process were something that was happening only to the mother-to-be. Like many men who feel threatened by women entering male-dominated aspects of the work force, many women fear the implications of sharing in an arena in which women traditionally feel more empowered. Men are also seldom, if ever, invited to baby showers and other birthing rituals even though the arrival of a child will affect the father's life as much as the mother's for the next two decades at least.

When men do get involved in parenting, they're often shamed as unmanly in some way. The columnist Mary Graber, for example, writes sarcastically that "there is even a commercial out there that has a daddy as spokesparent for a baby wipe. Men have become overnight experts on raising children. It makes one wonder how women ever managed before Wonderful New Men came along."

Is it any wonder that men often feel they have no place in the early stages of birth and child-rearing? Men are rarely given paternity leave from work. Flex time is also less likely to be considered for working fathers than for working mothers. The movie *Kramer vs. Kramer* depicted the sort of discrimination fathers often face. The divorced father found himself stretched between the rock of an employer unsympathetic to the demands that he faced as a single parent, and the hard place of his ex-wife's constant attempts to undermine his credibility as a parent. He was strained and harried while attempting to balance his career with his parenting. She wanted to take away his custody rights even though he was a totally dedicated and loving parent to his son, who was happy to live with him.

Although many statistics are compiled by the government concerning the needs of working mothers, *none are kept on behalf of fathers,* including the special needs of the nearly 3 million American men who are single parents. Many family-oriented men wish they could modify their careers in order to have more intimacy in their lives and—as did men in preindustrial societies—spend more time with their families. They may have a good job, for which they are qualified, but don't necessarily want to make it the focus of their whole life.

I hear many women argue that men are threatened by the idea of a woman being more successful or more involved outside the home than they are. This sentiment is contrary to the experience of men in the Dennis Thatcher Society (named for the husband of the former British prime minister), who have married women who are "deservedly more prominent and influential than they are." According to one spokesman interviewed by the press, members feel that "this is a very enviable position." Their central ideological principle is that "the women's movement is the best thing that ever happened to men."

In our men's group, both Rodger and Carl find some aspects of the life of a homemaker enviable. Rodger said, "At some time in my life I'd love to have the opportunity to stay home more, have time to take better care of myself, pursue avocational interests, and have more time with the kids." Carl feels that his status as the primary wage earner for the family is oppressive: "It prevents that fantasy from ever being possible." Many men feel wounded by the meager support and acknowledgment they receive for attempting to be involved parents. It's natural to feel that way in a society and cultural context that, for the most part, tends to drive men out of the home.

THE INEQUITIES OF DIVORCE

Even though men are often depicted as abandoning their families at the drop of an overdue bill, the reality is that divorce is frequently just as destructive to the lives of men as it is to those of women. This phenomenon may be underscored by the fact that wives are actually twice as likely to file for divorce as husbands. This seems to indicate that, once committed to marriage, men are generally more reluctant to end it than are women. Why is it that in popular literature and the media we usually see the reverse?

Jack told us, "My first wife left me for another woman. Yet, for some reason, most of her friends decided the breakup was all my fault. She also took the kids, and then took me for every cent she could get. She and her girlfriend even wound up living together in the house I built. I was the bad guy because she had needs I just couldn't satisfy. There were other issues, of course, but that was the main one."

Infidelity is often cited by women as a major complaint against men. It's often depicted as one of the essential character defects of men in general. Once again, a review of the latest information contradicts popular opinion. According to the sociologist Annette Lawson, who recently surveyed over six hundred men and women, modern women are usually the *first* partner to develop sexual liaisons outside their marriages. They begin sexual relations with other men on the average of 4.5 years after getting married—somewhat earlier than men. This reverses the trend of past generations in which women generally waited several years longer than men before straying from the marital bed. Is this progress?

Warren Farrell has, at times, called the women's movement *divorce training*. With rising divorce rates over the last several decades, men have never been more at risk when it comes to maintaining a long-term relationship with a woman. The privilege and opportunity for remaining an involved parent are thus also increasingly placed in jeopardy.

Men are generally denied the right to custody of their children in divorce, even though there is no clear body of research that demonstrates that single women are better parents than single men. Even in those rare cases in which men do win physical custody, their parenting decisions are often called into question in court, and the vast majority of these men lose custody again within two years.

Men are also treated unequally by spousal-support laws, which restrict them from being *active* parents. About 20 percent of the 13.3 million single-parent households are now headed by a male. This number is steadily increasing as more men challenge established customs. One difficulty that full-time fathers face is that they seldom receive child or spousal support, even in those cases, like Brad's, where their ex-wife's earnings are greater than or equal to their own. In one recent case a judge even threatened a man with contempt and fines for raising the issue of spousal support for himself. The Latin word for "nourishment" is *alimonia*. Although thousands of men are jailed every year for failing to provide this financial nourishment as mandated by law, women are seldom held equally accountable.

Many men report that when they demonstrate interest in being a full-time parent, their wish is often met with suspicion and the intimation that they must have some unnatural, perverse motive for wanting to be with their children so much. The sad irony, however, is that, contrary to the myth of men's untrustworthiness as single parents, the majority of violent child-abuse incidents, resulting in tens of thousands of injuries and hundreds of deaths every year, are perpetrated by women. A majority of these victims are boys averaging two and a half years old.

Rodger's first wife moved to Canada with their children after their divorce. Since then he has seen them only once a year. Even though he is now remarried, with three new children, he still has lingering grief over the loss of his first son and daughter. He told us, "They hardly even know me now, they're growing up so fast. She only lets them come visit at Christmas, and with all the demands of my new family, I just don't have the time, energy, or money to fight for shared-custody rights. Jenny [his eleven-year-old] wants to spend the summer with us, but her mother refuses to even consider it. Jenny is her prisoner."

Men are twice as likely to commit suicide or have serious mental and emotional problems following divorce as are women. One study puts the suicide rate for divorced men at about four times the rate for divorced women. This may be because men have become dependent on women to support them emotionally and, like good mothers, to keep track of their health-maintenance needs.

Men are also more likely to develop their social contacts through women. This often results in their being left alone and isolated when the couple's friends choose sides after a divorce. Single men in general are also less likely to be invited to social gatherings and parties hosted by couples than are other couples.

The loss of children in the home is another major reason men suffer from more emotional problems in the years following a divorce. Rodger told us, "The reason I started drinking in the first place was that I got totally depressed when my wife left the country with our kids."

FALSE ALLEGATIONS OF CHILD ABUSE

The inaccurate accusation of child abuse is an ominous new trend in our culture that is also separating fathers from their children. Andy, whom I know well, is a very devoted and conscientious father. Recently he was reported to police for child molestation by his ex-wife, with whom he was engaged in a vicious custody dispute. He had touched his six-month-old son's scrotum while diapering him in her presence. The child-protective services informed the police, and a warrant was issued without so much as a phone call to verify the circumstances. It's hard to imagine a mother being similarly charged or forced into expensive, time-consuming psychological evaluations and court proceedings.

Andy was initially barred from visiting his son, which is what the mother had been attempting to accomplish for months, and was essentially regarded as guilty until proven innocent by all agencies involved. He was allowed visitation, after a time, but only in the presence of a court-approved observer for whom he had to pay about forty dollars an hour.

Thousands of dollars later, after months of investigation, Andy's ex-wife was finally admonished to cease from these blatantly abusive tactics and spurious charges. Visitation rights were resumed and increased. The charges, however, continued to work their way through the criminal-justice system, because once a complaint is made it must be acted upon regardless of its merit. Many innocent men walk away from this type of encounter, having neither the time, money, stamina, nor courage to face the stigma of being publicly shamed as a child molester—thus losing a precious lifetime relationship.

In this particular divorce, the mother later acknowledged that such a tactic was encouraged by a women's support group. She was disturbed that the father wanted to be involved with the child because she didn't want him in *her* life anymore.

This is not an unusual story. Andy was devastated during the process. "Can you imagine?" he asked me one night. "Someday I'm going to take my kid to a local ball game and people are going to point and say, 'There's that guy who messed around with his kid when he was a baby.' Or worse, some kid could approach my son on the playground and say, 'Hey, I heard your daddy likes to have a good time with you.'"

The Association of Family and Conciliation Courts, which reviewed these types of cases in twelve states, concluded that approximately *one-third of child-abuse allegations in custody disputes are probably false*. It also concluded that at least *14 percent are deliberately falsified*. In most cases this falsification is an attempt to discredit any claim for parental rights that a father may have. The columnist Bob Vacon interviewed a number of people on this topic, including the first director of the National Center on Child Abuse, who calls this issue the "atomic bomb of custody litigation because it is so hard to prove." Vacon observed that a number of professionals in this field feel this "superweapon in custody disputes" is often also misused because ambiguous physical signs or behavior changes are overblown by well-meaning professionals who have only partial training in clinical assessment.

These sorts of false charges have resulted in several child-protective services around the country becoming the objects of lawsuits. In one such incident reported to me by a source who wishes to remain anonymous, a caseworker systematically ignored evidence contrary to the claim made by the child's psychologist. She believed the abuse must have happened. As a former victim herself, she was certain that she knew the signs even though the child and everyone else in the family consistently denied the allegations.

Over one hundred thousand cases of real sexual child abuse *do* occur every year. We need strong laws and procedures to protect our children from abuse by *both* of their parents. However, some female writers, even though primarily concerned with the recovery of female victims, admit there is a taboo against speaking out about abuse perpetrated by women. This denial can make their victims feel as if they are crazy—that they are the only ones with this experience.

Ellen Bass and Laura Davis cite early studies indicating that at least "20 percent of the perpetrators who molest boys are female" and that "a number of girls are molested by female caretakers as well." They conclude that "women do abuse, and if it's not put out there the healing can't happen." Other, more recent studies indicate that as many as 47 percent of sex-abuse victims are male and that of that number, approximately one-third were abused by women.

I have surveyed a number of male therapists who work with men who have been sexually abused. They also report that about 30 to 40 percent of their clients were molested by women. This information has been in the dark for a long time. Many therapists never even ask men if they have been sexually abused by a woman or a man, even though the subject is almost always raised during initial psychological interviews with women. Men are conditioned to think that if an older female seduces them as a child or adolescent, they got lucky. Perhaps this is true in some cases, but men are often reluctant to talk about this issue.

It doesn't feel very heroic to admit to this wound. Yet it requires real heroism to break the spell that childhood abuse has cast upon many of us by coming out of denial and admitting that it did hurt us in a variety of ways. Many men who had these sorts of early sexual encounters with women have had various difficulties in their adult relations with women and other problems as well. We are often quick to recount the sins of our fathers. Yet the most hardened men, capable of ignoring almost any taunt or insult, can usually be provoked into a fight by even mildly denigrating comments about their mothers. In many cases, our tendency to overidealize women influences us to refrain from speaking out about the abusive mother, sister, aunt, grandmother, or babysitter.

When boys have been victims of a male perpetrator, feelings of shame, doubts about their sexual identity, and fears of being perceived as having acted in an unmanly way often keep them silent. Some studies indicate that much of the data concerning male victims, regardless of the perpetrator's sex, has often been ignored by health professionals when reported in the past. Most treatment programs have been concerned only with female victims, who are three times more likely than boys to tell their parents about abuse when it occurs. This is not surprising since girls have been better educated and supported for speaking out on this issue than have boys.

The current abuses and manipulations of the system by some divorce lawyers and social workers who hold a presumption of perversion toward fathers has the tragic potential for actually undermining child-protective services in general by eroding their credibility. Many men who view their traditional role as one that protects the helpless and vulnerable have been wounded by false allegations about their character.

We need not abandon the rights of fathers, or reinforce the illusion that all men abuse their wives and children, in order to gain social justice and protect the rights of victims. Ninety-nine and a half percent of us are not child molesters. We do not need to feel, as some men do today, ashamed or uncomfortable about fighting for our children. Many men, for various reasons, abandon their families. But many more are exiled by legal and social forces inimical to fathers' rights.

THE WOUND OF THE EXILED FATHER

The psychologist Phyllis Tyson, in her analysis of how male gender identity is formed, observes, "If their [the mother's and father's] relationship is fraught with ambivalence, with a devaluation of the father, the boy may fear that, as a male, he will be devalued and belittled by mother as father is. . . . He may then remain in a passive, dependent, infantile role . . . with defensive aggression directed toward the mother, with the view that all females are potential castrators."

As we will discover in the next chapter, both these traits—fear of women, and male passivity—seem to be growing in this culture. So it's important to understand the consequences when the divorced father is exiled from the home by the mother or prevented from maintaining a relationship with the child. Many boys whose parents have been divorced prefer to be with their fathers. This becomes increasingly important to them in later childhood, and even more so in adolescence.

In some cases fathers also can be exiled by the courts. For example, unwed men who become fathers also have important parental relationships that should be preserved. Yet according to a Supreme Court decision several years ago, a man who impregnated a woman during a casual affair could not prevent her from putting their daughter up for adoption. Strangers were allowed to adopt the child over the natural father's legal protests. His request for visitation rights was also denied. The mother could lose her right to be legally recognized as a parent only if she was found unfit by a court. According to this decision, the father never had any rights in the first place. The child also had no right to be loved by and known to a *biological parent* who was motivated to have at least some degree of a parental role in her life, even though he could not assume custody at that time.

This ruling is significant in that approximately 25 percent of all children born today are born out of wedlock. Additionally, about 50 percent of marriages end in divorce. Women get custody in about 80 percent of these cases. Thus, well over half of the fathers in America are now outside the home. Once outside, they tend to become increasingly estranged from their children as time goes on.

A study of one thousand children from disrupted homes showed that about half of them had never been in their father's home, 40 percent had not seen him in the previous year, and only one in six saw the father once a week or more. Men often have difficulty separating their relations with their kids from their relations with their former spouses. When they no longer live with the children, they are often dependent upon the custodial mother's goodwill in order to maintain a good relationship with them. Many men simply give up.

In the ghettos, an even higher percentage of fathers are exiled from the home and discouraged from having a presence in the family by social-welfare laws that threaten reduced aid to families with fathers. Young men in these communities are increasingly forming violent gangs. The absent father is one of many social causes of this phenomenon. Adolescent males inevitably search for some sort of masculine identity and male community wherever they can find it.

Drug abuse among adolescent males is epidemic in our culture, and one factor many adolescent addicts share is an absent father. One study concludes that the abuse is higher when "youth feel that they receive less love from parents, especially the father." As we will see later, there are several other very important developmental reasons that a boy needs to spend time with his father at this time of his life.

One of the deepest and most prevalent wounds many men carry concerns the actual or emotional absence of their fathers when they were growing up. This issue has come up repeatedly in our group as we have tried to sort out where our first images of masculinity came from.

Jim recalls, "My old man clobbered me for stealing his car when I was sixteen. I was so pissed off that I moved away from home and didn't see him again for twenty-five years. I recently started working on a wooden bust of him. During the work I remembered how he taught me how to use tools and gave me my first chisel set when I was eleven. I suddenly missed him a lot and looked him up. He was kinda cool at first, hurt I guess, but he was really glad to hear from me. We've started visiting and have both apologized for the past. He's retired now and pretty mellow, even wise in some ways, I guess. Anyway, we see each other about every other week and are going fishing next month. Maybe it's true that it's never too late to have a happy childhood."

There is no shame in feeling this longing for our fathers. It is quite natural to feel unrequited grief about this separation, especially if they died before we could ever get to know them. Our fathers also may have been conditioned to hold themselves somewhat apart from us. Yet many of us, like Jim, experience a good welcome when we make the effort to reconnect.

ABORTION IS ALSO A MAN'S ISSUE

Regardless of whatever solidarity they may feel with champions of women's rights, men today have *no* rights in deciding the fate of their unborn children through requesting or preventing abortion. This reality is reflected by a Supreme Court decision in November 1988, according to which a husband does not have the right to block his wife's abortion. The attorney argued on behalf of the husband that a woman's abortion right is not absolute. He believed that expectant fathers should have some means to protect unborn children for whom they are prepared to be responsible. The court did not agree. Obviously, men cannot have children without the cooperation of a woman. But women can and do choose to be single, male-free parents. Thousands of lesbian couples and single women are even becoming impregnated anonymously through sperm banks.

I am struck by the enormous depth of grief men in my groups have expressed over the abortions that have occurred in their lives. A recent survey indicated that men often suffer *more* long-term guilt and regret about abortion than many women. Previous to working with men at this level of intimacy, I was completely unaware that other men felt that way.

From the opposite perspective, men are also held financially accountable for unwanted, unplanned children whom they feel unprepared to father—for whatever reasons—and would otherwise choose to abort. One woman recently sued for custody rights to her frozen eggs, previously fertilized in vitro by the husband she was now divorcing. He no longer wanted to father children with her, yet the woman claimed that the eggs were subject to community-property laws and that she had the right to have them implanted and bring a child to term, despite her husband's expressed wishes to the contrary.

Either way, men are treated inequitably under the law and in the culture at large. It's true that women are physically affected and endangered by pregnancy and should therefore have the inalienable right to choose—to protect themselves, their bodies, and their futures. This does not mean, however, that men who are emotionally and economically affected, and thus also at risk, should have no rights in the matter.

Women want to break the so-called male conspiracy that has denied them economic power in the past. In the same manner, men want to change the social order that denies them the opportunity to be parents, with or without a partner in their lives. Many men have felt wounded by the loss of their unborn children. Others have resented being made responsible for children they did not want or felt unable to care for.

VIOLENCE AGAINST MEN

Another arena in which the needs of men have often been disregarded by society is that of the millions of men who are victims of violence every year. In recent years there has been a great deal of attention given to the serious problem of violence toward women in our society. Much of the increase in public awareness about this important issue has been due to the dedicated efforts of feminist activists. Violence toward women is often cited as one aspect of women's oppression and inequality.

And men bear the responsibility for perpetrating the majority of physical violence. But what seems to have been overlooked is that men are also the *primary victims* of violence in our culture: men make up about 80 percent of all homicide victims, are victims of about 70 percent of all robberies, and make up 70 percent of all other victims of aggravated assaults. Even rape, which is primarily held to be a crime against women, victimizes incarcerated men in numbers matching or exceeding those of free women. The fact that these statistics have apparently been ignored inflames the wounds of men by making their victimization seem less important than women's.

In the Vietnam War, men were killed eight thousand to one over women. In films and television, more than 90 percent of the characters who die are men. In romance novels, written primarily for the entertainment of women, the degradation of men and violence committed against men are such frequently recurring themes that they have inspired more than one writer to dub this form of literature *women's pornography*.

During a Sally Jessy Raphael talk show on the subject of men who have been victims of violence perpetrated by women, the women in the audience mocked a man who was a victim of his wife's abuse, and they applauded her actions against him. Yet an incident in which a man abuses a woman is almost always perceived as shameful and criminal, regardless of the provocation. Men have at times been known to step in, even at significant risk, to aid a woman being attacked by another man. But it's rare that women, other than police officers, respond in kind on behalf of a man in any kind of danger.

Men die from all causes combined an average of nine years earlier than women. Although death comes to us all, it is a more present reality in the mind of the man who knows it is he, in his role as defender of women and children in a moment of danger, who will be expected to die first if necessary. Women are still rescued first in time of emergency. Many disaster statistics, from homelessness to the sinking of the *Titanic* to various hostage crises and wars around the world, reveal a disproportionate number of male victims. Men know instinctively, from their biological evolution as hunters, that they are the first to face danger, dismemberment, and sudden, violent death.

Violence against men is a form of entertainment in our culture. Boxing, football, hockey, and car racing often feature men being wounded, maimed, even killed. Although many films depict violence toward women, the physical abuse of women is seldom perceived as funny. Yet a lot of physical comedy is based upon violence toward men. This brand of humor ranges from Abbott and Costello through the Three Stooges right up to numerous recent films that feature the death, dismemberment, or torture of men in supposedly funny ways. The comedy *I Love You to Death* featured a plot, based on a true story, about the various ways in which a wife and mother-in-law conspired to murder a man. He was a loving father and a hard-working provider who, essentially, loved his wife. They decided he deserved to die because he was habitually unfaithful. Comic violence against men takes on a much larger dimension in films like *48 Hrs, Harlem Nights, Batman, Lethal Weapon,* and most Schwarzenegger action films, in which the actor often makes a few gleeful kills in cute ways for occasional comic relief from the more serious gore.

THE SECOND TASK OF MEN: TO BEGIN HEALING ONE ANOTHER THROUGH EXAMINING OUR WOUNDS

The list of male-specific inequities, inferiorities, and wounds is more extensive than any of us realized when we began our group. The above reports represent only a small sampling of articles I've reviewed and information I've received from the new knights and other men. The purpose of this section of the book is not simply to complain about the problems of male oppression—another activity men are discouraged from engaging in—or to make the reader angry (which I hope in fact to have done). The intent has been to demonstrate, through a small survey of problems, that contrary to popular myth, men do not have all the advantages and are suffering in many ways that are sex-role specific. That suffering is often expressed through behaviors such as abuse, addiction, poor health maintenance, and violence toward ourselves and others.

There are no easy solutions to many of the problems we face. The first step seems to be to become aware of our own wounds— the pain, isolation, grief, oppression, anger, and frustration. We can then heal whatever shame we may carry through sharing that knowledge with one another, and supporting one another through the dramatic process of social reformation in which we find ourselves today.

The archetypes of the Martyr and the Hero are clearly engendering pathological responses in many men. These old roles are programs for losing soul. We hope that a revision of the underlying psychological structures that give substance to our culture may produce a different relationship to masculinity and to new roles that are soulful, joyful, nurturing, generative, creative, and fully alive.

Many of us welcome most of the changes that the women's movement is making. By encouraging women to become more self-reliant and self-sufficient, the women's movement paves the rough and pitted road to men's liberation as well. Ultimately, I hope both these wings of freedom and social justice will beat in synchrony. Until that time men must begin to support one another in claiming their rights wherever they are abridged, while simultaneously supporting the rights of women—to the degree that they do not inequitably discriminate against men. We cannot make compensation for the sins of our fathers by martyring ourselves.

For the most part, men are still having to face discrimination on their own, case by individual case. Many of the wounds of men have been self-inflicted. Others have been created by the neglect, abuse, ignorance, or indifference of other men. Yet as we examine these wounds we find that some of them are also caused by women. These often leave a different sort of mark upon us.

We need women to understand, as the next chapter will reveal, the ways in which some women inflame the wounds of men. This has made it difficult for many of us to find a place of solidarity with them that does not hold our own self-abasement as a prerequisite.

> *Beginning to heal our wounds through revealing them was our second task. Understanding some of the ways in which we become shamed by women, and rebuilding our self-esteem on deep masculine foundations, was the third task we faced.*

CHAPTER 3

Angry Women and Feminized Men

In the old time women's cunts had teeth in them
It was hard to be a man then . . .
If your woman said she felt like biting, you didn't
* take it lightly*
Maybe you just ran away to fight Numuzoho
* the Cannibal.*
            From old Paiute poem

A book attempting to redefine femininity today would have scant need for the type of information we've included about masculinity in the last two chapters. The historical and contemporary wounds of women should be well known to anyone but the most recalcitrant misogynist. The National Organization for Women and other women's groups maintain lobbyists to create legislation that protects women's rights. They also further women's aims through the courts, literature, the media, and public education. They have been working for equal opportunity in jobs and education, for rights to sexual freedom and abortion, and for child-care centers, maternity leave from work, and a fair share of political and economic power. Many women also have been reforming our social and religious institutions.

The men's movement in this country is about twenty years behind the well-organized and more vocal women's movement. The men's movement is still an amorphous and diverse entity. What seems to be a common thread, however, is a concern about the ways in which men are wounded and a search for new models, images, and myths of masculinity connected to depth of soul and breadth of spirit. In this respect, our goals are not in conflict with women's agendas.

One way in which political, religious, and social groups have historically found their identity and cohesiveness is by sharing a common enemy. But men don't have an easily identifiable scapegoat to rail against in order to create instant solidarity with one another. The men's movement seems to be growing along less reactionary lines than the women's movement, which initially laid many of its complaints at the feet of the misogynist, chauvinistic, or patriarchal male.

The men's movement is not a mere reaction to feminism. For the most part, we don't view our male predicament as having been created by women's misandry (hatred or fear of men) or reverse sexism. Male oppression is much more insidious, subtle, and pervasive than that. For the most part we need to look to ourselves as men for positive solutions and transformation. However, some discrimination does emanate from women's attitudes about us, and we need to confront that as well. We can't blame women for our situation. But it's important for women and men to understand the ways in which men, as we have documented, are often equally at risk for being wounded. Until now, most of us have remained silent, caught in the Hero/Martyr image.

TURNING AWAY FROM THE GODDESS

I haven't always been, as my partner Liz has playfully started calling me, a radical masculinist. During the earlier years of the women's movement I was quite intrigued by its aura of empowerment, fierceness, sociopolitical relevance, and vision. A sense of awakening spirituality, mobilized passion, and environmental consciousness also spoke to a deeper aspect of my being—the young man in search of his soul. I felt that most men around me were relatively superficial, even crude. I felt I understood women more and was in turn more understood by them. I identified with their righteous social indignation and enjoyed the poetic and emotional nature of their gatherings.

I had few close male friends then, priding myself on being the kind of man who could have many women in his life who were just friends. Sooner or later, several of these friends wound up intimately involved with me. But it was a nice platonic illusion for a while. For a long time I felt that women were going to save the world with the help of a few of us *enlightened* men. I looked to the women's movement for leadership in the social transformation that seemed to be upon us.

Women taught me hymns and rituals of invocation to various goddesses—chants to Isis, Astarte, Diana, Hecate, Demeter, Kali, Inanna, and the ever-ubiquitous Earth Mother. It was the time for the Goddess to become the new sacred image of humankind. The Goddess would lead us into a more compassionate world that revered life, protected the environment, and ended war.

But one night about ten years ago my feminized spiritual beliefs were dramatically changed. I had been performing and recording with a ritual-music band called the Circle. We decided to attend an antinuclear protest at Lawrence Livermore Laboratory, where some of the primary nuclear-weapons research is conducted. We felt the time had come for us to *walk our talk* more—to be more active in the expression of our environmental and political beliefs. For years many group members had tried to help the world through prayer and meditation, letter writing, and public education. These still seemed like good ideas. But as some of us learned during the antiwar movement a decade earlier, there is no substitute for direct action and media events.

The night before the demonstration, we were invited to a pre-event rally being held in a remote field. It was supposed to be a ceremonial invocation by a currently well-known ecofeminist leader, writer, and teacher of women. We walked a long trail through the woods to a clearing in which several hundred people had gathered. It was the deep of the night and very dark.

As we approached the center of the clearing, where everyone had gathered, I began to see the outline of a huge shape. As I drew near I could see that it was a statue of a man, at least twelve feet tall, made of sticks and branches lashed together. Songs were sung, rattles shaken, and drums pounded while the processioners decorated this statue with flowers, handwritten prayers, and colored pieces of cloth. Speeches were made against the military-industrial complex. There was a call for the end of nuclear proliferation and a return to respect for the earth—all sentiments that I still share today.

It was beautiful and peaceful in that special time, a few hours before dawn when almost everyone is still asleep. Then there began a long litany of the evils committed by men against women and the earth. At some prearranged signal, torches were lit. Some women set fire to the wicker man. As it began to blaze a number of the women took off their shirts and began to dance, swaying bare-breasted around the fire. "Death to the patriarchy! Death to the patriarchy!" several cried. As the large stick representing the man's penis caught fire, one woman cried aloud, "You're not so tough now, are you?" The whole ensemble laughed and cheered. They continued dancing and singing hymns to the Goddess, crying "Blessed be She! Blessed be She!"

I looked around the gathering, which was almost half male. The faces of the men indicated that they were as disturbed as I was. We had come a long way to make a political statement as allies and brothers of the women present. I felt nauseated and shaken by what had occurred. I realized that when these women said they hated men, they were essentially talking about me as well. Somehow along the way, I had disidentified myself as a man. I wasn't like *those* men who were wrecking the world with their chain saws, bulldozers, and war machines. The reality, however, was that, much as I might, as Jungians believe, have a feminine soul, my body and orientation toward life were and are very male.

In a Communion-like ritual, the women strolled through the assembly, placing bread in our mouths. I spit mine out. The road of my initiation into Earth Mother mysteries had ended. I knew instinctively, years before conducting the research for this book, that the phallus was also holy. It was no better to burn wicker men than it was to burn witches. Suddenly I no longer found amusing the antimale bumper stickers I had seen on women's cars as we hiked in. They said, "If god created men, who can you trust?" "The more I get to know men, the more I love my dog," and, more ominously, "Dead men can't rape." I had heard of SCUM, the Society to Cut Up Men, but never believed, before that night, that they existed outside of some media hype. The Goddess showed a dark face that night, which felt just as dangerous as the so-called patriarchy.

ARE MEN REALLY TO BLAME FOR EVERYTHING?

Most feminist initiative does not so blatantly express the attitude of female superiority and misandry I experienced that night at Livermore. Women have a valid litany of wounds, comparable to those I've listed for men. Additionally, women experience a number of serious, gender-specific problems, like steadily increasing levels of sexual assault. After several decades of feminism in America, there still remains much work ahead to create a culture that honors women's lives.

Women have suffered enormously in the past. Only in recent generations have they reclaimed the power to reshape the culture and their individual lives. But in addition to empowering women, raising their consciousness, and educating men about the inequalities women face in this culture, something else also has taken place. A unilateral, gender-polarized approach to society's ills, with a stance that is often degrading and inimical toward men, has been injected into many levels of the culture.

Many women complain that men are self-centered, sexist, and lazy. Or oppressive, oversexed, and violent. A recent survey of American women reports that a majority of women hold these significantly sexist ideas about men *as a group.* These perceptions have steadily grown among women over the last twenty years.

Over fifteen years ago, the pioneering feminist Betty Friedan warned that the faction of the women's movement that "preached man-hating sex/class warfare" was in danger of "driving out the women who wanted equality but who also wanted to keep on loving their husbands and children." She felt this "orgy of sex hatred" was in danger of splintering the women's movement, potentially as disruptive as any agent provocateur deliberately attempting to diffuse it. She worried that gender polarization could slow down women's progress in achieving their agenda.

The majority of feminist women may indeed want to work in partnership with men for equitable social change. But as Betty Friedan feared, it is the more strident voice of opposition, blame, and degradation of men that often greets even the most concerned and responsive male.

Carl, who did graduate work at the University of California-Santa Cruz in the early seventies, was a campaign worker for several liberal politicians in the area. He said, "I got so tired of the constant antimale rhetoric from the women I was working with that I finally just had to quit. Who needs to go to work every day to hear about how screwed up men are from your coworkers? It practically turned me into a Republican."

In addition to the wide body of scholarly profemale/antimale feminist literature as represented by the landmark books *The Women's Room, Sexual Politics,* and *Against Our Will,* there also now exists a plethora of popular books such as: *Smart Women, Foolish Choices* and *Women Who Love Too Much.* There are *Wild Women with Passive Men* and women with *The Cinderella Complex,* who find *No Good Men* while facing the *Don Juan Dilemma* in relationships with men who have *The Peter Pan Complex* or *The Casanova Complex.* They wonder *Should Women Stay with Men Who Stray, Men Who Can't Love,* or *Men Who Cannot Be Faithful?* There are also *Men Who Hate Women and the Women Who Love Them* and

Men Who Hate Women and the Women Who Marry Them, who have given rise to the *Men Who Hate Themselves and the Women Who Agree with Them.* One book, now at press, simply proclaims, *Maybe Men Are Just Jerks.*

In his best-selling book about his midlife crisis, *Dave Barry Turns Forty,* Barry notes that these popular psychology books have helped us to understand that "underneath their brusque 'macho' exteriors men are all basically slime-sucking toads."

Male-bashing is rampant in most feminist literature, ranging from subtle insinuations to blatant rancorous language. In *Pure Lust,* Mary Daly says, "This book is being published in the 1980s—a period of extreme danger for women and for our sister the earth and her other creatures, all of whom are targeted by the maniacal fathers, sons, and holy ghosts for extinction by nuclear holocaust." Charlene Spretnak attempts to make the case that neurophysiologists have *proven* that men are "manipulative animals." A commonly repeated theme is that masculinity represents war, machines, and the death principle, while femininity represents life, nature, and beauty. In this vituperative mode, Daly says male sexual energy is

> phallic lust, violent and self-indulgent, which levels all life, dismembering spirit/matter, attempting annihilation. . . . This lust is pure in the sense that it is characterized by unmitigated malevolence. It is pure in the sense that it is ontologically evil, having as its end the braking/breaking of female be-ing.

This perspective is shared by Susan Brownmiller, who believes that "man's discovery that his genitalia could serve as a weapon to generate fear must rank as one of the most important discoveries of prehistoric times. . . . One of the earliest forms of male bonding must have been the gang rape of one woman by a band of marauding men." According to this point of view, male obsession with death and power over women and nature—also labeled the *patriarchy*—is the cause of the endangered environment and the root of war and aggression.

Even the planet Earth has been increasingly anthropomorphized as a female entity—a single mother. This has not been the case, as will be seen in chapter 6, in many other cultures and ancient mythologies, which include the Earth Father as cocreative deity with the Earth Mother. Concurrently, it's often suggested that women share a deeper connection and alignment with the earth than men. This popular, New Age, feminist-influenced belief is expressed by Lynn Andrews, who states that "everything must be born of women. . . . Men are interlopers."

Women are more in tune and possess greater elemental power, according to Spretnak, who also says that "in achieving balance, as in perceiving holistic, spiritual truths, women again have the advantage." Consequently, the growing belief of many feminists seems to be that it is through the female gender alone that our salvation will come. Can the human race be redeemed merely through the instilling of feminine values in both men and women? The antinuclear activist Dr. Helen Caldicott, whom I otherwise deeply respect, also has expressed the sentiment of many women that "it's up to the women now to save the world." But I believe that a united effort is needed.

The 1990s have been referred to as the she decade. According to Joyce Brothers, women will be "writing the script." Many of the above beliefs are becoming pervasive throughout various areas of the culture. It is, without doubt, part of a powerful and necessary process of women reclaiming their power. But it is frequently reversing the very sexist attitudes that women have attacked men for displaying in the past. Over forty years ago Margaret Mead warned that if we perpetuate the habit of focusing on women's issues in a vacuum, we will "fail to recognize that where one sex suffers, the other sex suffers also."

Many men feel wounded by the unrelenting wrath of the new matriarchy. During the last few decades, according to the poet Robert Bly, women have been expressing "forty generations of repressed rage." This is often more than any single man can face. In the early days of the men's movement, Otis Adams published comments describing his anger about the "ladies-first syndrome," which leads some women to take advantage of the training that men often receive to be chivalrous. He felt that many women believed, "I can hit you but you can't hit me back because I'm a girl." His experience was that the social trend of the past few decades has been restricted to "unilateral liberation. Everything I had ever believed, my every thought, everything I had ever tried to express was lost, drowned out in the roar of feminism. . . . The unidirectional forcefulness of their assertions blotted out all other points of view on sexual roles and stereotypes."

Of course, beneath these gender conflicts we all seek deeper and more balanced partnerships with one another and with nature. What degrades any one of us clearly degrades us all—woman and man alike. Most men today do not openly advocate the oppression of women. With the exception of some raunchy jokes, it's also rare that I hear denigrating or derisive sentiments about women expressed at men's gatherings. There is, however, a lot of confusion and resentment. Some of these feelings develop from powerful antimale trends in our popular culture.

THE MALE-BASHING MEDIA

Male-bashing has become a popular exercise. One can observe this daily on television or in print—in ads, cartoons, articles—and even in entire films that present men in a demeaning manner. Frederic Hayward, a researcher for the Sacramento-based advocacy group Men's Rights, Inc., conducted a one-year study on how men's roles are being depicted in television advertising. He concluded that because advertisers gear their ads toward women consumers, and are hearing a lot of anger from them these days, "it's politically chic to dump on men. Advertising copywriters feel free to insult men in a way they would never do to women. . . . Despite the changing roles of men, advertising continues to ignore their work as care givers and parents."

Donald F. Buzzone, the president of a research company that studies hundreds of commercials every year, concludes that ads with male-bashing themes *work*. "They seem to do more to turn females on than they do to turn males off," he states. If racial minorities or women were used in the same denigrating ways as men, a torrent of protest would result.

The Associated Press reviewer Kathryn Baker commented that in the original television miniseries produced by Oprah Winfrey, *The Women of Brewster Place,* "men who tune in will see their gender portrayed as mostly bullies, brutes, and no-account losers. One of the only nice guys in the movie winds up getting beat with a two-by-four wielded by a lesbian." The visual media are merely perpetuating a long tradition in Western literature represented by the popular genre of the anti-male novel. Its readership, accounting for sales of millions of books each year, is almost exclusively female. These stories have a repetitive theme involving violence perpetrated against at least one male character, who is often an oppressor of women. Usually it results in his death—and her rescue by a stereotypically heroic male.

Men have been notably silent about being so frequently depicted as inept, impotent buffoons or aggressive, dominating, alcoholic, child-abusing, raping, sexist, greedy, wife-beating, power-monopolizing, narcissistic, unfeeling jerks. Within the revolution in the social fabric of Western culture has arisen a recurring theme of degradation of all things male. The well-published radical wing of the women's movement has evolved into an adversarial force of women against men. They appear to espouse the belief that since women have felt powerless in the past, men must have all the power—and it must be seized from them by any means.

Ironically, the majority of men do not feel powerful. In fact, men are just beginning to understand the degree to which we, too, have been powerless in the past. Herb Goldberg, in *The New Male,* observes that "the [feminist] diagnosis of chauvinism is superficial. More often it is a gross and misleading distortion. Closer examination of a man's behavior reveals a powerfully masochistic, self-hating, and often pathetically self-destructive style." He believes that "self or other abusive behavior" is not symptomatic of "the chauvinistic 'bad boy' behavior of the inherently 'evil' man"; rather it is indicative of the "frustrated, trapped male."

Many men are coming to realize the extent to which they have been in denial—anesthetized to the abuse they silently bear. Brad told us one night, "I've got this growing feeling that men are just being hung out to dry. I mean, who's out there politicking for us? I'm getting kind of sick of listening to college-educated women who are making four times as much as I am complaining about how unfair everything is. I'd like to put down my hammer and go back to school. But there are no programs for re-entry men."

Columnists Angela and Richard Miller received no male responses from a survey of readers' reactions to a series of newspaper articles about the new superwomen. They noted that "after years of being berated, blamed and intimidated, and faced with media who treat relationships as if they were only a woman's issue, most men are understandably quiet about the issue." This stance is consistent with the male self-concept that it is not masculine to feel or, much worse, to express pain or shame. Our silence as men has perpetuated the cultural illusion that, for the most part, women are victims, and men are the victimizers.

FRICTION BETWEEN WOMEN AND MEN AT WORK

In chapter 2 we reviewed some hardships men encounter in the workplace, such as the repression of emotion many feel they must practice to survive. One result of this is the development of limit-testing behavior, which men first engage in as adolescents and refine on the job. Sexual discrimination toward women certainly exists throughout our culture; but many grievances of women are in response to the hazing, practical joking, and testing of limits that men regularly encounter.

Some of this joking starts as a compensatory reaction to the strain of the workaday world. Men continually insult and test one another, usually in a somewhat good-natured way. It is a way of affirming that the man they are sharing danger with can handle it, that his skin has not become too thin, that he can be trusted to endure whatever trial confronts his interdependent group. The ability to face challenges with a light spirit is a *positive* quality of masculinity. It breaks up heavy aggregations of immobilizing stress.

The shock many women experience at encountering boisterous jiving and razzing by men is exemplified by the complaints of a recent graduate of the California Maritime Academy. One woman claimed sex bias there because, among other events, "a young woman was badly shaken when a group of male students jumped out of their beds naked as she entered their cabin on wake-up rounds." Another classmate complained that she "found my life goals and ambitions destroyed as I experienced uncontrollable hazing." Others complained about being subjected to "sexual wisecracks." The attitude of the men was challenging: "Hey, what are you going to do when you get on a real ship?"

These men were succinctly expressing their reality: right or wrong, men are frequently and regularly subjected to much more severe testing of their sensibilities at work, yet have no forum for complaint that doesn't make them seem weak, overly sensitive, or ridiculous. Men quickly learn that in order to be respected they must give tit for tat when challenged. Then the hazing stops. A plant worker at the Monsanto Company in Hahnville, Louisiana, was recently awarded $60,000 in damages because she suffered from anxiety attacks after her foreman cursed at her. It is hard to imagine this same result for a male petitioner against a male—or, even less likely, a female—employer.

Three NFL players for the New England Patriots were fined $72,500 for sexual harassment of a female sportswriter. They exposed their genitals and made lewd comments to her while she was in the men's locker room. Even though their conduct was offensive and wrong, two players had previously complained that she was spending a lot of time just hanging around the locker room, not interviewing anyone. They said they felt she was a "looker." The owner of the team agreed that women reporters were "intruding" in the locker room.

It is true that this so-called sex harassment affected the reporter's ability to do her job. However, it is hard to imagine a male sportswriter pressing the same claim against women athletes who exposed themselves or taunted him as he stood around watching them in the women's locker room. He wouldn't be there in the first place. Perhaps the way to ensure women's rights to equal access for interviews is to deny both men and women access to locker rooms rather than subject players to tests of their sensibilities through violations of their privacy in the name of gender equality.

On a similar front, women are increasingly invading men's restrooms when women's are full. It would be better, however, for women to lobby for more facilities rather than insist that men give up their privacy. The few court cases against women for trespassing in men's rooms have acquitted them of any wrongdoing. It is hard to imagine that men exhibiting the same behavior would be treated accordingly.

The columnist Susan Harte observes that men are increasingly cautious and cynical in their dealings with women on the job. They perceive sex-discrimination laws as making them "afraid to even compliment a female or engage in any sort of friendly banter since some women will run to the union with any kind of grievance." Men are "ruthlessly suppressing certain aspects of their personalities at work." According to Harte's observations, "current law is such that if a female wants to use this procedure to settle something [i.e., personal, nonharassment issues], it can be done." She quotes Elizabeth Fox-Genovese, who she says presents the prevailing feminist view: "If men feel bad, that's an unfortunate price we have to pay."

One member of our group, Jack, observes that "sexual harassment cuts both ways. Many women are not above using their sexuality as a tool for advancement. Some even advocate sleeping with the enemy as a means to gain power. My executive secretary was my lover for three years. When we broke up, we couldn't work together anymore. She threatened a sex-harassment suit. She seduced *me,* for chrissakes, inviting me over to her apartment in the beginning and everything. She knew I had just broken up with my wife. I *was* vulnerable, if you can believe it. Anyway, I had to give her a huge cash settlement just to avoid a scandal. I knew that any man, especially an employer, who cried foul would just be laughed at."

Jinie Sayles is a consultant who teaches women that the best way to get wealth is to marry it. In her well-attended *gold digger* courses, she says, "One of the best places to meet rich men is on the job." She advises women not to be too nice and suggests they present men with lots of little problems to solve. This makes them feel important. She also advises women to try to keep men isolated from friends and family as they attempt to snare them. She says, "The woman who controls the man controls it all."

In addition, as Warren Farrell has documented, a review of almost any working women's magazine will show a much greater emphasis on looking sexy in the workplace than one will find in men's business publications, which are more likely to emphasize educational, technological, and informational skills as keys to advancement.

Women cite unequal pay for equal work as another major inequity between the sexes. According to the U.S. Commission on Civil Rights, however, this phenomenon is largely due to the fact that women are more likely than men to leave their jobs to care for children. They forfeit the higher salaries, seniority, and other economic benefits men may have gained from sacrificing family ties and health to focus solely on a career. In 1989 *twice as many men worked over fifty hours a week as women.* This is another reason men appear to make more money—they work more hours. Women have also made great gains in recent years. Women attorneys now start out with annual salaries about two thousand dollars higher than men. More than 50 percent of managers are now women.

Carl says, "I'm often afraid to say anything about the behavior of some women supervisors. In many cases, they're picking up the very characteristics of the older, dominating, executive males that we're trying to transform in ourselves. I guess this is often the only model they have for wielding power. They'll even cross personal lines that a man would never cross. He'd get clobbered if he did. It seems that feminism is sometimes used by certain women as an excuse to be rude to men. If you say anything at all, you risk being regarded as sexist by every woman in the department. I've heard women say that one of the aims of feminism is to bring a more caring attitude into the workplace, but I sure haven't experienced it. Some female superiors even stifle our work through being more detail focused, rule bound, and bureaucratic than people oriented, broad focused, and compromise seeking."

Of course, the system in the past often has been prejudicial toward women. This can have the effect of making women defensive, ill at ease, and—in reaction to what they perceive as a hostile, male-dominated ruling class—more aggressive than necessary at times. It is not necessary, however, to shame, dominate, manipulate, or attempt to control men in order to be powerful in relationship to them. This understanding becomes more important as increasing numbers of women develop parity with and even advantage over men. Women can demonstrate leadership by becoming compassionate victors where they make gains.

It is a curious phenomenon in human history that once an oppressed minority begins to gain power, it often takes on the characteristics of the former oppressors. The masculinization of women would not be so bad if women had better access to positive male images from which to draw. As it stands, the denial of feelings inherent in old male roles numbs women's souls just as readily as men's.

Jack told us, "Contrary to popular myth, not every man is dedicated to oppressing women. Many are willing to become mentors to women or other men with whom they sense a feeling of mutual respect. Many opportunities are thus given or taken. No affirmative action or other legislation is going to change that. Some women are actually more ruthless, unfriendly, and willing to wound than men are. They often don't play the game the same way we do. I think it is one of the issues that keep women out of the inner circle.

"As a businessman, I'm pragmatic. I want the best person for the job, male or female. But many of us are stressed out at work. We're reluctant to work with others who might add to that strain. An easygoing, flexible attitude and fierce loyalty are just as important as the right education or skills. Sexism surely exists, but the exercise of this trusted-ally criterion isn't the same thing—it keeps out many men who are not team players as well."

On the other hand, men now perceive women who are more successful than they as being less willing to provide them with opportunity. Many young men on the way up experience a sort of reverse sexism. This is underscored by the fact that successful women also rarely socialize with, date, or marry men who don't have greater economic status than their own. I recently interviewed a local leader of the Soroptimists, a social club for successful women. I asked her how she and other women who were economically established felt about giving young men a hand up. She said, "You've got to be kidding. They're on their own, honey. Us women are sticking together."

At the same time, there are thousands of women who are taking Betty Friedan's second step in feminism: they are attempting to forge partnerships and alliances with men. Many men actually appreciate the changes feminism has brought. Women who move out of dependence and take more responsibility for their own self-sufficiency free us to take our own journeys of self-discovery. Men will also clearly benefit if women can actually make the workplace and our other institutions more healthy for *both* genders.

THE REAL WAR BETWEEN THE SEXES IS VIOLENT, ABUSIVE, AND DEADLY

As the myth of Man the Monster advances in our culture, men are increasingly blamed for women's crimes. This is exemplified by the federal judge A. Andrew Hauk's lenient sentencing, in 1989, of Dannielle Tyece Mast, who robbed five banks and claimed as her defense that her lover influenced her to do it. Hauk, in handing down a two-year sentence to the so-called Miss America bandit, said, "Women are a soft touch, particularly if sex is involved. . . . Men historically have exercised control over the activities of women." No evidence was submitted at the trial to substantiate this belief.

For centuries women have been treated more leniently under the law for perpetrating, under similar circumstances, the same crimes as men. Statutory-rape laws, which imprison men for having sex with girls under the age of eighteen, are almost never applied to the many women who seduce boys. In California, it wasn't until 1990 that this law was even made applicable to women. In most other major-crime categories women serve significantly less time in jail or prison than their male counterparts.

Once imprisoned, women are treated better and are significantly more protected from rape, assault, and murder than are men in prison.

Of the 195 executions performed at San Quentin, 191 have been of men. Of the 2,124 prisoners under sentence of death in the country today, 98.9 percent are male, yet women account for over 15 percent of all arrests for murder.

In El Dorado County, California, a pair of women were not prosecuted for shooting to death a man who was their shared lover. They fired six bullets into him, from a total of thirteen shots fired by a rifle, a shotgun, and a pistol. They claimed he was abusive. This is only one of many recent incidents in which women have apparently gotten away with murder by saying, essentially, that the man deserved it. The governor of Washington recently granted clemency to a woman who hired a hit man to kill her husband of seventeen years. Documents were submitted to the clemency board that showed the man was abusive.

The governor of Ohio followed suit by granting clemency, during the last month of his term of office, to twenty-five women in prison for murdering or assaulting their abusive husbands or boyfriends. He ordered twenty-one of them to be immediately released. This decision was assailed by judges and prosecutors throughout the nation, many of whom feared that women were being encouraged to use violence to solve the problems of abuse. However, Dr. Lenore Walker, the director of the Domestic Violence Institute, said, "This is a signal to the rest of the country that women will no longer permit themselves to be battered and abused by men."

Another battered woman in the San Francisco Bay area shot her husband five times as he lay asleep in bed. She was sentenced to probation and advised to get counseling. The news report on the day of her sentencing featured an interview with two women who ran a battered-women's shelter. One said, "It is hard to believe that more women don't do this [murder their abusive husbands]." The other warned that this could easily happen to other men. Were they insinuating that women now have a license to kill? In all the public reports of these cases, no concern whatsoever was expressed for the male victims. Nor was there any discussion about the circumstances that may have provoked these men to violence. Often the male victims are not even named.

Dehumanization of the enemy is a classic technique used throughout history for one group to justify its abuses of another.

They become gooks, krauts, kikes, or niggers—no longer human, therefore easier to kill. Has the dehumanization of men as a group given rise to a growing sentiment in our culture that male offenders are not entitled to the same protection under the law as women?

Should battering men be arrested and punished? Of course. Do they need treatment? Yes. Should women leave abusive men who will not change? Without a doubt. Should women be encouraged to report their behavior to the police, seek safety in battered-women's shelters, and seek restraining orders or other protections under the law? Absolutely. And if the laws are insufficient to provide this protection, we have an obligation as a society to change them. But it is wrong to assume that murder is a psychologically valid response and that the premeditated homicide of a man not threatening a woman in the moment is justified. Well over one-third of spousal murders are committed by women.

It is important that society finally has begun to recognize that the abuse of women is a serious problem in our culture. But we go too far when we condone murder. Even war criminals and mass murderers are entitled to due process under the law. Are dysfunctional, even violent and abusive, men any less entitled?

Justifiable homicide on the basis of spousal abuse would be a ludicrous defense for a man. As prison statistics demonstrate, vets and thousands of other abused men are generally not absolved of crimes committed in reaction to their post-traumatic-stress disorders—their battered-male syndromes. It is deeply ingrained in our collective psyche that women's lives are more valuable than men's.

Men's expression of violence is often considered independent of the system that provokes it. There is more of an attempt by society to understand women's violence as a product of their prior experience of victimization. Treatment for the violent man is usually behavioral conditioning of some sort, or prison—neither of which does much to help men heal the underlying wounds that drive them to acting out in the first place. Often the battering male is himself a victim of poverty or mental illness. Alcohol and drug abuse is associated with 90 percent of all these incidents and about 50 percent of *all* murders. Men need treatment for these conditions, which make them prone to loss of control, but adequate facilities for substance-abuse recovery and classes that teach anger management to men at risk are in short supply.

Feeling guilty about committing violence is the proper response of a healthy psyche. Feeling ashamed for angry or violent thoughts, as many feminized men do these days, is a product of psychological repression. So is feeling ashamed about providing compassionate treatment for men who become abusers. Many men *feel* angry and violent for good reason. There is no shame in this, only the need for healing.

It is important to remember that each year over 97 percent of husbands—about the same number as wives—do not resort to violence in their relationships. Also, violence of women against men and against other women and children frequently goes unreported and unheralded. Some surveys indicate that husbands are physically abused as frequently as wives. Men are not unequivocally bigger, stronger, or more violent and abusive in any given relationship. Because of feelings of shame, men usually report physical abuse to police only when there are injuries severe enough to require medical attention.

Women are more likely to use hard objects and knives than men. They are likely to say these weapons were used defensively. The throwing of hard objects is often not counted in surveys of violent behavior. This is another way in which women's violence is underreported. Other studies conclude that patterns and frequency of violence between husbands and wives are about the same. Yet men, by virtue of their greater strength, do more damage.

For those who doubt that women have the capacity to be just as violent as men, the *San Francisco Chronicle* staff writer Scott Wilson, who has done a historical survey of female mass murderers throughout history, concludes that "a handful of women have murdered so many with such viciousness that their deeds easily match or exceed those of male mass murderers." We need to look more deeply into the roots of violence between the sexes and begin to treat it as a system-wide problem for which both sexes share responsibility.

FEMINIZED MEN

When I refer to *feminized* men, I do not mean feminine, limp-wristed, or hip-wriggling men. Feminization is largely a product of women's attempts to modify or control men's thinking and behavior. There have been other influences in this feminization.

Urbanization has disconnected men from their traditional, earthy masculinity. The absence of the father in the post-industrial-age home also has aggravated the feminization of men. Men have lost touch with masculine soul and forgotten how to initiate their sons into masculine depth. Many boys have grown up almost exclusively in the domestic domain of women. Others, repulsed by the excesses of men in power, have thrown off the heroic-male characteristics of previous generations in search of a model of masculinity that is more in accord with nature and women.

The psychiatrist David Gutman believes that industrial society damages men and causes the "psychological depletion of men in urban settings. . . . While urbanization appears to sponsor male passivity, it has the opposite effect in regard to women and spurs their liberation." Two *Washington Post* columnists observe, while noting the increase in rugged male-image consumerism, that "the urban man has lost the most territory in the war of the sexes. . . . The gradual encroachment of women on the terrain once exclusively men's is almost complete. Now we are beginning to see the last bunkers clearly, now that the smoke of the feminist advance is clearing. . . . Men of all classes in the post-feminist world are reestablishing their psychological territory in a myriad of curious ways."

One of the "curious" ways in which men are coping is by shutting down, becoming numb and silent. Another is by displaying more rugged male-image products, like four-wheel-drive trucks and guns. Some men become more dominating, hostile, uncooperative, and even violent toward women. But many more have followed women's directives that they attempt to get in touch with their feminine side.

All these strategies for coping with the modern changes in men's roles are *reactionary*. They are not affirming positive, creative choices for men generated out of men's own inner search and inspiration. They are merely attempts to adjust to the changes women have made. Reactionary roles do nothing to further men's psychological and spiritual development, heal our wounds, or increase the range of our personal freedoms.

Sadly, much of the move toward so-called femininity is a product of shame. The shame of being male is aggravated by the type of feminist invective cited in the preceding pages. Some men are actually quite afraid of women's power to make life diffi-

male style of codependency. Others become more like women, in an attempt to both avoid their wrath and connect with their social power, while simultaneously disassociating themselves from the modern stigmas accompanying masculinity.

Carl once told us, "I'm embarrassed to say it, but I'm actually afraid of my wife's women's group. There are twelve of them, and I'm afraid that if we're not getting along for some reason, and she shares it in her group, half of the women in town will think I'm some sort of jerk. It's a small town, and ever since she joined the group I feel like I'm living in a glass house."

Generally women do not want us to become ineffectual and disempowered in the process of redesigning ourselves. Just as we don't want women to become ruthless, competitive, dominating, and rigid, they don't want men to become so flexible, receptive, gentle, and emotional tht we lose our power and assertiveness. We have examined at length the debilitating dangers of conventional, heroic masculinity. There are pitfalls on the path to integration as well.

In reaction to *patriarchy* (the sociopolitical belief that the rule of men is a higher authority than that of women) and in response to feminism (which often promotes women as morally superior to men), many men have sought initation into soul through the feminine. There even exists an active wing of the men's movement that is still pursuing these aims. This has resulted in a more sensitive, receptive, gentle, conscientious, and socially responsible male. Yet many of the so-called new, changing men are often powerless and ineffectual in the world. As a result, women today are asking, "Where are all the real men?"

Robert Bly comments upon this nationwide development of the so-called soft male:

> The male in the past twenty years has become more thoughtful, more gentle. But by this process he has not become more free. . . . He's a nice boy who now not only pleases his mother but also the young woman he is living with. They're lovely valuable people. . . . They've no interest in harming the earth or starting wars. But something's wrong. . . . Many of these men are unhappy. You often see these men with strong women who positively radiate energy. Here we have a finely tuned young man, ecologically superior to his father, sympathetic to the whole harmony of the universe, yet he himself has no energy to offer.

The strong, deep soul of men has been, for the most part, repressed, neglected, and denied. In my gender-conflict workshops I often hear women complain that men just aren't manly enough anymore—robust, self-reliant, rugged, and courageous. This doesn't mean they long for a return to the heroic, dominator ethic. They want to encounter strong male, *yang* energy, just as we enjoy dancing with the receptive, fluid, and evocative feminine *yin* in women. Just as many of us regret the loss of feminine grace in some women, they mourn the loss, in the new males, of that ineffable *uhhhmph* that makes a man exciting and desire-able (able to be a sire).

The dark face of the patriarchy is well known, especially to the sensitive men and boys dominated by the unconscious males of the generation now in power. Some male writers rethinking male psychology today, such as Eugene Monick, caution that "it is important at this time to differentiate masculinity from patriarchy to prevent both from going down the drain together." This need is evident from the grief, numbness, and confusion I hear men express in my practice, at conferences, and in groups. There has been a lack of direction posed by the dearth of visible, positive male images to counteract this trend.

One young man came up to me after a talk I gave for psychology undergraduates. He said, "I just wanted to thank you personally. This is the first time in over three years of college that I have heard anyone, in any classroom, say anything positive about men. I'm really tired of being made to feel ashamed for being male."

In his pioneering book on American manhood, *A Choice of Heroes,* Mark Gerzon suggests that, once "freed from the burden of continually promoting their sex's superiority, men who embody the emerging masculinities can develop a deeper awareness of the mutuality of the sexes." However, before we can move forward in society with a much-needed reconciliation of gender issues, men, as well as women, may need to reawaken their relationship to that which is deeply buried in the *male* psyche.

SEPARATION FROM THE FEMININE: A STEP TOWARD MUTUAL BALANCE

In the last few years I've attended a number of meetings with groups of New Age and feminist-affirming men. There is often a lot of good drumming and singing at these gatherings, yet I am struck by how often the discussions are about the concerns of women. This is in contrast to my experience with other groups of men, like the new knights, who are mostly focusing on their own recovery and private healing. For a while I attended the monthly meetings of a loose-knit group of about forty men exploring male healing rituals. The first night I was there, Brian, an environmental activist in his forties, said, "My wife's women's group wants to know what men fear most about women. They want us to prepare an answer to this question." The entire night was spent discussing her request.

The next month David, an artisan in his thirties, brought a letter from another women's group. He said, "The women want to know what we are going to do about sex abuse in this culture. They're concerned about pornography. They want our group to confront R_____ [a local spiritual teacher rumored to be sexually irresponsible]. I think it's our responsibility, as conscious men, to take on these issues. What should we do?"

From my private talks with some of these guys it was evident that underemployment, substance abuse, relationship problems, and low masculine self-esteem were problems for many of them. Yet these topics were seldom, if ever, addressed in the group. The next few months were spent talking about the letter and drafting a response to it. So much energy was spent in this way that the men rarely said anything about their own personal issues.

Feminized men often seem to feel that responding to women's pain is the primary agenda for men's work. Their concerns are put forth as examples of changes they have made to become more conscious and caring than past generations of men. They seek acknowledgment from women for these changing attitudes. They have embraced the cult of the female victim and are apologetic for men in their historical role as victimizers. It is as if they feel guilty, by gender association, for all past abuses committed by men, and need to present themselves to women in a way that seeks absolution for those sins. They also clearly fear the power of women to shame them.

A number of the new books on men's issues are from this camp of male apologists. One writer on so-called new male sexuality even cautions that "reinforcement of the paternal figure is ill advised during this transition toward matriarchy."

Is it important to be concerned about the needs of women? Of course. Do men need to start focusing on their own pain and victimization and reclaim their deep and ethical masculine power? Clearly.

Cultural pluralism, the old American ideal of a melting-pot society, has influenced some men and women to move toward androgyny. This is the ideal of the feminized man. He rejects the dominating hero and associates femininity with the affirmation of life. A number of modern philosophers and psychologists have written entire books promoting this idea, proposed as a solution to age-old gender conflicts.

The more recent, cultural-anthropological view, however, is more of a tossed salad. This up-to-date analysis says, "Vive la différence." We need to relearn how to accept, enjoy, recognize, and honor one another's gender differences, just as we are learning to enjoy the richness that diverse cultural origins bring to the culture at large. Our differences do not make one sex superior or inferior to the other. Men and women *are* very different. We possess gender-specific characteristics that, when better understood, may be seen once again as complementary.

We live in a time of extreme envy, tension, and distrust between the sexes. Each seems to think that the other has what it lacks and for some perverse reason is unwilling to share it. Thus many women are becoming hard, like the old male model, and men are becomng soft, embracing the old feminine model. The reality is that both sexes have lost a deeper connection to nature, myth, and the common rituals that bind most cultures. A living, vital mythology should create a sense of cohesiveness and mutual respect for the *different* ways in which each gender contributes to the whole. If there is an enemy, it is neither men nor women. Rather, it is our cultural attitudes and the religious and mythological beliefs that underpin them.

Men need to experience some separation from the feminine in order to connect with the deeper ground of masculinity. Women often have cultural consent to draw boundaries around their availability. Men are often regarded as being always available, requiring only an invitation from a woman to respond. When a man can't lose awareness of himself through merging with women, however, repressed feelings of aloneness, alienation, separation, and unresolved issues with his father and other men often emerge.

Through attending to our issues and our wounds, in the company of other men, we become better able to return to partnership with the feminine without becoming submerged in it. We can return secure and established in our own essential manliness. This is different from returning to the mother as a wounded boy in search of healing. This is also different from becoming more feminine in some sort of attempt to please her, make her feel more secure around male energy, or carry her pain for her.

THE LAST ANGRY MEN

When men meet alone, profound feelings often arise that do not come as easily in mixed-gender dialogues. Grief is one. Anger is another. Many men's groups have been working on the expression of grief. And this is a good thing. But most of us have repressed anger as well, which needs to find expression. The women's movement has effectively encouraged women to contact and express rage. Men, on the other hand, are often told their anger is dangerous. We are encouraged by spiritual teachers and women to repress, give up, or somehow transform it, without expressing it.

We *are* angry: some at our fathers, some at our mothers, some at others, both close and distant. Mostly we are pissed off about the double standards our society holds for men. When unexpressed, this feeling gets internalized, and repetitive patterns of self-abuse emerge.

Men's anger, when it finally does emerge, is often expressed violently. This has given anger a bad name. Another way it develops is in the self-destructive, self-hating behaviors described in previous chapters. When a system doesn't have a means for ridding itself of stresses a little at a time, they build up to the point of blowing it apart. So we have a fear of our anger. This fear is exacerbated in feminized males who often repress anger out of deference to women whom they believe are more entitled to be enraged.

But becoming apologetic for our anger or self-effacing, timid, or intimidated in our dealings with women is psychologically self-destructive. Ultimately this behavior is degrading to the very women we are trying to please. It buys into the old heroic belief that women are not as emotionally tough as men. Then, in our protective role, we cannot confront them with our strong feelings. Men must be able to stand up to women, as well as to other men, in order to limit the sorts of abuse documented previously. In order to develop and grow as men, we must embrace our anger with respect.

Men's anger has a very healthy component. When the people in our lives are subjugated to violence and oppression, it is natural to be angry. When we see the environment being destroyed by ignorance and greed, it is appropriate to be angry. When children suffer starvation and sexual abuse, and women as well as men are not safe to walk in the streets, we *should* be angry. Anger has a socially relevant, spiritually correct component.

In the vision of masculinity we are moving toward, a man expresses his rage through empowered and compassionate *action*. We have all seen the failure of the politics of confrontation. Violence breeds more violence, whereas the expression of anger through creative action is personally and socially healing. We need to love and respect our capacity to be angry, experience the impetus toward healing that it engenders in us, and enjoy its course. No one really wishes to breed anger or dwell in it. Yet to deny it is to lose vitality and passion—to suffer and die.

We are angry that our cultural conditioning has inhibited us from being emotional, spiritual, and joyful. We are angry that our culture accepts the degradation of men and the destruction of their bodies as normal, acceptable, and even entertaining. We are angry at the women who try to control or shame us. We are angry toward those who do not recognize the existence of what is deeply masculine and continue to depict *all* men as violent. We are angry about the general global condition of distress and the irresponsibility of many men now in power. We are trying to find ways to stay mobilized, active, empowered, sane, and even happy while facing the world as it is, with all its horror and beauty.

THE THIRD TASK OF MEN: TO REBUILD SELF-ESTEEM ON DEEP MASCULINE FOUNDATIONS

This book is not about becoming a sensitive New Age guy. In order to meet the challenges ahead, a complete reimagining of ourselves as men is required. We need our physical prowess and our rational, inquiring minds intact, our sensitivity and emotional bodies healthy and vital, our spirituality awakened, our souls integrated with the rest of our being, our creativity and wild magic flowing. We need these gifts so that we can meet the challenges of overpopulation, global pollution, spiraling violence, hunger, drug abuse, disease, and political repression.

Wimps need to yang up; dominating jerks need to open up. We all must support one another in claiming our birthright as eclectic, fully functioning men. We must change—not because women demand that we do so, nor even because the world needs us to. We must change because our lives are unfulfilled, limited, constrained, and circumscribed by restrictive role models of masculinity that don't work for anyone. We must change our hearts and minds. If we don't catch up to the changes that have occurred in the world around us, we may not survive—individually as men, collectively as a society, or even as a species.

I have said some hard things about the dysfunctional sides of male roles. This has been a necessary deconstruction of anachronistic ideas and dead visions. I've done this to open the way to new ideas, not to exacerbate existing shame; we've all had enough of that. We're through considering the problems of the old male roles. Now we can move on to greater things.

Men are full of beauty. The next section of the book will turn its attention to that beauty. One of the ways that beauty becomes apparent is through an increased appreciation for our diversity and multiplicity. The heroic male actually has a lot to offer: strength, perseverance, courage, and capability. The wounded male, through his connection to feeling, draws us into the depth of soul, humility, and grace. And the feminized man offers sensitivity, gentleness, and a supportive attitude toward life.

All these male modes, as well as many others, have qualities that are vital and essential to life. The masculine soul is a composite of many different images, often seemingly contradictory ones. Problems arise when one aspect becomes repressed out of shame or ignorance. Then destructive elements can dominate the personality. The hero can't feel much, the wounded man feels too much, and the soft man can't act powerfully; none is whole. The old hero and the new feminized antihero cancel each other out. No progress.

It's difficult to make changes in a vacuum, in the absence of a vision. In the next section we will attempt to move closer to a vision of the whole. This process embraces the best of men in an integration of old and new ideals.

> *Separating from the feminine and discovering some of the ways in which we get shamed has steered us toward rebuilding our self-esteem on deep masculine foundations—our third task. Breaking out of old stereotypes to claim our diversity and multiplicity was the fourth task we faced.*

PART II

Reclaiming the Masculine Soul

CHAPTER 4

Authentic Masculinity and the New Male Manifesto

What a piece of work is a man! How noble in reason!
how infinite in faculty!
in form, in moving, how express and admirable!
in action how like an angel! in apprehension how like
  a god!
the beauty of the world! the paragon of animals!
    William Shakespeare

One evening, after our new knights of the round table had been meeting for about two years, Ben brought in a photo of the great former Soviet ballet dancer Mikhail Baryshnikov. He had made copies for each of us. It showed the dancer leaping through space, arms outstretched, palms facing the sky. One leg was fully extended, upward and forward of his body, the other angled beneath, as if not needed for the return to earth. He was impossibly high off the floor, almost in flight, it seemed.

Baryshnikov's pose combined strength, agility, flexibility, purpose, and discipline. It created an image of archetypal, timeless, masculine beauty. We gazed at this photo for a while. It spoke to each of us, moving some place deep within. "This is an image of the life I am seeking," said Rodger finally. "Not the life of a ballet dancer, of course, but one that expresses the same degree of freedom, joy, and unabashed masculine glory captured in this picture."

Then Jack said, "I have an announcement. I've been holding off making a decision, but tonight, with this picture on the table, it seems like a good time to do it. I'm retiring. I'm turning over the business to my partner and hiring a manager to take over my duties. I'll remain chairman for now, but I am not going into the office anymore. The business is stable and prospering. I'm sure that if I continue at the helm for the next ten years I could easily triple its worth. It's not that I hate the work. No, I love it. But there's so much I want to do with my life that has nothing to do with making money. I'll be fifty-five next month. My dad died at sixty-five. So who knows how long I really have left?

"I don't even know what I'm going to do yet," Jack went on. "But I know it has something to do with reclaiming my soul. I'm sure gonna take some time to just quiet down, listen to my inner voice, and let it guide me. I want to use the years that remain to have more fun, spend time with my friends and family, and play some music. I want to do this while I'm still healthy and strong. Who knows what the coming years will bring? I also want to try using my skills to make this a better world somehow. That's the sort of legacy I want to leave behind—no regrets! My kids already stand to inherit too much. Why should I go on making more?"

"Right on, Jack!" cried Jim.

"Yeah, it's about time," said Carl, amid scattered applause, hooting, and whistling from the rest of us who approved Jack's decision.

We were all starting to feel more free to change our lives. Sobriety helped us become more attuned to the voices of our deeper desires. The strong support we gave each other was equally empowering. We were beginning to lift our heads above the haze of our day-to-day lives and catch a glimpse of other options life may offer. During the next few meetings we talked at length about how this image of Baryshnikov compared with other male images we had been fed over time—emotionless gunslingers, a healer nailed to a cross, tireless workers, pain-negating sports gladiators, driven business heroes, ruthless, equivocating politicians, and slick secret agents.

Carl said, "I feel better about my life than ever before. For the first time in years I can try new things, wrap my mind around some new alternatives. I'm not so afraid to risk failure, not so hung up on having to be perfect all the time. I feel that if something doesn't work out I've got you guys to come to. I never had that before. More than that, I've got more of myself than ever before. I'm not so afraid to be different or alone.

"My wife, Jennie, is wonderful," Carl continued. "Very supportive. But she depends on me, too. I don't feel comfortable sharing some of my wilder ideas with her. I know she wants me to be happy, but she feels threatened when I talk about changing work. I'm not sure she's really ready to change her lifestyle so I can have more freedom."

Six months later Carl was working for an international environmental organization at half the pay he was making before. He told us, "I'm enjoying my work for the first time in fifteen years. I'm working with a great bunch of people, doing something with my life I can feel proud of. We are selling the house and moving to a smaller one. The money we make and save on the move will keep us afloat for years on my current salary. Jennie had to choose between a big house or a happy husband. She chose me. Our girl is getting old enough now that Jennie can take a part-time job if we need more. It's all going to work out."

In our culture, with its pervasive Protestant work ethic, a man is often defined by his profession. We are often quick to say, "I am a doctor" (or lawyer, plumber, or carpenter). But we're much more than what we do for a living. Many of us have found that the achievement of obtaining a profession has not brought about a corresponding sense of freedom and fulfillment in life.

What is freedom? Is it having lots of money, the prestige and power of a profession, or the time to pursue your dreams? Some men are fortunate enough to combine all three. But for most of us in the group, pursuing our dreams was geting higher on the list of priorities. None of us wanted to die rich. We would prefer to live richly.

Even Brad, who was facing the greatest financial struggle in the group, was becoming more concerned with enriching his life than his pocketbook. As a result of his increased stability, enhanced self-esteem, and our encouragement to try new approaches, he got a job supervising construction instead of performing it. He told us, "It feels a little weird not wearing my tool belt every day. But now I'm actually making more money per hour. I don't have to work as much overtime to get by. I could keep up the old pace and make even more. But now I have enough energy left to read a book in the evening. I'm thinking I could probably start taking some classes at night. Who knows where that might lead?"

Brad laughed before going on to say, "My body can't take construction anyway, now that I'm not drinking to squash the pain. Shit, I used to just come home and crash on the couch. It was hard to make dinner, much less enjoy my evenings. I could have been doing management five years ago, but I was hung up on my hard-driving working-man image. My old man only wore a suit at weddings and funerals. Swingin' a hammer was the only way I thought I could be manly."

After this conversation we started to collect all our thoughts into some form that expressed the new principles that were beginning to affect our lives. We began to construct a way of thinking that would replace the old rules we grew up with—a new male manifesto that expressed what we were discovering about being men. After a few weeks of talking and taking individual notes, we came up with the first draft on the following page, which we wrote up on sheets of butcher paper tacked to the wall.

AUTHENTIC MEN WHO HAVE INSPIRED US

For over two years our group had systematically rejected many of the conventional images and ideals of masculinity from the old male manifesto: the armored, rigid hero; the cool success object; the wimpy nice guy. We were beginning to wonder what might replace them. One night Jim asked, "Who stands out in the world as exemplifying the type of men you want to be?"

At first we found it easier to talk about individual qualities in ordinary men we knew as friends and associates. Although we could think of many mythological and historical persons, ranging from King Arthur and Merlin (my favorite) to John Lennon and Gandhi, there seemed to be a real dearth of contemporary public figures who inspired us. But as we kicked this idea around, a few emerged.

Jack mentioned Cecil Williams, the founder of Glide Memorial Church in San Francisco: "Cecil doesn't hide behind a pulpit. He's out there every day working on behalf of the disenfranchised and disheartened people in his community. A few weeks ago my girlfriend and I went to one of his services. We wound up marching through one of the most crime-ridden, crack-infested housing projects in the city. Cecil called people out of their apartments and into the street. He called for a rebirth of community, getting isolated neighbors to talk to one another. He embraced the dealers, too, saying they were also victims—a radical idea. He brought a gospel of love into the street and into the community."

In the weeks that followed, the crime rate went down in that neighborhood. Some former crack dealers are now working for the church. They are trying to help the others—not by shaming, punishing, condemning, and controlling, but by offering viable alternatives, showing the young men a way to gain self-esteem, glory, and membership through serving the community rather than destroying it. This is something all the police, government leaders, think tanks, legislators, and social agencies have been unable to accomplish.

The unshakable belief that unconditional love can heal drug addicts, dealers, and whole communities is a radical idea. It flies in the face of conventional approaches, which at this time are fail-

THE NEW MALE MANIFESTO

I Men are beautiful. Masculinity is life-affirming and life-supporting. Male sexuality generates life. The male body needs and deserves to be nurtured and protected.

II A man's value is not measured by what he produces. We are not merely our professions. We need to be loved for who we are. We make money to support life. Our real challenge, and the adventure that makes life full, is making soul.

III Men are not flawed by nature. We become destructive when our masculinity is damaged. Violence springs from desperation and fear rather than from authentic manhood.

IV A man doesn't have to live up to any narrow, societal image of manhood. There are many ancient images of men as healers, protectors, lovers, and partners with women, men, and nature. This is how we are in our depths: celebrators of life, ethical and strong.

V Men do not need to become more like women in order to reconnect with soul. Women can help by giving men room to change, grow, and rediscover masculine depth. Women also support men's healing by seeking out and affirming the good in them.

VI Masculinity does not require the denial of deep feeling. Men have the right to express all their feelings. In our society this takes courage and the support of others. We start to die when we are afraid to say or act upon what we feel.

VII Men are not only competitors. Men are also brothers. It is natural for us to cooperate and support each other. We find strength and healing through telling the truth to one another—man to man.

VIII Men deserve the same rights as women for custody of children, economic support, government aid, education, health care, and protection from abuse. Fathers are equal to mothers in ability to raise children. Fatherhood is honorable.

IX Men and women can be equal partners. As men learn to treat women more fairly they also want women to work toward a vision of partnership that does not require men to become less than who they authentically are.

X Sometimes we have the right to be wrong, irresponsible, unpredictable, silly, inconsistent, afraid, indecisive, experimental, insecure, visionary, lustful, lazy, fat, bald, old, playful, fierce, irreverent, magical, wild, impractical, unconventional, and other things we're not supposed to be in a culture that circumscribes our lives with rigid roles.

ing hopelessly. In our work together as men we're also trying to love that which is outcast, both within us and without. We encourage one another to speak about our shadowy inner desires. And we help each other find ways to make amends for past behaviors that hurt others. Both of these approaches are routes toward forgiving ourselves, healing shame, and restoring self-esteem.

Jack now works occasionally with Cecil Williams as a volunteer. He finds this and other types of community service more personally fulfilling than being the boss of a large company.

Carl mentioned Lech Walesa: "Here is a man who has consistently stood up to the forces of repression in his society with a firm resolve. His courage has inspired an entire nation to demand and claim a free society after decades of totalitarian rule. He was one of the hot torches that cut down the iron curtain. Where are those deeply committed statesmen in America today? Where are the Abraham Lincolns—the impassioned advocates of freedom and social justice? What has happened to our leaders?"

"What about Jesse Jackson?" asked Jim. "I saw him when he came to speak here during the last campaign. This is a guy who really seems to care about the poor, the outsiders, the oppressed, about racial and sexual discrimination, the environment, the very soul of the nation—something all the other guys seem to have abandoned. I don't know if he has any ability to run a country, but shit, the man is full of passion. He *feels*. He's committed. He listens. He's present. He risks being his full-blown self. He's the first politician who ever moved me to tears. He was full of feeling, but he was very fierce, strong, and masculine. There's nothing wimpy about him."

I mentioned Ram Dass, a spiritual teacher. He was a professor of psychology at Harvard University who left a life of privilege and prestige to do outlawed research on altered states of consciousness. His curiosity about the outer limits of human potential ultimately led him to twenty-five years of committed spiritual practices, which brought him into relationship with his own soul. He was one of several modern psychologists who reintroduced soul into the field of psychology. Psychology means the science of psyche, and the word *psyche* actually means *soul* in Greek.

Ram Dass started the prison-ashram project, which helps prisoners use their incarceration time for spiritual development. He also helped found the SEVA Foundation, which provides medical care and health maintenance in some of the poorest regions of the globe. He works with the homeless and other disadvantaged people in America. All his questing for enlightenment led him to some very simple revelations: love everyone, feed everyone, do what you can to help. He's a very unpretentious guy and totally outrageous at the same time. He keeps a sense of humor about the ironic predicaments we all find ourselves in. He's made some major mistakes along the way, admitted them, and used them as part of his teaching. The model he represents says it's okay to fall and fail and keep on trying—no shame.

Brad's vote was for Nelson Mandela: "This guy was in prison since I was a kid. Even when the South African government was responding to international pressure to release him, he refused to betray his commitment to the liberation of his people in order to get out of prison. This took enormous manly resolve, courage, and commitment to his beliefs. He could have been out years earlier if he would kowtow to the white leaders, even a little, but he refused. He waited until he could be released on his own terms.

"I was surprised and excited when such a broad segment of the American public lionized him during his visit here," Brad continued. "I don't think it's just his courage or his cause alone that inspired us. His authenticity and straightforwardness, his dignity, gentleness, and fierceness set him apart from most national leaders. Obviously a lot of people today are ready to embrace a man who displays these authentic male qualities."

Rodger offered up the poets of the world. "It's hard for me to name any particular public figure, but the men who have moved me most deeply have been poets. Gary Snyder, Robert Bly, and other contemporaries have touched my life at various times. They helped me to see the richness of life. Bly is concerned about men's souls. He reminds me that it's okay to grieve, to be deeply moved by the bittersweetness of life. Gary Snyder, like Thoreau, has helped me remember the importance of staying connected to nature and wildness.

"Others from the past, like Emerson, Blake, Rilke, and Rumi, have reawakened my spirit at times when it was low. All these men have stood outside the conventions of the societies in which they lived. The world of poets is radical. It's far from my world of dentistry. Yet I find poetry in my work and in my family life as a result of my connection with these men. I've started reading poetry and mythology to my kids at bedtime. It's a special time we share."

As we went around the room talking about men we admired, I began to feel concerned about overly idealizing these guys. I knew from personal experience that even existential heroes have feet of clay. During my own questing years I spent time with a number of well-known spiritual teachers and luminaries in the field of psychology. They all had their dark sides. Some were so-called celibates who slept with their students. Some were irresponsible, even unethical in their administration of large sums of money. Some were manipulative, neurotic, and insecure. Substance abuse was also not unknown, even by those who professed abstinence.

Some of the current leaders of the men's movement also have disorderly personal lives. In short, underneath their bigger-than-life personas, all leaders are as vulnerable as the rest of us mortal men.

It's important not to overidealize any men. We really don't need new heroes. But what is it about these public men that touched us in the group? What is it we imagine they represent, which inspired us as ordinary men in extraordinary times? Who touches your soul as a man, deepens your sense of self, inspires you to greatness, gives you hope?

John Sununu, President Bush's chief of staff, says his boss "is on an even keel all the time—neither laid back nor hot." As for himself, he says, "Whatever emotion other people see, I use as a tool, whether it's humor or having to be stern. When showing a little emotion helps get something done, I'm not uncomfortable showing that emotion."

This voice reflects the old heroic ideal of the current political and corporate leadership in this nation. It leaves us cold. It inspires nothing but distrust and contempt. Yes, we want the man with his finger on the trigger to have a cool head. It's important to be able to be cool, to be able to master your emotions in the face of danger. But as a general model of masculinity it's a far cry from the potent and embodied voice of authentic masculinity as we are coming to envision it.

SHAPING A NEW IMAGE

As I learned in the building trade, it's easy to cut a little more off a board to make it fit, but it's impossible to add a little to one cut too short. In the same manner, it seems important, as we try to imagine new ways of being men, to have some image of what it is we are moving toward. Otherwise we may cut away portions of ourselves that are essential to our development. We may lose or discard certain abilities that may have no apparent use at the moment but could be essential at another time in our lives.

The heroic male in quest of strength cut away his softness. With it, he also lost sensitivity. Life was diminished. Feelings became less rich. The feminized male, in cutting away his hardness, lost his fierceness, his capacity for committed action and success in the world. So we must be careful.

Individual freedom is ultimately expressed by our ability to become what we truly are. That process—what Jungian psychologists refer to as *individuation*—is about becoming our unique self in all its depth and complexity. This is different from attempting to become more like a particular image—even if that image is one society holds dear. Even so, it feels worthwhile to explore what images—other than the ones we have grown up with—might lie about, within and without us. Then we have greater choice about what we might incorporate into our own particular self-image. That is one major aspect of freedom—choice.

The anthropoligist David Gilmore has done research on masculinity all over the world. He believes it is society's needs for survival, rather than biological imprinting, that evoke certain roles such as the hunter, the worker, and the soldier. He believes that masculine roles, though "paradoxically the exact opposite of what we Westerners normally consider the nurturing personality," have "a criterion of selfless generosity, even to the point of sacrifice." In reviewing Gilmore's insights, Beryl Benderly observes that "male sternness, toughness, acquisitiveness, and aggressiveness serve, in circumstances of threat and scarcity, the same social ends as female tenderness and gentleness." Gilmore believes that manliness is not just one set of aggressive characteristics but "a cultural construct" that is "endlessly variable."

If, indeed, masculine roles are primarily a reaction to society's needs, what are the roles for this time of radical change in every arena of life? Of equal importance, what are our personal needs as authentic men attempting to discover who we really are—in our endless variability—independent of society's demands?

RADICAL MASCULINITY

The adjective *radical* means "proceeding from, or pertaining to, the root or foundation; essential; fundamental; inherent; basic." As a noun, a radical is someone who carries his convictions to their furthest application. In mathematics, etymology, and botany, *radical* describes the qualities of things associated with the roots of numbers, words, and plants.

However, the word *radical,* like the word *liberal,* has gotten a bad name in American politics. What *radical* actually means in a political context is "one who advocates governmental changes and reforms at the earliest opportunity."

What are the qualities of masculinity that are associated with its roots, that are essential, fundamental, inherent, and basic? What are our deepest convictions as men at the edge of a new millennium? What needs to be changed at the earliest opportunity? These are a few of the questions provoked by our image of radical masculinity. The knights began to use the word *authentic* to describe the radical of masculinity. It seemed the best way to describe the quality we were looking for in our quest for new visions of manliness.

After we wrote our manifesto, we started to list qualities that we associated with authentic masculinity and that we believed were at its core. These are qualities that we admire in one another and in other men, qualities that we feel within ourselves and are trying to learn how to cultivate as ordinary men in extraordinary times.

It is ironic that we experience the very principles that strengthen our self-esteem as radical. Our ideal may appear outside the norm for most of our culture. But authentic masculinity is actually very basic. It may be closer to an ancient center of the male psyche than so-called normalcy is today.

The chart on the following page compares some differences between the old heroic, emotionally dead, manipulative model, the newer antiheroic, feminized model, and the emerging model of authentic masculinity as we are coming to know it. Please note that the attributes we ascribe to feminized men are not meant to describe the attributes of women or gay men. In fact, homosexuality traditionally has had little to do with feminization. Male homosexuality has been a prevalent manifestation of masculinity throughout time and across all cultures. It is generally more concerned with men loving other men than men wanting to be more like women. The qualities of the feminized male are reactionary and just as likely to affect straight men as gays. Feminized men are in rebellion against the old heroic model but have not yet affirmed or been initiated into that which lies deep within men—the root, the radical. Whereas femininity is a life-affirming force in women, it can represent hypomasculinity in men. In this form it is just as toxic as the hypermasculinity of the heroic male.

	UNINITIATED		INITIATED
ARENA	HEROIC (HYPER) MASCULINITY	FEMINIZED (HYPO) MASCULINITY	AUTHENTIC (INTEGRATED) MASCULINITY
	old male principles	transitional male principles	ancient/new male principles
PHYSICAL	Hard	Soft	Flexible
	Dominating	Submissive	Capable
	Tough	Gentle	Strong
	Soldier	Pacifist	Warrior
	Killer	Gatherer	Hunter
	Coercive	Pliant	Firm
	Controlling	Controlled	Vigilant
	Lord and master	Consort	Husband/partner
	Destructive	Immobile	Generative
EMOTIONAL	Closed	Unprotected	Receptive
	Numb	Flooded	Feeling
	Codependent	Dependent	Interdependent
	Demanding	Smothering	Nurturing
	Aggressive	Passive	Assertive
	Cynical	Naive	Fresh/humorous
	Sex partner	Pleaser	Lover
	Defensive	Wounded	Deep feeling
	Repressed	Contained	Wild/playful
	Bastard	Nice guy	Fierce
MENTAL	Compartmentalized	Merged	Eclectic
	Penetrating	Diffused	Insightful
	Analytical	Synthetic	Discriminating
	Splitting	Joining	Holds paradox
	Linear	Circular	Holonomic
	Hierarchy	Anarchy	Community
	Exploitive	Conservative	Resourceful
	Rules and laws	Procedures	Personal ethics
	Doctor	Magical thinker	Healer
SPIRITUAL	Patriarchal	Matriarchal	Polytheistic
	Absolute	Dualistic	Paradoxical
	Uninitiated	Seeker	Initiated
	Immobile	In flight	Grounded
	Single self	Selfless	Braided self
	Divided	Disassociated	Embodied
	Dogma	Belief	Direct experience
	Exclusive	Inclusive	Selective
	Priest	Guru	Mentor/elder

For several weeks we left the sheet of butcher paper on the wall in our meeting room. We periodically added and crossed off various items on the list. One night Rodger said, "As I look at the way our list is growing, I notice that our authentic man displays many of the traditional male's qualities: courage, strength, capability, endurance, perseverance, undauntedness. But unlike his heroic, dominating counterpart, he uses his strength in the service of the community—to protect, serve, and support it. I think this is something feminized men, who associate assertiveness with negative aggression, are often unable to do."

"Yeah, but these days it seems that our strength is often put down as something negative," said Brad. "If we aren't assertive then we're wimps. And when we are, then we're macho." He gestured toward the chart on authentic masculinity and continued, saying, "But I think our willingness to face danger and to protect and support life is one of the truly wonderful things about men."

"Yes," I agreed, "machismo is actually a very misunderstood concept. The heroic male is often called *macho*—a racist word in our culture that stereotypes certain characteristics of Latin men. [I've avoided using that term in this book, preferring the term *heroic*.] But the Latin understanding of machismo has little to do with the Americanized idiom. Rosa Maria Ortiz-Gruhn, a social-worker colleague of mine, is from El Salvador. She told me the term *macho*, as it's used in America, would be regarded as shameful and cowardly in her culture. Machismo actually represents masculine courage, honor, resolve, protectiveness, stoic dignity, and strength in service of the community."

"That doesn't sound like the stereotype of macho men," Ben said. "They're coercive, dominating, controlling, bullying, self-destructive, and pumped up with a false bravado."

"You're right," I replied. "The traditional meaning more accurately describes qualities of the empowered, authentic male than our old American hero model."

"The way I see it," said Carl, "unlike the hero, the authentic male allows himself to feel and to express his feelings to others. But he's not flooded or dominated by his feelings like the feminized man. He retains his stoic warrior qualities while reclaiming his capacity to feel. He attempts to relate to women as equals, without overidealizing them as the source of his positive feelings or demeaning them as the source of his pain, He's more likely to be an involved and nurturing father to his children. He is sensitive to others and to nature, yet he's spontaneous, lively, and acts consistently with his true feelings. He can act heroically in the face of danger or adversity but does not exhibit the hero's habitual control and domination, or the apologetic inferiority and naive sincerity of the feminized man."

Then Jim said, "For me, of course, the radical male is like an artist—wild, playful, intuitive, creative, and expressive. Humor, music, dancing, and play are important. Hey, I want to fool around and celebrate life! Get loose, have fun, laugh and sing a little. So let's not get too serious about our quest. The authentic male is a fun lover, too. Our playfulness is something we are trying to revive along with our strength, self-esteem, and spirituality.

"You stuck a lot of ten-dollar words up on the wall as usual, Aaron," he laughed. "Even though I'm not sure I know exactly what *holonomic* means, what I do get from our ideas is an image of a man who lives from his center."

"Exactly," I replied. "The reason I use some of these words is that for me they are like eggs or seeds: they contain whole concepts. *Holonomic* essentially describes a style of awareness that is interconnected with and touched by all things, rather than isolated in a bubble of individuality or separated from life."

"So this is a guy who takes his cues from his inner self, while still staying connected to everything around him," said Jim. "He believes in himself and listens to his inner voice, while still listening to others and being sensitive to his environment."

"Right," I replied.

"But," Jim continued, "I think he could be a revolutionary just as easily as a healer. The important thing for me is that he's found the balance between outrageous personal freedom and responsibility to the world around him. It seems like most of us in the past have chosen one or the other. Living both together is what I think you mean with terms like *paradox* and *braided self.*"

"Yes," I agreed. "The braided self weaves many different images of self into an integrated whole. Our notion of the authentic male seems to represent a style of consciousness—an archetype—that is very repressed in the modern psyche. Yet it's a source of what makes life exciting and vital. He is irrational and intuitive—an artist, as you say. Like nature itself, he lives according to natural law, which may be quite different than the law of society and civilized man. He may be a revolutionary or even an outlaw like Robin Hood. He may not be home for dinner. He is primitive, but not savage. Our great-great-grandfather, he is to the modern urban male what wolves are to dogs, what the magnificent wild panther of the deep, dark, primordial jungle is to a house cat purring by the fire."

THE NEW RENAISSANCE MAN

"The image coming up for me," said Jack, "is of the old Renaissance man. During the Renaissance men prided themselves on their self-expression in many different arenas. They were expected to be able to write a poem, compose and perform a song, fight a duel with a sword if necessary, be a good lover, speak several languages, and understand the newest scientific and political ideas of the day. They prided themselves on being great artists, lovers, warriors, thinkers, inventors, and statesmen.

"But one of the unfortunate things that has happened in our technological society is its increasing emphasis on specialization. People aren't doctors anymore, they're gastroenterologists, hematologists, and dermatologists. The treat bowels, blood, or skin, but not the whole person."

"Yes," I added. "Psychologists are Freudians, Jungians, behaviorists, or object relationists. They focus on personality, dreams, behavior, or relationships; few have a holistic approach. Examining boards encourage specialization. Eclecticism is regarded suspiciously."

"Some wonderful discoveries have come out of this type of finely focused attention," said Jack. "But we've lost a vision of ourselves as being composed of multiple feelings, desires, ideals, and abilities. We've also lost, for the most part, an important ecological perspective that keeps us aware of the interrelatedness of all fields. What is discovered in quantum physics affects our understanding of psychology. The innovative new gene-splice may also carry as yet unknown diseases. As we are now learning, the pollution of one nation affects the environment of another."

Men often feel they have to focus all their energy on one skill or ability in order to remain competitive and secure a place at the table. We wear blinders, unconcerned about the effects our specialization may have on the world as a whole. We become like the overdeveloped muscle man who can no longer bend down to tie his shoes. The old jack-of-all-trades was not "a master of none"; he was a master of multiplicity.

But the world is beginning to experience a new Renaissance. Authentic masculinity supports the idea of a new Renaissance man to meet that new world—a man who has access to the full range of diversity and multiplicity that lies within him. We all have physical, mental, emotional, and spiritual needs. When we focus on any one to the exclusion of the others, life suffers. It is as if some vitamin is missing: we feel incomplete, but we don't know why.

We can't all be like the old Renaissance men in our daily lives. Most of us are not Michelangelos, Benjamin Franklins, or Leonardo da Vincis. Someone has to sack the corn and pound the nails. Yet the ideal of the Renaissance man resonates with the authentic male's ideal of multiplicity, flexibility, and diversity. We can all be new Renaissance men inside, psychologically and spiritually—men who embrace a wide range of feelings and images that enhance the richness of our individual and collective lives.

The authentic male paradigm attempts to integrate many paradoxical attributes of masculinity, inherent in both ancient and modern cultural ideals. To recover our roots we have to examine ancient history, mythology, and our experiences deep within the human psyche.

THE FOURTH TASK OF MEN: TO BREAK OUT OF OLD STEREOTYPES AND CLAIM OUR DIVERSITY

We ended this stage of our sessions by expressing a lot of love and appreciation to one another for the beauty we saw in our own diversity and differences. We had each benefited from the different perspectives on our personal lives, as well as each member's individual contribution to the quest. We acknowledged each other for the attempt we were making to become our real selves, distinct from social constraints that had been layered upon us. Mostly we began to affirm to one another that men really are wonderful in many ways, something we had forgotten or perhaps had never even known.

Many of the attributes we had come to feel ashamed of are actually fine qualities that have been misunderstood or misdirected. We gave one another a lot of support for experimenting with new styles of relating to life. We came to believe that in their core men are not only good, but noble and magical as well.

By our second year, the knights were beginning to develop many ideas about new directions we were interested in pursuing. We began to realize that the sociological and psychological images based on the old male principles had roots deep in the collective psyche of our culture. Our old heroic conditioning is pervasive and vast.

As we looked underneath the surface of our culture we found certain religious principles that gave birth to these ideas, and we found mythological images that gave rise to the religions in the first place. The old, Heroic/Martyr male principles have their source in the predominant religion of Western culture—monotheistic Judeo-Christianity. In order to understand how these images have imprisoned our masculine souls, we first had to understand how these religious ideals gave birth to our culture. Our self-image and the myth of our purpose and destiny as men are related to these religious ideals and the myths that underlie them.

We decided that in order to reimagine ourselves as men we would need more than a list of qualities we admired, a few dubious role models, and a picture of a levitating Russian dancer. We would need other myths from older religions and cultures with different ideas about what it means to be a man. This need brought us to our next task.

> *Breaking out of old stereotypes in order to claim a new vision of our diversity had been the fourth task we attempted. Reclaiming ancient, sacred masculine images that could help us reconnect with our bodies, our souls, the earth, and the people in our lives, was the fifth task we faced.*

❧ CHAPTER 5

Beyond Patriarchy and Matriarchy: Our Ancient Roots in the Earth

The first man is of the earth, earthy.
　1 Corinthians 15:47

The new knights came to realize that we had inherited a very skewed view of masculinity, based on a limited selection of male role models. Regardless of our individual religious beliefs, we had been influenced by the major archetypes of patriarchal religions presented to us by our teachers, parents, peers, and the media. We began to look at the mythological foundations of our culture in order to understand the fundamental, archetypal forces that shaped it. Those forces have left a strong imprint on our psyches and, in particular, influence how we see ourselves as men.

According to archetypal psychology, which began with the thinking of Carl Jung, archetypes are universal patterns or images within the psyche that symbolize life experiences that all humans share. These images occur in every culture and time. They represent eternal forms: the Wise Old Man, the Soul, Death, Mother, the Hero, the Eternal Child, and so on. Recently the Jungian psychologist Robert Moore described the primary images of the mature male psyche as Lover, Warrior, Magician, and King. And, as we began to discover during this stage of our quest, there are many other archetypal forms of authentic masculinity as well.

In subtler forms archetypes may represent more abstract feelings, instincts, and other psychological tendencies such as Desire, Envy, Grace, and Wisdom. At still deeper levels archetypes can represent the fundamental forces of nature itself. They precede and underlie human consciousness and exist independent of it.

Some thinkers, like the archetypal psychologist James Hillman, simply call these archetypes *the Gods.* They may be seen in the mythological images of all cultures, in literature and the arts. Our individual dreams link our modern lives to these ancient forms through the unconscious.

The new knights often brought up their dreams during our weekly group meetings. As we discussed them we discovered that they contained themes, stories, and symbols that mirrored specific myths—recurring dramatic patterns we read about from many different epochs and cultures. For example, Jim had recurring dreams about a man with wings on his head. We later discovered that one of the ancient gods of men was Hermes, a messenger of the gods who wore a winged helmet. Was Jim's dream figure a messenger coming to teach us more about authentic masculinity? At times, as he told us about these dreams, it seemed so.

We are all moved by images that have the power to disturb us—monsters, angelic spirits, or gods. These images may also lie at the core, or root, of our individual psychological complexes, problems, and patterns of behavior. They are also the characters in the mythological stories that give rise to our religious beliefs. As we began to bring our attention to the archetypal field of consciousness, we started to identify and compare ourselves with these larger-than-life entities from mythology. Brad still had occasional nightmares about Vietnam. In several dreams he saw a terrifying, angry figure with a sword or a lance in his hand. Was this Ares, the god of war? If so, why was he appearing now? What did he have to say? What claim had he made on Brad's life? What did he want? We wondered.

At times we talked about ourselves being like a particular god in various ways. In time, however, we begin to understand these archetypal forces as autonomous—having a life of their own, independent of our imagination or will. The new knights began to feel that through establishing relationships with these ancient images resonating in our modern psyches, we could deepen our experience of ourselves and of life around us.

The contemporary post-Jungian perspective holds that our individual consciousness is actually composed of a number of distinct and separate archetypal identities in relationship with one another—a myth or story in progress. The characters and their relationships may change as our lives change, or through our relationship with the gods we may affect them and in turn be changed by them.

Our consciousness actually may not be a *thing* but rather a *process,* the result of the ongoing relationships of diverse psychic elements, like an ongoing conversation in a play. We can imagine that we are not the individual characters, but the play itself. As we began to think of ourselves in this way, the knights began to look at the voices that have dominated the play of our psyches. And we started to reach out toward those voices that have been silenced within men for a long, long time.

THE ROOTS OF PATRIARCHY

There are a few prominent mythological images that have served as our Western cultural foundations for masculinity. These characters have been the major actors in the play of men's psyches for the last several thousand years. One has been the all-conquering, invincible *youthful hero,* like Hercules. The strong *elder male,* like Moses or Abraham, is another prominent ideal of manhood. He leads his tribe with absolute authority. He rules in the name of the all-powerful god in the sky, who demands there be no other gods before him. Another major image is that of a *superhuman healer and caretaker.* He becomes a suffering, victimized, wounded, and murdered man nailed to a cross—the martyred Christ. He, too, is related to and derives his power from a distant father in the sky.

Even though omnipotent, the distant sky god, or solar god as he is sometimes called, was also capricious, wrathful, possessive, jealous, dominating, and devaluing of the feminine. He was known as Kronos, Zeus, Apollo, and Uranus by the Greeks, Jupiter or Jove by the Romans, Indra by the ancient Indians, Jehovah by the Israelites, Allah by the adherents of Islam, and by many other names in different cultures. He was the Thunderer, the Light Bringer, the Sun, and the Lord of the Universe. The belief that males should be the primary rulers—the patriarchy— evolved from the mythologies surrounding these male deities.

In Genesis, the Old Testament proposes that we are made in God's image. In depth psychology this belief is mirrored in the theory that our individual ego reflects an archetype, or more precisely, a complex of archetypal forces in relationship with one another. Our lives may enact the story of a particular myth or a collection of stories, instead of reflecting the nature of one single god or goddess. Regardless of the relative merit of these theories, men who draw *only* from solar images or images of Olympian patriarchal deities for their inspiration of sacred masculinity are condemned to conceive of their own divine nature as distant, abstract or transcendent, erractically wrathful, and superior.

Unfortunately for all of us, the heroic myth of the man who rules over all by virtue of a manifest destiny granted by the one true solar sky god has prevented the development of an authentic, holistic masculine image. A holistic image supports men's spiritual and psychological development independent of the popular religious or social ideals of the time.

Our new image of authentic, sacred masculinity is of a creative, fecund, generative, nurturing, protective, and compassionate male, existing in harmony with the earth and the feminine, yet also erotic, free, wild, fierce, and undomesticated. This image is a far cry from the invincible, rigid, patriarchal, war-making hero of old, or the suffering martyr. On the positive side, the old image has a solar aspect that presents an ideal of warmth and light. It helps things grow. But problems arise when there is *too much* sun. That is the condition of many men in our culture: too dry, too distant, too brittle—disconnected from the body and the earth. A global warming of the psyche has taken place. A masculine sort of moisture is needed to end this drought in the male psyche.

There are myths that reveal masculine archetypes that appear more fluid, essential, grounded, and life-affirming. *Mythopoeisis* means the making of myth. The knights began to realize that this was the work we were engaging in: the making of a new myth of masculinity. But first we had to reclaim old myths that were lost, repressed, and hidden from view.

AUTHENTIC MASCULINITY AND THE GAIA HYPOTHESIS

Until now most of our masculine images have emerged from the patriarchy. More recently, the renewed matriarchy has offered a feminized vision for men. Some of these visions stem from ancient matriarchal times. In our work together, the new knights of the round table began to move beyond both those limiting ideas. Our quest is for an image of masculinity that springs from our depths.

Most patriarchal solar deities, like Apollo, Jehovah, and Zeus, descend from on high; they are in the sky and over the earth. The archetype of the Goddess, on the other hand, is generally depicted as an earthy or lunar-related deity. The symbolism these mythologies create involves the masculine over the feminine, whose light is thus imagined to be merely a reflection of the masculine sun. Missing from the current vision of soul and gender has been a view that embraces masculinity as earth-based or lunar—soulful, receptive, sensitive, and transforming.

Gaia was the Earth Mother or Mother Nature in ancient Greece. She is often regarded as the prototype or grandmother of the earth goddesses. The modern Gaia hypothesis posits that the earth is a living organism that is feminine. This increasingly popular metaphor exemplifies the predicament of our current vision concerning the relationship of culture, soul, and gender. To envision the earth as solely feminine does the same injustice to the male psyche as the exclusively male, Sky Father hypothesis does to women. This perspective also ignores many ancient myths that depict the feminine as solar and the masculine as earth based or lunar based. This way of thinking has been confusing for many men in quest of soul, who came to believe that the only alternative to the heroic image was a feminine one.

Cultures that have promoted the image of a male sky god have disempowered women socially, politically, and spiritually. They had no sacred feminine image that was not subservient to men. Many men, moreover, felt they had to be heroes or martyrs to keep the angry, abstract, distant Sky Father happy. In a similar manner, viewing the soul of the earth as a feminine entity, Gaia, divorces the male psyche from its own fecund, life-affirming nature. Men often feel they have to become subservient to women in order to become connected to deep feeling, pleasure, and life itself.

In psychology, this problem is well articulated by the Jungian analyst Eugene Monick, who notes that when men are not connected to Phallos (archetypal earth-based masculinity), everything is feminine. Since men are different from women, when they experience their source of life as solely feminine, "castration has begun. . . . The feminization process in a male is inimical to his psychological connection with Phallos. . . . A fundamental differentiation must take place." This means that unless the male can discover his link to archetypal masculine energy, he risks becoming devoured by the feminine. For a differentiation from the mother to take place, he needs contact with the archetypal father, who is also in the earth.

Many men today have been attempting to become more

balanced by getting in touch with their femininity. Yet a man's individuation is in danger if he bases his development solely on a return to the mother—whether through worship of a female earth or a goddess image, or by idealizing a particular woman or feminine characteristics. He risks becoming dependent and disempowered, as have many feminized males. The radical male perspective holds that a man must enter the archetypal field of the masculine if he is ever to coexist with the feminine in partnership. *Partnership* means being neither dominated by the matriarchy nor, by virtue of our fearful reaction, dominating it.

The male initiation process, through which young men in earlier cultures connected with the masculine powers in the earth, is for the most part lost in this culture. Consequently men are in danger of reentering a son-lover-victim relationship with the Goddess, as may have been the case in ancient matriarchal times. In those times, for instance, the wooden statues of wicker men had living men bound up inside them to carry messages to the Goddess after they were burned. Old matriarchal icons often show a mature goddess with her young son/lover, but rarely depict her in relationship with an adult and equally powerful male.

A new monotheism, with an all-powerful goddess as its only sacred image, would be no more appealing than the old patriarchal dominance. If new goddess spirituality is not to be a mere reaction to centuries of domination by the patriarchy, the Gaia hypothesis must be expanded to include a concept of the life-affirming, grounded male in soul embrace with the feminine as an equal partner. Then we may be able to welcome a new ecological perspective that includes the principle of sacred masculinity.

"Save the Earth Mother" is a proclamation we see frequently these days. This thinking reflects the male-degrading fashion of our time. It ignores the ancient connection with the earth that men always have had. It makes us appear as outsiders, intruders who don't really belong to the earth or care for it. Many men may unconsciously disregard nature for that very reason. The Gaia hypothesis reinforces the patriarchal notion that whereas women may draw power from the earth, men are answerable only to some higher power in the sky or to a king on earth who represents that power.

The mythologist and storyteller Michael Meade observes that in our culture the mythological ground that supports the development of separate, distinct, yet complementary genders has eroded to the point of becoming a huge chasm between the sexes.

Any one of us may fall into it. Yet there are many ancient myths of the Earth Father and Mother in sacred marriage with one another, such as the Hindu gods Shiva and Parvati. As men and women rediscover these old myths, we may then find our common ground as allies in the preservation and protection of the earth—the Earth Parent.

The earth contains sacred elements of both genders. The concrete aspects of earth, from its subtlest quantum-mechanical basis to its most defined geological forms, display a wide variety of structures. One can characterize these elements metaphorically, according to certain myths of gender, as feminine or masculine.

Mountains have a thrusting erect maleness about them; they thunder and make wild weather at their peaks, while valleys have an embracing, nurturing, inviting fertile femininity. There exist deep, moist caves and tall, erect trees. The magnetic poles are distinct and opposite. At the quantum level this is also true: creation arises through the interaction of distinctly different and opposite forces like electrons and positrons. Most biological life arises through the combination of male and female genetic materials. If one examines the earth in this manner, it seems clearly composed of both male and female qualities. *If* the earth is a living being, which embodies a feminine soul or consciousness called Gaia, it must also embody a male consciousness.

One of the tasks our new knights began was to return the Earth Father archetype to our psychology, philosophy, and spiritual lives. In response to the historical dominance of the Great Mother in archetypal psychology, Hillman says, "We are able to recall that oceans and rivers belong to Oceanos and Poseidon; that Eros is also a male figure and force; that a lord of vegetation and zoetic life, and of childhood too, is Dionysus; and that even the earth itself can have, as in Egypt at the historical roots of our symbolisms, a masculine personification."

One night, our group worked together in clay. We made various figures and masks that expressed how we had been feeling for the past week. Jim, a single man, made a penis that stood straight up from the center of the table. We laughed. It was clear what had been on his mind recently. We left it standing there as we talked that night. Carl said, "You know, I just realized that I never see images of the erect penis anywhere. Not in art, not in magazines, at least the ones I read, not in films, and certainly not on television. Yet there is something powerful about it."

"Yeah," said Brad. "I see images of voluptuous, hot, swollen women everywhere, but rarely a picture of a fully aroused man except in porno. Why is that?"

Jack noted, "Several women I know have altars with goddess figurines on them, wide hipped, big breasted, and nude. Yet I've never seen an altar or a religious painting depicting a man or a god with a hard-on. What is so shameful about the phallic image?" In an attempt to answer this and other questions, I volunteered to conduct some research and report back to the group.

EARTH MOTHER, STONE FATHER: ANCIENT TRACES OF EARTH-BASED MASCULINITY

I began to do formal research—going to many museums, combing through books, interviewing scholars, and visiting a number of historical sites. I discovered that there are numerous prehistoric sacred images of a man who is different from the solar, heroic Lord of the Universe. Often these ancient paintings and sculptures show him in animal dress, wearing horns, practicing magic, or perhaps just dancing, making music, and hunting. These images frequently depict him as fully sexually aroused. For the most part, the sacred male images that remain from ancient, pre-Christian cultures are phallic: cave paintings of prehistoric hunter-shamans, pre-Socratic statues called herms, the standing stones of pagan Europe, the lingams of pre-Aryan Indus cultures, and numerous other masculine relics from around the world.

In the cave called Les Combarelles, in France, among the wall engravings dating back to 15,000 B.C., and next to an engraving of a woman's vulva, is a clearly defined phallus. Also, in the Fourneau de Diable, there is a Stone Age wall painting of a man with an erection, dancing inside a bull skin. This is very similar to images found in other Stone Age French caves, as well as in Spanish and Swedish ones.

From the second millennium B.C. in Mohenjo-Daro, predating patriarchal Aryan invasions in the region, comes a small, square stamp seal with the image of a man wearing a bull-horned helmet, seated in a cross-legged, meditation posture. He has an erect phallus and is surrounded by male elephants, rhinos, oxen, antelopes and other horned animals. This famous image was found in conjunction with a number of other seals whose most frequent recurring image was a huge bull—the ubiquitous representation of the Earth Father. Icons of this phallic earth-bull-father god are also found in ancient Hungary, Mesopotamia, India, Sumeria, Egypt, Crete, and Greece.

The remains of large stone phalli—the Bauta stones—are found all over Denmark and date back to the Bronze Age. These images are also found in paleolithic Norway, as well as Bronze Age Sweden. The national museum in Copenhagen even has a rare wooden image of a phallic god that dates back to the Celtic Iron Age. There must have been many others that have decomposed.

In ancient Japan, centuries before Buddhism repressed the native religions, there were numerous phallic images. Many were placed in roadside shrines. One of the earliest known stories of Japanese mythology tells about the magic power of the phallus to prevent or cure agricultural disaster and disease.

There are remains of prehistoric phallic standing stones all over England. Like the early Greek phallic herms placed at crossroads and along roadsides, many of these were placed upon *lay lines*—telluric currents or energy flows in the earth. They connected various distant points and earth-based religious shrines along straight lines that can still be seen today. In addition to these large stones there are vast quantities of small phalli from all over prehistoric Europe, carved out of stone and bone. Many of these bone images were carved from the remains of aurochs bulls. These huge bulls (six feet at the shoulder) were a primary source of food, bone for implements, and hide for clothing and shelter. In many ancient Earth Father cults they represented the embodiment of the generativity and generosity of the Earth Father.

At Maiden Castle in Wessex, England, are the remains of ancient earthworks that marked the boundaries of a neolithic camp. From the air one can still see the outline of a giant phallus (almost a half mile long), complete with a detailed head and urethral opening. Ritual burial sites were found in the chalk between two long furrows outlining the urethra.

In Dorset there is another giant phallus in chalk that can be fully appreciated only from the air—the thirty-foot penis of the one-hundred-and-eighty-foot-tall Cerne Giant. There's a depression worn in the head of this penis from people copulating there over the centuries in hopes of enhancing their fertility. This practice continues today.

The New World has many of these images as well. They range from Aztec clay figurines of music-making dancers with erect penises, to carved-stone Mayan temples devoted solely to the phallic image.

In earlier times hunting and gathering cultures were more related to the earth. Attention was turned more toward the ground. The generative power of the earth was represented by these phallic images placed in and upon it. It seems evident that for thousands of years, in many different cultures, the cock was holy.

Although archaeological finds from early agricultural cultures depict some violence of humans toward each other, even cannibalism, organized warfare seems absent. As time went on, agricultural society turned increasingly toward the heavens as harvest issues predominated religious life. And along with this shift toward the heavens as the home of the gods came a new sky-god culture. Things began to change for the men who honored the sacred male power in the earth.

A BRIEF CHRONOLOGY OF THE RISE AND FALL OF EARTH-BASED MASCULINITY

One night we began to sort out the information I had gathered about ancient masculine images. There was a lot of material to go through, so we worked up an outline that briefly told the history of sacred masculinity as we were coming to understand it.

Writers such as Maria Gimbutas, Riane Eisler, and Merlin Stone have produced creative and scholarly feminist revisions of this period of human history, with the intent of reclaiming lost images of the Goddess. Their work is intended to empower and enrich the psychology of modern women by returning ancient sacred feminine iconography to their lives.

This brief guide roughly represents our vision of what might have happened to the psyches of ancient men, based on the images we have uncovered from various overlapping stages of the development of human culture around the world. We were trying to understand the impact of technological culture on men, how things had changed for them, and what might have been lost to them along the way—something feminist revisionists have, for the most part, overlooked.

The chronology that follows does not accurately represent the cultural evolution of all peoples throughout time. Rather it is included simply to give a broad and general view of the evolution of human society in many parts of the world: from hunting and gathering through the development of agriculture to the rise of technological culture such as our own today.

2,000,000–8000 B.C.—Paleolithic (Stone Age)

The sacred masculine image was a hunter/dancer/healer/wild-bull man in *partnership* with the great goddess. Attention was turned toward the earth.

Nomadic man did not accumulate material; no warfare, no territory or wealth to seize. Men had time to dream, to sit around the fire telling stories to one another. There were no hierarchies. The work of male hunters and female gatherers was equally important and their sacred images were equally powerful. Men and women lived together in small tribal bands. Population was stable.

8000–3000 B.C.—Meso/Neolithic (Agricultural Age)

The hunter slowly develops into a soldier guarding new, accumulated wealth. The great agricultural earth goddess takes predominance over the wild, hunting earth gods and wild nature goddesses. Cultivation becomes more valued than hunting and gathering. Narcotics and alcohol are mass-produced for the first time. Men become subservient to the Goddess. They become complacent agricultural workers. The *scapegoat* sacrifice of male animals, and ritual sacrifices of a male *dying god* emerge.

Nature becomes increasingly subordinated. Sacred male images become feminized, and animalistic images become humanized. The wild bull is tamed; he pulls a plow. Partnership between men and women turns into *consortship*—men serving the Goddess.

Earth-father mystery cults decline; matriarchy rises. The nomadic band gives way to larger, more complex, and differentiated social culture. Attention begins to move skyward, concerned with the effect of rain, sun, and seasons on crops. Population starts to grow.

4500–1000 B.C. (Copper, Bronze, and Iron Ages)

The horse is domesticated. Sky-god religions arise in some isolated and wasteland areas, along with organized warfare. Nomadic, horse-mounted, dominating, warlike men overrun the sedentary matriarchy and also destroy the last remnants of the declining earth-father cults.

Partriarchy rises and the urban culture begins to grow. *Dominance* becomes the primary male image—the birth of the Hero.

1000 B.C.—Present (Technological Age)

The Sky Father religions consolidate power; the Earth Father is destroyed or transformed into a symbol of evil. The Goddess is dominated. The phallus becomes a symbol of dominance rather than a generator of life.

Monotheism becomes the primary form of religion. Nature becomes defiled. The current ecological crisis begins when the first forest to be clear-cut (to build ships for ancient Phoenecia) turns into a desert. Polytheistic religions are persecuted; sacred groves are cut down; Christian churches are built over the ancient shrines of earth-based religions.

Materialism rises; men lose connection to soul and to the earth. Large cities grow. Men feel alienated from nature, women, and one another. Warfare becomes a way of life. Population explodes.

THE DESTRUCTION OF THE EARTH FATHER CULTS

With this brief chronology before us, we began to pore over background material. We learned that the old, pretechnological, earth-related deities were not the unapproachable, remote images associated with the male god today.

Earth-related deities were not abstract or transcendent. They were more likely to be related to specific places—a mountain, river, great tree, or clearing in the woods. The patriarchal Sky Father, on the other hand, evolved in conjunction with the development of advanced agriculture, metallurgy, and other high technology.

The domestication of the horse allowed wide-ranging marauders and organized warfare to flourish. Nomadic horse-mounted men developed the notion of a transcendent sky god, who could travel with them from place to place.

When they conquered an earth-based religious culture, they tended to substitute the iconography of an overlord who ruled over the local earth-related deities. This is one of the methods conquerors have used to subject and enslave people up to today. First they defeat and defile indigenous sacred images. Then they forcefully instill a belief that the indigenous sacred power is inferior to the conqueror's god.

The Christian church performed quite a bit of this activity all over the world. In this country African slaves and Native Americans were subjected to the will of their conquerors for centuries; it's no coincidence that along with the growth of the civil-rights movement came a growing interest among these people in restoring the ancient religious beliefs and cultural practices of their ancestors. Those beliefs were polytheistic and connected with the earth.

Once settled, agrarian cultures became wealthy enough to become more stratified and specialized, with large holdings of stored grains to account for. To administer control of this wealth, a hierarchical priestesshood may have evolved in early matriarchal cultures. With the development of a more urban culture, something precious to male experience was lost—earth-based masculinity in partnership with the earth goddesses.

Perhaps the Earth Father religion was already in decline when the destruction of the ancient world began. Adele Getty suggests that when castration was introduced as a technique for domesticating herd animals, something traumatic happened to the male psyche that witnessed it. There was a transformation from wild hunting man in relationship with wild animals to domesticated herding man in relationship with emasculated animals. Men began to conceive of the one fertile bull who ruled the herd—the dominating patriarch who also had power over the other domesticated males.

Marauding, nomadic Sky Father men overran the unwalled, egalitarian cultures of old Europe, the Indus Valley, the Fertile Crescent, and other sites. The defenseless, agriculturally based men who lived there, peace loving or not, were most likely slain or enslaved.

We don't know what forces created the marauders or exactly where they came from. As the new knights discussed this, Ben suggested that they may have been hunter men outcast from the agricultural societies for being too wild, who banded together in exile. Wherever they came from, the accumulation of wealth in these old agriculturally based communities was too great for the lean outsiders who rode amid wastelands to resist. They may have perceived these communities as a herd of fat bison waiting to be hunted and harvested.

Perhaps the men of these ancient, so-called matrilineal cultures already had become dispirited and vulnerable to dominance, as have many of today's sons of controlling mothers. Alcohol and drug abuse came about through the cultivation of the vine and the poppy. Alcohol and drugs, produced in large amounts for the first time in human history, helped keep docile the large work forces needed to support a privileged class. If men were dominated by a powerful, wealth-controlling, agriculturally based matriarchy, they may have lost the warrior powers their paleolithic forebears needed to fight off invaders.

Whatever the cause, the image of the Earth Father was profaned, disfigured, repressed into the underworld and the unconscious, or forgotten altogether. This repression continued into historical times, although in pre-Christian Greece there remained some remnants of Earth Father images in relationship to the cult of Pan.

According to Eva Kuels, in early Greek culture we find, for the most part, "a display of the phallus less as an organ of union or of mutual pleasure than as a kind of weapon; a spear or war club, and a scepter of sovereignty." The image of Phallos, although widespread, had by this time lost the sacred, generative, life-affirming symbolic aspects it had had in earlier ages.

The perversion of the phallus from a sacred image of the Earth Father in union with the Earth Mother into an image of the intellectual, unfeeling man who dominates the feminine culminated in the early Christian era. Plutarch said the reason that herms (sculptures dedicated to the god Hermes) were featureless below the head, except for erect penises in bas-relief, was that *the body was not important.* He believed that in order for a man to be potent only the brains had to be alive and fertile. Men began to become disconnected from their feelings, which have their roots in the body. Intellectualization and splitting from the body were encouraged.

Plutarch was merely reflecting the Platonic/Socratic philosophic traditions of his predecessors. He also heralded the death of the last extant Earth Father cult. He paved the road for the later Christians to transform the phallic Earth Father into the embodiment of evil—the Devil. The phallus began to become depicted as *bad,* shameful, dangerous. This sentiment persists into the present. Today phallic images are considered either pornographic symbols of patriarchal dominance or objects of homosexual fascination.

The women who were enslaved and forced to interbreed with the men who overthrew the Old World earth-based cultures were at least able to preserve some fragments of their Earth Goddess religions. These then became interwoven in the culture, religion, and mythologies of the victors. For example, the Virgin Mary still remains a powerful force in Christianity today. The priests of the ancient Earth Father religions, however, were most likely enslaved or slain to the last man. Thus even less knowlege remains about these religions than about the ancient goddess cults.

THE TAMING OF THE ANCIENT WILD BULL-MAN

Curiously enough, I found a lot of information about the Earth Father through reading literature about the ancient goddesses. One night I read aloud an ancient poem to the new knights. We felt moved by its story about the demise of earth-based masculinity.

It comes to us from clay tablets from ancient Sumeria that have been dated back to approximately 2000 B.C.—over two thousand years before Plutarch heralded the death of Pan—and is one of the most complete eulogies concerning the destruction of the old Earth Father religion to have survived over the ages. It expresses the great regard in which the Earth Father was once held, and also gives us a glimpse into the feeling of a woman and man in sacred partnership. The goddess Inanna sings to her consort Dumuzi, the god of the harvest and fertility:

> My honey-man, my honey-man sweetens me always.
> My lord, the honey-man of the gods,
> He is the one my womb loves best. . . .
> He laid his hands on my holy vulva,
> He smoothed my black boat with cream,
> He quickened my narrow boat with milk . . .
> I will decree a sweet fate for him.

Unfortunately, not even the power of this ancient Queen of Heaven and Earth was able to prevent him from a dark fate. In the following excerpt, the *eagle* and the *falcon*, the *wind* and the *flies* from the steppes are icons of the invading sky god. It poignantly expresses not only the despair of the defeated earth-related male, but that of his feminine counterpart as well. Dumuzi speaks:

> In a wooded grove the terror of tall trees rises about me.
> Water is poured over my holy hearth
> The bottom of my churn drops away.
> My drinking cup falls from its peg
> My shepherd's crook has disappeared.
>
> An eagle seizes a lamb from the sheepfold
> A falcon catches a sparrow on the reed fence
> My sister, your goats drag their lapis beards in the dust
> Your sheep scratch the earth with bent feet.
> The churn lies silent; no milk is poured
> The cup lies shattered; Dumuzi is no more.
> The sheepfold is given to the winds.

Inanna wept for Dumuzi . . .

O, you flies of the steppe,
My beloved bridegroom has been taken from me
Before I could wrap him with a proper shroud.

The wild bull lives no more.
The shepherd, the wild bull lives no more.
Dumuzi, the wild bull, lives no more. . . .

The jackal lies down in this bed.
The raven dwells in his sheepfold.
You ask me about his reed pipe?
The wind must play it for him.
You ask me about his sweet songs?
The wind must sing them for him.

Dumuzi was both a wild male and a husband of the earth—a shepherd. He was like the wild bull who protects the herd from predators. He is an archetype that elegantly balances wildness and responsibility, the very thing many of us are struggling with today. The paleolithic and early neolithic cults of the wild bull, which honored the untamed generativity of men, were eventually completely transformed during the so-called matriarchal, agricultural ages. The bull became a domestic beast of domestic men.

Sacred phallic images became less evident, even absent in places like Crete, which cradled early Greek culture. There the bull-man was called a monster—the Minotaur. A hero, Theseus, came along to slay it millennia before the church turned Pan into a hideous monster as well. Man became completely tame or, in reaction to the forces of domestication, violent—split off from life.

Gods like Dionysus began to emerge. In his rituals, the raw flesh of a sacrificial bull or goat, representing the mana or power of the god himself, was ripped apart and eaten. Its blood, and/or wine representing his blood, was imbibed. Dionysus's followers were reportedly then able to commune directly with the god, who would enter them in a trance possession. Dionysus had wild-women followers who carried phallic images in processions. The bull and the phallus were no longer the icons of male mystery cults.

With the noble wild bull tamed, the sacred hunter also was no more. He became replaced by the soldier. The new gods, the

Olympians, were heroes with human forms. They lost connection to their animal forms and the earth, except for gods like Pan, who were soon also repressed and forgotten.

The phallic, half-animal, magical, wild, dancing, music-making man was no more. Only remnants of him are seen in wild, phytomorphic (vegetation) gods like Dionysus, who in time gave rise to the more humanized Orpheus. Eventually, with the advance of urban culture, a sanitized Christ emerged out of these Dionysian and Orphic roots as the new sacred image of men.

So the new knights discovered, through looking at this historical information, that there once existed a sacred image of masculinity distinctly different from the one that dominates our collective consciousness today. And we hoped, through a variety of means, to recover some connection with that latent, underlying psychic field. One aspect of our quest was to rediscover these images; another was to learn how to reconnect with these ancient archetypes in a manner that would enrich our lives as modern men.

What became of these Earth Fathers, these former deities of men? What was lost when men turned away from hunting side by side and began stalking wealth and hunting one another? Their unfettered lives as hunters became distorted. They began using their weapons to protect their wealth—stored grains, animals, and artifacts—or to seize the wealth of others; they became soldiers. Something happened to the male psyche when domesticated animals and grains became more essential to society than the wild meat that hunting men formerly provided. Men lost their connection to the inner richness of soul, to their old magic, shared stories, and myths. As they became more empty, they attempted to fill themselves up with more conquests and material goods.

Ultimately, most of what we may infer about prehistoric Earth Father or Earth Mother religions and cultures is simply conjecture. Yet there is sufficient archaeological evidence to support this idea. There are artifacts and threads of myth and ritual that can be combed out and coaxed to yield at least an outline of the ancient Earth Father, and Moon Father as well. And we do know that there is an image of masculine soul buried deep in the psyche—because we feel it.

To whom do the symbols for the horned bull, the magical hunter with an erect phallus, and the wild, free, dancing, music-making man belong? Where are they now, and what do they have to offer to our modern understanding of soul and gender? The importance of mythology for answering some of these questions is suggested by James Hillman:

> The personages of myth are not mere subjects of knowledge. They are living actualities of the human being, having existence as *psychic realities* in addition to and perhaps even prior to their historical and geographical manifestation. . . . The soul still re-dreams these themes in its fantasy, behavior and thought structures. . . . We cannot touch myth without it touching us.

This is the point of recounting the myths in the chapter that follows. We are trying to touch and be touched by myths, to discover what literal truth these mythic truths may offer our lives. Something can awaken when we hear the stories and the names of the ancient gods of men. In a book we try to awaken the masculine soul with words. When we meet together as men, as we'll discuss later, we utilize drumming, dancing, storytelling, music, poetry, ritual, ceremony, visual arts, wilderness experience, and dreamwork.

I SEEM TO BE AN US

In order to effect a radical reformation of ourselves as men we may also need to redefine our basic ideas about the nature of the self. The vision we are working toward goes against many traditional formulations.

In the West we have the idea of a single unified, central self. Traditional therapies attempt to move one toward that goal. This thinking evolves out of the image of the old Judeo-Christian patriarchal god. It emerges from the belief that man was made in that god's image, that one big old man in the sky. Yet when we examine this dominant religion, which has so deeply influenced the formulation of our self-concept as men, we see that monotheism has another aspect.

In addition to the old man in the sky, there is a young man who was on earth. He also had a father on the earth who, like many modern fathers, is mostly forgotten and ignored. His mother, on the other hand, retained the evocative qualities of some of the prepatriarchal goddesses. In fact, most of the churches I visited in Europe were dedicated to Mary and full of her icons. Since it's pretty hard to contact the fierce, warlike Jehovah, New Testament believers generally call on the young man and his mother to tell the old man to lighten up a bit and ease their load.

Not only is there the Trinity, but also the devil and a whole host of archangels, saints, demons, and other denizens of the transhuman realms. Traditional psychology, with its trinity of id, ego, and superego, mirrors the New Testament view of how human consciousness is organized: superego equals god; ego equals human; id equals devil. Therefore, even so-called monotheism has multiple images contained within it. Likewise, polytheism offers men a wider range of sacred images from which to gain inspiration, definition, and direction.

In our work together as men we have been attempting to host a dialogue between these different selves, or gods, as we come to know them. We are entertaining a model of mental health that the psychologist James Fadiman refers to as the "braided self." Traditional psychology considers the idea of multiple personalities as pathological. Yet pathology arises only when the selves do not communicate well with one another and act independently. Thus, a breakdown of the inner ecosystem occurs. In the same manner, when we act independently of other natural forces in our environment, the symbiotic, natural balance may be lost. We create problems.

How does this idea affect our self-concept as men? In earlier chapters we saw how the archetype of the Hero has wreaked havoc in the world. Domineering, aggressive, polarized male energy has exploited the earth, causing widespread ecological imbalance and danger. The continued existence of life itself is threatened. The heroic male feels spiritually impoverished. He is empty inside—dry. He is always hungry, trying to fill up the lost inner richness of multiplicity with more and more material goods and exciting experiences that *momentarily* make him feel alive again.

The old psychological notion of the unified self reflects a dominator/heroic model. It oppresses and numbs the deep psyche of men. What we consider normal behavior for a Western man may be the product of a mass psychosis, a cultural sickness caused by severe repression of the diverse aspects of self and a callous disregard for the rich inner ecology of the psyche.

Problems in our environment and culture have arisen from a

lack of understanding of the interrelatedness and interdependence of all things. Problems also arise when various aspects of the self are unconscious of one another. These issues in the culture and in the inner life of men mirror one another and create one another. Some archetypal psychologists believe that the condition of the world actually reflects the collective condition of our human souls and vice versa. Thus we speak of the Anima Mundi—the soul of the world.

The journey toward healing is a journey into the wilderness of the self. We need contact with the inner richness of life that multiple images can offer. We are moving toward the mythical, archetypal, and ancient core of men. This is the fundamental source of our energy and creativity in life.

THE FIFTH TASK OF MEN: TO RECLAIM THE ANCIENT, SACRED IMAGES OF MASCULINITY

The new knights of the round table decided to continue our search for images of masculinity that did not emerge out of the dominating, heroic, patriarchal religions, images that recent revivals of matriarchal religions do not offer. Matriarchy is as smothering and oppressive as patriarchy to our process of self-discovery as men. We each made a commitment to find sacred images from ancient times that speak to us today, a variety of different models and archetypes that mirror our emerging vision of authentic masculinity.

> *Reclaiming some of the ancient images of men was the fifth task we attempted. Learning how to work with these archetypes and apply the myths to our daily lives was the sixth task we faced.*

❧ CHAPTER 6

The Forgotten and Forbidden Sacred Images of Men

And that dismal cry rose slowly,
And sank slowly through the air,
Full of spirit's melancholy
And eternity's despair!
And they heard the words it said—
"Pan is dead!—great Pan is dead—
Pan, Pan is dead!"
        Elizabeth Browning

Unresolved issues with our fathers were central to most of us in the group. Many of us remembered our fathers as distant, emotionally inaccessible, or absent altogether. Several of the men's fathers had died before the men could develop a strong, satisfying relationship with them. As our work continued, though, we realized that our need to activate the missing father within us was as important as resolving old childhood issues with our own parents. We were attempting as adult men to become protective and nurturing parents to our own inner child, still alive within our psyches. As long as we continued to depend solely on women to nurture and protect our inner child, we ran the risk of becoming powerless and dependent, remaining perpetually immature.

Women are often willing to mother us, as a result of their own traditional conditioning. But as awareness of their own oppression has grown, they've often come to resent this dynamic. They want to be in relationships with mature men, not needy boys. Yet each of us has a needy boy within him. How do we meet the needs of that inner child?

One way is through the type of work we do together in men's groups like the new knights. We give each other permission to express fears and vulnerabilities, to be silly and playful. In other parts of our lives, these childlike behaviors are often met with judgment or rejection.

Another way we are healing ourselves is through connecting with our own inner fathers. We reparent one another by being fatherly to one another, extending a helping hand when a group member is feeling low, supporting one another's growth. We also reparent ourselves individually by paying attention to the voice of the child within us and giving it expression in a supportive environment.

Like the inner child, the archetype of the Father is one of many images we are learning to access directly in our psyches through both inner, imaginal dialogues and our conversations with one another. Most of us were unaware of this fatherly presence within until we had children of our own. As Wordsworth once said, "The child is father of the man." Yet as we have seen, a major aspect of the Father archetype has been absent in the psyche of most modern men. Whether parents or not, few men these days have a good relationship with the archetype of the Earth Father.

Our consciousness is not something that merely resides within us. Many depth psychologists believe that it is contiguous with the consciousness of others and the world as a whole. Therefore, the Earth Father has roots not only within our individual psyches, but also deep in the collective psyche of all people, in the dark mystery of the world psyche (the consciousness of nature), and in the earth itself. He is a source of diverse imagery and inspiration for a variety of masculine roles. He is a different sort of sacred father than "our father who art in heaven, hallowed be thy name." He offers a different perspective on how to relate to our own fathers, how to access the father within, and how to parent our children.

THE LOST FATHERS OF THE EARTH

Aspects of the Earth Father may be seen in the myths of many cultures. We've already looked at a bit of the archaeological record that the knights reviewed. As we continued on our quest, we turned our attention to the oral and written literature of mythology in an attempt to better understand the nature of the ancient core of masculine soul.

One night Rodger brought in a book called *The Father: Mythology and Changing Roles,* by Arthur and Libby Coleman. The Colemans write about a number of earth gods who are depicted as giving birth to the earth and/or its inhabitants. They also mention a number of "more complex gods who are also associated with fertility and the earth but who are not the primary creator."

Freyr, for example, of Norse mythology, is a god of agriculture and the underworld, like the Egyptian Osiris and the Greek Pluto. Freyr stands for peace; no weapons are allowed in his temple. The Australian Earth Father, Karora, gives birth from his armpits. The Norse giant Ymir gives birth from his feet; when he dies, his body is turned into the earth. The Vedic Purusha is the progenitor of the earth, as is the Chinese Pan-ku, who is depicted with children crawling all over him.

We took turns reading aloud about some of these deities. Over the next few weeks, each of us searched out and brought in various pictures, statues, and masks of earth-based masculine icons that spoke to us. We added them to the collection of images and charts growing on the wall of our meeting room.

In addition to the myths mentioned by the Colemans, we discovered a multitude of other deities from various cultures and epochs. They reflect a very different ideal of masculinity than those presented by the archetypes of our modern Judeo-Christian culture.

Dumuzi, for example, mentioned in the preceding chapter, is the agricultural god of ancient Sumeria. He is the husband of the goddess Inanna. Enki is an earthy, magical Sumerian god of depth and wisdom who aides Inanna on her epic journey to the underworld. Both these sacred male figures are connected to the earth; they have a powerful relationship in alliance with the goddess of heaven and earth as well.

From Africa we found Ogun, the dragon slayer, who, like Iron John in Robert Bly's recent book, is a wild man of the woods. With the advent of urban culture, however, Ogun was transformed into a tool maker—a traditional occupation of men. The African god Elleggua is a trickster, like the Native American Coyote. Similar to the Greek Hermes, Elleggua is also a messenger and magician associated with the penis and the crossroads. Obatala, who is most revered in the African Yoruba tradition, is an androgynous creator god associated with the high mountains.

As we continued to read and talk about these sacred images, we developed a growing sense of wonder as we realized just how pervasive and numerous these earth-based images of masculinity have been throughout time.

Many pre-Christian, Greek masculine deities were also connected to the earth. Hephaestus works deep beneath mountains, creating wondrous works upon his forge. Orpheus is associated with music and wild animals, as is Pan. Hades dwells deep beneath the earth in the place of souls. Fertility and riches spring from the depths of Pluto, the Roman Hades. Dionysus, an ecstatic lord of vegetation and the vine, dances, dies, and is reborn each spring. Hermes, the great communicator, can go deep into the underworld and return to the world above. He also brings down the word from the Olympian gods on high.

Geb was one of the earliest, earth-based creator gods in the Egyptian cosmology. He is usually depicted in connection with his twin sister, Nut, the sky goddess, who is arched over him. Also in Egypt was Osiris, discoverer of the Nile river. Each year the river would overflow, depositing fresh alluvium to fertilize the crops. This was depicted in several ancient paintings as Osiris's ejaculate fluid flowing directly from his phallus into the mouths of the people. He represents the fluid, cyclic style of earth-based masculinity that engenders and supports life.

Why is it valuable to understand or embrace earth-based masculinity? Because the heroic, solar, heavenly model, taken alone, is dominating and oppressive. The solar gods are abstract and often inaccessible to our imagination—the very image of the remote or disembodied father. Christ, for example, stood for many fine virtues—unconditional love, healing, and forgiveness. However, he was not a father or a husband. His heavenly father was also without a feminine consort or partner. What can these male, monotheistic images communicate to us as men concerned about issues as important as raising our children, relating to women, and preserving the earth?

The Earth Father is not the Lord of the entire Universe. He is a more personal god who is a progenitor of life on *this* planet. He is concerned with life's evolution and preservation. He is an image of a father involved with the day-to-day life of his family. He is not out running around the entire galaxy. He presents a sacred image of masculinity that embodies many of the qualities now ascribed to the feminine: life-generating, fluid, emotional, wild, playful, nurturing, and connected to the earth—an image of a present and embodied father. These are qualities the new knights began to ascribe to authentic masculinity as well—not as an attempt to claim feminine virtues as our own, but as fundamental qualities of many diverse sacred images of men that were worshiped throughout time. They are in our collective unconscious, in our mythological heritage, and in our bones.

MOON FATHERS

In pretechnological cultures, the gods were associated with many different domains. There was no chief executive officer who ruled over all worlds. These deities interacted with one another as a council, a family, or a tribe. Men enjoyed a *personal* relationship with these deities, who were close to their lives. There were gods of the sea, forest, rivers, mountains, desert, sun, sky, and moon.

The moon has not always been the symbol of femininity it is today. There was once a Man in the Moon. In ancient Egypt there were numerous inscriptions referring to Osiris as lord of the moon. His son Horus, also known as Old-Man-Who-Becomes-a-Child-Again, has the moon as his left eye. Thoth, a god of wisdom and spokesman for the gods, was also a lunar-related deity. Hermes, who is more familiar to many of us, is a Greek personification and later evolution of Thoth and Min, the phallic god of upper Egypt who was a protector of travelers.

In ancient Sumer, in the city of Ur, the Moon Father was worshiped as Nanna. He is known in Serbian myth as Myesyats, the Bald Uncle. He's been revered in the far-flung outreaches of Greenland, as well as in Malay and amid the Maoris of Australia. In India he is referred to as Soma and Chandra, great liberators from ignorance. In Australia, he is called Japara. In ancient Babylonia he was known as Sinn. Among the ancient druids of Ireland he was called Saint Luan, Dugad, and Moling. The Eskimos of Baffin Island speak of Brother Moon, who wears the black handprints of his sister, the sun.

Why is it valuable to become aware of lunar masculinity? The heroic, solar model is very consistent. The sun rises and falls every day, always the same. It is a model of the man who remains the same throughout time. This has its value in establishing a model of discipline and consistency in our lives. However, that consistency can smother other aspects of our being.

The ebb and flow of the moon, on the other hand, reminds us that only at times do we feel completely full and luminous. Sometimes our brightness is on the wane. Sometimes we want to be completely dark, withdrawn, and alone. At other times our light starts to grow again; we feel expansive and move outward.

If we envision masculinity as changeless, like the sun, we become alarmed when we get moody, when we fluctuate. We try to modulate our behavior with the abuses discussed in Part I. Lunar masculinity provides a more authentic masculine model that is in emotional flux. We ebb and flow. We don't have to be hard, brave, and outward all the time. Sometimes we, too, can be soft, vulnerable, and inward.

There are countless examples of masculine deities who are more related to the earth, moon, or sea than to the sky, stars, or sun. It's not possible, within the context of this book, to explore all these myths. So we'll examine just a few, which are representative, to some degree, of them all. This may help us see how any of these old gods can be reknown, reclaimed, remembered, and reintegrated into our consciousness. This may suggest how new gods may be born or invited into our collective consciousness—in *this* time, for *this* culture.

RETURNING TO THE EARTH

Some of the major tasks faced by the new knights were (1) restoring our ability to feel at home in our bodies without numbing our feelings; (2) learning to love, laugh, and play again; (3) recovering from shame by accepting ourselves for who we really are; and (4) discovering new sacred images of masculinity that inspire us.

There are many different masculine gods. We decided to focus on a few that speak to these issues. Some popular writers, such as Jean Shinoda Bolen, have thoughtfully suggested that various gods and goddesses exist within the human psyche and that it is both possible and potentially beneficial to connect with these inner archetypal forces. As we entered this mythological way of seeing, we came to realize that not only are the gods within us, but we are, as it were, within them as well.

These archetypal forces are bigger than our individual egos. In learning to work with archetypal energy, we have come to realize that to a significant degree we are all powerless. The forms of the gods are infinite in their variety and vast in their complexity. We cannot control them. Often we are possessed or even destroyed by them. If we're lucky we may learn how to commune with the gods and receive an occasional gift through catching a glimpse into this mystery. Perhaps, through our attempts to know them, we will gain some insight into the myriad forces that move our lives from within and without.

The gods may demand expression upon the stage of our individual lives. They make a claim upon us. If we ignore that claim, we get possessed—driven. Learning how to host that claim—to welcome the expression of potent forces of transformation into our lives—is a large portion of our work together in the knights.

Alcoholism, for example, is related to possession by the god of ecstasy—Dionysus. Robert Johnson warns that when we lack the "spiritual nutrition" that emerges from communion with Dionysus, we wind up chasing the phantoms of "ephemeral happiness": sex, food, money, drugs, and drinks. In the knights we are attempting to learn how to commune with and honor our archetypal need for ecstasy and getting loose, without entertaining the behaviors that destroy our lives and the lives of others.

This is one of the paths an authentic male walks: learning how to approach and honor the ancient gods of men. Through this work we may also learn about how to approach the Goddess without becoming devoured. The poet Robert Bly believes that the male journey, at this time, is a downward one, into the underworld, the world of soul and deep feeling. The new knights are concentrating on the deities connected with those realms, though the gods of heights and light have much to teach as well.

WILD GODS OF DEEP, FLUID FEELING

Masculinity is frequently depicted as dry. Femininity, by virtue of emotionality, milk giving, menstruating, birthing, and lubricating the route to coitus, is often associated with moisture.

The solar gods present an image that is hot, dry, high, and far away. Apollo, for example, is a god of the intellect, the aspect of self that has the capacity to distance itself from feelings and physicality. This has its value. Therefore, we don't want to abandon our relationship with the solar powers altogether. However, there are other gods, like Poseidon, the Greek god of the sea, who present a different image of masculinity—a fluid masculinity that has been lacking in the psyche of most modern men. It's important to remember the ways in which we are men of deep feelings. These feelings make our lives rich.

Poseidon, who was called Neptune by the Romans, was the husband of Amphitrite, a daughter of Oceanus. Although some feminist mythologists name him as a patriarchal god, he once joined with Hera and Athena to overthrow the sky father Zeus. He is unlike the other Olympian gods who rule from on high. From his watery depths he reminds us of the ways in which a man is *moist*. With tears a man grieves for what has been lost. He embraces soul and endures loneliness on his journey to the underworld. With his sweat he shelters, protects, and overcomes adversity. With his semen he quickens, engenders, and enlivens. With his blood he nourishes, defends, and gives back to the earth.

Ram Dass once said that many spiritual seekers, through meditation and other practices, wind up connecting with a dry, dispassionate soul. They lose their juice. For him, the real work was to stay connected to a "juicy soul" that was passionate and engaged with life. Although we are not here to praise the old patriarchs, it was said of Moses that part of his greatness was that at the age of 110 he still had all his juices—something worth aspiring to.

The moist male is not solely the son of the Earth Mother, like today's feminized male. He is also the Earth Father's progeny, allied in a manner in which a son may never ally with the mother, by virtue of her otherness. During the process of a male's evolution, there comes a time when the boy must leave the mother and be initiated into the magnetic field of the father. A whole generation of men who have rejected the dominating solar myths and the dry soul of patriarchal spirituality have been reluctant to make this transition. Yet by staying allied to the field of the mother, they lack the vitality of the authentic male in sacred relationship to the earth.

Many men who feel dry turn to alcohol or drugs for lubrication. They want to loosen up. But this Dionysian strategy is also fraught with the potential for drowning. We may attempt to drown our sorrows, or cool our rage, but it doesn't really work. The knights have been trying to help one another swim with our sorrows and creatively express our moral outrage, surfing upon its huge, empowering waves. We feel, acknowledge, share, and embrace both grief and rage as components of our renewed capacity for deep feeling. The heroic, armored male phobically avoids realms of deep feeling. If we enter Poseidon's realm with our armor still intact, we may sink, never to return.

The authentic, moist male can draw inspiration from Poseidon—a wild, raging god of depth. We are coming to understand our emotional fluidity as rooted in a deep inner strength and power. This is distinct from an image of the watery emotional man who floats on the surface of deep feeling or is overwhelmed and possessed by the oceanic inner feminine. Misdirected, uninitiated heroic male power is one force that is destroying the planet. An equal but opposite force of destruction is watery passivity, narcissism, numbness, and irresponsibility.

The Christian, Asian, and New Age ideal of spiritual flight—ascended masters, angels, going into the light, communing with the higher power—encourages men to try to get *beyond their bodies and off the earth*. This ideal presents another danger to the earth. If we see our bodies and the earth as prisons of spirit, we may lose respect for the inherently sacred nature of matter. If we perceive body and earth as vessels both containing and composed of soul, which is accessible to us in the here and now, however, they are more likely to evoke feelings of wonder and reverence.

To embrace nature is to be in communion with the typhonic—the primordial and uncontrollable monsters of the deep—as well as the flowers, babbling brooks, and butterflies. Nature is noble, beautiful, and wild—but it's not *nice*.

Poseidon offers us a source of wild magic and empowerment. These powerful feelings also have inherent possibilities for abuse. Our challenge is to learn to surf the waves and not be drowned. Carl said once, "As a man who's lived on the northern California coast for many years, I know the greatest danger comes when you turn your back on the ocean. That's when the giant sleeper waves appear from out of nowhere. They break high on the shore and sweep you away." Possession by archetypal forces may occur when we turn our back on them as well. Our lives become driven by obsessions and compulsions. We lose the ability to flow in harmony with, or even be aware of, the deep currents flowing through our lives.

The images of the ancient masculine earth gods are sexually well endowed. By contrast, as the Jungian analyst Eugene Monick has observed, the icons of the solar fathers have tiny, hidden, or even absent phalli. Poseidon's trident is a symbol of his phallic nature. The swelling and contracting of tides, the upwelling of currents, the ocean's generous abundance, and its terrifying capacity to sweep away, overwhelm, and drown are metaphors for Poseidon's generative, phallic power. This trident is also seen in the hands of Satan as an instrument used to torture souls. Certainly, possession by Phallos can be torturous to a man—we become sex addicts or rapists. But communion with Phallos can be ecstatic—we become wild lovers and generators of passion, pleasure, life, and creativity.

Poseidon is contiguous with Gaia. He is a partner with the Earth Mother. His realm, the sea, surrounds and embraces the earth. Although we may fear his typhonic nature and the sea monsters of his abyss, he is also the Lord of the Deep, wherein lie our deepest emotions, our most profound inner stillness, and the dark, fecund mysteries of soul.

The feelings of an authentic male are drawn from a deep well.

This is why we're sometimes slow to share them; often we need a little time to let them rise. In order for an ocean wave to rise high, without breaking up, it must continually expand its depth. When it hits the shallow shore, it shatters. One way we expand our masculine depth is in silence. We give each other a lot of space when a member of our group is trying to express himself. This is one way we're often different in our men's meetings than when we're with women. Women's feelings often seem more accessible, on the surface. As men, we sometimes get overwhelmed by women's immediacy around feelings in our relationships.

We are not quick to analyze, fix, question, or give feedback. Nor do we try to speak for one another. Sometimes we just sit with one another's pain, as men have done together through the ages. Silence itself is a masculine mode of feeling, which Poseidon also represents. The depths of the ocean are silent and dark; the silence is not of emptiness, but rather of depth.

SHIVA, THE WILD, DANCING GOD

One night Carl brought in a poster of Shiva, the Indian Lord of the Dance, which he found in a religious bookstore. "Aaron, you were in India," he said. "What do you know about this god? He looks so potent, graceful, and energized. Nothing like our Western god images of a young man dying on a cross, the stern, desert patriarchs, or a distant old man in the sky."

"Yeah, he's hot, sexy, audacious, and fluid," I replied. "He transforms the universe by dancing and making love."

"What a wild concept," replied Carl. "I've always thought I could only change the world through hard work. But as I think about this, it occurs to me that one of the reasons I burned out on my last job was I had forgotten how to dance. I had lost my flexibility and capacity to enjoy life."

In this picture, Shiva, like Poseidon, carries a trident. His followers in India still draw this trident on their foreheads today. He's indigo blue in color, like the deep of the sea. Also like Poseidon, Shiva is depicted, in some Indian temple carvings, as the earth shaker, the creator of earthquakes. He's a consort of Kali, the dark, terrifying, wrathful, destructive death goddess, and also of Parvati, the beautiful, nurturing great mother.

Shiva is known to us in the West as the dancing god within a ring of fire. He dances with one upraised foot and one hand in a mudra, or pose, that signifies "fear not." His cult goes back at least ten thousand years. It vastly predates the Aryan invasions of patriarchal Vedic culture from Europe, which brought a pantheon of warlike sky gods into the peaceful agrarian cultures of the Indus Valley.

Throughout the ages Shiva has been universally represented by a lingam—a phallus. It often has an image of the god on it carved in bas-relief. More often the lingam is simply a large phallic-shaped stone. It is frequently placed in a vulva-shaped stand or container called a *yoni,* much as a pestle might be placed upright in a mortar. It thus represents the union of Earth Mother and Earth Father. These images of the Earth Father are still worshiped in parts of India today as symbols of generativity and fertility.

While in India I witnessed Shivite women pouring oil over these lingams and rubbing them during the course of a Shiva *puja* (a ceremony or service). Shiva is an earlier incarnation of Krishna. Like Pan, but more refined, Krishna is a shepherd who plays his flute and charms the nymphlike milk maids. As an expression of his fecundity, Krishna is often reported to have made love to thousands of women at a time and satisfied them all. The Hindu culture is full of ecstatic poems and songs generated in response to his fluid sensuality, powerful beauty, and role of protector of life—like Dumuzi, a shepherd and guardian of the flock.

From the icons of myth, it appears that when Shiva performs the dance of eternal transformation he's found in consort with the beautiful goddess Parvati. She is benign, sensual, playful, and life-giving. She's frequently depicted in ecstatic sexual embrace with him. It's when he becomes inert, when he is immobilized, that flesh-rending Kali, in all her horrific glory, arises as his other consort. In one of Shiva's less-known forms, he's depicted as a corpse. Kali is mounted upon him in sexual embrace. She sits astride his supine body with his phallus—erect even in death— inside her.

We may wish to remember this image as we seek balance with the women in our lives. Men who find themselves repeatedly encountering Kali in one manifestation or another may have forgotten how to dance. If you're already dead in your life, it's no surprise the Goddess of Death would choose you as a consort. "God respects me when I work, but loves me when I sing," said the ancient Chinese poet Basho. When we become frozen, immobilized by the weight of our armor, inflexible, or afraid to keep facing life's changes as they appear, the face of the dark mother turns toward us with her long, sharp, armor-piercing teeth dripping blood and says, "Change or die." She is in service of life's continual dance. Shiva is also known as Maheshvara, the great destroyer of ignorance. He breaks down rigid boundaries and helps us move out of stuck places.

Shiva reminds us that dancing isn't just a pastime. It's our sacred duty to celebrate life and to revel in our wildness and potency. A few weeks after this meeting, I placed a statue of him on my computer. He reminds me now to shut it off once in a while and take a Shiva break—put on some tunes and rock around the room. It's easy to forget.

GODS OF LAUGHTER AND SACRED PLAY

The following week, Jim brought in an old tattered book from his childhood with the story of Brer Rabbit. He read it aloud toward the end of the evening. It got us talking about the Trickster archetype deep into the night. The next week, on a lark, we went out to see the movie *Who Framed Roger Rabbit?* Although entertained, we were also somewhat disappointed. Unlike Brer Rabbit and Bugs Bunny, Roger was no trickster. He was more of a sap, a victim. "Does the trickster energy help us from becoming saps?" wondered Jim as we continued our talk in a coffeehouse. "Where do humor and goofing fit into this serious work of recovering the masculine soul?" he asked. Good question.

The Trickster is an archetypal and mythological figure present in almost every culture, present and past. Almost always male, he represents a complex aspect of the psyche. He is paradoxical, uncontrollable, iconoclastic, and in many ways difficult to fathom. He is playful and spontaneous. As a breaker of boundaries he tends to deflate those who are pompous, egoistic, controlling, dominating, and inflated.

Unlike the war-loving Greek figure Ares, he doesn't usually destroy the people he vanquishes. He merely brings them to ground, where they can continue to evolve with restored humility. In this manner he serves as an individuating force that assists the psyche in moving out of stuck places—whether inflated, depressed, or fixated. He has things to teach us about the nature of the dream, certain aspects of men's work, and the individuation process in general. In many ways he appears to be an archetype of the unconscious self.

In order to understand what this figure may represent in the male psyche, it's useful to examine his mythological roles.

According to the anthropologist Paul Radin, the Trickster "dupes others and is always duped himself. . . . He acts from impulses over which he has no control. . . . He knows neither good nor evil yet is responsible for both. He possesses no values . . . yet through all his actions values come into being." Basically, the Trickster possesses no well-defined or fixed form.

Radin further speculates that the myths concerning the Trickster address "man's struggle with himself and with a world into which he had been thrust without his volition and consent. The reaction of the audience, in aboriginal societies, both to him and his exploits, is one of laughter tempered by awe."

Joseph Campbell tells us, "The mythological Trickster is immediately recognizable in whatever cultural costume he assumes; voracious, phallic, stupid and yet sly, what he signifies is the spirit of disorder, the enemy of boundaries." To Carl Jung he is "god, man, and animal at once. He is both subhuman and superhuman, a bestial and divine being whose chief and most charming characteristic is his unconsciousness."

In his book on Omaha Indian Trickster tales, Roger Welsch notes that

> he is simultaneously the creator and the destroyer, savior and corruptor. In one episode he saves a tribe from the ravages of some terrible, evil, supernatural force and then he goes through an equally strenuous exercise of his powers to seduce the chief's virgin daughter. . . . The clever trickster sometimes fails despite his wile and the stupid trickster sometimes succeeds despite his slow-wittedness. . . . Sometimes there are no answers; there is no logic. . . . He is an accurate reflection of the perversity, ambiguity, and contradictions of life, needing no further explanation or analysis.

Robert Pelton, who has done extensive work on this figure in African mythology, observes that the Trickster

> opposes the gods and mocks the shamans. In seeking this mastery of the world and the creation of a secular sacredness, the trickster often fails. In his follies he becomes a joke, yet in laughing at him men are set free, for they are laughing at themselves . . . . Loutish, lustful, puffed up with boasts and lies, ravenous for foolery and food, yet managing always to draw order from ordure . . . seemingly trivial and altogether lawless, he arouses affection and even esteem wherever his stories are told.

As we started talking about the Trickster figure more regularly in the new knights, we began to realize that he had much to teach us about living paradoxically. We were learning that many of our problems had no clear solutions, but rather that we could embrace contradictory notions without having to move them toward resolution. We could be both tough and tender, respectful and irreverent, receptive and assertive, serious and silly, lustful and reserved, engaged and detached. In his book *Crazy Wisdom,* Wes Niker says, "Conventional wisdom is the habitual, the unexamined life, absorbed into the culture and the fashion of the time." Crazy wisdom, however, "is the challenge to all that; it dismantles assumptions accepted as truth, unmasking ourselves and our societies." This crazy wisdom way is exactly the path of discovery we felt we must walk upon our quest for authentic masculinity in an unauthentic culture.

Many contemporary Jungians, following Jung himself, regard the Trickster as an immature force in the psyche that represents a more primitive, less mature aspect of masculinity. This European, urban perspective is quite contrary to the view of authentic masculinity. In a manner aligned with the African and Native American perspective on the Trickster, we knights began to see his capacity for "two-wayness" and paradoxicality as a highly desirable state of mind to cultivate.

Thinking paradoxically allows us to embrace contrary notions concerning our authentic character as men. The heroic mind is always attempting to reconcile opposites into clear, rational patterns. Life, however, like the Trickster himself, is full of contradictions and surprises. The less we attempt to conquer and control it heroically, and instead strive to live with it as it is, the more pleasure, delight, and energy for transformation we seem to have. Instead of trying to reconcile the many contradictory aspects of our masculinity into polarities like maturity/immaturity, masculine/feminine, spiritual/mundane, we are seeking a more integrated and authentic self-concept, which the Trickster seems to embody in his many different manifestations.

One of the fears of a knight without armor is that he will become, like the feminized man, defenseless. This is why many heroes choose lifestyles that lead to immobilizing heart attacks or substance addictions rather than risk taking off their armor and living with more sensitivity to the needs of their bodies. On a national level this is expressed by choosing war over a style of diplomacy that can openly admit our failings. Rather than being solely an undesirable image of deviousness, the Trickster presents a nonheroic, unarmored model of masculinity that can be quick, decisive, and a potent transformer of the world, without getting caught or slaughtered by the spears and arrows of its armored hordes.

PLAYFUL COYOTE AND OTHER SLY ROGUES

Myths and stories concerning the adventures of Coyote, and other *tricky* animals, permeate Native American cultures and many others. Among the Blackfoot he is the respected Old Man, who, according to George Grinnell, is "a combination of strength, weakness, wisdom, folly, childishness, and malice." Old Man Coyote, like Prairie Wolf, is a god of hunters. In some myths Wolf is a creator god, and Coyote is either his assistant or his nemesis. There are many creation myths involving Coyote. Feces often serve as the medium with which he creates.

Mercurius is the alchemical name for the trickster Hermes, who is the Greek predecessor of the Roman god Mercury. Jung notes that he also is

> found in dung heaps . . . a god of thieves and cheats . . . and revelations. He is *prima materia* . . . He represents the self . . . the individuation process . . . and the collective unconscious. He stands in a compensatory relation to Christ.

In our men's group, those aspects of life that we feel shitty about often serve as our *prima materia,* the primary material for the focus for our work together. It's those tricky psychological or emotional forces that feel out of control and contrary to social norms that often motivate us to seek help or attempt to change our lives. In India there is a common saying: "out of the dung and muck grows the beautiful lotus." By embracing the darker, dirtier parts of ourselves, we may stimulate or fertilize the growth of our beauty.

The Trickster also alerts us to shit in others. He's not naive. He represents that part of the psyche that can easily discern truth from falsehood. It's hard to trick a trickster. He's savvy and alert. He may let people think they're fooling him, but then—whoops!—they're caught in their own trap. He thus protects our less discriminating inner child.

In Jung's analysis of the fairy tale "The Spirit in the Bottle" he likens the "spellbound spirit," Mercurius, to a pagan god who is

> forced under the influence of Christianity to descend into the dark underworld and be morally disqualified. . . . He becomes the daemon of mysteries . . . forest and storm, he bestows wealth by changing base metal into gold; and like the devil, he also gets tricked. . . . His gifts are not ephemeral like the "cheated devil" who is tricked out of a soul. He is only tricked into his own better nature.

In this old story, a boy frees Mercury, thereby gaining wealth and the power of healing. (The caduceus, Mercury's staff with two entwined snakes, is still the symbol of Western medicine today.) In our men's work we may discover gifts through a similar process of freeing repressed forces in our psyche. This is not without risk. It often requires a willingness to move beyond our cultural values and limited ideals to apprehend and commune with images of the psyche in their uncivilized authenticity.

In the Pacific Northwest the Trickster is known as Raven. He's impudent and greedy, as well as a world transformer and creator of the world. He accidentally created light while playing as an infant. Many other Trickster figures have Prometheus-like myths, as light or fire stealers. For the Eskimos the Trickster is Crow. In other tribes he is Buzzard.

Jung notes that the buzzard or vulture is a bird of Hermes. Hermes, as a figure who can move between the upper and lower worlds, brings the dream images that connect our unconscious experience to consciousness. In our men's work we elicit his aid in our search for understanding through dreams and the images of mythology.

Kokopeli is another Native American trickster. He's a wandering, dancing, Pan-like flute player who plants trees wherever he goes, from South America to the great Northwest. He rarely misses an opportunity to seduce a local maiden along the way.

The Trickster appears in cultures all over the world. In Africa, Ashanti is the name of the spider trickster of the Ananse. African Bushmen have Kaggen, a praying mantis who is a creator and trickster. Legba represents wild sexuality and is a master of the spoken word. Eshu likes to stir things up and disturb the social norms.

Islam's stories of the irascible Nasrudin are not unlike many tales concerning rascal Zen monks, who violate all the rules of their orders and confound students with koans (paradoxical stories) designed to exhaust their rational minds. Thus they evoke a transrational state of perception called enlightenment. Zen enlightenment has many similarities to the paradoxical mind welcomed through work of authentic masculinity.

The Trickster is also embodied in the Scandinavian Loki, Shakespeare's Puck, and the European Jester throughout Western history and fable. And he is represented by the alchemical Fool and the Magician, still seen on tarot cards today.

As the knights continued reading different Trickster stories we were somewhat overwhelmed by how vast and pervasive this archetypal figure has been throughout the world. We felt there was something essentially masculine about him that we have lost touch with in our modern culture. We found ourselves enjoying his stories, as well as the laughter, and the zaniness they brought into our discussion groups.

THE TRICKSTER AS OUTLAW, PEACEMAKER, AND JESTER

For many weeks I pondered Jim's question: where does joking fit into our recovery work? In the West, laughter in public has been socially acceptable only within the last hundred years. Many medieval and Victorian physicians cautioned against the coarseness of laughter. It was contrary to Christian philosophical notions of silence, gravity, and sobriety. The Pilgrim settlers in America looked upon laughter with disdain. It was seen as lacking in decorum, primitive, and uncontrollable. This is our national heritage.

Psychology groups are often very serious and deliberate. Likewise, some of the spiritual gatherings I've attended have been more tedious than a leaky-tire exhibition. We have all been wounded and therefore, at times, may tend to be overly cautious in our dealings with one another. Yet there is a clear difference between being sensitive to the needs of others and complacently tolerating their habitual stuck places. The figure of the Trickster reminds us that there is an important place in our men's work for humor, paradox, irony, and tricks.

We need not become so bound by fears and conventions that we don't dare on occasion to step off the edge. In the fashion of the Fool we may discover psychic dimensions that lie beyond the rational and logical. This is one form taken by the spiritual aspect of radical masculinity. Sometimes we goad, tease, and jive one another with parody, satire, and black humor. There's a special kind of male humor that is dark, gross, even surrealistic. This is one way men deal with the grief and pain of life. Tears are one way to grieve. We also heal the shame of our worst failures with laughter.

Our digs at each other test limits, assess our character, and shake us out of depression, ego inflation, and other stuck places. Joking, however, can easily become a defense against intimacy. So we need to stay sensitive to others. In our group we're as quick to offer tenderness, compassion, or silence as humor, jesting, or a challenge to "get off the melodrama and on with the life, mate." This is how our group experience differs from our typical experience as men, where we encounter only the jest and rarely receive loving sincerity and support.

Tricksters defeat the ego in the service of the self. They can't be controlled or domesticated. Our masculine style of humor, as we've seen, is unsettling to some women. The Trickster often seems more welcome when men meet alone. In mixed-gender groups we may become reluctant to evoke him. "Ugh, you guys are gross!" is a comment more than one of us has heard. But our men's lodge is one place where we can encounter and commune with the outlawed and profaned images of the male psyche with no shame or blame.

Often it is the outsider, the radical, the jester, or the outlaw who gives us the impetus and courage to laugh at ourselves. He challenges our conventions and rigid ideas about life. He is unafraid to make fun of the conventional because he is not dependent upon the dominant culture for his sense of definition and belonging. He belongs to life itself, from which he can't be exiled, shunned, or excommunicated.

Hermes, for example, is a god of outlaws. He's also one of the few gods who can go anywhere, with access to all realms. American culture is replete with images of the outlaw who is both feared for his unpredictability and idealized for his freedom. Movies like *The Sting, Butch Cassidy and the Sundance Kid, The Outlaw Josey Wales,* and the more recent *Family Business* often endear us to the outlaw. Many of the most popular musicians of the past few decades—Bob Dylan, the Beatles, the Rolling Stones, Willie Nelson, and M.C. Hammer—have built their popularity on artistic expressions that embrace outlaw themes.

Creativity is often a product of an outlawlike consciousness. For successful artists it's often experienced as outside normal constraints—intuitive and nonlinear. Trickster energy is outlaw: it's not contained or constrained by conventionality. Yet it operates from a code of deeper law—like the fabled honor among thieves. It honors the spirit of life. It passionately challenges confining, rigid social conventions that bind and diminish life. It serves the development of authentic masculinity through expanding the possible boundaries of our lives.

Rabbit man, the Algonquian trickster, is found in petroglyphs in Ontario. He's known as Nanabozhom, the Great Hare. The Creeks of Alabama and Georgia had Rabbit and Tar-Baby. These stories mingled with African trickster tales and evolved into modern rabbit tales, from *Watership Down* to stories about Brer Rabbit (who started the new knights thinking about the Trickster in the first place). Quickness, good hearing, and a good nose are among his attributes. These, too, are qualities the authentic male seeks to cultivate: a quickness of mind, an astute nose for following the trail of psyche, and a long ear to discern the whispered story of the soul.

In some stories, the trickster is Turtle. In Aesop's fable, Turtle tricks the trickster, Hare, by simply keeping to his natural element of perseverance. Steadfastness, the capacity to withdraw, and self-sufficiency are also important masculine qualities of the Trickster.

In one story, when caught for some misdeed, Turtle arranges to get punished by being banished into a body of water—his natural element. Brer Rabbit also gets his captors to punish him by throwing him into the brier patch—his home. The Trickster often gets others to think they control him when he is actually getting them to do as he wishes. In an aikido-like manner, he steps aside when trouble comes to crush him. He lives to play another day. This represents a different sort of life philosophy than that of a hero. The hero uses his will to get what he wants through force, domination, and control. If that doesn't work he frequently destroys that which opposes him—a poor game at best. The feminized, soft man tries to meet every situation with sincerity. He often gets smashed or ripped off as a consequence.

In our culture today the images of Coyote, Raven, and Hare have all found their way into American cartoons. There's Wile E. Coyote and the Road Runner, Heckle and Jeckle, the Magpie Brothers, and the greatest modern trickster figure of them all, Bugs Bunny. The Trickster is one of the most pervasive archetypes from ancient times and is also one of the most misunderstood and repressed figures in modern culture.

Tricksters induce laughter. Thus they are peacemakers. They end war, or prevent it, by changing the direction of anger's flow. They break up its heavy concentration. In Japan, for example, there are several tales about Impetuous Male, who was always mischievously disrupting the imperial, war-making plans of the solar goddess Amaterasu, his sister. The Trickster may diffuse overheated, polarized arguments in the men's lodge when they occur. Through humor we return our confrontations in the group to balance. We get extricated from the traps of our personal melodramas.

One night Jack was having a protracted, heated debate with Brad about the ultimate virtues of capitalism. We were all bored, but no one protested until Jim finally cowered under the table in mock fear and submission, crying to Jack, "Yes, Boss, please don't whip us. We all get back to work right now."

It cracked us up, including Jack. Jim got us off abstract politics and back to our personal issues about money and power, which had started the talk in the first place. He did it without attacking, controlling, or insulting Jack or Brad. He was just so absurd that it changed the whole atmosphere in the room. They could have told him to bug off, but it was immediately clear to them they had lost the here and now of our work together. It brought them back to the present and to the group.

Satire is an important, traditional aspect of masculine humor in many cultures. The Tibetan folk character Uncle Tompa has a whole cycle of tales about him with a central theme of phallic humor. He often satirized imperial persons and scandalized the lives of austere monks and nuns. A colleague of mine, Lobsang Sherpa, is a Tibetan monk. He tells me that in Tibet, once every thirteen years a monastery performs several plays that ridicule the entire government and spiritual hierarchy. They address themes of corruption and ineptitude without fear of retaliation for their acts.

This ritualized form of irreverence often contains a lot of ribald humor and satirization of public figures. It helps ensure that the leadership doesn't get too deeply entrenched in the seriousness of its positions. We could use that sort of ritual healing in our culture as well. In the West, the revelries of carnival reverse the hierarchical order, as does April Fool's Day. Friars Club roasts of public figures attempt this type of work in a good-natured way. The Trickster is thus a force that can deflate pomposity if it arises in our work as men. He is a force that is sorely needed on our national political scene. The jester should be a mandatory part of every president's cabinet: the Secretary of Humor.

In our new knights we frequently take our work and our recovery much too seriously. This is also true for some leaders of men's gatherings. So the knights periodically stage our own carnivals, times of buffoonery and play. We paint our faces, swap jokes, trade lyrical and florid insults, and conduct tall-tale competitions. One night we wound up in a pond and covered each other with mud, and we now occasionally evoke the spirit of the mud men. It kind of puts things back in perspective when someone starts to get too sanctimonious. We might threaten to carry him back to the pond or simply challenge him to tell us a new joke on the spot. And it has to be a good one, too, something that will make us smile.

Although there's not enough room in this book for abridgments of the thousands of trickster tales, the references at the end of the book will lead the reader to many excellent texts. Sometimes we read these and other stories at our group meetings. They often provide an interesting and playful foundation to stimulate and give form to our discussions.

The pervasive belief in many diverse cultures is that sacred myths must always be told correctly, and only to the initiated, at proper times. Most trickster stories, however, can be told in various contexts—at mixed-gender gatherings or those of the initiated and uninitiated together. They can be elaborated upon and changed by different tellers at different times. Similarly, like the knights, men don't really need initiation into male mysteries by a council of experts, elders, or other illuminati to help them engage in reclaiming the masculine soul. The Trickster is a promethean force that can take our men's work out of the realm of the special few, the workshop elite. Ideally, men's soul work is nonprofessional and community based—common and available to all.

Altogether, the work of rediscovering masculine depth and healing the masculine soul is a tricky business. For the most part we are all still stumbling around in the dark. We grope around the boundaries of the soul, like the blind men describing an elephant, and report to one another what we feel is there. Sometimes we find a jewel. Sometimes we stub our toes. Often we have more a felt sense of what we are doing, rather than a concrete, rational knowing.

The Trickster reminds us that on the quest for masculine soul, there is much we do not know or understand, that everything is subject to entropy and change. Humor, paradox, spontaniety, foolishness, and human sexuality are all powerful forces of transformation and healing. There is always an imp in the shadows who, once released, is quick to restore balances. He can take us beyond known boundaries of the conscious mind and egoic will, into the boundless wilderness of the soul.

THE NATURE GOD OF SHAMELESS MASCULINE SENSUALITY

Pan is a wild, unfettered god of nature who was popular prior to the advent of Christian culture in ancient Greece. Also known as Faunus/Satyr/Silvanus and Ephialtes, he was one of the latest gods introduced to the Greek pantheon. He has the lower body of a goat and the upper body of a human, except for the small horns and pointed ears on his head. He has a sly but handsome face. He may be the son of Hermes. Yet his parentage is also ascribed to many other fathers. His maternal lineage is equally obscure.

There are only a few myths surrounding Pan. In one story, Pan's mother was so horrified by his goat body that she abandoned him and ran away. Hermes recovered the infant and introduced him to the Olympians, who were fond of him. Hermes is a shepherd of the soul, and Pan is also depicted as a shepherd. He dances in the fields, cavorting with the nymphs and playing his pipes, like the Native American Kokopeli. He represents the most recent, final diminutive echo of the ancient cult of the wild bull.

There are brief references to a warrior aspect of Pan. He overcame enemies—the Titans and others—with a shout. He would infect them with panic. Similarly, fierce Scottish warriors went into battle playing pipes designed to strike terror into the hearts of their enemies.

Pan is uncivilized and part animal. Like the Green Man of Celtic and other ancient European lore who is part plant, Pan was a god of the forest. His temples—unlike the elaborate structures built to honor the more prominent Olympians—were simple rock grottoes and caves. He is known for his connection with fear and the panic associated with flight and nightmare. But the aspect for which he ultimately was most rejected was his fundamental embodiment of Phallos.

In the second century A.D. Plutarch declared, "The great god Pan is dead." This announcement heralded the final demise of old pagan earth religions in the Western culture. They already had been repressed for centuries. Early Christianity was in the service of a growing urban consciousness. It solidified the Platonic ideals of culture and state, separated from the untamed and unpredictable passions of nature and the body. This dancing, goat-bodied, musical god with his earthy sensuality and playfulness was relegated to the underworld. He was redepicted as the embodiment of evil. To this day the Christian devil resembles ancient images of Pan in great detail. And he is still known as Mephistopheles, whose name the comparative mythologist Wilhelm Roscher etymologically connects with Pan.

The urban culture's fear of the wild man and his untamed sensuality caused the repression and defilement of the Earth Father images. Pan and other earth gods became a threat to the hierarchical control of the church-based state. The result was that men increasingly felt they must conform to a narrow ideal of manhood approved by the dominant religion. This new ideal of the rational, urban male precipitated the loss of soul in Western males. In Greek, Pan's name means "he who feeds." Men who are no longer connected with some aspect of Pan in their own psyches may feel hungry for something they sense is missing from their modern lives.

Saint Paul's early influence on Christianity further repressed men's traditional earthy sensuality, distorting it into a satanic image. Eventually, European pagans were denounced, harassed, tortured, and even murdered by the thousands. In many other cultures, however, horns and Pan-like symbolism were used in religious images as *positive,* life-affirming icons. Native Americans, for example, frequently wore headdresses with horns, which were considered to be symbols of earth wisdom and the evocative power of animals like the wild bison. These people also were condemned as heathens by the so-called more civilized Europeans.

Many of the neolithic and Bronze Age Earth Father cults mentioned earlier had a horned god as their primary deity. Even Moses descending from the mountain with the commandments is depicted in some iconography with horns symbolizing his wisdom. But in most cases these representations of man's animal, earthy, embodied, or sexual nature were repressed and vilified by the solar, monotheistic patriarchy, along with images of women's sexuality.

Old Pan was demeaned, repressed, and depicted as the embodiment of evil. The characterization of evil as a masculine entity, a god to be feared, avoided, and denied, has shadowed male psychology ever since. Pan is a natural man and yet he is also part animal, an unnatural monster. This is consistent with the experience of many of us in the group.

The new knights have come to experience ourselves as relatively socialized, normal men in the world. We also, however, struggle with passions, compulsions, and fantasies that at times have made us feel monstrous, guilty, and ashamed. As Bob Dylan once sang, "If my thought dreams could be seen they'd probably put my head in a guillotine." One of the ways we have been healing our shame is by discussing our forbidden and socially unacceptable fantasies with one another. Interestingly enough, we all have them. That realization alone has been helpful to us.

The word *panic* has Pan at its root. But heroic men frequently see the expression of fear or panic as unmanly. In the horror movies it's usually a woman who sees the monster in the dark. The man says, "Heh-heh, don't you worry, little lady, it's only the wind," or some such thing. This always happens just before the monster actually sneaks up and splatters him. Men often tend to meet fears heroically by overpowering them, pushing through them, or numbing them out. In mythology Pan was said to be the force of nature that caused animals to stampede in time of danger. The fear he generates is a call to action and a basic inbred, biological survival mechanism.

Inattention to the complex delicacy of nature has resulted in an ecological nightmare. Yet heroic leaders consistently try to overlook tremendous damage. "Don't panic, everything is fine—no problem," they say. They justify the rape of nature in the name of heroic progress, conquest, greed, and short-sighted economic exploitation while turning deaf ears to the fears of informed and alert citizens. The fact is, panic may be an appropriate response in some cases. One cannot be attuned to nature in this day and age without feeling at least some panic about what is happening to it: the growing ozone hole and warming of the atmosphere, the poisoning of the air and water, the rapidly decreasing forests and advancing deserts, and the extinction of species worldwide.

This same dynamic may be true of our relationship to the inner ecology of mind. Many of us feel we have been emotionally raped, poisoned, and deadened by our culture. In this manner, the soul in the world—the Anima Mundi—may reflect the condition of the individual souls of men and women and vice versa.

Some of the pain or violation we feel within us is an echo of the distress we have created in the environment.

"Fear, like love, can be a call into consciousness," says James Hillman, who also informs us that Pan is the creator of the nightmare. Pan turns our attention toward the unconscious. It is often the experience of nightmares that brings a man to the psychologist's consulting room. Pan, as a shepherd, watches over the flock and causes flight of the herd when danger approaches. He alerts us, through the nightmare, to the danger of ignoring the soul. He gets our attention. Fear and anxiety are not just bad feelings to get rid of; they are calls to action—whether in our environment or the inner wilderness of psyche. We defeat nature if we regard this call as merely metaphorical or a personal neurosis that needs to be fixed or tranquilized.

This is one of the reasons the new knights abstain from drugs and alcohol. In addition to keeping us in touch with the feelings of our bodies and our positive emotions, sobriety also keeps us in touch with our fear. When we don't numb ourselves to our fears, we have to act in response to them. We have to attend to whatever is generating those fears rather than ignore it. Denial becomes much harder when you're sober.

Pan is also depicted in myth as a rapist. Hillman believes this represents the "compulsive necessity within and behind all generation" and the "divine penetration and fecundation of the resistant world of matter." When Pan is repressed, like any archetypal force denied or ignored, he possesses.

What can we learn from Pan, as a god of compulsive sexuality, to understand that aspect of masculinity that is unsocialized and out of control? The reed-blown music of Pan is a call to nature, a call to return to our senses, our spontaneity. The anxiety that modern man experiences outside the urban container is also the quickening excitement of our wild, unfettered nativeness. One question Brad has been asking in our group discussions is "What does it mean to be alive, free, wild, impassioned, and empowered without becoming sexually coercive, dominating, or brutal?"

To demean Pan as merely a rapist is the same literalistic thinking that led millions of men over the millennia to fear and distrust women as seductive Eves or witches. If men are ever to prevent rape in our culture we must talk about, reimagine, and come to understand this force of wild, physical, phallic sexuality within us. Shame and repression are not satisfactory strategies.

Forcible rape is primarily a pathological act of rage,

stemming from fear and hatred. It should never be condoned by men. Rape actually has little to do with sexuality or authentic masculinity. Yet fear of deep, wild, masculine sexuality has caused many feminized men to adopt a passive and restrained attitude toward their phallic power, which does not leave them feeling truly alive. However, Phallos has an upright integrity and impeccability that is life-supporting, energetic, and evolutionary. In and of itself, it is not violent. Even so, many men carry deep, even incapacitating shame around the phallic aspect of manhood. One way this is expressed is through the high incidence of male sexual dysfunction in our culture.

Pan is also the god of masturbation. He represents sexuality that is done not for procreation or to please another, but simply for one's own pleasure. Masturbation harms no one; it's merely asocial. The women's movement has done a great deal to educate women in this area. Yet it still remains an arena of shame and complexity for men. Pan sexuality, unlike Eros sexuality, is more connected with life force than romantic love. Eros is a god of love who's more involved in relationships.

Men find that relatedness, as defined by women, doesn't always fulfill their sexual life. If you look at male sexuality straight on, there is an aspect of it, often expressed in the masturbatory fantasy, that is not oriented toward pleasing others. Women have a similar feminine archetype in their consciousness, but that is not our tale to tell.

There are many shadow forces we are afraid to face: rape, masturbation, panic, fear, instinct, intimacy, war, nature's wildness, life's unpredictability, and the horror of ecological destruction. We fear our spontaneity, uncontainment, wild abandonment. We fear being alone outside the walls of normal society. These fears and more lie within the archetypal constellation of Pan. As we look in this direction, back to the earth, for insights into these issues, healing may emerge.

THE SIXTH TASK OF MEN: TO APPLY THE MYTHS OF MASCULINE SOUL TO OUR DAILY LIVES

"Well," said Rodger, "as I look back over these images I feel most drawn to the luminous, changing moon gods. I like the idea of masculinity expressing changing moods. I used to feel embarrassed about my need to withdraw from time to time. My wife can say it's her hormones when she needs a little time off, but I'm just *moody*. Next time I feel like holing up for a few days alone with my books, I'm gonna tell her that I'm just going off to commune with the Moon Father, but that I'll be back."

"I'm going to carve a statue of Pan to remind me that it's natural to get horny," said Jim. "He makes me feel like masculine desire has a truly sacred quality, that it's nothing to be ashamed of. I like the idea of worshiping a god that loves dancing, nature, music, and sex. That's my kind of guy."

"I'm drawn to the images of the Earth Father," said Ben. "I like that Chinese Pan-Ku, who has children crawling all over him. My son, Eric, loves to crawl on me and ride on my back and be swung through the air. His laughter is like music. Our romps are high points in my day. As I think about it, being an Earth Father isn't just about being more wild, erotic, and free. It's also about being present, being home more, making time for Eric, working in the garden, not being off in the faraway sky of workaholism."

"Yeah, I'm feeling that way, too," said Brad. "Dumuzi seems to embody my ideal of a man who is wild and free yet still present in his home and with his family. I no longer see these ideals as mutually exclusive. I also love the way his sexuality was appreciated as part of his spirituality by the goddess. That's the kind of attitude I'd like to have in my next relationship with a woman."

"It's the sly, funny trickster gods who seem to call to me these days," says Jack. "Getting out of my business hasn't been as easy as I thought. I'm having to learn to get real slippery. I can't just walk in without getting clobbered with a million questions and also discovering a bunch of details that need attention. Now when they turn around, I'm gone—surprise! Nothing's going to fall apart; it's just not going to run quite as efficiently as when I was looking after every detail."

"I relate to the moist, deep, juicy sea god and the wild dancing Shiva," said Carl. "I've been so straight and contained most of my life, I want to loosen up and *feel* more, not be so predictable. Letting my anger about the environment come to the surface, in the last year, has moved me to change my life around. I feel that one of the deep feelings Poseidon contains is holy rage. When I was trying to be a nice guy all the time, I just stayed stuck in my old job and fretted a lot. Now I'm doing what I want to do and enjoying it more. First it took letting that big wave of feeling rise up from the deep."

"Hermes is the figure I'm working with now," I said. "Like

African Elleggua, he's the master of words. When I get stuck in my writing I imagine and welcome Hermes. He's one of the few gods who can move into the underworld, dance on the surface, fly up to the heavens, and return. So Hermes keeps my writing moving. I ask for help in staying connected to all realms so that I can range deep and high but also keep reconnecting to the surface of our daily lives."

The gods and images that our new knights recovered and identified with in the last two chapters are but a few templates for masculine psychology. Each man is a myth in his own right. Attention to our own experience of archetypal energies may aid us in recovering our souls. Authentic masculinity encourages the practice of psyche-centered dreamwork, ritual, and myth making. Polytheistic spirituality, paradoxical thinking, and communion with archetypes are also a few means for reclaiming the masculine soul.

In the next section we'll explore myths that touch us in our daily lives as sons, lovers, husbands, workers, visionaries, and elders. We'll try to understand ways in which we're related to images that are different from the ones we've grown up with. We'll also try to develop new understandings of our changing roles as men in a changing world.

> *Learning something about how ancient myths and images connect to our modern lives was the sixth task we attempted. We then concluded this period of research and focus on other cultures and old myths. We wanted to spend more time looking at our own lives and culture with some of the new perspectives we had gained. Trying to understand how we first came to feel that we had been initiated into manhood, in our own time, was the seventh task we faced.*

PART III

Revisioning Masculinity: Men's New Roles in a Changing World

CHAPTER 7

The Nurtured Son and the Initiated Young Man

Build me a son O Lord who will be strong enough to know when he is weak and brave enough to face himself when he is afraid . . . whose wishes will not take the place of deeds.
    Douglas MacArthur

One of the things Brad's son, Jamie, wanted for his seventeenth birthday was to attend a session of our men's group. We had discussed the possibility of working with younger men in the community for some time, and this seemed like a good place to start.

Brad and Jamie used the opportunity to talk in the group about one of their conflicts. Brad was upset about Jamie's decision to go to an expensive art school in the city. He thought his son should do something more practical, like go to a less expensive junior college, in which case he could live at home and study art while working toward a conventional degree. Jamie was completely uninterested in any sort of academic study. He was certain that he wanted to be an artist. He was honored that his portfolio had been accepted by a prestigious school, and he wanted to leave home and "go for it."

After some discussion, we took sides and role-played their positions while father and son watched. It was an opportunity for them both to get some insight and support from other men. Through our play and discussions, Jamie began to understand his father's point of view more deeply. Brad had been the single parent of his two sons since his wife had left seven years ago. Suddenly, the maternal grandparents were willing to foot the bill for this elite school. It was difficult for Brad to condone this support for something he viewed as a privileged lifestyle. On his salary, he couldn't afford to send Jamie to a fancy school. For years he had struggled with providing the very basics of food, clothing, and shelter without a penny from the mother's family. Now, all of a sudden, they were dream makers. He felt usurped.

Meanwhile, Brad realized he was carrying some lingering resentment toward his ex-wife and her family, then taking it out on Jamie. With choked emotion he reaffirmed his love for his son and told him that he wanted to support him in following his dreams. He also acknowledged, with difficulty, that he would miss his son living at home, which had been part of his resistance to Jamie's plan.

Jamie expressed his appreciation for everything his father had done, realizing that he had taken a lot for granted. He always had seen his father as some sort of an "iron man" and was surprised to encounter his undisguised pain. He assured Brad that nothing could ever replace his affection for him and that he still wanted to come home during weekends and holidays. However, he was "stoked" to have this opportunity. And his attitude was, "What the hell? Grandma's going to pay." It didn't matter to him where the money came from, just that it came.

At the end of the meeting, Jamie understood why his father had been "so uptight" about the whole thing. They gave each other a big hug and left the group at peace with each other. Jamie said he wanted to come back at some time in the future. Later, he told his father it was the first time in his life that he had felt accepted and respected by other men. We had shown genuine interest in his plight and taken the time to address his concerns.

For Brad, including the knights as uncles in his family system took off some of the pressure to be everything for Jamie. We could offer a new perspective on issues around which they had been stuck. Although we didn't engage in any sort of formal rites of passage that night, Brad related to us that Jamie seemed to regard this simple experience as some sort of initiation into manhood. We had included him in our secret adult male society.

We had originally limited our group to men over forty, and still felt it was a good idea to keep it that way. But a number of younger men in the recovery community had expressed interest in the group. So in the months that followed Jamie's visit, we helped organize groups for younger men. Several of the new knights served as mentors for these groups until they got going. Then we withdrew, remaining available for consultation if needed. This continues to be one of several outreach services in which the knights are still engaged.

We were beginning to reach beyond our self-centered concerns about our personal recovery. We were discovering ways in which we could be of service to other men. We started to talk more about the young men in our community and became more curious about initiation in general. And we began thinking about our own roles as fathers and as sons. We asked ourselves, "What do fathers actually *do* for a child, an adolescent, a young adult?"

OUR FATHERS, OUR CHILDREN, OUR SELVES

This turned out to be a difficult question. Most of the new knights' fathers had been pretty distant. Jack's was an executive with a power company. He traveled a lot and was frequently gone for weeks at a time. Brad's dad had worked in construction eight to ten hours a day, six days a week. At home he had been too tired to spend much time with the kids. He was killed by a fall on the job while Brad was still a teenager.

Ben's father, an award-winning scientist, was totally devoted to his work. He was rarely visible at home except at mealtimes, after which he would disappear into his study, where he was not to be disturbed. Jim's father was often drunk and withdrawn. At other times he was abusive.

Rodger had had a good relationship with his father, who took an active interest in his children's lives. But he died when Rodger was only nine. Carl's father, a roofer, also died when Carl was a boy, from a lung disease incurred from years of inhaling toxins on the job.

My father was a professional handicapper for the horseracing industry. Since my parents were divorced when I was three, I was either in his custody, in my mother's, in foster care, or in various state facilities. Altogether I spent only a few years with my father, for a few short months at a time. Many people thought his lifestyle was inappropriate for a young boy. But the summers I spent hanging out with him at the racetracks stand out as some of the highlights of my childhood. He occupied a rich, exciting, and engaging world of gangsters, gamblers, con artists, jazz musicians, and exotic women. They were some of the most interesting people I'd ever met. I loved being by his side and taking it all in.

One night Jack asked us to recall what portion of the home our fathers occupied. Most of us reported that in addition to their being absent most of the time, there was little in the home that marked their presence. A cursory inspection of most homes will not show much evidence of the father. The man may have a favorite chair or couch, a drawer in the bathroom for his toilet kit, or an office in a nook somewhere. Men may work alone in the garage, in their studies, and in their offices. But most household space is usually filled with the wife's heirlooms, belongings and furnishings, which she selected for the entire family.

All the knights grew up with father hunger. Just as we receive milk from our mother's body, there is some sort of invisible milk of the father that emanates from his being. We all felt something ineffable when we were physically near our fathers, and we missed it when they were gone. It didn't matter so much what we actually *did* with our time together. The milk of our fathers seemed to flow into and nourish us merely by their nearness.

ZEUS: THE UNINITIATED SKY FATHER

One of the earliest father gods in ancient Greece was Kronos, who had the habit of swallowing his children. His wife, Rhea, was upset about this. She conspired to keep her last son, Zeus, from this fate by feeding Kronos a stone dressed like the child. Later, Kronos was forced to regurgitate all the children and was overthrown by Zeus.

This myth has been interpreted by numerous writers as an example of the horrible nature of patriarchal fathers: they swallow up their children's autonomy, and have to be overthrown by a son who is under his mother's control. However, there is another perspective on this story.

Swallowing is *not* the same as devouring. In this story there was no digestion but rather a gestation, a sort of male pregnancy and rebirth for the children. Zeus was denied this experience by his mother and was improperly fathered as a result. Zeus's two brothers, however, Hades and Poseidon, went through this process. We've already talked about Poseidon and the wild depth of feeling he represents. His other brother, Hades, became another nonheroic, soulful god, a god of the underworld. Something happened to Zeus's elder brothers through being held within their father's body: they became potent gods of depth.

Zeus, however, who conspired with his mother to overthrow the father, missed this nurturing developmental period in the masculine field of the father. He became one of the primary sky-father images—the patriarchal tyrant who is disconnected from the earth. Zeus's relationships with women were also full of conflict. The overmothered, underfathered Zeus became the image of an uninitiated man who seizes power through force, domination, and control—a patriarchal male.

THE GROUNDED FATHER

In the new knights we have fourteen children among us. In various ways we're attempting to be different sorts of parents than our fathers. Yet we face the same obstacles that they encountered: divorce, custody disputes, economic hardships, lack of community, and the powerful demands of the workplace, which often take us outside the home.

But those of us with children are committed to being active, engaged parents. We're also healing our own childhood wounds by ensuring that our children don't grow up with the same loss we felt. Unlike our fathers, however, we now have a community of men that supports this ideal and acknowledges it as a masculine activity in every way.

Parenting was something for which our fathers rarely got any acknowledgment or support. In the new knights, however, we support one another to become the best possible parents we can be. We share advice and information about parenting with one another. Previously we received most of our information about being a parent from the women in our lives. They were the experts. Unlike the meeting we had with Brad and Jamie, our masculine conversation in the past was mostly restricted to topics of sports, work, politics, and technology.

Psychological theory concerning child-rearing historically has been dominated by the primacy of the mother. Only about 5 percent of all studies done on parent-infant relationships include the role of the father. In addition to exiling and ignoring the father and perpetuating his absence, this thinking has done a great disservice to the mother as well. It identifies her as the primary cause of the child's psychological problems later in life. In actuality the father, absent or not, is *always* an issue.

In the last few decades some theorists have proposed that there really is no such thing as an infant alone, but rather a dyad—a child/mother relationship. Today we can go a step further and say there is no such thing as a dyad; there is always a triad—a child/mother/father relationship. Even if the father was an anonymous sperm donor, he is a significant influence on the mother and often a troubling question for the child as well. A mother will often resent an absent or unknown father. She may lose her capacity to hold the child in a safe, stable, and nurturing environment if she is not also held by the influence of a loving, engaged father/husband—or worse, is disrupted by an invasive, erratic, disturbed one.

A mother who's not supported by a loving and present mate

may begin to resent her infant. If she lacks serenity and the capacity to hold her own pain or loneliness, she may either invade the infant with excessive needs for contact or neglect it. The infant can become traumatized by this. He can be smothered and overwhelmed by her attention or feel frustrated by her neglect. As a result he can develop an attachment to an inner state of minimal excitation or deadness, which the onslaughts of the outer world, perceived as disturbing or hostile, cannot penetrate. This is one of the ways many psychologists believe that narcissism is induced—a self-involvement that excludes intimate relationship with the world.

Most of us in the new knights felt that our mothers were overly involved in our upbringing in a well-meaning attempt to compensate for our fathers' absence. When we take a hard look at ourselves we realize that, like many men these days, we, too, have been narcissistic in our lives. We had been so preoccupied with careers, needs for validation, self-gratification, and other self-interests that we often excluded intimacy with other people and responsibility to the world around us. We perceive this self-involvement as one of the major factors that led us to substance abuse: it supported our need to feel special and separate, insulated from the world around us.

The psychologist Hans Kohut observes that "it is not so much what the parents do that will influence the character of the child's self, but what they are. . . . Some parents are not adequately sensitive to the needs of the child but will instead respond to the needs of their own insecurely established self." He feels that when a child's world lacks secure parents, "it is a dangerous world." So if we experienced intimacy with our mothers as unbearably dangerous, we may drink, drug, fuck, and work ourselves numb so that we can't be touched by intimacy in our adult life.

The narcissism-inducing mother is unsupported by a present, involved, and concerned father. She's in danger of becoming overwhelmed by the child's demands. On some level the child realizes he's troubling her. He begins to pick up the mother's pain. He may become overwhelmed with guilt and conflict, then become the caretaker of the mother. He becomes the codependent son, metaphorically her lover, and ultimately her unintentional victim. If he cannot separate from her, he may never experience his sense of autonomy from women as a mature, adult male. If, as Robert Bly tells the tale in *Iron John,* a boy cannot seize the key hidden under the mother's pillow and free the wild, earthy male in the cage, he will remain domesticated, controlled in his mother's house. Self-involvement, or narcissism, is a radical attempt to both avoid going through the necessary pain of this separation and remain submerged in the good diffused feeling of the mother within.

Those of us who grew up with our mothers as the most involved parent noticed that we were quickly turned into mother's little helpers. This was especially true of those men whose fathers were completely absent due to divorce or death. We often had to fill the shoes of the absent father, being mother's little man—someone she could lean on, confide in, even flirt with in some cases.

The movie *Look Who's Talking* is about an infant boy who's trying to get a man he likes to become his father and mate with his single mother, Kirstie Alley. John Travolta, who plays the man, says, "Being a good father is keeping the mother happy so she doesn't drive the kids crazy." Not a bad way of putting it, in our opinion. By being present, caring, and involved fathers, we can bring an essential balance to the growing child and enhance the mother's ability to nurture as well.

Men don't seem to nurture in exactly the same manner as women, but that doesn't mean that what we offer is any less significant. It's separate, different, and equally important. At times Rodger carries his little boy tucked under his arm like a sack of potatoes. The boy seems to delight in this, yet it's very different from the more intimate way his mother holds him. On the other hand, Jack remembers that when his second child was crying, he was more able to soothe him than the mother, who was going through an anxious and exhausted postpartum period.

Men are just as able to cuddle, care for, and comfort children as women, but we're also more likely to engage our children physically with the outer world. We toss them in the air, rough-and-tumble with them on the floor, and introduce them to tools, musical instruments, computers, and sports. We teach them how to defend themselves from violence. We get the family outings on the road, set up the tents, and teach them wildcraft—fire and shelter building, how to hunt and fish.

We serve as examples for our sons about how to become men. This is something no mother, however well intentioned, can do alone. We also keep mom from smothering our sons with good intentions. Through loving interactions with their mothers, which openly display respect, fun, and sensuality, we model relations that will guide them in their own adult relationships. Boys who grow up without a healthy, grounded father or other adult male who is present and involved in their lives often have a very distorted notion of what it is to be a man or how to relate to women.

But it isn't only our sons whom we initiate into the outer world; we do this for our daughters as well. When I drive to the dump on back-country roads, I let my eleven-year-old daughter sit close at my side and take the wheel of the truck while I control the pedals. I just slowly putt along and also keep my hands ready in case she should oversteer. This slightly horrifies her mother, Liz, but thoroughly delights Noelani. It has built her confidence in her ability to engage with the world at large. Noelani also has begun to build things out of scrap wood and now takes pride in being able to use my glue gun, hammer, and power drill.

In this way we provide our daughters an opportunity to have a positive relationship with a man. I believe that most of the anti-male invective today comes from women who have had a negative relationship with their fathers. A girl's positive relationship with a present and involved father builds the foundation for balanced relations with the men in her adult life.

In our lives we knights felt that the absence of our fathers was a real factor that led to our substance abuse. We often drank in an attempt to cover up the low self-esteem we felt as men who were unsure about our adult male roles, or about how, actually, we had become men. Becoming men did not seem like something that came naturally to us. Girls, for instance, start menstruation and then automatically become young women. We could not recall hearing girls be told to *be* a woman or act like a woman. We have many memories, however, of admonitions to be a man. Becoming a man felt more like something we had to earn, or in many cases, keep rewinning after we had earned it.

TO BECOME A MAN

"When did you first feel that you had become a man?" asked Rodger one night.

"At sixteen, when I got a summer job working with my old man in construction," Brad replied. "It was about a year before he got killed. One hot Friday, after the first week of work, he tossed me a cold beer. I sat up on the ridge beam we hoisted that day, drinking with a couple of other guys and gazing out at the view across the canyon. I can still remember the smell of sweat mixed with the sage and tarweed on the breeze. . . . Yeah, that was it for me."

Ben said, "I sort of felt that way the day of my bar mitzvah, at thirteen, reading from the Torah in front of all my friends and relatives. But the next day I was just a little kid again. What a comedown. They said I was a man at the ceremony, but nothing had really changed. My mother still ran the home, set my bedtime and all the other rules. It wasn't till I left home for college at nineteen and got accepted by a fraternity that I *really* felt like a man."

"For me it was the first time I had sex," said Jack.

Carl agreed. "Yeah, that was it for me, too. Amanda Sue, whew! First we got drunk, of course. Sixteen and I thought I knew everything about life and being a man."

I talked about how during one of my stays in my mother's home, I fought off my stepfather's frequent assaults on me. I'd been toughened up by life in the Youth Authority and was no longer afraid to confront the violence of other men, regardless of their size. "He left me alone after that," I said. "Now he was afraid of me, a fourteen-year-old. For the first time in my life I no longer felt defenseless."

"I don't think I felt like a man until after I graduated from dental school and opened my practice at twenty-seven," said Rodger. "I remember wishing that my father could have been there to see my office that first day. I was so proud."

"For me it was the day my father gave me a set of chisels of my own," said Jim. "He was a real SOB. Often he ignored me, and several times he beat me. But those tools made me feel that I had the ability to shape my own life. Just like you did for Jamie last month, Brad, my old man honored me for my artistic ability. That meant a lot then and still does now."

Work, independence, combat, sex, alcohol, and our fathers' approval had been significant markers of our transitions from boys to men. Only Brad, who was acknowledged by other men in his father's workplace, felt that his transition had been noted by the men in his community. Ben's initiation was hollow, and our others, while representing triumphs of some sort, were never marked by the other men around us. Not a single one of us felt that our manhood had come from our mothers. They nurtured, comforted, educated, and sang to us; they nursed us when we were sick, taught us manners, and protected us from various things, including the abuses of our fathers. But they couldn't teach us how to become men.

For the most part we had initiated ourselves as men. But without that acknowledgment from other men, something was missing. We began to provide that missing connection by talking about these transitional experiences in the group. We acknowledged the wounds we had endured, the failures that taught us the measure of our limitations. We also shared the triumphs we had achieved and the sense of possibility they created within us. We affirmed one another for transitions we had made in our lives that had previously gone unheralded, experienced alone in a silent world. So the new knights became a further initiation into manhood. Our work in the group had a solidifying effect. We refathered each other through our love and acceptance. We felt this even more strongly as we discovered our ability to be of some service and support for younger men struggling around us.

There's a lot of talk about initiation in the men's movement today, but not much information. What we do know is often borrowed from other cultures, which may have little to offer us. Also, many tribal initiations were designed to prepare young men for the hardships of war, something we're not so keen about encouraging today. What does seem clear, however, is that throughout the ages young men have gone through some rites of passage that let them know they're men. These rites also have connected young men to the depth of the masculine soul, the spirit of nature, and the community as a whole—something *none* of us had experienced in our youth.

The only remnants we have of these ancient rites in our modern culture are initiations into the masculine cult of the hero. Football and other competitive sports, fraternity hazing, the military, entering work or corporate life, sexual conquest, gang initiations, and drinking at the bar are events with which many young men measure their worth as men. Little is said by the elder men to the younger ones about soul, nature, tenderness, health, the body, sexuality, desire, dance, poetry, beauty, deep feeling, suffering, weakness, fear, or failure.

The film *Dead Poets Society* poignantly addressed this issue. It tells of an inspired and passionate English teacher, played by Robin Williams, in a private boys' school. He uses poetry and literature to arouse his students' masculine depths and appreciation of the mystery and beauty of life. It's a story that shows one of the many ways in which male initiation is lacking in our culture. Can this be recovered, reclaimed, and remembered in our postmodern society? I believe so.

INITIATION AND THE MASCULINE SOUL

My interest in male initiation began about twenty years ago when I was an undergraduate in psychology. I was working my way through school as a counselor for a residential treatment center for disturbed and delinquent adolescent boys. I wound up in charge of the emancipation program, which focused on helping older wards make the transition from institutional life to living on their own in the community.

I was not unfamiliar with some of the problems that faced these boys. I had been a ward of the state of California for many years off and on. I learned the codes for male conduct on the streets of Los Angeles and in the institutions of the juvenile justice system: be cool; never show fear, weakness, or pain; never back down from a fight; don't be a squealer; get your piece of the action any way you can.

Like me, most if not all of these boys had absent fathers for a significant portion of their lives. Many were institutionalized to such a degree that they seemed incapable of independent thought and action. They frequently tended to act out primitive impulses with little or no control. My assignment was to prevent them from actualizing their prognosis, which called for them to become chronic inmates of the adult correctional system.

There was a constant attempt on the part of the staff to socialize these wild boys according to the mores of white middle-class society. But wild animals, who behave according to an integrated code of conduct for their species, often develop neurotic and destructive behavior when confined. The same is true for the modern urban male. At some point it occurred to me that what they needed was connection with some deeper sense of honor, in a context that accepted their wildness as something of potential value rather than merely a social threat.

I began to wonder just how many of my wards' difficulties stemmed exclusively from individual psychological problems. To what degree, I wondered, were their problems aggravated and perpetuated by a highly structured, controlling environment peopled by well-meaning social workers, probation officers, teachers, school counselors, parents, therapists, police, and judges—all of whom scrutinized and controlled their every move?

This is the old nurture versus nature quandary. I decided to take them out of the institution and into the wilderness for a while. There they could experience who they were independent of their immediate cultural context—a home for dysfunctional boys. This would also temporarily remove them from their ever-present social identity as outcasts and throwaways.

The program was funded under the guise of teaching boys independent living skills, which in fact it did. Although this is now a regular component of many rehabilitation programs, it was fairly controversial at the time. We wrangled for parental and jurisdictional permissions, funding, and insurance. Finally, we went out to the wilderness. Over the next few years, I went on to lead many of these trips for various institutions.

The first thing we would do after arriving at the trailhead was to dig a hole in the ground to bury our collective past and our personal histories, including our names. We would agree to stay together for the next eight to fourteen days, depending on the trip, and to attempt to work together as a group or tribe. Everyone agreed to finish the trip, and no one was allowed to get hurt. The understanding was that there was no such thing as accidents. My naive ideal was to have no other rules. I wanted to deal with whatever came up as it emerged, in an egalitarian fashion.

Later I realized that adult male authority always has its essential value and can't be simply discarded. I made other conditions: no indiscriminate damage to the wilderness or its inhabitants, including the members or the counselor, could be permitted.

Thus agreed, we hiked into the wilderness. Many of these young men had never cooked a meal for themselves, built a fire, or slept outdoors. Urban bravado quickly faded with the arrival of a bear at the edge of camp in the middle of the night. An unexpected thundershower would demand quick shelter building and mutual cooperation.

Stealing no longer became a targetless event, because the boy who had no food for supper would be exhausted the next day on the trail, holding everyone back. Or a boy missing his knife would not be as helpful building shelter or fire, making more work for others. There were good, worthy, and exciting places to get to—high mountain lakes where the fishing was good, where there was still snow on the ridges to make Kool-Aid slushes with. We went cross-country, off the trails, and learned to navigate with a topographic map and sighting compass. The boys took turns leading, and sometimes we got lost. Eventually, though, we always found our way again. Great triumph.

New names came up along the way. I was hiking razor-backed granite ridges in the moonlight with Whistler, Lame

Dog, Gort, Cisco, Redwood, Daniel (formerly Timmy), and Bigfoot. I became Spoon-shaper, Dakota, Hawk, and Abalone (which the boys pronounced Ah Baloney).

As we sat around the fire, it seemed that this was what we had always done. After a while the bitching and whining seemed to pass away. Stories developed, tales of the strange old tribes we had come from before we stumbled into this valley of the lost warriors. In the mornings dreams began to be shared. The unconscious psyche found a context where it felt safe enough to reveal itself. Often we would have common elements in our dreams. Dreams rarely had been shared at the home, even in the frequent "group therapy" sessions, such as they were, with their cynical joking and resistance.

As the days passed, we got stronger. Our tender feet hurt less and we survived. No one got hurt and we had fun. We were moved by the beauty, engaged with the wilderness, interested in learning and observing. Something touched our souls. Some boys became friends for the first time, and in the night, at the edge of camp, there were often one-to-one talks with me. We touched deeper truths, revelations, and intimacies than had been experienced at the home.

There was no one to blame for failures. No cops. No probation officer. No stupid teacher. If your sleeping bag got wet, it was your fault. If your macaroni burned it was because you didn't watch the fire. If we ate fresh trout, sautéed in oil, wild herbs, and garlic, it was because we caught it. Dinner wasn't just what the house counselor had picked up on sale at the Safeway. No dessert? Maybe we shouldn't have eaten all the candy bars the first day out.

We built sweat lodges, got hot, and jumped in the rivers. We tracked animals for the fun of it, made up songs, plays, and stories, and performed other rites. But mostly these initiations did not have much to do with rituals or ceremonies one can read about in various ethnographies. They were more about staying loose while growing strong and walking in the footsteps of the ancestors—something that just doesn't happen in the city. They were about feeling our relationship to something ancient in nature that resonated in the deep emotional body of a boy. This is something that no amount of counseling, reparenting, transactional analysis, or behavior modification is going to accomplish. For millions of years our young men went hunting with their fathers and uncles. Something in our bones remembers that. We still have a deep and abiding hunger for it.

It was always hard coming back. True, there were the joys of missed TV and a hot shower. But for months later I would often hear, "When are we going back?" Although a sense of tribal membership often waned, it remained to some degree. Some kept their new names. Poems were written by those who had never written poems. In the weeks following one trip, a huge garden was planted in the backyard of one house. "We can grow our *own* food, man."

One of these boys, now a grown man, works at the local hardware store. Another, a night dispatcher for AAA, recognized my voice on the phone ten years later and kept me entertained with jokes and reminiscences until the tow truck arrived to pull my car out of the ditch in the middle of a stormy night.

Not all of them made it. Some went back to locked institutions. Many I never heard about again. But every one of those boys learned that he could feed and house himself, find his way when lost, and carry on his own back everything in the world he needed to survive for a whole week.

Each young man learned the value of cooperation and mutual support. Each learned that he could rewrite his personal history, at least for a time. He learned that he could belong to a group whose members depended upon each other for survival. He learned that his toughness, fortitude, creativity, stamina, and sense of adventure had value. Most of all, he learned that he belonged to the world of all the men who had gone before him. He was not merely a waste product from a decayed urban nightmare.

A BOY NEEDS A TRIBE AND ELDER MALES

Some years later I was initiated into the rituals of the Native American church. During the course of those dusk-to-dawn rituals there was usually a tremendous expression of grief, an honoring of the earth, and a mourning for the wounds of the planet. There was an exposure of personal pains from the past and a humble account of indiscretions and transgressions toward others. Sincere prayers for self-forgiveness as well as expressions of compassion for the struggles of others were offered.

The *road chiefs* for the ceremonies had the responsibility to ensure that the ritual was conducted in a respectful and proper way. They created a strong container in which the participants would be safely held during the experience. Together, a lodge of people could hold something—a spiritual force and presence—greater than anyone could hold individually.

One night, along with a handful of white men and women, I was sitting with one of the elder chiefs and several other men from his lodge. I was privileged to witness a ceremony during which the chief initiated one of his nephews into the medicine ways and sacred teachings. Toward the end of this night, the road chief passed the eagle feather around the circle to his nephew. The medicine men use these feathers for channeling the spirit energy and directing it for healing. The acquisition and handling of eagle feathers is done according to ancient traditions, and their magical properties are taken quite seriously.

The chief explained that the feather he was passing on to the younger man was a down feather. It was all white and much smaller than the huge quills I had seen the other men use for prayer. He explained that if a young man tries to channel power with a rigid quill it may shatter and cause things to go awry. A young man needed to start working with a downy quill because it was flexible and would bend without breaking if he made mistakes at first. In this simple event was transmitted the entire essence of male initiation.

The role of the adult male initiator is to wound a young man's typical sense of unlimited ability without inducing shame in the process. The young man was acknowledged as a member of the adult male clan—capable and worthy of producing magic, yet still protected by the strength and guidance of the elders. In this ritual he's told he will fail repeatedly as he tries to master new powers; that's why he doesn't start out with the big quill he would really like to have. In this manner he is encouraged to enter new experiences without risking shame. He is taught the limits of youthful endeavor and given a vision of his potential in the future. He's both limited and encouraged at the same time.

Rarely in my life have I seen a young male radiating as much wholeness as did this nephew at the end of his initiation. I doubt that any bar mitzvah or first Communion ever came close to communicating the teaching of this simple ceremony. *You belong. You are welcome. You have magic. You don't know how to use it yet. You will learn. There is a place for you by the fire.* Who among us, man and woman alike, has not longed to feel this sense of membership in some form?

I have participated in a number of these ceremonies, both with Native Americans and with white neo-shamanic chiefs. A few of these nontraditional teachers have tremendous gifts and the capacity to perform a good ceremony—to hold a good road. Even so, I have never witnessed one who had the capacity to activate the emotional body of a young man—to wake up a connection with deep feeling—in the same manner as native teachers. This is not because native teachers have some special racial ability; the same power and compassion are present in our community. What has been lacking for us until now, however, is a sense of a *traditional male brotherhood into which young men can be initiated.*

The masculine *field* to support that experience—the underlying mythological ground—has not been lively in the collective consciousness of contemporary Western males. Weekend workshops cannot fill the gap. We need to build real, lasting, ongoing community. Western culture today is tragically impoverished. The mythological ground is barren. What has been lost, however, can be recovered. Our work is to help reverse the soul-crushing trend of modern times, to plow those fields of the masculine soul and rediscover that essential, sacred relatedness we have to other men and all life.

HAMLET: THE UNINITIATED MALE

One of the tenets of archetypal psychology is that through the study of myth one can gain insight into various human psychological complexes. Mythology gives shape to the dimensions of various human tendencies, possibilities, and so-called pathologies. Mythology can lend insight into etiologies (origins and causes) as well. That is one of the reasons we regularly read myths, literature, and poetry in our men's group. This way of seeing through myths and stories is also a way of thinking—one that we're trying to share in this book. This way of thinking has more to offer than any information we could share.

With this in mind, we went to the local junior college with Brad one night to see a performance of *Hamlet,* in which Jamie was playing a supporting role. Briefly, the story of this mythic Prince of Denmark goes as follows:

Hamlet's father is secretly murdered by his uncle Claudius, whom his mother marries a month after the death. Hamlet grieves for his father and wants to leave the court to go away to school. His mother, Gertrude, implores him to stay. Then the ghost of his father appears to inform him that he was murdered by Claudius. Hamlet attempts to avenge the wrong but is ineffectual. Along the way Hamlet spurns the love of a beautiful maiden, Ophelia, who kills herself after Hamlet kills Polonius, her father. Through a variety of misadventures emanating from

Hamlet, just about every other major character in the play, including Hamlet, eventually dies as well.

After the performance we gathered at a coffee shop to discuss our reactions to the play. We agreed that three forms of masculinity were exemplified in this tale: (1) deep, authentic masculinity, expressed by the life and ghost of the old king (it has at its basis a nurturing, generative, ethical power); (2) polarized, heroic, dominating masculinity, expressed by Claudius's murderous deceit (it has no connection with depth; it's merely self-gratifying and egotistical, not life-affirming and fathering); and (3) feminized, uninitiated masculinity (Hamlet is immobilized, ineffectual and, when he does act—deadly).

"Hamlet kills, directly or indirectly, everyone who threatens him," noted Ben as we continued analyzing this tale.

"But a man who's initiated into masculine power can stand up to life without violence," said Carl.

"Yes," Brad agreed. "In most cases, he need only show his sword, not use it."

"That's how I see it," said Rodger. "Violence is usually an expression of weakness, not strength. This is where the feminist perspective on masculinity goes askew. Men are violent, especially in the senseless way Hamlet kills Polonius, out of a sense of powerlessness—not as an expression of life-affirming masculine power."

"Exactly," said Jack. "A good king, secure in the masculine field and in possession of Phallos, doesn't rule through domination and violence. He exerts leadership. He displays a sacred relationship to the forces of nature. He possesses wisdom, insight, and the loyalty of committed allies. Hamlet lacks this type of strength. His feminization keeps him in the posture of an ineffectual son."

"And his mother, Gertrude, wants to keep Hamlet under her control at court," offered Jim. "It's as if she wants to keep him in the role of a son to satisfy her own needs."

"Her marriage certainly prevents his rightful ascension to the throne," Ben agreed. "She may need him to diffuse the dominating masculinity of Claudius. Or she may want him to somehow share her burden or help carry her pain—the repressed guilt she feels about the events surrounding the death of her husband."

"So, in this story," Rodger summarized, "instead of the son succeeding the father, the throne has been seized by the brother. The natural order is upset. There's no mourning for the lost father. The tragedy is hidden or repressed, just like it was with my father. The son, instead of growing in generative power, becomes immobilized, self-absorbed, and unable to steward the life within the kingdom. When I was still in denial about my grief, I used to be consumed with rage. It's no wonder that Hamlet could only bring death."

"It's Hamlet's sacred duty as a son and prince of the realm to find an appropriate means to avenge the wrong and thus protect the kingdom from corruption," observed Ben. "The rules of war state that if you attack a king, you must slay him; otherwise, surely he will slay you. Hamlet, as an uninitiated man, is incapable of being a warrior and slaying Claudius. He is a scholar who's more concerned with words and ideas than committed action."

PROBLEMS WITH THE UNINITIATED MALE

In Hamlet's case, almost everyone around him dies. Robert Johnson believes that "most men are Hamlets today." He observes that Hamlet has "no roots in the instinctive world," and that even though he can touch the divine, "he makes only division and tragedy of it, not paradox and synthesis." The narcissistic male, unable to wield the power of the father, cannot generate and protect life or transform the world, only devalue it. This is often the position of the modern, new male. He's educated, sensitive, and aware of the corruption in the world. Yet he can't establish himself in the world, hold the reins of power, and effect dynamic change.

The ghost of Hamlet's father is fierce. His apparition can "freeze thy young blood." He attempts to rectify the wrongs that have been done, advising his son from a position "more in sorrow than in anger." He reflects the perspective of authentic, deep masculinity. But he cannot initiate his son. He is disembodied, beyond this world, an absent father. Hamlet retreats into immobilization as a defense against the conflicting emotions he feels. The narcissistic man perceives others as disturbing to his innerness, his self-involvement. "To be or not to be" is exactly the question.

The feminist perspective is that Hamlet is dominated by patriarchal, masculine values and unable to respond to feminine, life-affirming influences. However, from the perspective of authentic masculinity, which affirms and protects life through the committed actions of an ethical warrior, just the opposite is true: Hamlet appears to be overly feminized, in the manner of many New Age men who are emerging from a culture in which the influence of an initiating, nurturing elder male is almost completely absent.

Hamlet idealized his father, in whose face "every god did set his seal." Yet Hamlet had not been allowed to grieve for his father, to fall apart, to go under. His mother had married within one month of his death. More than possible incest with her son or complicity in the death of her husband, the real crime of Gertrude was that she requested that Hamlet "cast thy knighted color off [cease grieving] . . . and not seek for thy noble father in the dust."

The expression of deep feeling is often regarded as unmasculine. There's a great deal of resistance in this culture to men acknowledging their pain and grief. Men are often expected to get on with business only a few days after the death of a loved one. We're generally depicted as heroically able to conquer all, like Claudius. Repression and denial of grief, however, merely provoke pathological responses—like the destructive behaviors displayed by Hamlet.

Hamlet was in late adolescence, toward the end of the time during which a young man traditionally receives initiation into the world of men. A young man must be protected and held by the magnetic field of the father or other caring adult males at every stage of his development—from birth and weaning through latency, puberty, and individuation as an adult male. A nurturing father can stand up to and limit both the violent aggression of the young male and the immobilizing attempts of the mother to control it. If he is successful, this violence will become transmuted into assertive and creative potency.

It's this lack of male initiation that may account for some of the life-negating forces in Western culture, which are now no longer merely subduing the earth, but destroying it. Hamlet also destroyed the kingdom that was his inheritance and that it was his sovereign duty to preserve.

Hamlet could not sever his ties with his mother, and thus was unable to seize power through committed action. This is a typical narcissistic predicament. He became enmeshed with numbness and deadness. His actions diminished life. He could not expand life with the phallic generativity of the ancient Earth Father.

The yuppie economy of the eighties in America reflected this problem on a national level. All the emphasis was on consumption and self-indulgence. Production, generation, and long-term planning were neglected, causing ruin on many levels.

There are many myths concerning sons who fail to grow into full maturity. Icarus and Phaëthon were destroyed by failing to follow the instructions of their fathers. Phaëthon almost destroyed the earth and the heavens as well when, against his father's warning, he attempted to command his father's sun chariot and it got away from him. Bellerophon's youthful sense of omnipotence resulted in his ignoble fall to earth from the back of Pegasus. Like Icarus, he flew too high. Orpheus lost his life as well as his love, Eurydice, when he failed to follow the dictum of the old Earth Father, Hades. Narcissus, whose father was absent, falls in love with himself and then concludes that only death will separate him from his wretched passion. This was Hamlet's solution as well.

In the changeless image of a Narcissus peering into a pool is a feminized face unaffected by the influence of adult male maturity. In nature, that which does not grow can only wither and die. In our mythologically barren culture, boys aged fifteen to nineteen now have a higher incidence of suicide than any other group in the country. Among white boys, whose communities are the most spiritually impoverished, the suicide rate is now five times higher than it is for girls.

Early in this century, the Greek scholar Jane Harrison wrote:

> At and through his initiation the boy is brought into close communion with his tribal ancestors: he becomes socialized, part of the body politic. Henceforth he belongs to something bigger, more potent, more lasting, than his own individual existence: he is part of the stream of the totemic life, one with the generations before and yet to come.

In her analysis of ancient Greek rites, she laments, "Young men (Kouroi) we know, but initiated young men (Kouretes) are gone forever."

As we approach the end of this century, perhaps we will reverse this trend and prove her lament no longer true.

THE SEVENTH TASK OF MEN: TO REDISCOVER MALE INITIATION AND HEAL THE WOUNDS BETWEEN FATHERS AND SONS

"Perhaps someday," said Ben, "the men of our community will show up at a boy's house on his thirteenth birthday. They'll take him from his mother, who may be reluctant to release him but also grateful they've finally come. After testing him and showing him his limits they'll give him a sense of his real possibilities, his responsibilities to the earth, his brothers, and the feminine. He'll then have a sense of place and relatedness to all life. When he returns home, he really will be a man. Then, perhaps, powerful women will no longer need to ask, 'Where are all the *real* men?' "

The ancient tales of Narcissus, Phaëthon, Bellerophon, and Icarus, and the play *Hamlet,* also may be interpreted as laments for the knowledge of the authentic, deep masculine, which became lost somewhere along the way for the Western male. What we can rediscover, through explorations of the archetypes within our collective psyche, is the work ahead. However, before we can effectively begin to properly initiate our young men, we must first build a community of adult men whom they can respect and wish to join.

What we've learned from one another about child-rearing and initiation is that there is an enormous value to simply spending time fully engaged with our children. We don't really need a lot of fancy rites and rituals. We do need to pay attention to and honor the lives of our children. Our young men need to know that there are men in the community, other than their fathers, to whom they can relate, from whom they can learn, and by whom they can be accepted and admired. Through creating brotherhood with other men we create community for our sons, and respect and protection for our daughters.

> *Coming to understand some aspects of young male initiation had been the seventh task we faced. Learning how to take the lessons of youth and initiations of adolescence into our adult lives, to love and work in new ways and make our lives vessels through which the archetypes of sacred, deep, authentic masculinity can flow, was the eighth task we faced.*

CHAPTER 8

Love, Work, and Dreams

As you go through life, my friend,
no matter what your goal,
Keep your eye upon the doughnut
and not upon the hole.
>As told to me by my mother in a
>doughnut shop in 1956

In the months following the new knights' meeting with Jamie, we continued to discuss various issues around initiation in our adolescence. We had all been trained to accept a very narrow range of preferred behaviors for men. So we were now trying to understand how these attitudes about love, work, and relationships had developed in the first place. We needed to develop new relationships to many of the basic issues we had faced as young men. We no longer took our prescribed roles for granted and were now attempting to change them in conscious ways.

So we began to discuss our experiences as young adults. What had it been like for each of us to venture out into the larger world, to start working, live away from home, form relationships with women, and develop careers? How did these early experiences shape us? What were our dreams then? To what degree did we realize them? What was sacrificed along the way? How did we deal with failure, disillusionment, and success?

We thought that by sharing the lessons we learned as young men we might understand how to deepen our current experience as mature adults. We were trying to learn from the mistakes and negative conditioning of our pasts (without rejecting the capacity for joy we also had then). Just as we have attempted to reclaim the inner child, there's also the voice of a young man within us. When that voice is ignored, it can be a restless and destructive force driving us back into adolescent behaviors. When that voice is attended to, however, life can be richer and more complete. Our inner young man can lend vitality and enthusiasm to our experience.

One of the primary concerns we had had as young men was relationships with the other sex. This continues to be an area of fascination, frustration, pain, and pleasure for us today. We are trying to improve our relationships with women, to have more balance and harmony while still keeping passion and pleasure alive. We want to avoid losing ourselves and our dreams in pursuit of women and to feel whole and independent of our relationships. Most of the information we started out with about love, sex, and relationships wasn't that great. We understood the mechanics of sex, but not the feelings that accompanied it. We had all taken a long and winding road through the field of romantic pleasures and sorrows. And we still had a lot to learn.

THE FIVE F's AND OTHER SEXUAL INITIATIONS

"How were you first introduced to relationships with women?" Ben asked one night.

"Find 'em, feel 'em, finger 'em, fuck 'em, and forget 'em," replied Jack.

"Yeah, in my part of the country it was the Four *W*s," said Carl. "Whip it in, whip it out, wipe it off, and worry."

"For me," said Jim, "sex and courting were relegated to a game like baseball. First base was a kiss. Second base was feeling her breast. Third base was a finger in her vagina. Fourth base—a home run—was when we finally went *all the way*."

Rodger offered, "Slam, bam. Thank you, ma'am." (At least Rodger was taught to say thank you.)

We went on to list the terms we had heard, as adolescents and young men, to describe the anatomy of women. They were almost exclusively hard, monosyllabic, and degrading. These words were spit out with machine-gun rapidity around the room: tits, jugs, boobs, cans, ass, cunt, clit, twat, slit, slot, slash, crack, snatch, pussy, beaver, poon, bush, booty, box, hole.

Most of us had wanted sex when we were young. And it truly was the most amazing thing when a girl actually would provide it. Yet the way we were conditioned to react when they responded to our incessant advances was to label them: chicks, pieces of ass, meat, whores, sluts, cunts, cheap, or easy lays.

"Yeah, and girls who didn't put out were stuck up, had corncobs up their asses, were prudes, snobs, frigid, ice queens, or dikes," said Carl.

As for our own self-appraisal, we possessed cocks, dicks, boners, schlongs, peters, peckers, pistols, pricks, one-eyed lizards, balls, nuts, and the family jewels.

"However, I do think that *skin flutes* still has a nice ring to it," said Rodger.

Jack recalled that the act of sex was elegantly referred to as fish and finger pie (for digital penetration), banging, humping, pumping, grinding, balling, laying, bopping, fucking, screwing, and chopping meat.

"Masturbation was beating, jacking, jerking, or whacking off, beating your meat, and whipping it," chimed in Ben.

In the vast lexicon of imagery around sex there was a notable dearth of terms denoting love, intimacy, tenderness, and sublime erotic pleasure. Although there are some poetic terms in Elizabethan literature and modern esoteric prose, for the most part all we have today are obscenities and scientific jargon. This phenomenon is peculiar to Western culture. Many other cultures possess a vast lexicon of erotic words exemplifying a different attitude toward sexuality.

Although they may have an equal litany of obscenities in the East, penises are also sacred lingams, jade stalks, jeweled spears, peaks or stems, joy sticks, and steaming stalks. Vaginas are yonis, palaces, pleasure or jade gates, golden gullies, little streams, black pearls, deep chambers, inner doors, sparkling pearls, and centers of the lotus.

Sexual union is referred to as silk woman spinning a cocoon, united fishers, mandarin ducks entwined, flying white tigers, and turning dragons. In India I saw vast temples covered with intricate stone carvings entirely devoted to images of the gods making love with one another. These depictions of sacred sex displayed every possible sexual act as an expression of the beautiful, holy nature of life itself.

We, however, were introduced to sex as a mechanistic conquest of women. A rite of passage to prove our manhood. A means to relieve complex frustrations and hormonal tensions. A way to become validated.

It's not surprising, in light of our conditioning, that some of us arrived as adults feeling frustrated, confined, and confused in relationships with women. We were taught to believe that their sexuality was somehow more valuable or desirable than our own. We had to compete to win their attention and affection. In reaction to this idealization, feelings of resentment, objectification, and contempt grew in the shadows of our minds. These feelings were expressed by that hard language we used. Perhaps degrading the feminine image made us feel more equal.

WOMEN GRACEFULLY DROP THEIR HANDKERCHIEFS AS MEN STUMBLE TRYING TO PICK THEM UP

Somewhere along the way we learned that because the girl was basically doing *it* for us, we should pay for it in some way. It was not merely sex for which we felt this obligation. It included compensation for her time, attention, beauty, affection, even her love. We often paid through various sorts of heroic services.

Brad recalled his experience of dating Wanda in his early twenties: "We were at a party. I initiated the first eye contact. Then I walked all the way across the room. I felt very self-conscious in front of a lot of people watching my move. She was chatting with a girlfriend. I introduced myself to them. Then I asked her to dance while her girlfriend sort of smirked at me. Afterward I kept the conversation going. If I didn't keep talking, there'd be an embarrassed silence. So I asked her questions. Then she'd answer. I told her amusing little stories about different people at the party. She'd laugh. I kept trying to think of things to say, but she never initiated conversation from her side.

"I finally asked her if she'd like to get together sometime, and I asked for her number," Brad continued. "She said okay. I called her up several days later but she was busy. I called again the next week. Same reply. I didn't want to rush her, but I didn't want her to just slip away, either. So I was trying to sort out the best approach. I thought about it every day. I couldn't tell if she was interested in me or not. If she was, why didn't she say, 'I'm busy now, but I'm free next week'? If she wasn't, why did she give me her number in the first place? Anyway, a record by the Who had been playing when we first met and she had said something about really digging them. So finally, after letting another week pass, I called again. I casually said I had a couple of tickets to see them in concert and asked if she would like to go. She said, 'Sure.'"

"Well, of course, I didn't have the tickets yet. So I paid a scalper over a week's wages for two good seats. I borrowed a friend's Chevy, because mine was this real funky VW, and I didn't want her to know I was so broke. I picked her up, paid for dinner before the concert, the tip, parking for the restaurant and concert, everything. She wanted a concert guide—okay, another five bucks. But the concert was fantastic. We both really enjoyed it.

"Afterward we had dessert and coffee. I paid. I drove her home, and walked her to the door. All the while I was trying to figure out if I should try to kiss her or not. Would she think I was an insensitive jerk or, worse, some inept clod if I didn't come on just right? Would she think I was a wimp if I didn't try? Earlier I had to decide if it was okay to hold her hand during the concert. 'Will she just pull it away?' I worried. She didn't. But it made me crazy trying to figure out the right moment. I experienced her as just concentrating on looking good and having a good time that night." As Brad continued telling his tale, many of us were nodding and making affirming comments in recognition of our own similar experiences.

"*All* the pressure of initiating conversation, planning the evening, executing the plan, paying for it, and even initiating intimacy fell in my court," he said. "I finally got up the nerve to kiss her as we stood at the front door. She let me kiss her for a long moment, then looked at her watch and suddenly said, 'Hey, I gotta go. I've got an early class tomorrow.' She cheerfully called out good night, slipped behind the door, and shut it. She didn't tell me she'd had a great night or say thanks or ask me to call again. But she'd let me kiss her. I was in love. I was also, as a result, two weeks short on my rent.

"We continued to date. Eventually we became lovers. This lasted about six months, till she went away to a four-year college. But it was always the same story. I paid for everything and I arranged everything and initiated every encounter. It was as if she was doing me a great favor by simply granting me her company. And I believed it. I gave up most of my friends and spent my spare time doing things for her, like fixing her car even though mine needed more attention than hers. I got an extra part-time job to be able to afford her. Even with that, I was a thousand dollars in debt by the time she left. I felt that unless I could always show her a good time on the town, she'd dump me.

"Recently, at a party, an attractive woman gave me her business card and said to call her sometime. Wow! That was the first time in my life a woman *blatantly* took the first step."

Rodger recalled similar experiences in the courting of his first wife. He put out all the initiative. She merely chose to respond or not. "I had to charge after her on my white horse for a long time," he said. "It was as if she had everything that was valuable and I was lucky just to have the opportunity to enjoy her beauty. After a few years of dating, we decided to get married. However, this dynamic never really changed throughout our marriage.

"She would remind me of the economic success several of her

former boyfriends had. Hell, the whole reason I suffered through dental school in the first place was because I thought I had to make a lot of money to be really loved and appreciated by her. It was also something that I knew would really please my mother. I certainly never decided to be a dentist because it was the deepest longing in my heart. I'm glad I did it, however. It's a great career. But as a young man I wanted to be a poet and sail the South Seas. And that voice hasn't ever died."

Rodger continued, "When I said I thought the kids were old enough for her to get a job, the shit hit the fan. I had just started my practice and was still paying off huge debts from school. The strain of the whole thing was driving me to drink and cocaine. She was still totally stuck in the princess role I had supported during our courting and early marriage. But I didn't want to be a white knight anymore. I wanted an equal partner and a mate.

"We had other problems," he continued. "But money was the main issue that drove us apart. She thought that it was enough for her to just be sexy for me on occasion and to be a good mother. She thought nothing else was really required of her. Unfortunately, I'd believed the same thing for too many years. I'd picked up the handkerchief too many times. It was too late for both of us to change. When we finally broke up, I felt like a total failure. I thought that if only I'd been more successful, I wouldn't have lost her."

MEN WHO GIVE TOO MUCH: THE MALE SIDE OF CODEPENDENCE

One night Ben brought in a clipping from the newspaper. It was about a survey that showed that the majority of women thought men were shiftless, lazy no-goodniks who never did their fair share of housework.

Carl said, "Yeah, my wife's been reading this book about the second shift for working women. Now all of a sudden she's taking me to task about the amount of housework I do. But I've always had a second shift. I'm the one who changes the oil, cuts the firewood, splits it, and stacks it, cuts the lawn, prunes the trees, and repairs everything that breaks—from a doorknob to a flat tire. Last weekend I put up a new aerial and almost broke my neck in the process. While I was up there, I cleaned the gutters and the chimney to boot.

"Isn't all that stuff housework?" Carl continued. "It sure isn't my hobby. It's true I don't shop, clean, cook, and take care of our daughter as much as Stacy. But I do all those things to some degree. And I hired a housecleaner to give her some slack. However, she doesn't do any of the repairs or maintenance to the home, our equipment, or our cars. I handle all the banking and bills. And she only works part-time, while I usually work overtime. So I sat down and counted up the hours with her.

"She had to admit that, all told, it's more than even," Carl continued. "But I resented even doing it. It made me realize how much the things I do have always been taken for granted by women. That's the issue for me. I don't mind doing these things for my family. I just resent it when it's not acknowledged. I realized that I've always done these sorts of tasks for the women in my life. My experiences as a young man conditioned me to believe that it was also my god-given role to solve *all* their problems."

We had heard a lot about women's codependency. But like many men's issues, popular writers and the media have failed to address the male side of this dynamic. For us codependency started out with our training to be mother's little helpers. This continued with the kinds of dating and relationship experiences we had. We began to realize that we've often been more concerned about women's unhappiness in any given situation than about attending to our own. We were often more aware of their needs than our own.

The literature on women's codependence has focused on *women who love too much,* women who invest their emotional power in a relationship to such a degree that they lose the ability to nurture themselves. Most of us, however, had become accustomed to habitually being *men who give too much*. We often betrayed our own feelings, hopes, and desires because we thought we could not be loved just for who we are—only for what we do. We measured our worth by our capacity to caretake a woman.

Unless a man is in contact with his own essence—his masculine soul—life is incomplete. He becomes like a vampire, sucking energy out of women because he does not have the ability to nourish himself from his inexhaustible depths. Many of us have been conditioned to believe that only a woman can supply that missing essence, that she is the repository of all good feeling, beauty, and mystery in life. In the media sexy women are used to sell everything from cars to power tools. The ads promise that if we buy the product, we'll suddenly reclaim something essential that has been missing from our lives. As young men who had not been properly initiated into the nurturing field of the masculine soul, we were always in pursuit of a woman who could make us feel complete.

To the degree that we lack a solid connection to a depth of soul within, we seek it outside. We feel incomplete without a woman. When we believe we cannot be loved for who we are, we try to be her hero. We try to solve all her problems. We feel responsible for her pain. We want to rescue her. Our total involvement with her excludes others. We invest all our energy in this one relationship. We jealously guard that relationship because we believe it provides us with an essentially limited supply of validation, love, and pleasure. This is the male side of the so-called Cinderella complex—the waiting-to-be-rescued fantasy from which many conscious women have been attempting to extricate themselves. It is also the root of sex and love addiction.

The frantic sex craving that many men feel grows out of a hunger for intimacy that we often translate into sex. If we grow up believing that a woman validates our worth, sex takes on an unrealistic value—far beyond its intrinsic pleasure. We get addicted when we feel that it's only when a woman is sharing her body with us that we're really acknowledged as being valuable or lovable. Intimacy, however, enhances life; it doesn't validate it.

For several years the knights have been continuously affirming our worth as men to one another. That alone reduces our dependency on women. Our perspective is that relationships complement, enhance, and enrich our lives. But they do not *make* us whole. Wholeness is something that emerges through contact with our own essential nature. It's this wholeness we're encouraging one another to claim. Now sex and intimacy with women are increasingly expressions of giving and receiving love, rather than gaining some sort of seal of approval. This changing perspective is giving us greater freedom in the choices we make around relationships.

For example, one night Brad discussed some conflicts he was feeling in a new relationship. He really liked Gloria but was afraid to get really involved with her. He said, "Hey, her house is falling apart, her car needs work, and she's only working part-time. I can just see it. If I move in with her, the next thing you know I'll be spending all my time repairing her decks, cutting firewood, and rebuilding the engine on her car. She'll provide sex, dinner, and company. That's what all my relationships were like when I was a younger man. Now I'd rather have my charms perceived as having equal value. Let her fix her own stuff. I want to be with a mature, capable, independent woman who wants me because sharing life with someone makes it richer, not because I can rescue her from her distress. I'm too busy rescuing my own soul now."

"Right on!" several of the knights cried in chorus.

When we were younger we thought we could get nurtured only by a woman. Now we're developing the capability to nurture ourselves and one another. We want relationships based upon mutual respect and shared self-sufficiency. It's not enough for a woman to focus on her beauty. We want mutual support, teamwork, and partnership. We want to be in relationships with women capable of generating their own wealth and taking care of their own things. We want to strengthen one another's wholeness and health. We also want to maintain our separate interests and friends instead of putting all our time and attention into one woman.

Of course, not all women are passive or insensitive to the performance pressures with which men must contend. In recent years there's been an increase in women's willingness to initiate sex or intimacy and take equal responsibility in relationships. Even so, most of us feel we've lost something of great value in our relationships with women—a sense of equal worth. We've also often lost our capacity for intimacy, spontaneity, and joy along the way. It's hard to be very happy or relaxed when you feel responsible for *everything*.

Our conditioning told us that every aspect of a woman's happiness is dependent upon our ability to perform well. This is why we often get so devastated when a woman cries. That means we've failed to make her happy, and thus we've failed as men. This belief that we're loved only for our capacity to perform heroically extends beyond dating, courting, and providing for a family. It enters the bedroom as well, where performance anxiety can lead to a whole complex of sexual neuroses.

THE WAY IT WAS

Too often in our early sex lives we were under extreme anxiety about the place and setting in which we had sex.

"My first time was in the back of a car," said Jack.

"I was at home, where my parents could suddenly return at any moment," recalled Rodger.

"For me it was at the beach, under the lifeguard station, one summer night," said Jim. "I constantly worried that someone would come by."

As we discussed our early sexual encounters, we felt we'd all been conditioned to get it over with quickly. We had the responsibility for finding the place and initiating every step. We were always in forward motion, always figuring out the next move. Girls were conditioned to be passive and also not to give up too easily even though they often wanted to as much as we did. We often felt we had to keep the pace of the sexual encounter moving.

"Yes," said Carl. "I remember saying things like, 'It's okay. We don't have to do it. We can just lie here together in our underwear.' But of course that was only another manipulation. It was like we played a game that we weren't actually doing it until we were. Then you didn't want to even stop and take a breath because it had taken so much planning and manipulation to get together and you just wanted to keep it all moving. Then it was suddenly over. It was often kind of a letdown after all that work."

"When I was with my first lover," Ben recalled, "I suffered a lot from premature ejaculation. I started to feel sort of worthless because I couldn't provide her with an orgasm. I still feel embarrassed about this tonight, like it somehow reflects on my manliness. I've never really talked about this before with anyone."

We commiserated with him and assured him that most of us had had similar experiences.

"But women can't be premature," Jim interrupted. "The experience of pleasure is always appropriate for her whenever it comes. All the pressure's on the man."

"Even so," Jack replied, "it's also important to be able to prolong sex. Both partners can enjoy it more."

"But lasting long and worrying about our performance aren't very compatible with receiving much pleasure from sex," observed Carl. "I used to go so far as rubbing desensitizing cream on my cock so I could last longer. I couldn't feel a thing, but I could bang away forever. I thought that was my duty as a man."

"Exactly," Ben continued. "That's what I was starting to get at a minute ago. I used to wear thick condoms to achieve the same result. So recently I've started experimenting with some new approaches to sex."

YOU *CAN* TEACH OLD KNIGHTS NEW TRICKS

Ben began to tell us about his discoveries. "After I broke up with Amanda, I felt like a failure. I couldn't bring her to orgasm even when I performed oral sex, which she enjoyed. Over the course of the relationship she had really made me feel ashamed about how quickly I came. She'd call me Quick Draw McGraw.

"Well, anyway, I met Tracy and we dated for a long time before we made love. I was actually reluctant for the first time in my life. But Tracy was really aggressive sexually. I mean wow, she was really into it. She started to put the moves on me. This was great but, well, you know, I was afraid that I would disappoint her, too, that she wouldn't like me. I didn't want to lose her. I wanted to give her time to get to know me before we had sex.

"Well, eventually," he continued, "she overcame my resistance. But when we were just about to do it, she sensed my anxiety. She stopped everything and held me. She gently asked what was going on. I had never been with a woman who was so tuned in and tender. So I told her. She just laughed gently and leered seductively, saying, 'Oh, that's not a *problem,* that just means you're very sensitive. That's good!" Well, no one had ever said that before. She then went on to teach me about climax hovering.

"She told me to begin making love with her and just before I felt like I was going to come, to stop moving. There's that point of maximum pleasure just before orgasm, you know? That's when we would stop. Just before the point of no return. Then we'd continue to move in intercourse after the impetus toward orgasm subsided. Then I'd start again for a few minutes, then stop. We would just hold each other, talking, kissing, and then start again. Well, we made love for over an hour that way. That was the first time in my life I'd ever lasted more than a few minutes. It totally freed me from performance anxiety."

Ben continued as temperatures kept rising in the room. "In time I found I was able to engage in intercourse for increasingly longer periods of time. Now I don't have the problem at all. Period. First of all, making love this way relieved me of the anxiety of having to *produce* an orgasm for Tracy. There was no product, no goal. So I was a lot more relaxed. Also, sex wasn't over when we reached that highest point of pleasure. We reached it repeatedly. In fact, each time we returned to the level of maximum intensity, our pleasure increased.

"It's as if the boundaries of my container of energy were

stretched. My capacity increased. Instead of blowing all the energy out through a genital orgasm, I began to experience it as enhanced sensuality over my entire body. Also, I'm not so tired afterward. I can make love in the middle of the day without feeling wiped out. I feel energized, healed. Hey, this is great. I'm in love. But why did it take me so many years to learn about this simple thing?"

Many of us were vaguely familiar with this concept as a means for prolonging the pleasure of masturbation. But few of us had had the cooperation of a sensitive partner like Tracy. As young men we never talked about sex with our partners. They seemed to think we already knew all about it somehow. But where were we supposed to have found out? Several of us shared this story with our current partners and began to experiment with this practice. We also continued sharing ideas about how to expand other limited notions we'd developed as young men.

"After the first three years of marriage our love life was going downhill," said Carl. "I began to realize that it's important to set apart a time and place for lovemaking where we won't be interrupted, rushed, or pressured. I'd gotten very busy. We had conflicting schedules and a kid. I planned for business, why not for love? As a younger man my romantic ideal was that sex should *always* be spontaneous. But, like most of our early sexual notions, that just doesn't work. What's often occurred is that the demands of the day left only time just before sleep, when we were both tired.

"So we've started to plan times for intimacy," Carl continued. "Just like other events in our daily lives. Instead of going out all the time we just stay home and take care of each other. We leave our daughter at the sitter's and go back home. We've also begun to exchange massages. They release stress and enhance our sensitivity. This increases our capacity for enjoyment and pleasure. Now we're more relaxed and present on those occasions when we do make love."

Jim likes to play expansive music, have candles and incense burning, and rub scented oils on his partners. He feels that "all these things awaken our senses. Lovemaking is an experience of giving and receiving pleasure. It's enhanced by enlivening *all* our senses, not just the head of our penis."

We used to associate sensuality only with the feminine. As young men out to prove our virility, we thought only women could be sensual. That's part of why we were so obsessive in our pursuit of them. But sensuality is also a fundamental masculine pleasure. We've been sadly undernourished in that department. Rodger recently bought a Japanese silk robe that he now puts on when he's "in the mood for love." His wife, too, enjoys his increasing sensuality. He also now keeps some sweet fruits, ice cream, or other treats in a little refrigerator in the bedroom. We're learning to use our eyes, ears, taste, smell, and touch to return to our senses. So much of what we do during the day is dulling, an assault on our senses. Making love is a time to enjoy, let go, and be renewed and replenished.

The degree to which intimacy can be experienced in a relationship is equal to its strength and health. We can have intimacy without sex or sex without intimacy. When we have sex and intimacy together, it's the most satisfying.

PAN SEXUALITY VERSUS EROS SEXUALITY

Both Pan, the Greek god of sensuality, and Eros, the god of love, make demands upon our lives. When we honor only Pan, our physical sexuality, then Eros suffers. Relationships are shallow and unfulfilling. We move from partner to partner, like Pan chasing nymphs. This is the archetype that seemed to dominate us as younger men.

However, when Eros dominates our adult life, pleasure may suffer. We may feel confined, domesticated, inhibited, or smothered. We need to make a place in our lives for the expression of both of these primal forces—sexual abandon and intimate relationship. We want to hold the playful young man and the mature adult together in our awareness. Then we have hope for a balanced relationship, both erotic and romantic.

In actual practice, many of us find we enjoy alternating between deep, holistic, relaxed Eros sexuality and purely physical, genitally orgasmic, wilder Pan sexuality. The important thing is not to be bound by one mode or the other. We want to have a greater range of feeling, possibility for expression, and fulfillment in life. If we reject either our Pan or our Eros nature we'll always feel incomplete, blocked, and unsatisfied in our relationships.

Making love provides a time to sigh and moan, laugh, growl, cry, or howl if we want to. We need a woman to communicate with us so we're not always trying to guess what she needs and wants. We also need to find safe spaces to discuss the hidden aspects of our sexuality—the dark side, the secrets. We need to consciously work at our communication with the other sex, especially around the taboo, politicized, and pathology-ridden arena of human sexuality. Talking's okay now. It's healing. It's fun. It's sexy. It's masculine. We aren't kids hiding in the garage anymore. We don't have to do it in the dark, literally or psychologically. We can express what we're feeling. Men need to give themselves permission to let go and not be so cool and keep it all together. We do enough of that in the world of daily work.

The experience of being in the new knights has given us a consistent opportunity to explore these issues in an atmosphere of support and understanding. We never had this opportunity as younger men. In those days our communications were largely limited to tales of conquest. Any failure or confusion was degrading to our masculinity. Now we encourage one another to stretch, grow, and experiment in our relationships. However, this isn't the only aspect of life for which we needed to develop a new understanding.

Making money has been another intense focus in our lives. As in the bedroom, goal seeking in the marketplace is fraught with disappointment. It often blinds us to the small, nurturing moments present in our daily lives because we get focused on the big score. As a result we may overlook the enjoyment our family, friends, and simple pleasures can bring.

RIGHT LIVELIHOOD: PRACTICAL AND SACRED DREAMS

"I got a job," Jim announced one night. He looked around as we all sat in shocked silence. Jim was the free one, the one man in the group who had been uncompromising in his sacred dream to be an artist.

"Yeah, I'm tired of living in that little hovel above my studio," he said. "I want a nice house like yours, Ben. I want a decent car, and to be able to travel on a budget of more than five bucks a day. I'm staying alive selling a piece now and then, but I've got to face it: I've been at this over twenty years; it's not going to get any better. Now that I'm sober, I can't keep living in the romantic illusion that poverty is noble or that I'll suddenly be discovered someday. My artwork's good, but it's not all that fashionable. Galleries just aren't that interested even though I've won my share of shows. Anyway, the junior college has hired me to teach art half-time. It's good, steady pay, with good insurance benefits. It's an opportunity to share my talents in new ways. And I can still keep sculpting part-time."

Most of us had taken exactly the opposite track in life. We had sacrificed the sacred dreams of our youth—those often-secret ideals of what we would really like to do with our lives—in order to secure our practical dreams. We rushed into careers or college with one thing on our minds: making a good living. We learned very early that no one was going to take care of us simply because we were cute or had a nice personality. We thought we had to succeed at work if we were going to be loved by a woman or respected by our families.

Now, however, most of the knights were trying to reclaim some of the hopes we had discarded in our youth, the sacred dreams. Our practical dreams involved financial or job security, a family, home, community. But our sacred dream was often irrational, unreasonable, illogical, impractical—even unmasculine.

Jack had abandoned his musical interests early in life to work and support a family. Now he's coming back to music after thirty-five years. He recently bought a beautiful baby grand piano and is getting private lessons twice a week. Carl now works for environmental protection after many barren years as a computer consultant. Rodger always wanted to sail around the world. He's got the skills and can afford a boat now. But he never felt that he could take the time away from his career or family.

"Why am I making all this money anyway?" Rodger asked us one day. "Just to pay bills? What's the point of all these years of work if I don't ever get to go wild and free at least once in my life?" Now, with our encouragement, he's planning to take a whole year off with his family. He's going to farm out the practice to an associate and rent out the house. He won't really lose much financially, and it'll be a great education for the kids.

"I could wait till I'm retired, but will I still be able to do this then?" he asked. "Will my wife still want to go when she's sixty-four? Who knows? What I do know is that we can do it now. I deserve to have this dream. It's been squashed inside me since I was a teenager. This group's reminded me that my life is more than just an exercise in responsibility to my clients and my family."

For me, a sacred dream has been writing. I wanted to be a writer in my youth, but it always seemed too impractical. It had bothered me throughout my life—an unrealized potential, haunting me at times. Now at least I can struggle with it, like many of us dreamers, amid caring for a family, rebuilding a house, teaching, and meeting daily with clients and groups. The knights have supported me in working fewer hours so I could write more. They could see that it fed my soul, and they would reflect that back to me at times when I lost faith.

Often the sacred dream and the practical dream are at odds. The repression of one dream or the other is a frequent cause of depression, alienation, and despair in a man's life. The attempt to satisfy them both can also be a source of tremendous conflict. Often we work at our practical dream in order to make the sacred dream possible—"when I retire." Sadly, we often get lost in the practical dream and wounded along the way, in many cases fatally. On the other hand, some men get completely submerged in the sacred dream and drown. They never pull it together on the material plane of work and relationships. This is the reality Jim was having to face in his forties.

Through the work we do in our group, many of us have gotten in contact with repressed aspects of our lives. We've found the courage and encouragement to transform our lives, by supporting changes in one another that help bring the sacred and the personal dreams together. Sometimes this requires that the family also be prepared to make changes.

Carl's wife had to choose between having a great provider who was unhappy and frustrated, and demanding less so he could perform more meaningful work, have more intimacy with his children, and take the time he needed to develop his soul. Ultimately, her support for this change produced more fulfilling relationships for everyone in the family. But sometmes it can be threatening to spouses, who, even though loving and well intentioned, may have a tendency to opt for the status quo, security, and the known. Rodger's wife had to confront many fears about his desire to sail around the world. However, the prospect of a lifetime without realizing the sacred dream is even more terrifying. This is one of the many reasons why men also need the support, understanding, and vision of other men in their lives on a regular basis. Lest we all forget.

THE ZEN OF WORK

As men, we're taught to be goal directed. Our sense of self-worth is often tied to our perception of how we perform—in the bedroom, on the playing field, on the job, in the boardroom, or in our creative expressions. We learn that it's the product, not the process, that counts—making the touchdown, striking the deal, winning the prize, and being first.

Rodger crewed an ocean-racing sailboat while he was still in school. He told us, "Although I love sailing and enjoyed the camaraderie of being out to sea with other men, I finally quit the team. The thrill of the race and the challenge of honing our abilities as a team were rewarding. But we'd lost the joy of simply being with the wind and waves, watching the changing sky, observing the sea life. We had few moments to be in silent appreciation of the astonishing beauty that surrounded us.

"We often sailed home with blood in the cockpit from skinned hands and knees," he continued. "The triumph of winning was celebrated, or the dejection of losing drowned, at the bar of the yacht club. For me the joy of the chase was never as great as the joy of simply being there. It's that relationship with the poetic beauty and inspiration of the sea I hope to recover through next year's journey. Yet, without that stated goal of competition and a prize to win, most of the crew I raced with would never set foot off land."

Most of the activities men do together or alone are formulated along these lines. The joy of simply being present with our experience of the moment is often lost. That's why our achievements often ring so empty. No one was really there to enjoy them.

We are learning how to transform the necessary work of the practical dream through using day-to-day life to become more conscious and healthy. Brad told us, "As a young man I beat up my body on the job, working long hours, shunning protective gear, thinking safety procedures were for sissies. I thought I was invincible. But I've seen too many guys hurt, even killed, over the years. Now I try to find a position while nailing off a roof that stretches muscles rather than constricting them. I try to find ways to shift patterns of work to different muscle groups throughout the day so I get balanced exercise. I don't work anymore when I'm hurt, sick, or overtired. I remember to look up from time to time, take a moment to tune in to what's around me, try to soak in a little beauty of the day as it unwinds across the sky."

Jack recalled, "When I started out as a young man in business I only thought about one thing—make a buck any way you can. I used people and competed against everyone as I tried to climb on top. I made a lot of money and wound up a pretty lonely guy."

Jack could have gone on to become Mr. Megabucks. However, as we talked about this in the group one day, he told us, "I recently realized that this drive to succeed at any cost was my father's voice, not my own. Just like Rodger, a lot of my career has been about pleasing my parents and providing security for my family. Not about clear choices I made based on my personal dreams. Today, however, I am choosing. And I'm a much happier man devoting my time to doing work that feeds my soul and play that lifts my spirit."

Most men cannot even entertain the fantasy of pursuing their sacred dreams and are locked into the binding necessity of providing the means of daily survival for themselves and their families. Even in this age of so-called equality, men still provide the significant majority of income for the average family. Some studies indicate that as many as 80 percent of male workers in our culture feel that their work is both meaningless and oppressive. Additionally, many men have forgotten how to play in their leisure time, to re-create. Instead we often fill our off-work hours with other survival-related activities or pursuits designed to deaden the pain of work. A dreary numbness permeates the lives of many men.

In the new knights we continually affirm to one another that, according to our new manifesto, our worth as men is not measured by what we produce. It's measured by who we are. Our recovery, our families, our relations to others, our connection to soul, and making space for the sacred dreams are as important as making our way in the marketplace.

The *most* valuable assets for economic success are our serenity of mind and physical well-being. If we abuse ourselves, we're abusing our best tool. As young men we often felt we had to sacrifice our lives for economic success. However, success gained at the expense of our health and mental well-being is the ultimate failure. There's almost always an alternative. We now encourage each other to get the rest, recreation, exercise, and self-reflective time we need in order to be effective in our daily routines.

We check in with one another and comment when it seems like someone's losing grace. When one of us is starting to have sudden cravings for old, destructive behaviors, we pay very close attention to the recent details of his life. Without balance in our lives, it's inevitable that we'll return to some sort of abuse to numb the pain. Pain accompanies work that is split off from the rest of our lives. The Martyr and Hero archetypes we tried to live out as younger men are programs for losing soul and the sacred dream.

We also encourage one another to find humor in our various predicaments at work. We advise each other about how to deal with specific difficult situations. We commiserate with one another about the pain that emerges from situations we cannot change. It helps. It's really good to be able to whine and bitch once in a while. It's very satisfying in an environment where we're not shamed for having limitations or fears.

We support each other now in finding ways to make a living that don't destroy our bodies or our spirit. We work with understanding our addictions to excitement, which have driven us into types of work that harmed us. For example, it wasn't easy for me to leave my life as a filmmaker. But staying away helped restore me to sanity. New doors opened up, closer to my heart.

We still often tend to feel down when our work doesn't go well. But now we know we don't need to be heroes to feel loved. However, after a lifetime of conditioning to be heroic, it is often hard to remember this. The weekly meetings of the new knights are a place where we remind one another of what we have learned and remember to count our blessings.

We sometimes ask ourselves what we would do if we were simply hunters for a tribe. We might feel bad if we didn't catch anything that day, but we'd still be in the tribe. We'd still have membership, a family, and community.

HUNTING: THE TRADITIONAL WORK OF MEN

Competition is something we've all experienced as an essential component of our training to be men. We competed in sports, business, for women, and just for the joy of it. Like many of our male institutions, competition has its roots in the hunter.

There's a deep place in us that strives to drive one another to excellence. It took a lot of courage, resolve, and finely honed skill for small groups of men to hunt a wild boar or bull with only stone-pointed spears. For several million years, up until the last few millennia, hunting is what men did together. Something deep inside us still remembers this, even hungers for it.

Ben says, "My little boy frequently makes overhand tossing, throwing, and striking motions. He uses stalks of pampas grass for imaginary spears. He follows animals and bugs around all over the place, tracking and trapping." Most boys seem to cultivate this ability innately, with little or no prompting. We also can see the reflection of the hunter today in the football toss, the swing of the racquet and the bat, clubbing the golf ball, and the actions of many other sports, which reflect the movements and energies of the ancient Hunter archetype.

Physiologically, very little has changed in our bodies in the last ten thousand years. This is true even though our culture has been transformed beyond comprehension. In our bodies we're still hunters. The problem in our society is that this masculine drive, like many, has become distorted. Now our competition is frequently dedicated to the destruction of another person, corporation, nation, or belief system.

Fear of competition keeps men apart. We're afraid to be vulnerable to someone who later may use our weakness to his advantage. So we're always hiding our soft spot. How then do we expose our wounds and receive healing from one another? Like much of our work together, it's fraught with paradox and involves a certain degree of risk taking. As younger men we frequently attempted to dominate each other. We were always trying to get one up on the other guy. Today, can we compete in ways that make each other stronger?

Ultimately, we want our hunting partners to be stronger allies, not subservient to us. We want to encourage one another to be the best we can be, to strive for excellence, to test our limits and go beyond them. Through the community we create with our men's group, we're now there to pick one another up when we fall. So we can reach a little further. We also challenge one another when it appears that we're choosing a path that is too safe and narrow.

Sobriety and maturity do not mean that life ceases to be exciting or challenging. Just the opposite. Life's richer. We're more aware. We can *feel* more. This enhanced ability to feel may keep us out of some formerly destructive occupations. And it will guide us into new, healthier ones.

Competition is nature's way of encouraging evolution, positive change. So that's how we measure it these days. Is this challenge I'm facing supporting my life and the lives around me? Is this a road with heart?

In Part II we talked about sacred images of men that emerged out of old hunter societies. In the new knights we're trying to understand how those images and our innate tendency to be hunters relate to our modern lives. We feel that desire to hunt, deeply. In the past we pursued women with the steadfast intent of a hunter. The quests for money and power have been other hunts that drove us.

As younger men we pursued these goals relentlessly and reflexively, with little thought other than to fill our hunger. But we've found that this hunger is never really filled. So now we're after bigger game. We're becoming hunters of the sacred, hunting the deep essence of our own lives—hunters of the masculine soul.

A hunter of animals must learn their ways. A young man may race after them at first. But with practice he learns how to track with stealth, wait with patience, and even attract the animal to him. Through our work together in the group, we're starting to move more slowly through our lives, to reclaim our feelings and our dreams. We're learning the peculiar and often silent language of the soul. We draw soul to us through our group work and the simple peace that comes with self-acceptance.

Through coming to understand the language of the hunter, we may restore balance to our lives, confused and convoluted by the complexities of our urban existence. Through listening to nature and returning to our senses, we restore our connection to the earth and to the body.

Stealth, courage, and synchronized movement are required by the hunter. It's not surprising that football has attracted such profound interest from so many men in our culture. Their former status and definitive roles as hunters have been eliminated. The man who spends his day at a computer terminal has a need to experience, even vicariously, the synchronized, precise, and aggressive movements of other men.

Men's bodies are used to hunting side by side, an ancient habit. Perhaps women's bodies also have the ancient habit of facing one another and talking while weaving and grinding grain. In any case, men often experience their intimacy more shoulder to shoulder. For men, being face to face often implies conflict or competition with the other team.

While watching TV, today's couch warriors are like the young boys and old or infirm men of ancient tribal cultures, who delighted in sitting around the fire hearing tales of the hunt from the returning men. This afforded an opportunity for children to conceptualize the day when they, too, would join the hunt. Old men took pleasure in remembering past glories and pride in their sons' accomplishments.

Today, however, watching football side by side in the living room or at the bar together is a sad vestige of our legacy as hunters. We've lost the camaraderie we must have felt when we faced real danger together celebrating and feasting when we succeeded, starving when we failed.

HUNTING IN THE TWENTY-FIRST CENTURY

The new knights have begun to spend time together in nature. Once every few months we go for long hikes or fishing day trips. Last summer we spent four days white-water rafting. The synchronized stroking of oars as we careened through rapids attuned us to one another in a silent way. Singing and drumming by the fire, telling stories deep into the night, and sharing our dreams at dawn awakened old magic in our bones. We honed our skills together against the demands of the river. It brought our group closer. This is a different challenge than trying to best one another, which drives groups apart. This experience gave us a taste of what it may have been to be a real tribe, mutually dependent for our survival.

In fact, we all *are* mutually dependent. All people, everywhere. The environmental crisis has made that clear. However, the fragmentation in our culture and the competitive stance that men are conditioned to take with one another often obscure that underlying reality.

On the other hand, in our quest to breathe new life into the male role model, we don't want to become wimps—uncompetitive, nice, mushy good-feelers. We want to receive one another as whole persons, not the two-dimensional, rigid heroes we used to display to one another in the bars and on the job when we were younger men. So, in addition to encouraging one another to live in balance with our work, we also uphold a new ideal for economic success: *personal prosperity has its foundation in increasing the health and prosperity of the world around us*.

Many new men have given up believing that they are entitled to own or administer large resources, viewing the pursuit of wealth as somehow inherently evil. In the new knights, however, we feel it's important for men of goodwill to command the resources of the planet. That means we need to be capable and powerful in the world of business and commerce. The quest for soul is not an attempt to escape our adult male responsibility to steward life and the resources of the planet. Just the opposite: we've found that as we recover our connection to the depth of feeling, we become more concerned and more able to act in a committed and conscious way.

For example, Ben started a new company to build low-cost housing. He told us, "I figured out I can make just as good money building low-cost units as the custom luxury homes I've been building the last ten years. I've enjoyed building these huge architectural beauties and don't intend to give it up entirely. But I feel this work doesn't really give my life meaning. These flashy developments were more a product of my desires to show off as a younger man. Now I want to use the skills I've gained and the assets I have to support a new way of doing business. I'm more interested in creating communities than fancy homes.

"I've discovered some ideas that worked in Europe for cohousing," he went on. "I think this is a solution to the lack of low-income housing here. Our plans also conserve energy and materials. The city council is excited by the project. I beat out a dozen other proposals for the grants and permits. I feel good about competing in this way. And I'm doing something that I can feel proud of. This improves the life of the whole community, not just the lives of a privileged few."

To the knights Ben's philosophy of business feels more appropriate to the needs of a new millennium challenged by dwindling natural resources and the rapidly increasing impact of human society on nature.

THE EIGHTH TASK OF MEN: TO LOVE AND WORK IN WAYS THAT HEAL OUR LIVES

As young men we kept our eye upon the doughnut but lost sight of the *whole*. We strove for success and often failed. The goal was everything. When we failed at love, in sex, or in pursuit of wealth and power, we were often devastated because so much of our identity was tied up in our achievements. If we failed to produce or score, who were we? We had never been told we could be loved simply for who we were. We had never been told that the process was as important as the product. We were undernourished by life because we couldn't take pleasure from the simple moments of our day-to-day existence. Everything was measured in terms of our ultimate production.

Many of us wound up as substance abusers because we went a little crazy trying to be heroes. We tried to pick up women's pain and solve their problems. We tried to live up to our parents' expectations that we would excel beyond their level of achievement. We sacrificed our dreams to become practical men in the world or abandoned the world altogether to be dreamers. We never believed we could do both.

Now we're challenging one another to strengthen many aspects of our lives: our courage, authenticity, commitment to a vision, our determination, flexibility, inner direction, ability to fly in the face of convention, our honesty, capability, passion, ferocity, strength, ability to create community, and openness about our wounds and failures. We are attempting to enhance our connection to nature, our capacity for pleasure and joy, our spirituality, soulfulness, capability for multiple modes of expression, access to a wide range of emotions, our life-affirming protectiveness, our ability to hold power as a trust while simultaneously empowering others, our kindness, generosity, receptivity, playfulness, and responsiveness.

These are some of the qualities we're encouraging in our lives as we become hunters of the sacred. So now we compete with our younger selves. We up the ante on one another when it comes to telling the truth, claiming our sacred and practical dreams, and being who we truly are, in all our divine eccentricity. We challenge ourselves to become whole men, strong men, potent men, alive men, gentle men, and wise men.

> *Bringing a new vision to the roles of our adult lives was the eighth task we attempted. After many years of living as if there were no tomorrow, we've started to think more about the future—the future of our families, our community, our planet, and our own lives. Learning how to age well and become wise elders who have something to offer life—with good reasons to live it—was our next task.*

CHAPTER 9

The Elder Male: A Nonrenewable Resource

Sleep after toil, port after stormy seas,
Ease after war, death after life does greatly please.
    Edmund Spenser

It's been said that life begins at forty. And for many of us in the new knights this old saying has proven true. We've just begun to get a *conscious* sense of how we want to live the rest of our lives. Carl Jung believed the individuation process didn't really begin until after forty, in what he called the "second half of life." As a student of psychology in my early twenties, I remember thinking, "What nonsense. I'm individuating right now." Today, however, twenty years later, like most of the men in our group, I've begun to see the wisdom in Jung's observation.

In our group we're all in the middle years. We have more opportunities for self-reflection now than we did in the past. More importantly, we have some substantial life experience under our belts to reflect upon. Without that experience of success and failure over the years, it would be difficult to have a sense of the true needs of our developing souls. Through the passing of the years we're also now more aware of our mortality. We want to make good use of the time we have left and to enhance the richness and character of our lives in the years to come. We want to deepen our souls.

One night, as we sat on Rodger's living-room floor in front of a blazing fire, we started discussing some of our fears and hopes about growing older. Rodger said, "As I start to push fifty, some of the illusions I had in my youth about what I might achieve have faded away. By the same token, new possibilities I never considered have recently emerged. I really am going to sail around the world in just a few months. Amazing."

Jim noted, "Since I took this new job at the junior college I'm now doing, in my forties, what a lot of men did in their twenties. But my work now isn't only an attempt to improve my current standard of living or play catch-up with other men my age. It's a gift I'm giving to the old man I'll be someday. I don't want to be an impoverished artist when I'm eighty.

"Just as we've had dialogues with our inner child and young man," Jim continued, "I've begun to talk to the inner old man, too. He lives within me as a developing potential. Whenever I'm feeling down or too caught up in my personal melodrama, he says, 'Hey, *relaaax.* Everything changes. Don't wear yourself out with worry. Enjoy your life.' When I imagine myself as this old dude, I also try to think about what regrets I might have, what I'll wish I'd done in my forties. This also helps me to separate what's really important from the daily busy buzz work."

Then Jack added, "The thought of death used to fill me with terror. Now it actually enriches my life. Until I turned fifty, I really thought I was going to live forever. Now each day is precious, too valuable to waste in pursuit of goals that only stroke my ego or fluff my bank account."

Carl said, "I'm also looking forward to growing older. My experience over the last three years in this group has been that the more I reclaim who I really am and express what I really feel, the more enjoyable life becomes. My priorities have changed. My future's no longer about climbing the corporate ladder. I now see the coming years as an opportunity to refine my capacity for loving others and to increase my ability for giving something back to the world."

As younger men, all of us had enjoyed the pursuit of romantic and material goals. We were trying to make our place in the world of work and love. Although those remain worthy ambitions, the primary focus of our lives is beginning to change as we grow older.

We've all had the experience of arriving at a goal: perhaps a personal achievement, making a sum of money, or something as simple as reaching a destination on a trip. After all the buildup, excitement, expectation, and sacrifices made along the way, we are often disappointed. "Is this all there is?" we may ask.

When we examine the lives of many successful men, it seems their ultimate material achievement in life was often not very fulfilling. This is especially true if intimacy and the ability to appreciate the small moments of life were sacrificed along the way. This is one of the sad realizations Jack shared in an early meeting of the knights. It led him to change his life.

Rabbi Harold Kushner observes this poignant phenomenon, which affects many men's lives, in his book *When All You've Ever Wanted Isn't Enough*. He suggests we need to develop new definitions for success that affirm, "You have lived as a human being was meant to live and . . . have not wasted your life." Carl Jung expressed this idea by saying, "We overlook the essential fact that the achievements society rewards are won at the cost of a diminution of personality."

The new knights have been attempting to reverse this diminution of personality in our lives. In years past the heroic quest for productivity, identity, or relationships took precedence. Now we're undertaking a different sort of quest, a quest for soul. We're developing new attitudes toward aging and beginning to see the second half of life as an opportunity for discovering *inner* riches.

THERE ARE NO OLD HEROES—ONLY WISE OR FOOLISH OLD MEN

Aging is anathema to the heroic male. President Reagan used to dye his gray hair in an attempt to present a more youthful image. President Bush gives the media endless photo opportunities to witness him at his workouts. Let there be no doubt about his virility—no wimp here, the new image seems to say. Increasing numbers of top executives and entertainers have made male surgical and prosthetic cosmetics a huge growth industry in America.

The heroic male attempts to appear younger than he actually is. But there's a charm and dignity that can come with age. For example, Sean Connery, who's now in his sixties, is one of the sexiest men in America. In many cases aging actually makes a man *more* interesting and appealing than he was in his youth. Even so, many men who are possessed by the heroic archetype of youth look ahead to their later years with dread.

There's a lot of depression, loneliness, and lack of incentive among our older men. Men over sixty-five are second only to adolescent males in having the highest rates of suicide of any group in the nation. The rate increases steadily with each year they age. Like their adolescent counterparts, white males have the highest rates of all ethnic groups. As men age they also die off from disease and accidents much more quickly than women. By their eighth decade *women outnumber men two to one.*

There's a treasure store of knowledge among older men.

Unless it's passed on to the younger generation, this wisdom, culture, and tradition becomes forever lost, like the rapidly vanishing species of plants and animals in the wilderness.

When athletic ability or stamina on the job is all we value, we develop a culture dominated by the heroic archetype of the Eternal Youth. That's exactly the situation in our culture. This is the media image most of our male leaders attempt to project. So it's understandable that when a man can no longer perform in that mode, he's cast aside. But as we've learned, there are many other archetypes, many valuable and fulfilling images of masculinity that do not uphold the youthful hero as the most valuable kind of person a man can be.

The hero is a good ally. He has stamina, fortitude, and courage. But on the journey into the mystery of masculine soul, he's a lousy leader. Such energy may carry us along part of the way, but it's not the hero who plumbs the depths of feeling. The heroic impulse actually can get in the way of the quest for soul, even though we do need heroism to face our depths and the wounds of the world. But the hero needs to be in control all the time. That's the problem. Reconnection to our depths requires nonheroic attitudes: surrender, sensitivity, humility, and a willingness to leap (like the archetypal Fool) into the unknown.

An elder man who's connected to his depth is a man of inestimable value. He can temper the aggression of younger men. He knows that the wounds of war never compensate for its glory. He knows that the gleam of the marketplace cannot compare with the beauty of nature's glittering fabric of life. In this mode he's a peacemaker.

The initiated elder male, however, still caught in the image of the hero, will long to reclaim past glories through the actions of younger men. These are the old men who send young men to war. These are the old men who devour the nonrenewable resources of the planet, with no thought for future generations.

My generation of men has had a lot of distrust and anger toward the generation of men who came before us. The Vietnam War, the squandering of natural and economic resources, global pollution, and many other ills have been part of their legacy. They've hoarded wealth and held tightly to the levers of power. Many of us have felt that opportunities that traditionally get passed along to younger generations have been withheld. This has made us suspicious of older men, the patriarchy, our fathers, and the political process. But now, as part of our recovery, we're trying to bridge that generation gap—for ourselves, for our fathers, for our children, and for our children's children.

The generations have not always been so separate. Many of our ancestral lineages have been broken in Western culture. Three generations ago there was a massive jettisoning of old-world culture, language, custom, and myth. Many of the immigrants coming to this country in the early part of this century abandoned cherished traditions previously held for centuries. They even changed their names to something they considered more American.

Long before the social impact of modern feminism changed the structure of the family, the nature of men's roles was changing in America. A number of scholars who have written about the historical development of masculinity in Western culture mark the onset of the industrial revolution as a crucial time in the transformation of men's traditional roles. Prior to this period in history, men were more connected to the home and family. Then, in increasing numbers, they left the home and farm for many hours each day to work in factories. Most men no longer work alongside their fathers, uncles, and grandfathers as they did in preindustrial society.

As a result many young males today no longer feel their place in the slow, long dance of time and evolution. Middle-aged males have been cut off from both the traditional elders and the younger postboomer generation. And many elders are completely isolated—no longer connected to the old world, yet with no place of honor for them in the new.

There's a great value to tradition. Old men notice the changes that modern culture has wrought upon the land and in the community. Their stories of days past remind us that the world was once richer. Wilderness was abundant. Life was slower paced and more intimate. Family was multigenerational and more intact. In our hurry to create a new society in America, we abandoned much of what makes life rich. So what do our old men still have to offer?

For one thing, a grandfather can offer a boy or young man a softer image of masculinity. This is not the softness of the new male who never masters his potency. Ideally, this is the softness of a male who has found his strength and then tempered it with wisdom. As men age, they generally become less competitive and aggressive. A number of studies indicate that their aggression levels actually sink well below those of aging women.

Robert Bly refers to this older, mentoring, nurturing type of man as a "male mother," but I prefer to think of him as a completely masculine transformation—the *soulfather.*

Elder men who've been caught up in heroic conquests in the past often become more available to their families as they age. In the movie *The Godfather,* Marlon Brando plays a Mafia don who as a young man in pursuit of wealth and power was ruthlessly violent. As a grandfather, however, he's content to play in the rose garden with his grandson. This is the real meaning of the word *godfather:* an older man who is closer to God, a soulfather.

Unlike the father, the grandfather is not so concerned with discipline. He's more concerned with the soul of the boy. The grandfather has a special quality that he can pass along to us. Just as the knights grew up with some degree of father hunger, those of us who've had little contact with our grandfathers developed another sort of deficiency as well. I think this is evident in the new men's mythopoetic community. Thousands of men have flocked to spend time with gray-haired elders like Robert Bly and James Hillman.

They're often not merely seeking the lost fathers in their lives. They're hungering after soulful elders. The elder can plant the seed of soul in a young man. He's closer to death, closer to the mystery, further from the illusions of youthful endeavor and heroic visions. Something as simple as a whimsical smile may communicate this, a sleeping memory that awakens as we begin to tread our own path toward old age.

As modern men, we liked to believe we were self-made. We also felt we were products of the time and culture we lived in. But our work with the old gods of men has taught us that we are also related to something ancient in the collective psyche of men. We began to wonder, "Are we also influenced by the ghosts and genetic resonances of our forefathers?" So the new knights began to talk to one another about our elders. We decided to bring in photos of our ancestors to share our cultural and genetic heritage with one another.

OUR GRANDFATHERS

As planned, the following meeting was devoted to a discussion about older men who had touched our lives. Ben started off by telling us that his life had been devoid of elders. He somberly revealed, "Both my grandfathers and one grandmother were killed by the Nazis. Not a single photo of my mother's father remains.

But here's a sketch my mother made of him when she was a child."

As we passed this tattered, yellowed image around the room, Ben continued. "I was born toward the end of the war and have no memory of it, of course. But I think there's a family, possibly even a racial, grief which I inherited. It still affects me today. I rebelled against my Judaism and family. They're all highly educated professionals. Dad was a Fulbright scholar, for chrissakes. Getting into the building trade was a way for me to distance myself from that collective grief, from that academically oriented Jewish culture I grew up in.

"But I also lost a lot," Ben continued. "I lost my heritage, my membership in an ancient tribe, my tradition, and my family's personal history. So, recently I've taken to visiting my uncle Morris in the city. He was my father's only brother. I'd had no real contact with him since Dad's funeral eight years ago.

"Morris speaks about eleven languages and has lived all over Europe and North Africa. He was interned in Romania during the war but escaped the death camps. He's like a living history book. He knows the history of my family dating back to fifteenth-century Greece. That's where they went after fleeing the Spanish Inquisition. It's fascinating to spend time with him. We walk through the park and occasionally visit with some of the cronies he plays dominoes with. They've got some wild stories to tell as well.

"Morris always asks about my life. He's interested in my plans," Ben went on. "One thing, though. He just can't understand my sobriety. He still belts down a couple shots of schnapps every day and is slightly offended that I won't drink with him. 'Look at me,' he says, laughing, 'eighty-two and strong as an ox.'

"I've started taping some of his talks about the family history. When he's gone, a lot of these stories will go with him. In certain ways he's becoming closer to me than my father was. He's always happy to see me. It's like I've found a long-lost friend. I've also reclaimed my connection to my family in a way I didn't think was possible. He's helped me to know my father from a whole new perspective. I've come to understand the drives he had to succeed and excel, coming as he did out of the poverty of the American immigrant community. For some reason that I don't completely understand, it feels good to get acknowledged by this old man.

"Sometimes I find being a third-generation American culturally bleak," Ben added. "I like the notion of us moving toward becoming global citizens. But that doesn't mean we should all become the same. That melting-pot idea in America has diminished our richness. I feel the need now to be more rooted in my cultural tradition. I don't think it's our cultural differences but our lack of respect for the richness and diversity of other traditions that creates so much conflict in the world."

Jack comes from a long line of Englishmen and Scotsmen. He told us, "When the Scottish games were held here last year, I was able to trace my family name, at one of the clan tents, back to its original county in Scotland. I saw pictures of the ruins of the manor house my direct ancestors lived in over five centuries ago. There were also pictures of the coat of arms they bore. It made me feel connected to something very old. I'm not going to run out and buy a manor house in the Highlands. But it's comforting to remember the noble and fierce tradition that came before me.

"When I went to the Scottish games I noticed that all the men, regardless of whether they were in martial dress, had a dirk [a small throwing knife] stuck into the top of their knee socks. I like the idea of a man being armed as a traditional part of his dress. Men are defenders of the clan, the chidren, and the land. I think we should be prepared for violence. Perhaps there would actually be less violence in our culture if *every* citizen was armed. . . ."

As usual, Jack didn't hesitate to express his personal views about the state of the nation, but he finally continued with his ancestral tale when Brad started pelting him with raisins.

"The other thing that really touched me, as I rediscovered my ancestral roots, was the music. I've always had a strange love for bagpipes," Jack went on to say. "But I've never really connected it that much with my cultural heritage. I mean I'm an American, tried and true, you know. But I was fascinated to watch the men of the Black Guard march in their traditional regalia, playing pipes in a stately parade. I could hear the mournful cry and ancient sorrow of war in their music.

"This was no glorious, bright, cheerful American brass band marching off to war to make the world secure for capitalism and a Christian god," Jack continued. "In the sound of these pipes was the memory of old men who'd lost their sons and brothers. Here was the loneliness of younger men who'd lost their fathers on the battlefields and grown up alone. Listening to this music made me feel connected to something old, something broader than the McDonalds/McSafeway culture I live in today." Perhaps the pipes of old Pan, the wild god of the pastoral highlands, are also remembered in this music.

"My paternal grandfather was a pharmacist," I told the men that night. "I used to hang out at the drugstore a lot when I was a kid. He'd always lay a piece of candy on me or some such thing. He also gave me a regular supply of books, which I could choose off the paperback racks. These were the source of my first library. They also introduced me to a more interesting genre of literature than I was offered at school.

"At times, I'd go behind the counter while he mixed medicines. He'd tell me stories about the people they were for, what their maladies were, and how the various compounds would help. That's where I developed an early interest in medicine. After flunking college chemistry, however, this interest moved toward psychology. I think he'd be proud of me if he were still alive today."

Jim never knew either of his grandfathers. Since he's renewed relations with his father, however, he's learned that his paternal grandfather was a merchant seaman. One day Jim's father gave him a small knife with a scrimshawed handle that his father had carved. Jim passed this solitary heirloom of his ancestors around the circle with pride. "It's the first gift my father's given me since I was a kid," he said. "It really touched me, because I know he values this knife a great deal. I never realized it before, but I'm the third generation of carvers in my family. This art is in me blood, mates—a tradition."

Jim's father also told him about a photo on display at the maritime museum. It showed his grandfather as a young man on the deck of a gaff-rigged schooner. Jim got a copy of this from the historical society and brought it to the meeting. We were struck by how similar they appeared. "If you took that huge mustache off your grandfather, Jim, you could be the same person," noted Carl.

Brad also had never known his grandfathers. However, Jim's story reminded Brad of an old shipwright he'd met on a custom home-construction job in his early years. "Yeah, George was a crotchety Italian, in his early sixties when I met him. He'd worked as a boat builder for over forty years. But since they weren't making many wood boats anymore, he was plying his trade as a cabinetmaker and finish carpenter. And he was the best I've ever met. He didn't work real fast. He just moved at a steady pace. But he rarely made a false move. There was hardly ever any wasted material around his work area, and his tools were always immaculately maintained. The funny thing was, he consistently outproduced men half his age.

"He'd learned his trade from men who built the boats Jim's grandfather sailed upon. And now he was teaching me. I learned a lot of tricks I'd never seen as a carpenter's apprentice. How to make a dovetailed joint, the mysteries of mortise-and-tenon timber joinery, and other old-world techniques. A lot of this stuff was of little value on production jobs, which have been my mainstay over the years. But I've consistently used these techniques on a number of custom jobs.

"George was always willing to take a few minutes to show something to a younger man," Brad continued. "A lot of what I learned from him was subtle. How to look at the grain of a board and work it or resaw it in such a way as to display its beauty. How to sharpen a plane, saw, or drill bit so you always got a clean, true cut. What's stuck with me most, though, is a standard of quality and a work style that uses a minimum of precise motion for a maximum of output. Through George I connected to centuries of European craftsmen, their knowledge, and their standards. This attitude was almost absent in most of the American carpenters I've worked with over the years. Yeah, George was more than just a mentor; he was a real grandfather to me as well.

"Recently, since I've been doing construction management, I've missed working with tools. So I've started making fine-furniture pieces on the side. I've got a lot more energy during my off hours than I used to. And it gives me pleasure to work alone in my shop. I just sold a maple dinette for three thousand dollars. I'm only able to do that today because of the training I received from George twenty-five years ago."

The rest of the knights shared their stories as well, and toward the end of the evening we made a little altar with the pictures and artifacts we'd brought in from our male ancestors. Rodger lit a small candle and we sat there for a few moments in silence, looking at their faces in the flickering light—reflections and forecasts of the faces we may someday have ourselves. It felt good to simply remember the men who came before us and to honor their memory.

THE Y CHROMOSOME: MEN'S GENETIC RESONANCE WITH THE ANCIENTS

The glorification of patriarchal lineage in Western culture has come under justifiable criticism from feminists. Their point is that it became a means for controlling wealth and glorifying sons over daughters. We agree. And we're not here to resurrect patriarchy. But we also need to question whether there's something valuable for us as men in remembering our ancestors, both male and female.

When I went through training to become a teacher of meditation, I was initiated into some of the ancient ceremonial practices of the Vedic tradition of India. As preparation for instructing a new student, we were first taught to recount the names of the teachers of our teacher. This litany went all the way back to Shankara, who, twenty-five hundred years ago, codified the particular meditation system I taught. It also included the names of historical and mythological teachers who came before him. This ceremony had been handed from teacher to student since the dawn of Vedic culture thousands of years before these things were written down. From the perspective of that culture it would be dishonorable to teach without honoring the lineage that preceded us.

The Old Testament, too, recounts the history of the patriarchs, going all the way back to the mythical creation of the first parents—Adam and Eve. Old Celtic mythologies and ancient Egyptian and Mayan history follow suit. Many lineages of tribal cultures, including modern ones, claim to have a god or godlike ancestor in their bloodline. They believed that his divine characteristics had to be preserved from father to son.

It's curious, in light of the above, to note the genetic anomaly between men and women concerning the Y chromosome. A woman may receive her sex-determining X chromosome from either her father or her mother, who possesses two Xs. But a man can receive his sex-determining Y chromosome only from his father; he possesses both an X, which can come from either his mother or his father, and a Y, which can come only from his father. This is the only human chromosome that does not cross over from one sex to the other.

Women can trace their biological heritage through the DNA in the mitochondrial cell lining all the way back to the Stone Age Eve. But only men trace their genetic heritage back through a gender-specific chromosome. What other genes may be encoded in this chromosome and how they may affect our behavior as men is unknown. Gene-mapping research is still under way.

Whatever the depths of this mystery, our bodies are certainly linked to our male ancestors through our genetic heritage. And perhaps we gain some connection to life and essential masculinity through remembering our ancestors in various ways. Are our souls linked to mythological personages as well? Can we also reconnect through them to archetypal masculinity?

PLUMBING THE DEPTHS OF THE MASCULINE SOUL

We've talked about some of the old gods of men and how they still resonate within our modern psyches. In order to understand both the predicament and the special gifts of the elder male in our culture, let's return to the literature of mythology and familiarize ourselves with one more forgotten archetype of authentic masculinity—Hades, the ancient Greek God of Death.

The work we new knights have done toward healing the psychological past has made our lives richer and more fulfilling. In the same manner, we can live life today better through coming into a peaceful relationship with aging and the end of life. As Jim mentioned earlier, there's an old man within our psyches. The old man is both our future and the racial, collective memory of all men who've grown old and passed before us. Just as the potential for a huge tree exists within a tiny seed, the wise old man exists as a latent, undeveloped potential in our mind and body. One thing that can make an old man wise is his ability to reflect on life from a broad perspective of time. Another is his nearness to death.

In the new knights we've felt compelled to face our mortality. We've tried to meet the old man within as a guide to the depths of masculine soul. However, since the depth of soul is infinite, there's never any arrival—no real goal, to become devoid of meaning the moment it's been seized.

The quest for soul represents a nonheroic style of relationship to life and also to death. There's no prize to win, no omega point, no enlightenment, no satori—only what Carl Jung referred to as "an endless circumambulation of Soul." This is a strange idea to the heroic mind. Soul is something never fully achieved, never lost, never gained. Its very ambiguity, paradoxical nature, and mysteriousness usually cause the rational, heroic male to turn his face away.

Jung admonishes, "The dread and resistance which every natural human being experiences when it comes to delving too deeply into himself is, at the bottom, the fear of the journey to Hades." James Hillman also says Hades represents the "archetypal principle of the *deepest* aspect of soul [my italics]." Following their lead, let's dive into the depths of this ancient masculine figure.

Hades is such an awe-full deity that, like Jehovah, in ancient times his name was seldom spoken. Many euphemisms were created to describe him. He's known as Aidoeneus (the unseen one), Trophonios (nourishing), Zeus Katachthonios (Zeus of the underworld), and Him Who Receives So Many. He was also less known as the Good Counselor, the Renowned One, the Hospitable One, and the Gate Fastener. The Romans called him Pluton, Dis, or Pluto (wealth).

Pluto is the god of wealth mentioned in chapter 6. He's depicted with a cornucopia—an icon of the Earth Father—the fecundating force beneath the earth from which the crops spring. He represents the rich, generative, ensouling quality of Hades.

But Hades is also an undertaker—the creep of Western culture. He takes us down. He's the great leveler of life. In the midst of our crowning glories he's silently watching, saying, "This, too, shall pass." Our careers, lives, children, accomplishments, and creative works all pale, withered by his gaze. We experience him in the pressing midlife question "Is this all there is?" It's no wonder that in the few instances where he's depicted in Greek art, his head is averted. The essential question he raises for many of us is "How can we live with the existential pain of our mortality?"

Hades is reflected in detachment from life, masking the grief and loneliness many contemporary men feel in their lives. Living as we do in a culture actively engaged in the denial of death, this predicament isn't surprising. As we've seen before, the dynamics of archetypal psychology indicate that we become possessed by that which we've failed to commune with. To the degree to which we are unable to face death, we deaden ourselves while still living.

Carlos Castaneda, however, suggests that we make an ally of death in order to live life fully. He suggests we regard death as an ally looking over our left shoulder and that we consult him in our lives. He quotes the sorcerer Don Juan, who says a man of knowledge

> knows that his life will be over altogether too soon; he knows that he, as well as everybody else, is not going anywhere; he knows, because he *sees,* that nothing is more important than anything else. In other words, a man of knowledge has no honor, no dignity, no family, no name, no country, but only life to be lived, and under these circumstances his only tie to his fellow men is his controlled folly.

In ancient Rome, triumphant heroes returning from battle in a processional chariot parade had a man standing to their left wearing the mask of death. This man was present to preserve the hero from the sin of hubris, reminding him that he was still merely a mortal man.

FACING THE FACELESS GOD

So how do we go about making death our ally? It's a difficult idea. Very little is written about death's personification—Hades. His name is synonymous with his location—the underworld. His realm, like Poseidon's, is at every point contiguous with that of the earth goddess, Gaia. He's a partner with the Earth Mother. Male interiority, however, is not the same thing as Gaian fertility. Remember, we're different. Hillman notes that the "deep ground is not the same as dark earth." There's a distinct difference between the "darkness of soul and the blackness of soil."

The realm of Hades is *not* simply the womb of the Great Mother. Nor is it actually physically located within the earth. It's *under* the surface of life, more a direction, *downward,* or *inward,* than a fixed location. Mortal bodies return to the physical earth. However, in ancient Greek mythology all departed souls journeyed to Hades, a place *beyond* the surface of the earth.

So Hades, like many of the male earth gods, is a paradoxical figure. He is (1) a god of death; (2) a place of souls; (3) a direction: inward and downward; (4) simultaneously a father in the earth, yet beyond it; (5) a quality of human consciousness: implacable, dispassionate, remote, silent; and (6) a perspective: "all this shall pass."

Soul is a rather metaphysical concept. It does not fit nicely into any single logical category. It's everywhere and nowhere in particular. How, then, could a lord of souls be otherwise?

Hades has few myths surrounding him. He is rarely depicted in art. In fact, there were no temples erected to him in ancient Greece. There were no rites in communion with him and no mythological progeny or lineages descended from him. Hades joins the ranks of male, earth-related deities who, like Pan, are shunned, feared, forgotten, or ignored in modern times. Hades truly is the faceless God.

In early Christian times, Hades was merged with the new imagining of Satan. His dark invisibility and mysteriousness became blended with Pan's animalistic image as the embodiment of evil—ruler of a torturous hell. In earlier times, however, Hades had never been regarded as evil. His realm was not a place of torment, but rather a mysterious, cheerless place where souls awaited rebirth. Prior to the preeminence of sky-father myths, the Earth Father was an equal partner with the Earth Mother. Hades represents the deepest aspect of the ancient Earth Father—grandfather of the soul. He's the soul of the world itself—the *Animus* Mundi.

The ancient pagan notion of soul as connected to Hades and to the earth was a very different idea than the Christian and New Age idea of spirit. Spirit is light, moves upward, and desires to fly away from the earth. If it goes downward, it's into a torment of hell. With this polarized concept of good and evil alive in our consciousness, it's no wonder that modern urban men became afraid to face their depths and began to feel alienated from nature.

One night the knights read aloud one of the few myths from ancient Greece that features Hades as a main character. Ironically, just as we'd discovered much about the Sumerian Earth Father Dumuzi by reading hymns to the goddess Inanna, we learned about Hades through reading the Homeric hymn to the goddess Demeter.

This story told us how Persephone, a young maiden, was abducted by Hades while playing on the surface of the earth—personified as the goddess Gaia, her grandmother. Just as she bends down to pluck a narcissus flower, Hades erupts out of the underworld and drags her down to his kingdom. Demeter, Persephone's mother, becomes depressed about her disappearance and leaves Olympus, wandering the earth in search of her daughter. She becomes enraged that no one will help her find Persephone. Eventually Hecate, the crone, tells her where her daughter is. But Demeter can't enter Hades's realm. So she decides to force the gods to negotiate Persephone's return to the upper world.

To accomplish this, Demeter threatens to destroy humanity and thus deprive the gods of human adoration and oblations. Through her powers as an agricultural goddess, she creates a long winter. Everything withers. Consequently the gods relent and send down Hermes, as chief negotiator, to work out her daughter's return. Hades relents and agrees to return Persephone. But first he feeds her a pomegranate seed to ensure that she'll return to him for one season every year. Now, legend goes, winter comes when Persephone descends; spring arrives when she emerges. Persephone is no longer merely Demeter's daughter. She's the queen of the underworld, a guide and comfort to souls as the wife of Hades.

Much has been discussed about the *rape* of Persephone as understood from the feminine perspective. In Jungian circles this myth is frequently referred to as illustrating patterns of feminine initiation and individuation.

But as the new knights considered this Homeric hymn, we began to see it in a different light. We began to realize that

Demeter, as one of many corn goddesses, helps maintain political and social stability. She affirms the status quo. She also may be understood as nature that is cultivated and controlled by civilization. Therefore when we look at life and death from Demeter's point of view, the underworld is related to her ethic of unlimited growth. Thus the underworld seems like a bad place because it puts limits on growth. This view of Hades, however, is not the most desirable approach to the individuation of the masculine soul. As Hillman notes, growth after forty is more a metaphor of cancer than healthy expansion. In the second half of life we're not seeking growth, but rather depth.

As we've maintained throughout this book, civilization has had a numbing effect on the souls of men. We must learn to apprehend archetypal images with eyes free from the clouds of modern culture's prejudices if we're to know them at all.

So as we continued looking at this myth from a less civilized perspective, we began to understand that Hades represents a more primordial, less differentiated aspect of nature than Demeter. Hades was born at the beginning of creation as Tartarus, the dark center of Gaia. Gaia is an undifferentiated, uncivilized goddess of nature, who later gives birth to the agricultural goddess Demeter. With her deeper understanding of the ancient cycles of birth and death, Gaia is actually a coconspirator with Hades in the abduction of her granddaughter, Persephone. She creates the captivating narcissus flower.

Hades is also encouraged by Persephone's father, Zeus. He advised Hades to abduct her because Demeter couldn't bear the thought of her daughter ever leaving home in Olympus. According to Ovid, Aphrodite also has a hand in the abduction. She wanted to instill love into the underworld through inflaming Hades with passion.

The abduction of Persephone is an allegory for nature's homeostatic mechanism of restoring balance. Demeter is unlimited growth. Hades is unmitigated death. Persephone and Hermes get these absolute polarities moving in a cyclic manner: birth and death, spring and winter. So this story encourages us as men to develop greater awareness of the cyclic nature of life.

For example, when our heroic abilities die, when we fail or when we become depressed, we may remember that "this, too, shall pass." It's not just our glories that pass, but our pain as well. Life is ever changing. When we get stuck in unlimited heroic expansion or total contraction and isolation, we get abducted by forces greater than ourselves. Archetypal forces tell us to change or die. Nature seeks to keep things moving.

Persephone in the underworld reminds us that there's something lovely in our soulful depths. Even Aphrodite admires her beauty. Descent into soul is not merely about drowning in grief and incubating in darkness. Through learning to face our mortality and embrace death as a perspective on life that gives wise counsel in our endeavors, we're enriched. Why, then, do we turn our faces away from the inevitability of death, pretending heroically that we will live forever? Stephen Levine says, "As long as death is the enemy, life is a struggle. Life becomes fractured into heaven and hell. The mind continues its incessant roller coaster of fear and stress, which ironically may even cause disease."

As part of our recovery the new knights have increasingly valued serenity as our most valuable asset. A major step toward cultivating serenity comes from facing death's relentless inevitability and from understanding the true limitations of our mortal lives.

DEATH THE RAPIST

We experience death as overwhelming. It's like rape. It comes on relentlessly, unwanted and unbidden. Our loved ones are dragged out of life, against their will and ours. Through the gap in the world that Hades rends, we the living are touched and infected by his essence of deep, concentrated grief. But it's only from the perspective of Demeter that Persephone's abduction can be understood as a literal rape, instigated by Hades, an evil patriarchal man. One of the reasons I make this point is to counter prevalent radical feminist assertions that insist that all men are rapists in their depths.

Hades is no more a god of rapists than Kali is a goddess of mass murderers or Artemis simply a goddess out to destroy young males hunting the stag of their manhood. We must broaden our imagination regarding the meaning of these myths. Through bringing the awareness of death into naive human consciousness we further the creation and deepening of soul. We invite death to sit as a counselor at our table. We circumvent our narcissism. It's no coincidence that it was the narcissus flower that Hades prevented Persephone from grasping. That is how this Homeric hymn to Demeter speaks to us as men.

In his graduate thesis in archetypal psychology, Ralph Hyde observed:

> Whenever our consciousness is dominated by the perspective of growth, nurturance, and development, without a corresponding cognizance of destruction, decay, and death, we are in danger of losing our soul, our most precious flower, to the incursion of Hades, invisible behind those shadow aspects of life which we see as the darkest and the most dismal. It is then we are thrown, like Persephone herself, into despair, searching and mourning. Yet it is just this incursion by Hades that opens us to the possibility of rebirth and renewal.

So through turning our attention toward Hades we may, as Hyde, Hillman, Castaneda, Levine, and many others suggest, open to the possibility of transformation in life.

One of the techniques for working with material in depth psychology is the use of active imagination. Dream images, mythological characterizations, personifications, ghosts, ancestors, and gods are given a forum to speak—if they will. Often this sort of work is done individually, in private. The new knights set aside time to pay attention to archetypal images that have been appearing to us. So the week after we read this myth, we discussed the voices and images it had raised within us. We each had a perspective to speak from, as if we were players in the drama of the myth itself. Several of us were moved to speak with the voice of Hades. Later we discussed the feelings that emerged as we let this myth roll around our minds like some fine wine on our psychic palate.

"I didn't experience this story as just a tale of feminine initiation," said Rodger. "I felt compassion, affinity, and identification with a misunderstood and maligned Hades. I experienced him as a masculine soul locked away for countless ages, alone in the underworld, but now seeking individuation through communion with the upper world and the feminine."

"What came through for me," said Carl, "is the loneliness of Hades. He's chosen an unheroic position. He's separated from the other gods of Olympus. He's cut off from deeds, actions, and adventures in the surface world of mortals or on the heights of Olympus. Yet his actions are founded at every step upon a deep integrity and action within the bounds of natural law. Hades acquiesces to Hermes's request to return Persephone, even though there's nothing in it for him. Demeter's rage can't touch Hades. He has nothing to fear. There are no offerings to him to be taken away. It's only heroic Olympians who fear destruction of the human realm. All souls are already destined for Hades. So why does he relent?"

"Out of a deep sense of responsibility," offered Jack. "He wants to be sure that order and balance are maintained in the universe, even if the price of this is his own loss or sorrow. He's kind of selfless, like Humphrey Bogart helping Ingrid Bergman to leave at the end of *Casablanca.*"

This is consistent with the secret, selfless sense of service many men experience in their lives. Many men feel that they, like Hades, are invisible, absent, and not considered in relationships to the degree that they feel women are. They're often unrecognized or taken for granted while forgoing their dreams, sacrificing their health and even their lives in service of their families, communities, and nations.

Hades is dispassionate. Yet as the god of death he's also a steadfast servant of life. His silent, invisible nature is reflected in stoic, unflashy, simple, ethical masculinity, which has a willingness to face death in order to protect life. Hades is underneath life, a foundation for life. Life and death are not at war with one another. They both equally serve the endless transformation of the world.

THE DEATH OF THE HERO: COMMUNING WITH THE DEEP

As we've seen, the underlying condition of many men in this culture is one of unreconciled grief. The expression of that grief is inconsistent with flashy, heroic optimism. There are many heroes like Heracles and Christ who go down to conquer Hades. Peirithoüs and Theseus try to rob him. Orpheus, Odysseus, and others come seeking favors. Few, however, commune with him. The descent into the underworld is unbearable for the hero. Heroes aren't happy there. The shade of Achilles, a classical Greek hero, tells Odysseus, who visits the underworld, that he would rather be a poor man's slave than rule as king in Hades.

This myth also reflects the predicament of the Hades position. It indicates why there's so much resistance in this culture to men admitting their pain and grief. They suspect that if they present themselves unheroically, with all entrances to their underworld open, they'll be rejected by hero-loving women and men.

Robert Bly has presented an analysis of the Grimms' fairy tale "The Gnome." It depicts the experiences of three brothers in search of three princesses who've been abducted and hidden in the underworld. Ultimately, it's the younger, less heroic brother who finds their secret location from a tricky gnome. Rescuing the princesses requires a journey down a long dark well to reach them. The older brothers, representing the more rational and heroic aspects of masculinity, attempt the descent. But they fearfully return, never reaching the underrealm.

The youngest brother, who's sensitive but also brave and resourceful, goes down. He slays the dragons and rescues the princesses, sending them up to the surface. But the older brothers prevent his return to the surface by cutting the rope by which he made his descent. He's left to languish, abandoned in the underworld—defeated and alone. Many years pass. He eventually discovers his capacity to make music. This attracts underworld denizens—the dwarfs. They free him to claim his due riches and the princesses, whom the elder brothers falsely claimed to have rescued.

The individuating style as suggested by this youngest brother isn't the traditionally masculine metaphor. He hangs out in the underworld for a long, long time. He achieves his destiny by surrendering to his fate, by making beauty out of it and thus winning the support of the Earth Father. He does not succeed through force, domination, or the duplicity of the heroic male. Bly notes that a lot of sensitive contemporary men may stay submerged in depression for ten to fifteen years. That's been true for a number of the new knights as well. Now we're learning how to return to life.

In the hymn to Demeter, Persephone can move between life and death, between the underworld and the surface. Hermes, by virtue of his fluidity, also has this ability. They, like this nonheroic, youngest brother, represent the only style of consciousness that can commune with Hades and return to life renewed and empowered. To touch our depths we must learn how to grieve as men.

In ancient times, winter was known as the time of the dying god. One of the gods of nature who died and was reborn each year was Dionysus, who some myths say was the son of, or the same as, Hades. When we name the pain of nature, now perpetually wounded by our technological culture, as only our mother's pain, we can't fully connect with it as men. Many of us already have been overwhelmed by our own mothers' pain. However, when we understand this feeling as also the concentrated sorrow of the masculine soul in the earth, something else in us gets mobilized. We're more response-able. We can identify with it more closely. We somehow have more permission to grieve.

Our group attempts to create a climate of unconditional support for the expression of deep-seated feelings—even those dark, putrid, perverse, and deformed sentiments that often find no other acceptable outlet in the civilized world. Often we meet a brother's grief with silence—not the silence of apathy, but rather the welcome silence of the Good Counselor, the Hospitable One who understands and willingly bears witness to our grief. This is healing.

SPIRALING DOWN INTO THE CENTER OF OUR LIVES

A man's connection to life and to nature is often invisible. A woman begins menstruation, which physically marks her transition to womanhood. It reminds her continually of the natural cycles of nature—the waxing and waning of the moon. But a man has no such indicators marking his place in the cyclical order of things.

Also, when a man loses his virginity, to a large degree, little has changed. Physically he remains the same, even if emotionally he has, in most cases, validated himself as a man.

Pregnancy and birth also leave a man relatively unchanged, at least in comparison with the dramatic challenge and transformation the mother experiences. After birth she undergoes lactation and resumption of the menstrual cycle. The man, once again, is still the same, at least biologically.

Menopause marks the end of mothering and the transition into the arena of the Old Woman. The male simply, slowly, and inexorably ages; he grows older, and that's it. A man often doesn't actually realize that his life is changing until his children are grown, or until he retires or is struck by impotence, divorce, heart attack, or some other major disability.

If a man who hasn't regularly gone in and out of the underworld suddenly finds himself approaching the shores of the

Styx—the cold, dark river that flows along the boundaries of Hades—the shock may numb his soul. But through surrendering our male conditioning to act as heroes, we can overcome our fear of falling apart and being dismembered. Yes, we're drawn down. But through communion with Hades we can deepen our soul. Some have called this journey downward *the dark night of the soul.*

Through finding our soul music, our means of expressing grief, the underworld may become our ally. We reenter life. Day breaks anew. Through the agency of Hermes, the communicator, we, like Persephone, can emerge and return again. Enriched by the deep, we enjoy life and are perhaps more prepared for the final descent when it occurs. We can be more present with the riches we have when we're not continually overwhelmed by the anxiety of someday losing them. We become more aware of the cyclic nature of our lives, something that our interest in the Moon Father has also communicated to us.

A man's relationship to nature may be more rooted in the underworld, unlike a woman's Demeter-like above-the-ground cycles of birth, scarlet moons, and nurturing, which overtake her with their numinous power. These feminine cycles confront a woman with changes in her body and her being to which she has no choice but to surrender. She's therefore intimately aware of her mortality. She regularly experiences her heroic ego being ripped asunder by the forces of nature and then reconstituted.

Although men comprehend the changing nature of life intellectually, there's nothing in our biological experience that intimately connects us with its cyclic nature. But through a connection to the Earth Father, a man can find access to the ground of his being, not upon the changing surface of life but deep within it—underground.

Stephen Levine reminds us, "Life becomes immense when we start recognizing that there is no assurance that we will live out this day. Our fantasies and presumptions that we will live forever confuse us as we enter death. In reality, all the time we have is right now."

So in the new knights we try to be aware of death as a counselor whispering in our ear. He's reminding us to live the day fully. We encourage one another to make amends where possible for anything we regret, so that at any moment we can die at peace. Death teaches us to know our limits and also helps us meet our challenges with less fear. When we remember how truly powerless we are in the face of death, our melodramas and inflated self-importance are put in perspective. Most of us now spend a period of each day in silence, meditation, and reflection. Through letting go of activity for a short while each day, we die a little, sink into our depths, and return to our lives renewed.

THE NINTH TASK OF MEN: TO RESTORE A CONNECTION WITH OUR ANCESTORS AND COME TO TERMS WITH OUR MORTALITY

The new knights have been stumbling around in the dark trying to find a deeper connection to life. We've employed meditation, active imagination, speaking with our dreams, and welcoming the ghosts of our ancestors. And we've reflected upon our feelings in response to old myths. We've been looking into our genetic and cultural tradition for heirlooms of the masculine soul, thrown out as junk by our modern culture, which values only what is new.

We're getting older and trying to understand how to approach that reality in a conscious way. When we die we hope to go with the feeling that we haven't wasted our lives, that we have fully lived as men, in all our multiple roles.

We're hungry for a connection to elder men, so we now seek them out in our lives. We also seek connection to the elder within—a guide and counselor for our lives. He's very important in the absence of a vital cultural tradition that embraces and upholds the development of men's spiritual lives.

We're trying to find solutions to a planetary crisis, attempting to change our culture into one that is more protective of nature, more nurturing toward children, and equally supportive of the lives of men and women. And so we've taken a new look at the stages of development in a man's life: childhood, initiation, love, work, sacred dreams, the quest for soul, and aging. This is so that we, our sons, and our fathers can find a context in which to bless the development of one another's souls. This is so that our daughters, sisters, lovers, and mothers can live with respect, honor, and safety in our communities.

> *Reconnecting with our ancestors and facing our mortality was the ninth task we attempted. Restoring the traditional institution of sacred men's lodges to our mythologically and soul-impoverished culture was the tenth task we faced.*

PART IV

Rebuilding the Community and the World

CHAPTER 10

Meetings with Ordinary Men

In the deep of the night, with their bellies full of meat, the men warmed their hands by the fire, rubbed each other's backs, told wild stories, and laughed until dawn.
        From a tale told by
        the men of the Dragon Lodge

In the years since the new knights began meeting, we've frequently been asked by other men, "How do you start a men's group?" or "What do you do in your men's group?" A number of men expressed interest in joining our group. But we wanted to keep the core group small and intimate, so we would invite them to visit our group just for an evening or two. As a result of their experience, quite a few went on to start groups of their own. Several of us visited those groups in the early stages. We would offer what we could in the way of support and direction, and then withdraw.

Through my work as a psychologist concerned with gender issues, moreover, I've initiated numerous men's and mixed-gender groups, visited many existing groups, and attended dozens of men's conferences. Most of the new knights also have attended workshops, visited other groups, and been mentors as well. Along the way we've compared our notes from these experiences and integrated them with our personal work in the new knights. It has become increasingly important to us as an element of our recovery to reach out and be available to other men. This book, too, grew out of that sentiment.

In our experience groups can form around many diverse issues. A few examples are:

1. Men's-rights groups, which address inequities in the social and legal system we raised in Part I of this book. A lot of this work centers around fathers' rights and advocacy for male victims of abuse and discrimination.
2. Mythopoetic groups that focus on ritual, men's spirituality, and building male community. These groups are reclaiming sacred images of masculinity, like the ones we discussed in Part II.

3. Groups that focus on gay rights and other gay issues, such as the three levels of coming out—personal, private, and public—overcoming internalized homophobia (building gay-affirming self-esteem); fighting discrimination; increasing intimacy (moving beyond sex addiction); understanding the complexities of same-sex couples; and building gay-affirming community.
4. Male codependency groups, which focus on the issues of men who give too much. These groups focus on different issues than the oft-repeated women's issues depicted in the popular literature. Men benefit from looking at their relationship problems through a lens that affirms masculine ethics and examines the ways in which women equally contribute to relationship problems.
5. Groups like our new knights, which focus on recovery in a very broad sense. This work also led us to men's-rights issues, healing the wounds of childhood abuse, and concerns with recovering soul—the mythopoetic query.
6. Other twelve-step-inspired groups work with issues of specific addictions. The principles taught in these programs and the guidelines offered for meetings also offer valuable directions for men's work.

You may not be addicted to alcohol, work, drugs, or sex or suffer other easily identified obsessions. But if you can relate to the problems outlined in the first section of this book you may be suffering from the more pervasive, toxic heroic-masculinity syndrome we've described. In addition to their stated purposes, twelve-step programs address individual symptoms emerging from a global, pathological response to our Western sex-role models.

From our point of view recovery issues underlie the work of all men's groups. It's doubtful you'll get much out of a mythopoetic quest or adequately claim your rights to be a parent if you haven't faced the tyranny of your own addictive behaviors. However, focusing *only* on pathologies may keep you identifying yourself as a victim, an adult child—not really a man. So it's important to take what you can from this twelve-step work and leave the rest.

As the men's movement grows, the distinctions between all the various camps are beginning to blur. We are finding more similarities around our issues as men than these different group designations might suggest. Regardless of your specific orientation, the most valuable focus in men's work is the expression of the truth of our own experience. It's through men hearing other men express the honest story of their lives that the most healing results. The suggestions for group work mentioned below are just that—suggestions or possibilities, not guidelines, rules, or even ideals.

Perhaps the most valuable thing you can do is find at least one other man to whom you can tell the whole truth of your experience. If you both can then connect with another, even better. Then you have a group. Jesus is reported to have said that when "three of you gather in my name, then I am there." There's something to this. Archetypal forces in the masculine soul have moved men to gather in small groups throughout the ages. Perhaps collectively we can host gods that are impossible for us to know individually.

The myth of the lone hero is dead. We've said good-bye to Superman. But many men still have to work through the fantasy that they can do it all themselves. As soon as a few men in a community raise the flag of male solidarity, healing, and fraternity, there's usually a rush to rally round. Many men are just waiting to come in from the cold. All it takes is one person to say, "There's a men's meeting tonight."

Your focus may be recovery, healing, individuation, ritual, creating a place to talk safely, having a special kind of fun, organizing around specific social or political issues, learning more about men, or simply making friends. Regardless of how you organize your group, though, certain sorts of challenges seem to face most men who start groups with an emphasis on healing and personal transformation. Let's explore some of the possibilities and problems that can come up.

BUILDING A MEN'S LODGE

In some ways the terms *men's group* and *men's meeting* are rather vague. They could mean anything: a task force, an encounter group, a sports team. A *men's lodge,* however, implies something more specific than a group. It brings up the image of a bonded, tribal unit that meets for more than just the accomplishment of a specific task. It implies male community, brotherhood, fraternity. In ancient times, the men's lodge was a place in almost every culture where men gathered to perform their sacred rites, deepen their sense of male fraternity, and delve into male mysteries. Unfortunately, today the term may also raise the image of the old Elks or Moose. Many of these organizations perform valuable philanthropic and social activities, and perhaps they were once also concerned with men's souls. But in their current forms they do not appear to have that focus.

We have begun to think of the new knights as something more than a men's group. We have an identity now, a collective consciousness, committed friendships, a community. Several years ago Keith Thompson wrote an article titled "A Man Needs a Lodge." He proposed the idea that men's lodges have been an essential part of most cultures throughout time, and are necessary for the well-being of men in our culture as well. So we like to think of ourselves as a lodge now. And it's taken thousands of hours of meeting together to find that solidarity.

Ken Druck, the author of *Secrets Men Keep,* notes that one of the many unspoken commandments given to men is "Thou shalt stand alone." Part of the work of men's groups is to overcome this and many other covert cultural dictums that interfere with our enjoyment of life. Boys generally tend to form teams, groups, bands, and gangs, while girls often tend to develop relationships with special best friends. So the forming of groups is not alien to us as men. But the skills for deepening friendships, based upon intimacy, often take more deliberate attention.

Taking the first step toward recovery and integration as a man can be frightening, threatening, and difficult. In order to go to an existing men's-group meeting or to start one of your own, you may have to face any number of obstacles. Ridicule or resistance from significant women and men in your life may emerge. You may also confront habitual patterns of dominance, narcissism, and masochism in yourself and others. These traits are implicit in the types of self-abuse we're attempting to recover from. You also must be willing to face your homophobia, if you have it. And most heterosexual men do.

Several years ago one man wrote, upon returning from a group, "I told my wife about a very intimate men's-group meeting. She said, 'Did it ever occur to you that you're the only member who doesn't know the other guys are homosexuals?' None of them were, but I couldn't sleep that night."

In women's groups, homosexuality does not seem to carry the same specter it does for many men. Most men are trained from childhood to regard homosexuality as unmanly—the worst sin a man can commit. Also, since men are conditioned to associate intimacy with sexuality more than women, many fear that intimacy with other men automatically implies homosexuality. I've attended many groups with men of widely mixed sexual persuasions. Ironically, these groups are not significantly different in any way I can detect from any other group of men. Differences in our sexual orientation are among the lesser issues we have to face.

As the men's movement continues to grow, many gay and straight men are finding commonalities around their gender affiliation that transcend their differences of sexual orientation. Straight men can better support their gay and bisexual brothers by affirming homosexuality as a traditional and normal expression of one of the many diverse aspects of masculinity. And gays can better support straight men by more actively affirming their gender-specific issues around divorce, fathers' rights, and other inequities they face in their relationships with women.

For many men the process of joining a men's group is not unlike an alcoholic finding the courage to attend his first A.A. meeting. The degree of risk will vary from man to man. But probably everyone has to work through some degree of apprehension, resistance, or fear before he can receive the support, solidarity, healing, wisdom, friendship, and fun that can emerge out of a good men's lodge.

When you do meet with men, then meet with men. Don't have a woman near the meeting space, no matter how much positive regard or relatedness she shares with you. Men's-lodge space is a private, *sacred space*. Since the dawn of time men in every culture have met alone and in secret to approach their gods and find their collective magic. Every little boy knows this instinctively—"No Girlz Allowed." Almost every time I've seen a woman come into a group's space, even if it's just a member's wife calling him to the phone, it's disruptive and inhibiting. Right or wrong, men are often afraid to express their deepest truths when a woman may overhear.

NOW THAT WE'RE ALL HERE, WHAT DO WE SAY? WHAT SHOULD WE DO?

Of course many of us are habitually rational, goal directed, and focused on the content and outcome of things. When men come together there's often a tendency to talk *around* issues instead of *about* them. We may tend to fill the space swapping old tales and discussing current events. Our early meetings of the knights focused more on the poker game in front of us, news of the day, and business concerns than on our sobriety. This traditional men's-club sort of activity is enjoyable and natural. It's also what comes easiest for us all.

The easiest route, however, isn't always the most direct road toward healing and transformation. For example, Carl Jung points out that the individuation process is an operation *contra naturum*—opposite to our nature. The same may be true about the process of claiming a new vision of masculinity.

Talking about our personal issues—our hopes, fears, frustrations, and weaknesses—is more difficult. Expressing our uncensored feelings to one another is even more challenging. But it's more healing, valuable, and a better use of the limited time we have available for men's work. Through revealing our wounds, we also engender support for whatever crisis or difficult challenge we're facing at the moment.

At any time we may be slipping in our sobriety; experiencing conflict in our relationships, problems with our children, or stress at work; confronting health or financial problems; or having some other form of distress. Through including the men of the lodge in our struggles, our load is lightened. We receive new perspectives and commiseration. We no longer feel we must face everything alone. Our relationship with a woman no longer has to carry the entire burden of our emotional needs. This alone can improve our relationships significantly.

Sharing our hope, strength, and experience with one another will undoubtedly affect our relations with one another, our families, and the community at large. For that and for many other reasons, it's important to hold confidentiality as a basic tenet of our work. We don't want to risk muddying the group's waters with gossip. So we don't share the details of our meetings even with our mates. This isn't easy. But it's a measure of respect for the other men in our group. On that note, all of the new knights have read this manuscript. And nothing's been included that they have not wanted to divulge for the benefit of the reader.

In addition to talking openly about our personal issues we also try, during a portion of some meetings, to incorporate some nonverbal work. Drumming, making music, movement, working with art forms to express our feelings, hiking, cooking for each other, and even dancing have found their way into our meetings. This gets us out of our heads and breaks the rigid hold of tensions or problems we may be carrying.

The major benefit we've all reaped, however, has been from our regular conversations about issues that are central to our lives and our recovery. In our shadowy, neglected, and funky places are often found the keys to personal transformation. Outside of private therapy, our group is one of the few places we've ever felt supported for discussing our addictions, depressions, failures, inferiorities, dark fantasies, fears, and wild, hopeful dreams.

Many men feel wounded by failures to live up to the heroic ideal and by the lack of support for radical change that we often encounter in our environment. Through sharing our failures with one another we've healed much of this shame. We now feel that our failures are badges of honor earned for trying to succeed at all. Our lodge is also a place to celebrate our successes and transformations. We acknowledge one another for our triumphs, both small and large. It gives our lives greater meaning when our accomplishments are heralded by others.

One of the anxieties many men encounter in groups is the feeling, deep within our bodies, that when men gather together there's always the potential for violence. As we came to know one another in our group, this inherent discomfort steadily subsided. In actuality men are never safer than when in a men's lodge. A group has the power to contain one man's violence, to mitigate it, to allow violent feelings that have no other safe context for expression to surface and vent. This is healing.

Jack made the following observation during the second year of our group: "It's taken me a long time to feel really comfortable here. In the past I've viewed most other men as my competitors for money, power, or women. Even my friendships and alliances with other men were usually based on competition against other groups of men. Or they were tainted by the feeling that men were just being friends because they ultimately wanted something from me.

"I know that sounds a little paranoid," Jack continued. "Maybe it is. But this is the first group of men I've associated with, since I was a teenager, where relationships are clearly based upon mutual support and shared interests rather than competition. It's a relief to be able to finally let my guard down."

That night, as the meeting was ending, Jack went around and gave every one of us a long hug. This may not sound like a big deal. But for most of us who had spent a lifetime experiencing a backslap, shoulder punch, or handshake as the main form of male contact, it was a profound experience.

Men have a different emotional language and mode of expression than women. Women appear more comfortable with face-to-face intimacy. Men are generally more comfortable with the side-by-side contact that is experienced working on a project, hunting, drinking at a bar, or watching or playing a team sport together. For men, being face-to-face often implies squaring off or sizing each other up—competition or conflict. In the face-to-face contact found in small groups, the focus shifts from *us and them* to *I and thou*. It can be anxiety provoking.

A factor that often inhibits us from forming close male community is the repression many men have been conditioned to engage in around the expression of emotions. We're often afraid that if we reveal what we really feel, we'll be rejected. And the consequences of rejection by male society can be quite serious.

Membership in patriarchal institutions has its privileges, of course. But it also has its price. When men feel that their only connection to the ancestral field of masculinity is through their job, church, or heroic status as a success object, they're compelled to remain affiliated with institutions that may support only men's old roles. Chronic loyalties to confining, anachronistic, and debilitating structures are often based on fear of loss of economic or social power. (Actually, these are often the same thing.) So the idea of change can be threatening.

For many men, conventional corporations, traditional churches, and other patriarchal fraternal organizations partially satisfy a hunger for membership, for being part of the tribe. But these sorts of groups have their own agendas, which may drown out the unique cry of one man's spirit or, worse, exploit it. They're not the type of lodge a group like the new knights represents.

SHARING POWER IN A MEN'S GROUP

There are many ways for men to work together in groups. In a small lodge of six or so, there doesn't seem to be much need for power-sharing techniques. This size seems to afford everyone an opportunity to talk.

That's been true for us in the new knights, who number seven. There have been times when one member or another may be overbearing. But someone always addresses it. We just work it out. Sometimes one member has a pressing issue. At those times it's not unusual for us to spend most of an evening simply working with that one man's struggle. It's inevitable that what touches one of us will touch us all in some way, anyway.

In larger groups, however, it's worthwhile to utilize some means for sharing power. This is so the process doesn't become dominated by any single, strong personality or lobby within the group. One method we've found effective is to use a power object such as a stick of wood, a smooth stone, or other item. We agree that whoever holds the power can speak for a limited time—two, five, or ten minutes. He then must pass it on around the circle. We agree to give our full attention and not interrupt him or comment unless he asks for feedback. This ensures a certain measure of safety for expressing sometimes painfully repressed material. Often we don't need to be fixed, merely heard.

For larger groups of twenty or more, we sometimes use what we call "Roberts' neo-rules of order." By following a few simple principles we've been able to maintain a coherent conversation in a group as large as one hundred. It works in this way: one person initiates a topic. He may speak for a minute or so. Other members wishing to speak indicate through hand signals the way in which they wish to participate. Based upon which direction the current speaker would like to see the conversation take, he chooses the next speaker according to his signal.

Holding up one finger means, "I have a comment to make on this topic." Two fingers mean, "I have a comment that is tangential to this subject." Three mean, "I wish to introduce a new topic." Four mean, "I have a question." And five indicate, "I want a moment of silence." We eventually added a ten, which means "Pass the power along to another speaker. . . now." This is a way, without shaming anyone, that we can collectively move the work along if someone gets stuck, lost inside himself, or power hungry. Believe me, as someone who talks as much as I do quickly discovered, having a thousand fingers waving at you is as sobering a response as any amount of hooting and hollering.

You may want to change the symbols or the form. For example, the vigorous extension of a single middle finger is not unknown. This means, "I have a somewhat different perspective on this topic than the speaker." The important thing is to allow everyone an opportunity to speak without getting lost in power struggles, stilted silence, or domination by those with the strongest opinions or guru status.

Many of the workshops we've attended are dominated by one or a few big leaders. This is a mixed bag. Someone has to get the ball rolling. But then it's important to get out of the way. The whole trend to make certain men the gurus of the male renaissance is a perpetuation of the old heroic model. When men stand up in front of an assembly of men and lecture for huge fees, it's usually not very empowering to the listeners.

All of our stories are equally interesting. Each man's life is a notable and epic myth. You don't need an expensive workshop to discover this. However, it can be worthwhile to attend one to pick up new forms, ideas, and inspiration. Different members of the knights have brought back ideas from various workshops and incorporated them into our group. But most of our work together has come out of our own imaginations.

Empowerment comes through all of us getting off the hero trip, the king trip, the leader trip, and the expert trip. There are no experts when it comes to reclaiming the masculine soul, including me. It's also doubtful that there are any real initiators with some special or magical power to heal masculine wounds. Entertaining that belief is a way of giving away your personal power and remaining a victim, a child, a wounded man. There's an old saying in the Zen community: "If you see the Buddha coming down the road, slay him." Not bad advice in our opinion.

Healing masculinity comes through creating a real, ongoing brotherhood with the men in your day-to-day life and an honest relationship with yourself. Workshops are places to rally around and get some inspiration about how other men are finding their way. Also, something can be awakened in the soul or the body by the collective force of a large group. But the men's movement is not about creating new dogmas, superstars, or personalities.

BREAKING THE SPELL

The inspiration we've found through our men's work has encouraged a number of us to try moving out into the world with new ideas. Books, a play, newspaper, journal, and magazine articles, conferences, workshops, lectures, and newsletters have all emerged from the small circle of men I meet with locally. And this phenomenon is being repeated in many areas across the nation. It's important, however, not to get so caught up in our enthusiasm for social transformation that we lose sight of why we came together in the first place: to give personal support to one another in our daily lives.

If you find that the majority of your lodge's attention is turned toward solving some outside problem, creating some performance, or making a product, chances are you've lost your purpose. That's what we habitually do as men: create works. However, if we do nothing in the world, our group may succumb to narcissism. So we need to find a balance.

The initial work of deepening ourselves occurs in private. It happens in the solitude of our own inner work and in small groups focused on the desires of members rather than some outside agenda. With that foundation we can make works in the world without losing soul or depth in our group. Then works in the world are not a means of avoiding intimacy, but a means of expressing intimacy and our love for the world. Then works make soul.

Social activism is one of the works many of us are involved in. This sort of self-empowerment is one of the ways in which we are turning our private grief into a positive force in the world. We're breaking the spell that keeps us numb to our own pain and to the suffering in the world around us. *Fierceness* is an excellent word, which Robert Bly uses to describe one of the qualities of deep masculinity. Fierceness isn't violence. It can be violent, just as a mother lion protecting her cubs will be violent. But it's not violent by nature. It's important to our self-esteem to understand this difference between fierceness, which is healing, and violence, which is destructive. Too often they're depicted as the same.

A man who wishes to live nonviolently will go crazy if he represses his fierceness as part of his transformation into a peacemaker. This is what happens when men attempt to live the feminized vision of the soft male. It's also why women complain that many new males are lacking in the special vitality that makes men potent.

Waging peace is a fierce activity. It took fierceness, courage, and resolve for Carl to climb two hundred feet up a thousand-year-old redwood tree last summer and say, "I will not allow you to cut down this national treasure." It took fierceness for Jim and Rodger to stand up and face jail for refusing to fight an unjust war in Vietnam. As I write this they, along with Brad, have re-engaged in committed antiwar activism.

It's taken fierceness for Brad to raise two sons alone. It takes courage for Ben to risk altering his successful business formula so he can be more socially responsible. Jack, too, was daring to quit his successful business so he could focus on community service and soul work. It takes fierce commitment to work for positive transformation in a culture that is equally sexist toward the roles of men and women. It takes fierceness to stand up to the violence of other men and women and to protect our children. It takes fierceness for all of us to remain sober and continue to encounter the world, in all its pain and glory, without numbing out.

Much of our fierce activity goes unsung by the culture at large because it's not traditionally heroic. Those who orchestrate war and are heroic on the playing field, the winners in the boardroom and those who succeed in the performing arts, the politically powerful and the rich—these are the men who captivate the imagination of the nation. So we must regularly sing to one another's invisible glory. This keeps hope and commitment alive.

Fierceness is aligned with innate healing power in men's bodies. When we drum, chant, sing, and move together in a powerful way, it engenders a collective force that connects us with the ancestral field of all men who've lived before us. Ritual is a context through which we may move into a deeper connection with the spirit of life, the delight of energy and vitality we all possess naturally as a birthright.

The authentic male perceives his interrelatedness with all life and experiences fierceness as a gift that nature provides for its own protection and preservation. The planet needs warriors and men of conscience. In the current state of affairs we have too many powerful men without ethics and ethical men without power. We need to teach the powerful to have ethics. And the ethical must learn how to become more powerful. Men who are trying to bring a positive spirit into the world need much more support from other men, and from women as well. Yes, authentic men need love and protection, too. Save the Earth Father.

BANG THE DRUM AND RAISE A JOYFUL NOISE

Not all our challenges are quite so dramatic. Fierceness is one quality we're trying to nurture. But frivolity is another. Many of the male gods we've mentioned—Zeus, Krishna, Christ, Pan, Hermes, and Dionysus—have myths concerning their exploits as infants and children. There's something sacred about the innocent, playful, mischievous, and energetic qualities of boyhood.

One night Brad commented, "Those very qualities that make men endearing in childhood are often scorned in adult males—silliness, sensitivity, wildness, unrestrained enthusiasm.

'Grow up.' 'Don't be a baby.' 'Take it like a man,' we're likely to hear. Yet if part of male divinity *is* our childishness, why must we be so quick to abandon it as we grow older?"

As if to answer this inquiry, Jack beckoned us into his new music room. We'd already seen the piano during other meetings at his house. But this night he had other instruments as well: drums, rattles, a marimba, horns, bamboo flutes, ceramic whistles, bells, and other primitive hand instruments. He explained that several years ago he'd subleased some of his commercial space to a tenant for use as a music store. When that concern recently went belly up, the owners gave him all this stuff to settle up on monies owed him.

Jack sat down on the carpet with an impish grin and began pounding out a simple beat on a large Native American-style drum. We joined in, each picking up an instrument, discarding some, trying others, just messing around. We just started feeling our way around with it. At first it was a cacophony. But then we began listening to one another, blending in or standing out as the moment seemed to call for. It wasn't great music, but it was wonderful. We had a good time.

A few weeks later we invited a friend who is a percussionist to come teach us a few simple drumming patterns. We now had something to build on with our own permutations. This isn't necessary by any means. But we found it useful to have a small repertoire of rhythms as a common language to work with in the beginning. Music started to happen.

The most universal, archetypal, and fundamental ritual of male society is expressed through drumming, singing, and dancing together. This is something that has been absent from the lives of most modern men. There are, however, activities like the military, football, and the workplace where rhythm has been an essential element, reflecting this ancient tradition.

Since antiquity, men have charged into battle to the accompaniment of drums and horns. In the modern military there's uniform cadence marching. Men's feet and voices keep the beat. In more formal parades there's also the accompaniment of a drum corps. Football has its chants and half-time drumming. In industrial occupations there's the rhythm of machines and hammers, and the coordinated movements of teamwork in lifting and moving loads. We hear this rhythm in rap music, which evolved out of spirituals and blues. They in turn had their rhythmic origins in the work songs of black slaves, which were transformations of traditional African chants.

Just like hunting, there seems to be a natural love and need for rhythmic immersion in men's bones. All life moves in rhythmic cycles: the ebb and flow of tides, the rotation of the planets and stars, the fluctuation of night and day, the alternation of the seasons, the in and out of our breath. The first thing we're aware of in the womb is the steady heartbeat of our mother.

Drumming seems to access a deep, archetypal layer in our masculine consciousness that's rooted in the natural rhythms of the earth. Drumming resonates with the lower part of our bodies and with something old in the soul. It affords us an opportunity to access our power in a way that is creative, playful, and nurturing. It allows us to be aggressive, loud, intense, and powerful without being destructive.

Micky Hart, the drummer for the Grateful Dead, has stated in his book, *Drumming at the Edge of Magic,* that he feels that drumming actually stimulates the brain in a specific way, which encourages trance states and other alterations of consciousness. Perhaps drumming was a way that ancient men attuned themselves to one another—and to their prey as well—before the hunt. Various rhythms may actually evoke different specific archetypal forces. There may be gods in the drum that can be released.

So we began to start our meetings with about half an hour of drumming. Once we got our drumming more together, we started incorporating vocal sounds, songs, other instruments, and movement. Jack was actually getting pretty good on the piano. I'd played a little guitar and keyboards in rock bands for several years. Ben had had flute lessons as a kid and was able to make some very nice melodies. And Jim was rapidly beginning to find his way around a conga drum.

Carl had no musical experience and felt sort of awkward at first. He'd just sit and listen, nodding to the rhythm, enjoying the show. But later, with a little encouragement, he got into keeping a steady beat on the big drum. Carl soon became rock steady as the bass-drum heartbeat of our new ensemble.

Although Rodger also had little musical ability he was pretty good at extemporaneous poetics—kind of like spontaneous rapping, but without necessarily trying to rhyme everything. "Try expressing your feelings of the day or the week while the rest of the circle drums with you," he suggested. "Don't by shy, it's okay, you can get away with it here, it's just us," he encouraged. "Are you *ahhhhh* or *arrrrgh* today?" he asked. "Give yourself the freedom to be inarticulate, just let it out, however it comes." Soon we were growling, sighing, hooting, and howling while the drumming went on.

Then Rodger taught us something he called *dream singing*. "Try singing about the images of a dream you've had recently," he suggested. "Don't worry about the tune or timbre. Croak or groan it out if that's the only way it comes. Experiment. Tell us your story in prose, a chant, or song. No more talking! We've talked enough. Now's a time for singing," he cried.

Boy, Rodger had become real bossy all of a sudden. But we just went along with it. Why not try something new? We went around the room, and each man would sing his heart song or dream song to the best of his ability, while the others kept a quiet, steady beat or embellished with melodic instruments. We connected with some deep feelings this way and had a lot of fun. We also sang pieces from a lot of old rock songs, dirty limericks, and childhood rhymes we hadn't sung in ages.

Brad had never played a lick on an instrument, either. But he turned out to be a wild dancer, something we'd never known about him. During the next week's drumming session Brad had us getting up and moving around the room. He suggested, "Try expressing how you feel tonight with your body. Or dance like an animal image from your dreams. Move from deep within. Keep your knees bent and stay low to the earth," he said as he led us in a circle dance around the room.

This is the way most native peoples move in their dances. Locked knees and rigid postures are an invention of the Western urban culture. Bent knees bring us closer to the earth. So now we were dream dancing, too, playing our hand instruments and dancing around the room. This was way-out for this group of guys. Most of us felt pretty awkward at first. But with Brad's encouragement, we got into it more and more. And we had a blast.

We don't do all of this very often. But this sort of play has taken many of us to some very good places. It's helped us to connect with the old gods and to access feelings we usually don't express when we just talk about things. We usually feel lighter, energized, and more open emotionally after a little bit of banging on stuff, vocalizing, and jumping around.

This sort of activity calls forth images of Pan, Orpheus, Coyote, Legba, Shiva, and Dionysus. Our men's lodge has become a place for relief, a place to drop our formal presentation to the world. So much of our lives as men is about performance and achieving excellence in all our outward expressions that we often lose the pleasure of doing things just for the joy of it.

One cautionary note: in some cases I've found that men can actually use this kind of activity to *avoid* the expression of deep feeling to one another. Men can use drumming and manic, festive dancing just like drugs, alcohol, work, and other forms to avoid the discomfort that can emerge in the face of real intimacy. So don't let your group process overwhelm your individual needs for healing wounds, inspiring and supporting one another to make positive changes, and deepening your relationship to soul. Becoming the best samba drummer on the West Coast or memorizing the most Rilke poems are worthy ambitions, but are not the same thing.

Men's ritual activity is more about communing with one another than performing. In fact it's important not to be concerned about performance. It doesn't matter how well you do it, just that you do it. All you need is a drum and some other guys with drums or other simple instruments. And don't forget to take off your tie.

DANCING THE DREAM AWAKE IN THE WORLD

One night, a few months after we started incorporating this sort of activity in our group, a bunch of us went out dancing with our wives and girlfriends. At one point we were all out on the dance floor. I don't know exactly how it started, but I noticed Jim bumping into Brad. Then he started dancing around Rodger, bumping into him. After a bit we all started kind of slam-dancing into one another in the center of the floor. The women kept dancing with each other to the side, looking our way occasionally, laughing and shaking their heads. Uh-oh. The guys had finally lost it completely.

I had seen women dancing together all my life, but this was the first time I'd seen men dance together in public outside of a gay bar. And I was one of them. Everyone in the club was looking our way, but we didn't really care. We were having fun. Then we started dancing as a group with the women. All ten of us dancing together, free style. Very tribal. Very free. It deepened our sense of community.

There are many people today teaching the rituals and ceremonies of various cultures. But we don't really need to learn rites and practices from other times or remote contexts. In some cases, incorporating symbols from some other cultural context can actually get in the way of learning how to access the knowledge in our own bones.

It's always seemed a little odd to me to witness hundreds of white, middle-class American men in various workshops across the nation performing African, Caribbean, or American Indian music as their primary ritual forms. Having rejected much of Western tradition, some men adopt the teachings of other cultures in search of meaningful reconnection with spirit, earth, and soul. James Hillman sometimes describes this mythologically impoverished condition as lacking a "nose," an animallike sense of direction that moves toward soul. This can create a tendency to romanticize cultural traditions far removed from our own.

Cross-cultural traditions can give us a sense of how other men from other times and places have found a way to celebrate *their* lives together. And we've learned some great chants from other cultures, which we've enjoyed incorporating into our repertoire of ritual music. But ultimately we must find our own way. This is a more challenging but more satisfying task.

Our personal and ancestral histories are also rich cultural resources. In our group alone we have ancestral songs and dances from Russia, Romania, Italy, Poland, Greece, Israel, Germany, and Scotland. Our American music, from rap and rock to folk to jazz, also has much to offer. It's evolved out of African tribal roots but has also transformed as it blended with the rhythms and images of our own time and modern culture. In fact, native peoples from Mongolia to Africa now delight in dancing to Western pop music. It's our indigenous shamanic music.

We also may begin to perceive deep structures in our consciousness containing as yet unrevealed forms and myths appropriate for us in this time. Therefore, our own individually unique movement and poetics, emerging from our own dreams and visions, shouldn't be underrated or seen as inferior to any other culture's exotic tradition. We all have the capacity to make our own medicine. Out of our dream singing and dream dancing we can evolve our own particular ritual forms.

Another way men have traditionally reaffirmed their integration with the natural, cyclic world is through periodic ceremonies that incorporate elements of sacred music, song, and dance. Ceremonies mark the passages of individual lives through birth, adolescence, success at the hunt, marriage, death, and many smaller, yet significant, events along the way. Ceremonies acknowledge changes in the community around us and in the natural world.

We all share a relatedness to the cycles and rhythms of nature. When we fail to recognize it, fragmentation, sickness, imbalance, and weaknesses may creep into our lives. A few decades of industrial society haven't erased our need for community, tribal connectedness with other men, and rituals that affirm our place in the natural order of things. The changing of the seasons, the cycles of the moon and stars, and other natural phenomena are also markers of our changing lives. We're trying to learn how to honor these changes in the natural world and our personal lives with self-generated rituals. We're learning to express ourselves directly from our depths, without always staying locked up in our heads. We're learning to reconnect with nature.

HEALING THE ANCIENT WOUNDS BETWEEN MEN AND WOMEN

As we've started to engage in community gatherings and celebrations, we've come into more contact with groups of women who are also doing ritual and recovery work. They have expressed a great deal of curiosity about our men's-lodge work. In some cases they've also voiced some apprehension. Betty Friedan has said that the men's movement is trying to get back to the cave man and that it's definition of masculinity is based on dominance. In that vein Carol Bly recently wrote:

> The men's separatist movement is frightening. Separatism breeds feelings of superiority and imbalance—male bonding usually offers permission to regress. It is disguised as getting-free-of-mother, but that's very likely a cover-up: It is getting free of being civilized.

Groups like the new knights are indeed severing many of civilization's psychological snares. However, this doesn't imply the barbaric threat Carol Bly or others may feel. Getting free of civilization—or mother, for that matter—doesn't mean abandoning ethical, responsible, or genteel behavior. In fact, just the opposite is true: there's something lovely, noble, generative, and kind in our uncivilized depths. Men who remain stuck in the destructive roles that civilized urban culture spawned are more of a threat to women than any regression that could ever emerge from a men's lodge.

I've rarely heard any statements at men's gatherings in which violence, domination, or any other frightening suggestions were made regarding relations with women. Mostly we are trying to work through our own struggles and restore a healthy, integrated sense of masculine pride and joyfulness. Concerns about women are often completely absent or occupy only a small portion of our discussions.

We need to begin creating forums for healing the ancient wounds between the sexes in a protected atmosphere of mutuality, respect, and goodwill. Ultimately this is the real work ahead of us. Women have changed in many ways. Men are changing as well. The women's movement inadvertently freed men from some of the burdens we've been carrying regarding the male gender role. Our work together as men will also inevitably support women entering a new era of equality and community with men. Members of the women's movement have discovered that there are limits to the degree of unilateral growth and societal transformation they can effect: they can only go so far without men. The men's movement will also need to enter this social dialogue to seek new common ground with women.

The foundation for a new community based on partnership, mutual goodwill, and a healing of the wounds between the sexes is beginning to develop. This is based on men and women in forum, coming from a position of equal strength, support, and intimacy within their same-sex group. For example, most of the women involved in relationships with the new knights formed their own group after we'd been meeting for about a year. This has strengthened them, brought balance to our community at times, and also made our lodge feel less threatening to them.

In conjunction with some other men's groups, the new knights have recently begun meeting on occasion with several women's groups. This work has been very valuable. It has deepened the intimacy and level of understanding in our entire community. This work also has improved communication between a number of the couples who are involved in each group.

Naturally, at first we heard a lot of fear, distrust, anger, and needs for control coming from a generation of women who've suffered under the domination of uninitiated men. We also heard that women really want us in their lives, are hopeful about the changes we're making, and want to know how to help. We've shared with women that we fully support the deconstruction of the old patriarchy. But we also feel we can't continue to bear the blame or apologize for two thousand years of men's domination of women. We can't be blamed for all the sins of our fathers.

We're completely willing, however, to be accountable for our own actions and to hear women's concerns.

We want women to look at the ways in which they cocreate or perpetuate many of the problems we face and to understand the ways in which men have been equally victimized by a dysfunctional culture. This was a more difficult idea for some women, who were attached to their role as victims and also felt that feminine principles were superior to masculine ones.

The work toward a polytheistic, culturally plural, partnership society continues to propel us forward. We're moving toward new solutions, a culture that holds sacred masculine images and sacred feminine images as equal partners. Then our personal relationships can mirror that equality. We can't simply overthrow patriarchy and revert to some matriarchal culture that we may already have experimented with in our human history and, for whatever reasons, rejected. Recent visions of partnership put forth by some well-meaning feminists still fail to embrace a vision of archetypal masculinity as a sacred and universal life-affirming force equal to the Goddess.

The transformation we wish to effect is the creation of a balanced partnership between men and women. However, it's important for us to develop ourselves as men without our soul work being defined, directed, or controlled by women. So we need to tread slowly on this path. It's important to hold a strong boundary around our men's meetings and not give them up to do this gender work. A lot of men, after meeting for a year or two, think, "Okay, we're all healed, initiated, conscious men now. Let's get back together with the women."

It's important not to enter the combat ground between the sexes prematurely or naively. If too much attention is given to this sort of work it can be at the expense of men contacting and healing their own pain. First men must find their own mythology, solidarity, alliance, brotherhood, and sacred relationship to other men and the earth. It's only through such healthy men, established in their own field of masculine soul, encountering women who've also found their own power that we'll ever find balance and equality. Healing and ritual work with women is something that should happen in addition to our men's-lodge work, not instead of it.

All told, though, we've found women to be very supportive of our work. And we've had a lot of fun dancing, singing, praying, and honestly confronting one another in these meetings.

Many of the collective gender issues discussed in these mixed gatherings affect the day-to-day lives of individual couples. Many couples report improved relations. Perhaps we can accept complaints collectively that we would reject if they were presented to us individually by our partners.

The principles of alchemy state that only that which has first been properly separated can later be fully joined. In chemistry this is expressed as the need to begin with pure, elemental ingredients in order to create more complex, balanced compounds that will remain stable over time. Brother/sister lodges that are engaged in dialogue represent a revival of the most ancient and natural human societies. A balanced society is one in which both men and women have the security of their own separate spaces and are firmly established in their own gender identity. Then they can cooperate without dominating one another. They can come together without depending on the other gender to provide all their intellectual, emotional, material, or spiritual needs. Perhaps the age of codependency and denial is finally at an end, and the new century will usher in an age of true partnership.

THE TENTH TASK OF MEN: TO BUILD MALE COMMUNITY AND BEGIN HEALING THE WOUNDS BETWEEN THE SEXES

Being a member of a men's lodge is not an end in itself. Groups will change. They'll come and go. However, creating a lodge can draw to us the allies we need at that moment in time on our journey of personal transformation. That transformation remains with us all our lives regardless of our membership, friendships, or relationships. This is our real treasure in life: our connection to soul.

The initiated man—a man in connection with his masculine depths—has a possibility for tremendous freedom in life. His decisions are based on choice, not some sick dependency or codependence on a dysfunctional familial, fraternal, social, economic, or political system. It's not easy to claim this freedom. Reimagining ourselves as men takes courage. We all need to learn how to support one another, be compassionate with each other, and consistently love ourselves along the way.

Many men organize around different issues. If the ritual forms help, try them. If not, discard them. But keep meeting. Play poker or go fishing. But keep communicating with one another and telling the whole truth of your experience. A men's group, lodge, or ritual space is a place where we can exercise our natural tendency and desire to be just with men once in a while.

Based upon our experiences in our lodge we began to examine all our social institutions from the perspective of authentic masculinity. During the course of our group we had often discussed our past experiences in therapy and stories we'd heard from other men. Most of us felt we'd gotten more out of our lodge than any past experience in one-to-one therapy.

We began to wonder about what might be missing for men in psychology today. This was a task more aligned with my personal, professional concerns. But the knights agreed it was something that affected them all as well. How do men get healed? Where else should men go for healing? We all still wondered, yet we felt we now knew a few things about this.

> *Building male community through reinstituting sacred men's lodges was the tenth task we attempted. Bringing some new vision to the field of psychology, based on our experiences together, was our next task.*

CHAPTER 11

Toward a New Male Psychology

The thousand and one statements that are made every day—"Isn't that just like a man . . . Women are more sensitive than men"—have to be swept from the mind like tattered autumn leaves from the garden-path before it is possible to think clearly at all.
    Margaret Mead, 1949

There have been some changes since Margaret Mead made the above comment over forty years ago. But not that much has really changed concerning our cultural stereotypes about men and women. As we have seen, many of men's physical and mental health problems still stem from our misguided attempts to live up to an unrealistic, anachronistic ideal of masculinity. In our quest for healing and our continued exploration of the masculine soul, the knights began to talk about our experiences, both positive and negative, when seeking help from mental-health professionals.

One night Jack told us, "I went to couples counseling before my second divorce. By the second session it was clear our therapist had aligned herself with my wife's problems. She clearly understood every little detail of why my wife was miserable. But she had very little understanding for the equally distressing issues I was facing. So naturally most of her suggestions were about what *I* could do to change the situation."

"That's pretty much what couples counseling was like for me as well," said Rodger. "The problem, as far as the therapist was concerned, was *me*—not the dynamics of our relationship. Before I quit going I asked if we could include a man as cotherapist. But somehow that wasn't possible, and my wife was unwilling to work with a man alone because she thought we'd gang up on her."

We've already discussed Brad's experience of being belittled by a social-services counselor he had gone to for help as a single parent. He also sought counseling from county mental-health services. "I was feeling really ragged the year before I joined this group," he confided. "But the first counselor I saw was a woman who was obviously uncomfortable with me, so I asked for a man. But he was such a wimp! I couldn't stand his mewling platitudes and left after one session. Finally I had a very good experience with the California Vietnam Veterans' Center. The guy there was a vet. He wasn't even a trained therapist. But he really understood my issues and wasn't afraid of my horror stories. I saw him regularly for almost a year. I don't think I would have made it through that time without his steady, patient support. It sort of primed me for our group."

That night I shared my own experiences in psychology. "In training there were a lot of courses and specialized seminars that dealt with issues of specific concern to women. But almost nothing focused on men except for concerns about violence. Practically everything I've learned about male psychology has been *outside* of my graduate training, internships, and continuing education in various treatment settings. In fact, I've learned more about the psychology of men in this group than I did during six years of graduate school."

Psychology has a profound influence on attitudes toward men and women in the general culture. Some writers have commented that psychologists are even beginning to approximate the function and power of influence that priests previously held. Psychological attitudes permeate how we think people should be—what we consider to be normal as opposed to abnormal. Through psychologists' influences on patients in therapy, and through research publications, public education, a multitude of professional and popular books, radio talk shows, movies, television, and the print media, the ideas of a handful of thinkers are propelled into every aspect of our culture.

The reworking of the psychology of women in the last twenty-five years has been an important transformation of the field. It's significantly altered our cultural perspective on women and supported women in their emotional, social, and political liberation. The revolution feminism brought to psychology, however, has been seriously unbalanced. There's been a vacuum in its wake. Very little attention has been given to the changing face of masculinity. The current cultural myth seems to be that since men have more privileges, their psychological issues are not as pressing as those of women. As we've seen, however, objective statistics and the subjective experiences of men show that this is not the case.

In the first section of this book we recounted many areas of physical and mental health in which men are actually *more* at risk than women. In fact a number of surveys indicate that women aged eighteen to sixty-five generally report greater happiness in life than men. Men outscore women only from age sixty-five to seventy, the early years of retirement. This subjective assessment of the differences between men's and women's mental well-being is underscored by the objective fact that 73 percent of all suicides are male. If one adds the disproportionately high incidence of single-car wrecks and other fatal *accidents* involving men, this suicide figure is even higher.

So men, as well as women, are having lots of problems with modern life. And men are changing in many ways. But male psychology is still far behind the times. We need to start looking with fresh perspectives at the ways in which society attempts to help men and the ways in which it fails. We need to develop new standards of normalcy for masculinity and new treatment methodologies that meet the gender-specific needs of men who are suffering.

THE GREAT MOTHER AND LOST FATHER IN PSYCHOLOGY

Many modern clinicians, writers, and researchers in psychology believe that since most of the pioneers in psychology were patriarchal men, the field has not adequately thought through women's issues. This is true. In many cases, women were categorized as pathological for expressing legitimate social protest against a sexist culture that denied women equal opportunities for self-development. The work of the fathers of psychology was unavoidably colored by their times, the cultural and political attitudes of their society, and the limitations of their worldview.

From the very beginning, moreover, men like Charcot, Freud, Adler, Breuer, and Jung, and the men and women who followed them, focused a disproportionate amount of their concern on women, especially the influential power of the mother in personality development. The study of hysteria, which was thought to be primarily an affliction of women, was the impetus for the development of psychiatry. Most early psychiatric publications were about female patients: Anna O___, Emmy Von M___, Dora ___, and others. Subsequently, hundreds of writers developed psychological theories, still used today, based upon early studies that were predominantly concerned with women.

Feminist revisions of Freud's ideas began almost as soon as his ideas came out. Some of his female students, like Karen Horney, took issue with various theories about the nature of women's psychology. They also began to consider the sociopolitical implications of condescending psychological ideas that pathologize women.

As more and more women have come into the field in recent decades, they, too, have disproportionately focused on women's needs. While it is true that psychological theory had considered some elements of male psychology, all told, the understanding of men's authentic psychological and spiritual issues has been poorly developed by both men and women in the field.

In many cases men have been ignored altogether. For example, today most psychological doctrine still holds the mother as the primary parent. The child's relationship with the mother—the *dyad*—remains the primary, major focus of attention. This mother-centered psychology implies that the father's role is secondary, incidental. But this is contrary to the experience of the millions of modern fathers who are as engaged with their families as are mothers.

There's little attention given to today's father as a care giver and to his relationship to the child and mother. Only a few psychologists have considered the *triad* as the primary developmental environment of the child. Psychology also practically ignores the concerns of the almost 3 million men in this country who are *single* parents. Over 90 percent of all the studies done on child development and parenting focus only on the influence of mothers.

Modern psychology is still rooted in the thinking of the nineteenth century, which drew from the Enlightenment and the more distant classical period of European thought. When it comes to considerations regarding masculinity and femininity, most of these ideas are now hopelessly anachronistic. Yet the most popular test of gender specificity in psychology today still characterizes femininity as *nurturing*—helpful, expressive, and empathetic—and masculinity as *controlling*—dominant, confident, and assertive.

Men in our culture today are undergoing a major restructuring of the basic paradigms governing masculine consciousness and behavior. It's important to understand and uncover those aspects of the inner psychic life of men that are essentially masculine in nature. We need to develop a working model that meets the needs of modern men on the basis of their own individual, personal experience. In many cases this is very different from the constructs that have come out of heroic, monotheistic, patriarchal thinking or the revisions of feminist theory.

The depth psychologist Eugene Monick notes:

> Masculinity is as much an enigma as femininity. . . . Because it is inadequately based in psychoanalytic theory, it becomes an enemy of the unconscious for Freud and consort for Jung. . . . Psychoanalytic theory, whether Freudian or Jungian, gives singular primacy to the mother as the basis of life. This is an error.

The father is almost completely ignored in Jungian psychology. In formulations considering the foundations of consciousness itself, masculinity is absent altogether. James Hillman addresses the problem that such overwhelming emphasis on the mother in psychology presents for men, "who [are] ever being told by analytical psychology that [they] must sacrifice intellect, persona, extraversion for the sake of soul, feeling, inwardness, i.e., anima."

In psychology today, even the more thoughtful literature is dominated by a feminine perspective. Depth psychology, as initially developed by Carl Jung, metaphorically designates the unconscious as feminine. It regards waking consciousness and the ego as masculine. Jung, who deepened the thinking of his predecessor Sigmund Freud, developed the idea of the inner man—the animus—and the inner woman—the anima. Over time, due to the influence of a generation of writers who followed Jung, *anima* has come to be used more frequently to mean soul, or psyche itself.

Eric Neumann, who had an early influence on the field of analytical psychology, refers to the origin of psyche as solely feminine throughout his writings, saying:

> The Great Round, the Great Container . . . the elementary character of the Feminine . . . almost always has a "maternal" determinant. The ego, consciousness, the individual, regardless whether male or female, are childlike and dependent in their relation to it.

It may have been useful to envision the soulful aspect of men as feminine during a period in history when men were, as depicted by Hillman, "rigidly patriarchal, puritanically defensive, extravertedly willful and unsoulful." However, as we begin to approach the next century, modern men must question some of these philosophical foundations.

In analytical psychology, masculine consciousness is mostly understood as *solar:* self-effulgent, egoic, dominating, above the horizon of consciousness, with no capacity for reflection and receptivity. Thus our model of masculinity is degraded and limited, supposedly deriving its fecundity from the unconscious feminine within. Men's capacity to feel, be touched, experience their interiority, and interact with the unconscious is expressed as occurring through connectedness with anima or the inner woman.

We need a more expansive psychology, which embraces the possibility of a moist, soulful, dark, authentic, mysterious, lunar, deep, and earthy masculinity. This search for a new language—a new paradigm—is in reaction to what the Jungian analyst Patricia Berry refers to as "the dogma of gender." Charles Poncé queries: "Is the concept of the masculine and the feminine a myth, a projection, nothing more than the deep psyche's tendency to personify?"

If so, may we now project the authentic qualities of masculine and feminine soul along somewhat different lines than have been drawn so far? I believe so. However, only a few depth psychologists have begun to put forth personifications of the masculine as deep and generative, full of soul and feeling.

NURTURE OVER NATURE: IS SOCIETY TO BLAME?

Feminist researchers assert that there are few *essential* differences between the sexes, that most of our differences in behavior stem from our acculturation. In general feminists tend to seek environmental reasons for whatever differences there are between men's and women's behavior, abilities, and psychological make-up. However, the authors of a comprehensive text that analyzed hundreds of studies on sex differences concluded, "Feminists deemphasize and devalue biological factors in sex differences for essentially *political* reasons [my italics]." And there's a good reason for how this ideology evolved.

In the past, male-dominated empirical science used sexist biological theories to justify the denial of women's equal rights. Women have been completely justified in their attempts to correct this prejudicial theme influencing early Western psychology.

As a result, today we've grown beyond the belief that women have inferior abilities based upon their biology. However, as we've seen throughout this book, some peculiar myths about men still persist.

The nature (inherited/genetic) versus nurture (learned/conditioned) debate rages on, with countless studies supporting both views:

1. Nature: men and women have different behavior based on biological predispositions.
2. Nurture: men and women have different behavior based on cultural influences in their socialization.

Most likely, though, neither of the above theories is correct. Rather, it seems the behaviors of women and men are influenced by a combination of psychological, physiological, endocrinological, cultural, and even transpersonal influences (from the archetypes of gender). But we can't even begin to attempt to reconcile this scientific quandary here. It's enough for us to know that, for whatever reasons, the sexes are different in many ways. Therefore, they may require differing approaches to their psychological problems.

The implications of these differences need to be better understood by psychology. We need to start giving men the same sort of consideration and attention to their gender-specific needs that women have received over the last few decades. We must begin to ask why so many behavioral problems, as enumerated in the first section of this book, are disproportionately centered around men.

The radical feminist response is that men are ontologically flawed. But this runs counter to the theory of no essential predisposed difference, coming from the same camp. Also, paradoxically, there's been an implied tone from many women and men that women are innately morally superior to men. This also belies the equality theory. The more moderate feminist view is that our problems arise from patriarchal influences in the cultural training of boys and men. Their prescription is for women to be more involved in the institutions that influence personality development.

However, as we detailed in the first section of the book, the primary parental influence in the home today is overwhelmingly feminine. Half our children have no father in the home; for the rest, he's often not very present. Additionally almost all childcare workers, who fill the gap for working parents, are female. In the field of education about 75 percent of B.A.'s and M.A.'s and well over half the Ph.D.'s are granted to women.

In psychology, women account for 70 percent of bachelor's degrees, 65 percent of master's degrees, and over half the Ph.D.'s. Female social workers outnumber males four to one. In primary education 90 percent of teachers are women. The majority of child psychologists are also women. Yet our problems with boys and young men are getting worse, not better. So women alone clearly cannot turn this around. We also need men's committed involvement.

There are more male educators at the college level. By that stage of life, however, a young man's behavior is already set to a large degree. What concerns us here is the cultural influence on a young man's character during the developmental stages of his life. Also, even though universities have more male educators, they usually lack even a single course in men's studies. Meanwhile, there are thousands of courses and over six hundred university departments devoted to women's studies nationwide. And this number is growing steadily. Not surprisingly, women entering college now outnumber men, who are the new minority.

Several colleagues of mine who have attempted to institute men's-studies courses have reported being met with the derisive sentiment that the last two thousand years of education already have focused on men. This perspective, however, is another sad distortion of the truth. Education has focused on patriarchal values, not the deeper issues of masculine soul—the authentic inner lives of ordinary men. There are now a few hundred courses addressing men's issues across the nation. But for the most part they are under the umbrella of women's-studies departments. The study of authentic masculinity has not yet claimed a forum even remotely equal to the feminist initiative.

The above statistics document what any man who has been educated in America or ever sought psychological or social services already knows. Men have abdicated equal responsibility and interest in the fields that most influence the development of character or try to modify its pathological expressions. The heroic model, into which young boys are molded, has not been instituted solely by some mysterious distant patriarchy. It also emanates from large numbers of women actively involved in the early education of boys. Parenting, primary and secondary education, social services, and counseling psychology are dominated by women.

Even at the lay level of self-help, parenting and pop-psychology books on women's issues fill the shelves. There are thousands of titles directed at women's interests for self-development and recovery. But even in the enlightened 1990s, with the emerging men's movement, there are still only a few books for men. Almost every bookstore has an entire section on women's psychology. However, only a few stores have even a small shelf of similar books for men.

Men have been either too preoccupied with heroic achievements, too numb to really face ourselves, or so shamed about being men that we've habitually focused on the pain of women while ignoring our own disorders. It's time men began to change this social trend and become more involved in parenting, early education, social services, and mental-health services for men. Neither our historical partriarchal attitudes nor more recent matriarchal approaches are valid or useful for us today.

ARE OUR SCHOOLS DEFICIENT IN MASCULINE SOUL?

Today the primary-school classroom is a very feminine environment. Neatness, conformity, quietness, politeness, verbal skills, and other historically *feminine* virtues are highly emphasized there. But boys are often more active, disorderly, and aggressive, and less verbal, than girls. Consequently boys have greater failure rates and are perceived as having more personality problems in school. Since they're socialized to be more autonomous, they're often less interested in pleasing the teacher than girls are. They're often frustrated by repetitive drills in skills at which they're the weakest. Then they're labeled as having attention-deficit disorders. But for many reasons it's often harder for boys to sit still in a classroom. They're restless and energetic, not wrong or deviant.

In too many cases drugs like Ritalin are used now to calm boys down, rather than educators taking a hard look at the style of teaching, values, and the structure of the classroom. We don't give complacent girls drugs to *normalize* them and make them more assertive. If boys are more *deviant,* it may point to a failure in our educational system to accommodate the differing gender styles and modes of learning of boys and girls. Boys are expected to conform to an environment that is often contrary to their masculine self-image. They usually lack a strong masculine presence that can nurture the development of their deep masculinity and contain their aggression with a fearless, loving firmness. They may rebel against the control or criticism of mother in the school.

If they rebel enough, they quickly come to the attention of social agencies and disciplinarians. Corporal punishment is an institutionalized form of child abuse still practiced in thirty states. This abuse is predominantly directed at boys and affects approximately 2 million students, with as many as twenty thousand of them seeking medical attention for bruises every year. This phenomenon is consistent with boys' home environments, where they are generally subjected to a greater degree and frequency of physical punishment and abuse than girls. Boys are also drugged, hospitalized, and locked up in juvenile institutions much more frequently than girls.

Wild, masculine hunting energy is translated as hyperactivity, nonconformity, and poor social adjustment. But most pathology is culture specific. What's considered normal behavior in one time and place is crazy in another. Restless hunger for action would meet with praise, be encouraged, and be *positively directed* by older men in a hunter society. But it's called pathological and is condemned in our urban culture. My *deviant* adolescent boys in the wilderness drove this point home to everyone who worked with them. Their personalities positively changed in response to their experience of themselves as successfully adapted for survival in the challenging context of the wilderness.

We need to take another look at coeducation and ask if it really is the best idea for all boys. If we persist in coeducation, then should we at least have some period of the day or week when boys are in the company of only other boys and men? And shouldn't this be something other than the competitive environment of sports, the aggression training of ROTC, or the punitive environment of social-adjustment classes?

In ancient Greece young men were educated while walking alongside their fellow students and teachers. This satisfied their bodies' need for activity and stimulation while simultaneously engaging their minds in abstract thought. This style of education may be more supportive to a male-specific, hunter-style of learning. A counselor and teacher in the Los Angeles school system recently told me that she has been experimenting with teaching boys outdoors. She reports that on those occasions they appear less agitated. They feel freer to move their bodies and are more stimulated by the surrounding environment. This makes them feel less bored. Rather than being distracted from instruction, she found that they act out less, that their attention span grows, and that their writing and comprehension significantly improve.

Boys need an environment where their rowdiness is occasionally given an outlet, even appreciated, where they're not shamed or controlled, repeatedly told to be quiet and sit still. Maybe we need to institute courses like boys' conga drumming, rap dancing, rock-band practice, or some other loud, physical, aggressive, disorderly, noncompetitive activity for which boys could get as much credit as for good spelling. Shop courses also need to be given greater status and perceived as being as laudable as college-preparatory courses.

Boys need to have their aggressiveness directed and limited in a way that does not shame them for being physically activated—maybe something like ropes challenge courses, in which participants climb on cables and ropes, combining risk taking with teamwork and trust building. Or boys might prefer to learn mathematics and geometry in the concrete context of building a house together, rather than the abstract context of the classroom where they must disconnect from the energy in their bodies.

Cooperative sports and projects like these also go a long way toward building foundations for soulful male community, instead of pitting young men against one another in ways that plant the seeds of future alienation from other men. Loneliness, isolation, and low self-esteem are devastating to young men's psychology. These experiences are the fertile ground from which the seeds of antisocial behavior grow. At this time in our culture we need to focus just as much attention on building masculine self-esteem as on academic skills. They go together. It is doubtful that either goal can be well accomplished without the other.

Consider the boy with an absent father, overcontrolled by his mother, with mostly women teachers at school. Much of the control in his life is directed by women, yet most of the discipline for resisting that control is meted out by men: vice-principals, coaches, his father when he comes home, or other men designated to deal with troubled boys. It's not unreasonable to suspect that a lot of boys act out just so they *can* attract some strong male attention in their lives, even if that attention is negative. This idea is consistent with the experience of most of the male counselors I talked to during the years I worked in residential treatment centers. Acting out is often a cry for masculine attention and limit setting, even if it's punitive. But a consistent positive, male-affirming presence would be much preferable.

In her book *The Feminized Male,* Patricia Sexton laments that most male teachers are themselves feminized and therefore can do little to offset the damage done to boys' masculinity by the feminized classroom. Unfortunately, men are generally socialized away from pursuing careers as primary-school teachers. Working with young children is often perceived as an unmanly occupation. Some studies even indicate that men who want to work with children are perceived by many people as suspiciously variant.

There's a persistent idea in our culture today that feminine virtues are somehow more positive than masculine ones. But this is simply a reversal of the old sexist thinking many women and men have been struggling to eliminate from our culture. We clearly have a need for *fierce* men to become more involved at every level of boys' education and development. We also need to look at bad-boy behavior from a perspective that attempts to meet boys as they are, instead of trying to merely resocialize them with soul-negating behavioral or soul-numbing chemical methods.

Increasing numbers of youth gangs may be forming as a misguided attempt to fill the need every young man has for male community. But more socially nurturing behavior will come from connection with our ethical depths, not from merely increasing levels of outside constraint and control. Ritual, initiation, male mentoring, wilderness work, and authentic male-lodge society may help young men connect with those depths.

NATURE OVER NURTURE: IS BIOLOGY TO BLAME?

Why do boys have more problems with verbal skills than girls? Why do they suffer more from dyslexia, speech difficulties, and other verbal learning disabilities? In chapter 2 we cited studies that show that boys generally get less tactile and verbal stimulation from their mothers than girls do. This may also actually inhibit boys' neurological development, since neural pathways and sheathing, still being formed during the first year and a half of life, respond positively to tactile stimulation by growing thicker and stronger. Parents who become more involved with their infant sons may reverse this problem. This is a provocative idea for future study.

It's also possible that modern men, like our ancient hunting ancestors, still share a different mode of feeling or a less verbal language of expression than women. Earlier in this book, we discussed the silent male language style and other male/female differences related to a distinct ancestral development as male hunters and female gatherers. This is not merely a romantic, anthropological notion concerning our differences. Female superiority in verbal skills and male superiority in spatial tasks may not, as many feminist theorists suggest, simply be related to socialization and prejudices in education.

Recent research on brain physiology demonstrates some significant anatomical differences in the structure of men's and women's brains. These gender-specific anomalies may reflect differences between men and women in their biological tendencies toward certain abilities. Portions of the corpus callosum, which connects the right and left hemispheres of the brain, are disproportionately larger in women than in men. Sandra Witelson, a neuropsychologist, now believes that the anatomical gender differences in the brain, as indicated by research on the corpus callosum, are "just the tip of the iceberg."

Each hemisphere of the brain controls different functions. Men are more lateralized: they tend to think with one side of their brain or the other. Some researchers think this might enhance men's ability to focus more one-pointedly on certain tasks. Women, on the other hand, appear to have a better connection between the two hemispheres. This may enhance their ability to think holistically, to integrate intellect and feeling more easily. The *New York Times* reporter Daniel Goleman summarized some of this research on the differences in men's and women's abilities as related to brain physiology, saying,

> Girls begin to speak earlier than boys and women are generally more fluent with words than men and make fewer mistakes in grammar and pronunciation. On the other hand, men, on average, tend to be better than women at certain spatial tasks, such as drawing maps of places they have been and rotating imagined geometric images in their minds—a skill useful in mathematics, engineering and architecture.

This whole area of research is full of claims and counterclaims. It's not clear whether these differences are caused by environmental influences—like the tactile and verbal deprivation of boys and the restriction of girls' physical activities—or are innate biological differences. At this time we really can't say definitively whether men and women are essentially the same or different in ways other than their sexual characteristics. But from our perspective, it seems evident that we're quite different in many ways.

THE SECRET LANGUAGE OF MEN

A few centuries of urban culture and a few decades of new social theory are not going to change the biological resonance from the past several million years of human culture. There are several separate ancient tunes still humming in our masculine and feminine DNA. There's nothing to suggest that either the traditional hunting role or the gathering role was in some way superior. In fact, in most pretechnological cultures, where men and women supplied a roughly equal amount of food, their social status was about the same. So we needn't be afraid to look at the possibility that men and women really are quite different in a number of ways.

Most pretechnological societies differentiated tasks along gender lines. Hunting demanded the greater physical strength and endurance of the male body. Hunting also required the development of strong spatial skills. This allowed men to travel long distances without getting lost. It made them able to communicate the location of distant places to one another and to find their way home after days of wandering. The development of refined visual acuity made spotting prey easier. Men's stronger hand-eye coordination and superior gross motor skills made bringing down the prey more likely. These are areas in which men still test higher today.

Historically, women's superior verbal skills were needed to organize and catalogue the many different foods, medicinal herbs, and plant materials they collected. Their superior fine motor skills were needed for finding, collecting, winnowing, curing, preserving, weaving, and otherwise utilizing these materials. Women also required a much more complex symbolic language to process this information and to transmit it to others. They required a more elaborate language for their work and child-rearing. Gathering also did not require that women remain silent at work. Unlike hunted prey, plants do not run away if they hear, see, or smell their pursuer.

Silence, invisibility, and stealth are all required by the hunter.

Hunting also required the development of a silent language of sensing or signs through which men could communicate complex ideas. This was needed to coordinate movements during stalking and other strategies of the hunt. Hunting a large animal like a mammoth or wild bull with spears and arrows was a very dangerous undertaking. It was essential that men were able to depend on one another's courage, stability, and capacity to communicate their intentions silently. As we discussed in chapter 8, very little has changed physiologically in the last ten thousand years. In our bodies, men are still basically hunters.

These elements of disparate style and language are a foundation for discord between the members of each sex even today. These gender-distinct proclivities need to be understood and freed from judgment, shame, politicalization, and repression. For example, the stoic, silent male is not necessarily unable to express his feelings. He may simply demonstrate his feelings more directly through actions rather than words.

Several of the knights have spoken to these differences in reference to domestic issues. One time, as we sat talking in an all-night coffe shop, Rodger told us that his wife "just doesn't seem to understand my silent moods or that I just need space once in a while. It doesn't mean that I'm rejecting her; I just don't want to communicate *all* the time. I need a lot of simple, quiet time in my life to maintain my serenity."

Carl also said, "I just can't express myself with words to the same degree as my wife. Whenever we have a disagreement, she talks circles around me. Often I just give up, withdraw, and remain silent. Then she says I'm sulking. That might be true. But it feels more like I'm just defeated. I can't really explain the way I feel in a way that she clearly understands. It's different with you guys, though. You'll usually get it right away with just a few words. It's funny. I mean, I live with her every day and only see you guys once a week. But when it comes to certain issues, it seems you understand me more easily than she does."

Men's feelings may be communicated from a more silent, less verbal foundation. The implacable and silent qualities of many men have given fuel to the popular notion that men are not in touch with their feelings. This perception of male psychology is fraught with paradox. It's true, by virtue of men's extensive cultural conditioning against expressing feelings, that we're generally not as demonstrative or as effusive as many women. However, the other side of this phenomenon is a gender-specific male style of feeling that is different from the way in which women express their feelings.

For example, Jack said, "I'm a lot more likely to express my affection by fixing something around the house or by buying a gift than saying, 'I love you.'" All the knights nodded in agreement with this one. We're more likely to demonstrate our feelings through actions. We feel dismayed when a woman complains, "You never *say* you love me."

Ben said, "I used to put in a lot of extra hours so that I could provide the things I thought my wife wanted. That was the way I expressed my love. But what she really wanted was more of me, something I didn't really know how to give then. Since I've been single, I've been working less. I notice that when I come to these meetings, I'm not as tired as I used to be and feel more like talking. I used to come home and not want to even say a word for hours. That used to drive my wife crazy. She thought I didn't love her. But I did. I was just so burned out at night that all I wanted was a beer, dinner, TV, or silence. She never suggested I start working less so that I could be more present with her in the evenings. It never occurred to either of us."

Just as it's difficult for most women to lift loads that their same-sized male counterparts can manage, it's a strain for many men to communicate in a verbal style that is more accessible to a female counterpart. This does *not* mean that men are stupid, sullen, conspiratorial, or chauvinistic. Men are often just not as verbal. Sometimes, for a man, a grunt or a shrug tells the whole story of his day at work. It's sometimes exhausting and frustrating for men to feel that they have to lay everything out verbally. It's also often tiresome for men to listen to a higher degree of verbal input from women than they're comfortable with receiving.

What women perceive as men tuning them out or not listening may actually be an expression of mental fatigue. This could have its source in physical fatigue of that weaker portion of men's brain physiology. Some men even fake listening so they won't be labeled as insensitive and unresponsive by women.

As we continued talking about these differences with women, Brad mentioned, "On the occasions I've worked on job sites with women, I've noticed that notions that could be communicated to another man with a slight nod, shake of the head, grimace, or hand movement often seem lost on women."

To some degree it must be true that women haven't learned the body languages of working men. They haven't been working with them in the past as much as they are today. So it's hard to say if it is nature or nurture that has structured this difference in the sexes. Either way it's a source of gender conflict.

In the fast-moving, noisy environment of team sports, in the industrial workplace, and in other high-risk jobs like logging and construction, verbal communications are often inadequate or lost. In these situations, a man may communicate complex spatial ideas through a silent language of posture, nuance, and gesture. A hand wave from a hunter may mean you-go-around-behind-there-and-over-the-ridge-while-I-circle-around-from-the-other-side-and-come-up-behind-you-through-the-canyon. Or a nod at a construction site may say you-hoist-this-beam-up-to-the-roof-while-I-hold-the-end-of-this-rope-and-counter-balance-you. A finger twirled in a circle says *start it up* or *move it out*. A clenched fist says *stop*! When shaken, it emphasizes urgency . . . now! Misunderstanding this language on the hunt, at work, or in battle can result in injury, even death.

MEN IN PSYCHOTHERAPY

In the psychologist's consulting room, the misunderstanding of gender-specific communication styles can result in men failing to receive the mental-health support we need. There are many circumstances in which men react differently than women in a variety of subtle ways. All these differences come into play in the psychotherapeutic relationship.

For example, most therapy these days is conducted with the therapist facing the client, one-to-one. Women are generally comfortable with this arrangement. But many men are more likely to face the one person in a room they dislike, orienting themselves toward a potential conflict, whereas women are more likely to turn toward someone they like most, a potential relationship. In general men tend to face each other less often than women do. A number of studies indicate that men react more negatively when approached face-to-face by a stranger than women, who are more uncomfortable with being approached from the side. In this respect our behavior is not that different from many primates.

Males tend to sit farther away from strangers than women, who sit closer, especially to other women. Women do more same-sex touching than men. Men generally like to have more personal space around them than women do. Women are more comfortable sitting opposite a strange man they're not expected to interact with than one with whom they're expected to interact. Men, however, prefer to sit opposite a stranger they're expected to work with than one who remains disengaged. Not surprisingly, from reports I've heard at numerous clinical case consultations, female therapists often express more discomfort dealing one-to-one with male clients than men do working with female clients.

Women use more eye contact and feel it's more important. They may interpret a man looking away from them as resistance, avoidance, or an indication that he's being untruthful. Paradoxically, though, a man's gazing at them is perceived as more of an unwelcome interest than the same behavior from a woman. Men like it more than women when the opposite sex gazes at them. But men often interpret a lot of eye contact as a challenge from other men or as flirtation from women. Men are frequently confused by signals from women, which, from their point of view, often have double messages. For example, men usually smile only when saying positive things. But women, who smile more often than men in general, frequently smile when saying negative things or even when expressing anger. This is often confusing to men.

Men are more talkative when they can't see who they're talking to. Women prefer to see who they're speaking to. For example, a man may talk to someone while pacing around the room with his back turned, on occasion, with no insult implied. Women are more likely to interpret this behavior as rude. It often seems as if men and women belong to completely different cultures.

In her recent best-seller on gender communication styles, *You Just Don't Understand,* Deborah Tannen concluded, after reviewing a number of videotapes of conversations:

> Boys and men sit at angles to each other . . . and never look directly into each other's faces. . . . The girls and women anchor their gaze on each other's faces, occasionally glancing away, while the boys and men anchor their gaze elsewhere in the room, occasionally glancing at each other. In one case the boys even chose to sit parallel as if riding in a car. . . . When a woman looks at her therapist . . . she is simply doing what she has always done. . . . A man is asked to . . . do something different—something he has little practice doing, something that might even seem wrong

to do. Proclaiming men "disengaged" on the basis of their body language seems premature and unfair. They are being judged by the standards of a different culture.

Even if men are sitting side by side and only occasionally glancing at one another, they often synchronize their movements, shifting positions and making hand gestures that depict obvious engagement with one another.

The above studies represent just a few of the gender distinctions in modes of feeling, communication, and social interaction. They hold many implications for the way in which therapists conduct psychotherapy. We cannot just dismiss them by telling men they are wrong for the way they are or attempting to make them conform more to a traditionally female mode of feeling and communication.

Tannen observes that inexperienced female therapists initially do better than inexperienced male therapists. But this difference evens out over time. She speculates that the reason for this may be that "eventually, perhaps, men therapists—and men in therapy—learn to talk like women. This is all to the good."

But we're not so sure this is all to the good. Tannen does go on to say that women should learn men's language style as well. But learning men's language requires more than the kind of assertiveness training that she suggests. The way in which we approach the healing of men's wounds may at times require a completely different style than what were used to.

Initiation into therapy is humiliating for many men. When women approach therapy, they're acting congruently with their gender identity. Women are supposed to be in touch with their feelings and seek help with emotional difficulties. Men, however, often consider psychotherapy as dissonant with their traditional gender identity of being competent in the world. Consequently, their pride and strength need to be honored and considered as a factor affecting their capacity to receive help.

For men coming into therapy, more often an admission of failure is involved: they've failed to live up to the heroic role model. So, rather than insist that men shouldn't feel that way, we need to start understanding masculine culture in a way that makes therapy more sensitive to men *as they are*. However, many therapists today are still attempting to resocialize men into a more androgynous mode. Women should assume that they do not fully understand the male experience, and ask their male clients to explain it to them. This request alone will be healing to many men who feel judged and misunderstood by women.

Men may have difficulty learning from a woman or a feminized man about how to cope with problems maturely. One of the things we've been working on in the new knights is overcoming our dependency on women for all our emotional nurturing. Many uninitiated men easily become infantilized in their relationships with women. Often a man's needs are for maturity and separation from mother, not returning to her. They may do better, during specific periods of their development, with a male therapist who has an authentic, masculine depth perspective.

In any case, regardless of the therapist's gender, making it clear to men that they are entering into a *temporary* relationship will help to ameliorate men's initial fears about becoming more dependent, fears that may keep them out of therapy altogether.

Men are usually more comfortable sharing intimacy with a woman, but paradoxically less comfortable with a woman when in a position of less authority than she. So men may feel a little more careful, perhaps even fearful, in a therapeutic encounter with a female clinician. This is especially true of men who are referred to therapy for crimes of deviance. When men get past this fear and seek help, they're also often more guarded at first than women. But this does not mean they are resistant to therapy.

Because of the antimale sentiment in the air today, many men such as Jack and Carl feel that in couples counseling they're more likely to be identified as *the problem*. Perhaps they'd feel better meeting with a man-woman team rather than a single therapist whose neutrality they doubt. For family-systems counseling, a man would also benefit from the presence of a male cotherapist.

In many cases group therapeutic adventures for men may be more effective than one-to-one therapy. When in the consulting room, men may feel more comfortable if the chairs are aligned at an angle to one another, more congruent with their traditionally preferred side-by-side communication style.

If psychology begins to take a more male-affirming stance we'll begin to see a lot of other changes. More men will start utilizing psychological services instead of suffering silently and alone. This has certainly been the case at our local men's center for health and therapy services.

There are many well-meaning, talented, masculine-affirming women in the field. I do not mean to imply that these women are not able to support the healing of men. In many cases or at certain stages of development, a man may even do better with a woman than with a man. For example, a man who's been wounded by men might stay away from therapy if no female therapist is available. And women may also be able to help men work through various issues concerning intimate relationships with women and issues with their mothers or other significant women that a male therapist cannot as readily facilitate.

But men should be careful of women or men who have not worked through their prejudices and negative projections concerning the essential character of men.

SEXISM TOWARD MALE CLIENTS

In light of the prejudicial attitudes toward men prevalent in today's culture, it's important to look hard at the field of psychology. Is it really meeting the needs of men's mental health? Why is it that men don't seek the help of a therapist more often?

Of course, hero training has got something to do with this: "I don't need help. I can do it myself. I am not a wimp." However, there's another factor that keeps men away from the help they need. Men often feel that the services they really need are unavailable. Or they're simply uncomfortable with the ones that are.

Jim told us, "You know, I've tried to get sober several times in my life. I even went into the county detox once when I got busted for drunk and disorderly. But I never felt that any of the counselors could really relate to me. No one ever seemed to really understand what I was going through. They framed all my problems as typical alcoholism. Maybe they were right. But for whatever reason, this group is the first thing that has really done the trick. It's the first time I've felt that I was seen as a beautiful, soulful, and artistic man with a few problems that had solutions, rather than just some sort of loser or deviant who had to be resocialized."

In the past there's been a lot of blatant discrimination toward men in treatment. Historically, depressed women in hospitals have been likely to receive more therapy sessions than men. Male patients were almost twice as likely to receive electroshock therapy as women with the same symptoms. Males were released from hospitals less often than women. In many cases a man would be released only if he had a job, whereas a female with the same symptoms would be released to a cooperating family.

Assertive or adventurous male patients were less likely to be released than those who were equally disturbed but docile. Ken Kesey's novel *One Flew over the Cuckoo's Nest* depicts how one man's wild exuberance for life and irreverence toward rigid rules caused him to be assessed as dangerously pathological.

Prejudice today is often more subtle. Most training programs attempt to educate fledgling therapists as to the dangers of bringing racist, classist, or sexist attitudes into the therapeutic encounter. There's an attempt to get trainees to look at their attitudes toward a client's economic status, sexual preference, race, religious beliefs, or gender—*if that gender is female*. But no attention is usually given to their attitudes toward men, their prejudices or stereotypical notions regarding masculinity. In fact, only about 1 percent of the studies on sexism in psychology address attitudes toward male clients. Yet at clinical case consultations I've heard numerous sexist, sarcastic, and derogatory comments about male clients that would have been vehemently challenged if they had been made about women or minorities.

White men in particular are exempt from any sort of consideration regarding prejudice. It's often simply assumed that they're more economically and educationally advantaged, have more power in any given relationship, and have better access to health care in general. This is true for some, but not for most. A sort of reverse sexism seems to be creeping into the training of therapists. Since the majority of trainees today are women or feminized men, this imbalance in the training of therapists is alarming.

Therapists who react to men's issues from their own conventional socialization may discourage men's changes away from their traditional role model. For example, they may be inclined to perceive a man's moving away from work to spend more time with family or self-development as downward mobility. This is especially true for therapeutic services offered as an adjunct to the work environment, where the stated goal is often just to get the man back to work. (On the other hand, it's usually seen as okay for a woman to move out of her traditional role and leave the home to work or get more training that will make her upwardly mobile.) Therapists need to give more support to unconventional options for men, which may be more personally fulfilling to them than upholding their traditional roles. For many men today, downshifting is a move toward sanity.

Weak masculine foundations undermine practically every edifice in psychology today. Regardless of whether a therapist takes the humanistic position as a friend with unconditional positive regard or meets the client with a gestaltist's creative indifference, a Jungian's psyche-centered perspective, a psychoanalytic interpretive stance, or the simplistic mechanical view of a behaviorist, there are certain encrusted ideas that color the nature of therapists' attitudes toward their clients in any context. Gender prejudices in psychology can lead to a man's disadvantage, even to his harm.

As the psychoanalytic field has evolved, the influence of the therapist's personal issues has become more important. There's now more concern with the development of a therapist-client relationship that reflects the various dynamics of a client's style of dealing with life outside the consulting room. There are times, in every therapeutic relationship, when a client is extremely vulnerable. At that time it's essential for the therapist to be aware of his or her own personal issues. D. W. Winnicott describes this situation as follows:

> In the work I am describing the setting becomes more important than the interpretations. The behavior of the analyst . . . raises a hope that the true self may at last be able to take risks involved in starting to experience living. . . . This is a time of great dependence, and true risks.

The male client is especially at risk today from the many therapists with antimale attitudes who've entered the field in the last few decades. Just as with any other attitudes we carry that may affect the course of therapy, it behooves us to become conscious of these prejudices and make adjustments accordingly. In extreme cases, if therapists can't come to terms with their prejudicial feelings toward men as a group, they should refer their male clients elsewhere.

As an example of how negative male images permeate the psychoanalytic imagination, I've included a brief selection of comments by Melanie Kline, a widely respected psychologist. Her ideas are especially popular today with many women who work with children. Yet her interpretations concerning the nature of male sexuality and the penis as an object may be fueling notions concerning the so-called monstrous male that are growing in today's culture. She tells us:

> The father's penis is an anxiety object *par excellence* equated with dangerous weapons of various kinds and with animals which poison and devour. . . . This concentration of sadistic omnipotence in the penis is of fundamental importance for the masculine position of the boy. . . . His mother is to be rescued from the father's "bad penis" inside her. . . . Her body is a place which is filled with a number of dangerous penises. Fear of the bad penis is derived from his destructive impulses against his father's penis. . . . The boy's inordinately strong introjection of his father's monstrous "bad" penis makes him believe that his body is exposed to the same dangers from within as his mother's. . . . Erection and ejaculation is a tremendous heightening of the sadistic power of the penis.

This is only one of many examples in which masculinity, male sexuality, or male-specific modes of being are negatively framed by psychologists. We need to become more aware of how professional language perpetuates antimale ideas and propels them into the culture at large. We need to challenge ourselves to perceive things in new ways and be aware of therapists' gender prejudices, especially when they are counseling men, toward whom they may have powerful projections. Iconoclasm benefits the psychological profession and should be encouraged by its clients and practitioners wherever possible. For example, Winnicott notes:

> One might have a slight propagandist tendency to think of all snakes as penis symbols. . . . A child's drawing of a snake can be a drawing of the self, the self not yet using arms, fingers, legs and toes. One can see how many times patients have failed to convey a sense of self because a therapist has interpreted a snake as a penis symbol.

So we need to stay loose about the intrinsic meaning of so-called male symbols if we are ever to know the male psyche in its authentic depth and complexity. We need to shake off encrusted ideas about men. The same symbols may mean very different things about different men in different contexts. Psychology is a creative art that tries to see a man as he is in the moment. It's not an exact science in which specific images always mean the same things.

We need to start training therapists to become more aware of the ways in which they limit men's growth by holding limited notions about their authentic character. Through gaining a greater understanding of masculine depths, psychological interpretations will likely gain a deeper insight. They will then affirm a therapeutic alliance that has its roots in a more positive regard for masculinity, a male-specific way of loving, and masculinity's relationship to all of life.

Men who are entering therapy should carefully interview therapists about this very issue. Have they read many books on men's issues or attended workshops or trainings that deal specifically with men's concerns? Do they have much experience working with male clients?

Are they male affirming? Do they have good relationships with the men in their lives? Are they aware of the ways in which men are victimized by a bisexist culture? Do they hold anachronistic ideas about men needing to become more feminine or get in touch with their inner femininity? Are they aware of the differing ways in which men and women communicate? Are they familiar with the archetypes or paradigms of deep or authentic masculinity?

If you are going into couples or family counseling or being evaluated in a custody battle, find out if the therapists really believe that women and men are fundamentally different, yet equal. Are they aware of ways in which women emotionally abuse men, and are they aware that women are equally capable of violence? Are they aware of the nature of gender distribution of crimes against children? Do they acknowledge that mothers are just as likely to be perpetrators as fathers? Are they aware of the many inequities men face around divorce, custody, abortion, and other parenting rights?

You'll have questions of your own, to be sure, but don't be naive about the danger of entering therapy with people who have not as yet had their consciousness raised about men's issues. And at this time, many therapists still lack this training.

ARE MEN REALLY MORE DEVIANT THAN WOMEN?

Men commit more crimes than women. One out of nineteen men in America has been through the criminal justice system. Among young black men, one out of four is incarcerated, on probation or parole, under court order, or awaiting trial. The reasons for this are complex, but it's indicative of a wave of raw social protest within a society in which men are very frustrated and angry. One of the reasons for this *racial* disparity is a racist governmental policy that focuses on minorities and the urban poor. For example, 80 percent of illegal drug users are white. Yet blacks account for 80 percent of the arrests for drug possession.

In contrast, only one out of every four hundred women is under the jurisdiction of the justice system. One of the factors in this *gender* disparity is sexism against men. In almost any circumstance, men are dealt with more harshly around issues of antisocial behavior than women. For example, in California men are arrested for drug violations six to one over women. When it comes to serving time for those charges, however, men are incarcerated more than ten to one over women. Women are more likely to be released or diverted to treatment facilities than men.

Women, moreover, are more likely to go to doctors, hospitals, psychotherapists, or outpatient clinics in the first place, rather than self-medicate themselves with nonprescription drugs. They are more likely than men to report symptoms of physical and emotional discomfort to physicians, interpret general malaise as psychiatric problems requiring treatment, and be well received by those health professionals they seek out. Their drug use is thus supervised by these professionals. Women account for the use of over 70 percent of all *prescribed* minor tranquilizers and 80 percent of all the legal speed (diet pills). They also use the majority of barbiturates and noncontrolled narcotics. They renew their prescriptions more often than men and use them with greater frequency.

So women get diagnosed as depressives and neurotics and as having more psychophysiological, stress-induced disorders. But these women are not classed as antisocial or deviant. They don't wind up in the penal system to the same degree as men. They're viewed more sympathetically—as patients who need treatment, not punishment and incarceration, for their subtance-abuse problems.

On the other hand, the private psychotherapeutic community may in some cases steer away men perceived as threatening. Men are more likely to be referred to public mental-health clinics, which are generally understaffed and underfunded and often have long waiting lists. In our county mental-health clinic, there is only one group for men, though there are about a dozen for women. Since many men feel that their needs are much less likely to be understood or served by the psychotherapeutic community and since they also don't want to be seen as weak, they frequently turn to illegal street drugs and alcohol in a misguided attempt to cope with their stress.

Street drugs are expensive as well as illegal, so self-medicating men are much more likely to be arrested for crimes of social deviance. They often wind up in jails and prisons instead of treatment centers. Ninety-five percent of all the inmates in the nation are male, and a substantial number of their crimes are either substance related or committed under the influence. So we need to start treating men's substance-abuse problems as a mental-health issue and build more treatment centers oriented toward men instead of continuously expanding the penal system.

The problems of male victims in all circumstances have been seriously understudied. Male victims make us uncomfortable. They run contrary to our cultural notion of men as heroes. For example, even though twice as many men are victims of violent crimes, those committed against women take much greater prominence in the arenas of sociological and psychological research. For every woman who is raped—the most widely studied category of victimization—twenty men are victims of violent assaults. Also, as mentioned previously, a number of studies indicate that incarcerated men are raped in numbers equaling, or exceeding, those of free women. They are seldom treated for this abuse.

Our society offers little support to men who have been victims of violent crime. This has also been true for male victims of childhood sexual abuse, who by many current estimates account for about 40 percent of all victims. This situation has slowly begun to improve in the last few years, however, as more men are speaking out about this issue.

We study eating disorders in young women and offer clinics, groups, and even entire private hospitals for their treatment. But society practically ignores the equally widespread problem of steroid abuse in boys, stemming from similar sorts of body-image problems. We don't need to abandon the concerns of young women. But what about young men? Why are they the subject of so few studies? Psychology seems overly fascinated with the female victim.

Most male sex offenders were themselves abused. This is also true for many violent criminals. Male victims are much more likely to respond to their abuse by becoming victimizers themselves. They're socialized to become enraged. Women are more likely to respond by becoming self-abusive, something that generates less fear and more sympathy from others. Male victimizers' monster status prevents most treatment programs from working with them to reveal and heal their own wounds of childhood abuse.

This is one of the many arenas in which cultural expectations that men will be emotionally tougher than women are dangerous to men's well-being and recovery from victimization when it does occur. Male victims are more likely to be seen as having asked for it or failed as men because they did not protect themselvs. But failure to treat the wounds of male victims may merely generate more abuse from these victims in the future.

WHERE DO WE GO FROM HERE?

We need a revolution in psychology today. Men need to shake themselves out of their slumber and begin looking at the many ways in which the field fails to respond to their needs. Any clinic not offering groups for men, any therapist who works with men without having been trained to understand them, any training program that overlooks men as a special category of client—are all failing to meet our needs. We don't want to take anything away from women; we merely need to provoke the entire field to become more responsive, thoughtful, and creative in dealing with the problems of men.

All of us in the new knights grew up with a lot of repressed emotional pain. We tried drinking, drugging, working, and fucking ourselves numb, but all that did was ultimately make things worse. Over the years we've tried a lot of different things to get our lives straight: E.S.T., T.M., A.A., A.C.A., and lots of other initials. We've tried psychotherapy, psychedelics, and prayer. We've sought healing from the women in our lives and made sacrifices at the altar of the Great Mother. I've even gone so far as to follow gurus to the other side of the world.

But it wasn't until we turned to one another and said, "This is who I am without my armor. Who are you?" that we found a healing power of real, lasting value.

There's a place for psychotherapeutic services and spiritual teachers for men, just as there's a need for surgeons and antibiotics. But men's mental health, like physical health, is primarily a product of preventive maintenance. Through creating strong, supportive male community we can create a field of masculine health that will circumvent the emergence of a multitude of pathological expressions. This is the real work ahead of us. And whatever spiritual leaders, educators, and mental-health professionals can do to support the building of male community will be a step in the right direction.

THE ELEVENTH TASK OF MEN: TO DEVELOP A MASCULINE-AFFIRMING PSYCHOLOGY

Taking the first steps toward a new male psychology was the eleventh task the new knights of the round table attempted. Much research, study, inquiry, and dialogue needs to be instituted on behalf of men in this arena. I hope this book will point the way for some further inquiry from a new generation of researchers freed from the encrusted, calcified gender paradigms of past generations, which will have been "swept from the mind like tattered autumn leaves from the garden." And I hope the next few decades will bring about the same revolution in our understanding of male psychology as has occurred in the recent past for women. Then together, as men and women in partnership, with mutual understanding, we can face the broader task of rebuilding our communities and the culture at large.

Conclusion

The new knights don't have any special chemistry or magic. We're not particularly brave, smart, cool, or lucky. We're essentially ordinary men who took the risk of reaching out to one another. We asked each other for help and offered it in return. We didn't go through any big initiation, exchange blood vows, or join a secret organization. We didn't pay anyone to be our expert healer. We just took turns. Fools and wise men all, stumbling along through the dark, being steadfast companions to one another on our journey in quest of masculine soul.

We did, however, start out with a little of that good ol' twelve-step religion. And we still value the guidelines we got from A.A. We've integrated a lot of the knowledge we gained from mythopoetic and men's-rights groups, as well as the insights gained from each member's personal quests. But we've come a long way from being just a recovery or therapy group. We're family now, a tribe.

What we have found is friendship, solidarity, community, and brotherhood. We've liberated a great treasure—one another—from the oppressive ogre of masculine shame. We've also discovered new connections to the earth, to life, to women, to our ancestral and psychological pasts, and to our bodies, our feelings, our sacred and practical dreams, our families, and our deepest emotions.

Each man is unique. No archetype of masculinity, ancient or modern, is going to serve us all. Psychological types, archetypes, personality types, standards of so-called normalcy or pathology, and other such classifications are a lot like astrological signs: they're simplistic and reductive. They're never true depictions of the paradoxical complexity of the human psyche, which is always in flux and transformation.

THE FINAL TASK OF MEN: TO CONTINUE REAWAKENING THE MASCULINE SOUL

Soul is vast, limitless, unbounded. We'll never plumb its depths. But we're striving for that ideal—the freedom to be who we truly are in all its complex, wild beauty and strange affliction. We're always in a state of *becoming*. The world is ever new. The metaphorical depictions of male archetypes in this book and in other current writings on masculine psychology are merely lenses through which to reexamine ourselves. They're *rough* generalizations.

However, it's useful to hold these notions to illustrate the further idea we are reaching for—a paradoxical, multifaceted image that, like nature itself, is consistently evolving and transforming. The popular idea that there exists some formula or ideal way of *being* can actually limit our opportunities for real freedom and self-development. We must continually ask ourselves, "What's true for me?"

The last thing we want is a new formula for reducing the multiplicity and mystery of the male psyche to yet another system of classification, be it Hero, Wild Man, Warrior, King, or Authentic Male. Through dialogue with our own dreams and one another we'll *each* discover a unique mythology for our own particular context of self, family, work, and society.

When I started this book four years ago, the men's movement was still pretty much a private affair. Now I'm getting calls almost every day from men wanting to know what to read, where to go, and how to set about joining a group, healing themselves, and reclaiming masculine soul. I'm encouraged by the speed at which this dialogue is heating up and going public.

But I'm also discouraged by how little is as yet available in the way of high-quality books, men's-studies courses, men's centers, and institutes or groups focused on men's issues, as well as research on male psychology. More blatant social activism is also needed, both on behalf of men's rights and against institutions that perpetuate social tolerance for violence against men.

Conscious men need to become more involved in every aspect of our children's development. We need to create rehabilitation alternatives for the increasing numbers of men who are in distress and coming under the jurisdiction of the penal system. We need to become more mobilized in our defense of the earth and better able to hold power, command resources, and administer institutions in a responsive, intelligent, and compassionate manner.

We still have a long way to go. But we need not wait for society to reorganize itself to become more responsive to men's needs. We each have the individual power to create a men's lodge wherever we are in the world. I've also included a few resources at the end of this book that might help steer you toward making good connections outside your immediate community.

For us in the new knights, telling the truth and revealing the wounds beneath our armor has helped us to heal those wounds. The tasks we have undertaken have given us glimpses of an authentic image of masculinity that is quite different from the popular images of the culture we live in. The tasks that beckoned to us are not meant to be any sort of formula or even a sequential list of suggestions to the reader. Our tasks represent a few of the many issues men are grappling with today. I hope you will undertake your own quest of similar or completely different tasks, according to the developmental needs of your own soul.

In the new knights we've fiercely confronted one another and at the same time been gently supportive. We've tried to reconnect to life, our bodies, our feelings, and the earth itself through getting to know a little about the various archetypes of masculinity. Many more remain to be discovered, and there's much we still don't understand. But by virtue of our lodge work and an increasing willingness to meet life authentically regardless of the consequences, we have found healing, strength, and increasing levels of happiness in life.

Now, after several years of this work, we're no longer merely trying to heal our personal wounds and the wounds between men. We're reaching out to women and becoming more concerned about our children and our environment. We don't seem to be able to evolve independent of the world we live in. The quest for masculine soul is just as likely to take us into the world of social activism as into our psychological imagination.

Through our discovery of the old gods of men, we've awakened an awareness of the sacred nature of masculinity. Our ever-transforming working model of authentic masculinity has served to inspire us to feel good about being male again. It's inspired us to try new roles and new ideas, to claim our multiplicity and reorganize our lives in many ways. Now that we've built our ship of soul, we're trying to learn how to sail it. The quest has just begun.

Men's Resources

Wingspan: Journal of the Male Spirit
Box 1491
Manchester, MA 01944

Features articles with a mythopoetic perspective and interviews with leaders of men's conferences. Good calendar of men's events around the country. Free; donation requested.

Inroads: Men, Creativity, Soul
Box 14944
University Station
Minneapolis, MN 55414

Literary journal with a mythopoetic perspective. Published twice a year. Subscriptions are $7.50 a year.

Transitions
Box 129
Manhasset, NY 11030

Male-affirming bimonthly publication focusing on the gender-specific social, legal, political, and psychological needs of men. Subscriptions are $30 a year.

Man! Men's Issues, Relationships, and Recovery
Austin Men's Center
1611 West Sixth Street
Austin, TX 78703

A blend of articles addressing recovery issues, men's health, and soul. Quarterly. Subscriptions are $11 a year.

The Redwood Men's Center Re-Source
705 College Avenue
Santa Rosa, CA 95404

Short articles on archetypal male psychology. Regular round-table discussions on topical issues by men with a masculine soul perspective. Lends insight into the development and life of a regional men's center. Quarterly. Subscriptions are $6 a year.

Men's Rights (MR), Inc.
Box 163180
Sacramento, CA 95816

A men's-rights organization with an emphasis on confronting sexism and discrimination toward men. Their IQ test is worth getting: in a few words it clearly demonstrates how "sex discrimination affects men's lives as negatively as it does women's lives."

Equal Rights for Fathers, Inc.
Box 90042
San Jose, CA 95109-3042

"Seeks to assure the enforcement of existing laws which give men and women equal rights to custody and the enactment of new legislation to preserve the rights of children to both parents."

Ally Press Center
542 Orleans Street
St. Paul, MN 55107

A good catalogue of men's books and tapes, plus speaking schedules for leaders of men's conferences such as Robert Bly and James Hillman.

The Pangaea Institute for Gender Studies
Box 862
Sebastopol, CA 95473

For additional resources, correspondence with Aaron R. Kipnis, and a schedule of his speaking engagements. Also a source for articles and male and female leaders for workshops concerning the art of partnership between men and women.

Notes

When quoted matter starts in the middle of a line, the line number indicated here refers to the first line that follows.

Abbreviations:
CW *Collected Works,* by C. G. Jung (1953), ed. R. F. C. Hull. 20 vols. Bollingen Series XX, Princeton: Princeton University Press.
ASI *American Statistical Index Abstracts (1989) A Comprehensive Guide to the Statistical Publications of the United States Government.* Washington, D.C.: Congressional Information Service.
SA *Statistical Abstract of the United States: The National Data Book (1990)* 110th ed. Washington, D.C.: U.S. Department of Commerce, Bureau of the Census.

CHAPTER ONE

P. 16, L. 10 Fromm, E. (1976) *To Have or to Be.* New York: Bantam Books. **P. 20, L. 25** Montagu, A. (1971) *Touching: The Human Significance of the Skin.* New York: Columbia University Press, p. 182. **P. 21, L. 2** Sears, R., and Levin, H. (1957) *Patterns of Child Rearing.* New York: Peterson, pp. 56–57, 402. **P. 21, L. 6** Coppa, G., et al. (1990, March 10) Preliminary study of breast feeding and bacterial adhesion to upoepithelial cells. *Lancet,* p. 569. Also: Henson, L., et. al. (1988) Antiviral and antibacterial factors in human milk. In Hanson, L., ed., *Biology of Human Milk.* New York: Raven Press, pp. 141–57. **P. 21, L. 17** Fagot, B. (1978) The influence of sex of a child on parental reactions to toddler children. *Child Development* 47:812–19. **P. 21, L. 20** Lambert, W., et al. (1971) Child training values of English Canadian and French Canadian parents. *Canadian Journal of Behavioral Sciences* 3:217–36. **P. 21, L. 26** Jacklin, C., DiPietry, J., and Maccoby, E. (1984) Sex-typing behavior and sex-typing pressure in child/parent interaction. *Archives of Sexual Behavior* 14:413–25. **P. 21, L. 29** Serbin, L., O'Leary, D., Kent, R., and Tonick, J. (1973) A comparison of teacher response to the preacademic and problem behavior of boys and girls. *Child Development* 44:796–804. **P. 23, L. 1** ASI. National Institute of Mental Health (1989) *Mental Health Statistics.* Washington, D.C.: Alcohol Drug Abuse and Mental Health Administration. **P. 24, L. 6** Montagu, A. (1974) *Life before Birth.* New York: New American Library. **P. 24, L. 7** Fine, R. (1987) *The Forgotten Man: Understanding the Male Psyche.* New York: Harrington Park Press, p. 5. **P. 24, L. 9** Money, J., and Ehrhardt, A. (1972) *Man and Woman, Boy and Girl.* Baltimore: Johns Hopkins University Press, pp. 147–48. **P. 24, L. 13** Pearce, J. (1977) *Magical Child.* Toronto: Bantam Books, p. 255. **P. 24, L. 16** American Psychiatric Association (1987) *Diagnostic and Statistical Manual of Mental Disorders.* 3rd ed., rev. Washington, D.C.: American Psychiatric Association. **P. 24, L. 24** Miles, T. (1983) *Dyslexia: The Pattern of Difficulties.* London: Granada, p. 160. Also Matlin, M. (1987) *Psychology and Women.* Fort Worth: Holt, Rinehart & Winston, Inc. Funucci, J., and Childs, B. (1981) Are there really more dyslexic boys than girls? In A. Ansara, M. Albert, and N. Gartrell, eds., *Sex Differences in Dyslexia.* Towson, MD: Orton Dyslexia Society, pp. 1–9. **P. 24, L. 34** Cherry, L., and Lewis, M. (1976) Mothers and two year olds: a study of sex-differentiated aspects of verbal interaction. *Developmental Psychology* 12:278–82. **P. 25, L. 1** Schacter, F., et. al. (1978) Do girls talk earlier? Mean length of utterances in toddlers. *Developmental Psychology* 14:388–92. **P. 25, L. 8** Hamill, P. (1977) NCHS growth curves for children. *Vital and Health Statistics: Series 11 No. 165: Data from the National Health Survey.* Washington, D.C.: Government

Printing Office. **P. 25, L. 10** Roche, A., and Davial, G. (1972) Late adolescent growth in stature. *Pediatrics* 50:874–80. **P. 26, L. 16** Clarke, K. (1976, November 22) *Time*, p. 61. **P. 26, L. 19** Powell, J. (1988) *Three-Year Study of 21,233 High School Football Players.* for the National Athletic Trainers Association. University of Iowa. **P. 26, L. 29** Mellott, R. (1989, September 1) The truth hurts: major injuries up. *The Santa Rosa Press Democrat.* Sports. C-1, C-10. **P. 27, L. 19** Matuszak, J., and Delsohn, S. (1989) *Cruisin' with the Tooz.* New York: Berkeley Publishing. Also *San Francisco Chronicle* (1989, June 30), p. a-7. **P. 27, L. 33** Congbalay, D. (1989, July 26) Pressure on athletes: steroid use becoming more common. *San Francisco Chronicle.* **P. 27, L. 35** KCBS News Report (1989, April 24) Report from Penn State University. **P. 28, L. 4** Congbalay (1989). **P. 28, L. 13** (1990, June 14) Mr. Universe arrested for smuggling steriods. *San Francisco Chronicle.* **P. 30, L. 34** Siskin, B., and Staller, J. (1989) *What Are the Chances?* New York: Crown Books. **P. 30, L. 37** (1979, March) Prison census: *Corrections Today* Laurel, MD: American Correctional Association. Also, additional information from inquiries to (1989) Swords to Plowshares (veterans'-rights organization), San Francisco; (1990) Vietnam Veterans of California; (1991) American Association for Suicide Prevention. **P. 31, L. 8** Harrison, J. (1978) Warning: the male sex role may be hazardous to your health. *Journal of Social Issues* 34 (I): 65–86. **P. 31, L. 11** Farrell, W. (1986) *Why Men Are the Way They Are.* New York: McGraw-Hill. **P. 31, L. 17** Baumli, F., ed. (1985) *Men Freeing Men.* New York: New Atlantic Press. **P. 32, L. 12** Farrell (1986). **P. 32, L. 27** Edmondson, B., and Cutler, B. (1989) Proportion of the American population aged 18 to 44 that is male by county. *The Atlantic Monthly.* Reprinted in *This World, San Francisco Chronicle,* March 5, 1989. **P. 32, L. 27** Ubell, E. (1989, January 8) Is your job killing you? *Parade Magazine,* pp. 4–7. **P. 32, L. 36** Johnson, J. (1989, May 28) *Man to Man.* KCBS Radio talk show **P. 42, L. 32** Ubell (1989). **P. 33, L. 30** Siegel, J. (1980) Recent and expected demographic trends for the elderly population and some implications for health care. In S. G. Haynes and M. Feinleib, eds., *Epidemiology of Aging.* Washington, D.C.: Government Printing Office, pp. 289–315. (NIH Document no. 80-969.)

CHAPTER TWO

P. 35, L. 2 Blake, W. (1982) "Auguries of Innocence." In *The Complete Poetry and Prose of William Blake,* ed. D. Erdman. Garden City, NY: Doubleday, p. 491. **P. 35, L. 25** Fossum, M. (1987) *Catching Fire: Men Coming Alive in Recovery.* San Francisco: Harper and Row. **P. 36, L. 33** United States Internal Revenue Service (1988, Spring) *Statistics of Income Bulletin.* Washington, D.C.: U.S.G.P.O. **P. 36, L. 35** SA, pp. 445–63. Also *Money Income and Poverty Status in the United States* (advance data from the March 1989 current population survey). Washington, D.C.: U.S. Department of Commerce, Bureau of the Census. Series P-60, no. 166. Series P-23, no. 159. **P. 36, L. 40** SA, p. 100. **P. 37, L. 19** Kirp, D. (1990, April 9) AIDS goes to Washington—Hollywood style. *San Francisco Examiner,* p. A-23. Also (1989) *Learning by Heart: AIDS and Schoolchildren in America's Communities.* New Brunswick, N.J.: Rutgers University Press. **P. 37, L. 26** Fahey, E. (1989, May 24) Homeless men fight Contra Costa policy. *San Francisco Chronicle,* p. A-24. **P. 39, L. 7** Philips, D., and Segal, B. (1969) Sexual status and psychiatric symptoms. *American Sociological Review* 34:58–72. **P. 39, L. 7** Kipnis, A., Morris, D., and Badiner, J. (1990). Unpublished survey of eighteen psychotherapists who work with men. **P. 40, L. 8** (1990, January) U.S. Department of Justice, *Bureau of Justice Statistics NCJ-H0021.* Washington, D.C.: U.S. Department of Justice. **P. 40, L. 16** SA, p. 85. **P. 40, L. 24** Grimes, D. (1989, March 12) The right to wear tights: men want to prance around to "Wild Thing" too. Reprinted in the *San Francisco Chronicle* from the *Los Angeles Times Magazine.* **P. 40, L. 39** Littwin, S. (1989, June 14) Shape up! When entering a women's world men should try to adapt. *The Seattle Times: Scene,* p. C-1. **P. 41, L. 17** (1990, March 9) No men allowed. *San Francisco Chronicle.* **P. 42, L. 24** (1991, Jan. 14) Cover photo. *Time* magazine. **P. 42, L. 34** (1990) ASI. U.S. National Center for Health Statistics. U.S. Department of Health Service. Washington, D.C.: Health Resources Administration. Also *Vital Statistics of the United States. Volume II—Mortality.* (1987–88) U.S. Department of Health and Human Services. Public Health Service. National Centers for Disease Control. Washington, D.C.: National Center for Health Statistics. **P. 43, L. 38** Erickson, J. (1987) *Sight without color, and other statements about circumcision by men circumcised as adults.* Newsletter

with quote from interview with Paul Tardiff in *Informed Consent,* a video by Marilyn Milos and Sheila Curran. **P. 44, L. 25** Thomas, R. (1990) *Counseling and Life-Span Development.* Newbury Park, CA: Sage Publications, p. 189. **P. 44, L. 27** Group for the Advancement of Psychiatry (1986) *Crises of Adolescence—Teenage Pregnancy: Impact on Adolescent Development.* New York: Brunner/Mazel, pp. 8–9. **P. 45, L. 10** Goldberg, H. (1979) *The New Male.* New York. New American Library/Signet, pp. 99–113. **P. 45, L. 25** Male Sexual Dysfunctional Institute, Chicago, IL (1988). Reported in *Men's Resource Hotline Calendar.* San Anselmo, CA: MAS Medium and Co., p. 3. **P. 45, L. 29** Public Opinion Research of Princeton, NJ. **P. 45, L. 39** Levine, J. (1976) *Who Will Raise the Children? New Options for Fathers (and Mothers).* Philadelphia: Lippincott. **P. 46, L. 10** Sheff, D. (1981, January) John Lennon and Yoko Ono. *Playboy.* pp. 75–96. **P. 46, L. 30** Brown, M. (1986, July) Why won't they let us help deliver babies? Discrimination against male nurses. *RN,* pp. 49, 61. **P. 46, L. 34** Dinerstine, D. (1976) *The Mermaid and the Minotaur: Sexual Arrangements and Human Malaise.* New York: Harper and Row. **P. 46, L. 42** Graber, M. (1989, March) The new breed of supermen: anything she can do, he can do, too. *San Francisco Chronicle.* p. B-5. **P. 47, L. 8** Schwartz, F. (1989, January–February) Management women and the new facts of life. *Harvard Business Review,* pp. 65–76. **P. 47, L. 31** Horner, C. (1989, April 24) Obscure husbands of capital's powerful women. Quoted by Robert M. Andrews in *The Santa Rosa Press Democrat.* **P. 48, L. 12** ASI. (1990) U.S. National Center for Health Statistics. **P. 48, L. 27** Lawson, A. (1988) *Adultery: An Analysis of Love and Betrayal.* New York: Basic Books. **P. 49, L. 1** Hayward, F. (1988) Newsletter. Men's Rights, Inc. Sacramento, CA. **P. 49, L. 4** Pangborn, K. (1985) Custodial fatherhood. In Baumli, F., ed. *Men Freeing Men.* New York: New Atlantic Press, pp. 155, 170. **P. 49, L. 10** ASI (1990) U.S. Bureau of the Census. **P. 49, L. 16** Hayward (1988). **P. 49, L. 27** (1990) SA, p. 176. Also, additional information from inquiries to (1986) American Humane Association (national study of child neglect and abuse), Denver, Colorado; and the National Committee for Prevention of Child Abuse. **P. 49, L. 40** Gerson, L., Jarjoura, D., and McCord, G. (1987) Factors related to impaired mental health in urban elderly. *Research on Aging* 9 (3):356–71. **P. 49, L. 42** Gove, W. (1972) Sex, marital status, and suicide. *Journal of Health and Social Behavior* 13:204–13. **P. 51, L. 14** Vacon, B. (1990, March 18) The superweapon in custody disputes. *This World, San Francisco Chronicle.* Reprinted from the *Hartford Courant.* Based upon a study by The Association of Family and Conciliation Courts, March 1988. **P. 51, L. 40** Bass, E., and Davis, L. (1986) *The Courage to Heal: A Guide for Women Survivors of Child Sexual Abuse.* New York: Harper and Row, pp. 96, 198. **P. 52, L. 8** Singer, K. (1989, July) Group work with men who experienced incest in childhood. *American Journal of Orthopsychiatry* 59(3):466. **P. 52, L. 37** Obrian, S. (1980) *Child Abuse: A Crying Shame.* Provo, UT: Brigham Young University Press. **P. 53, L. 13** SA, p. 176. **P. 53, L. 19** Tyson, P. (1986) Male gender identity. In R. Friedman and L. Lerner, eds., *Toward a New Psychology of Men: Psychoanalytic and Social Perspectives.* New York: Guilford Press, pp. 10, 18. Reprinted from *The Psychoanalytic Review* 73(4):1–21 (Winter, 1986). **P. 53, L. 33** Norton, A., and Glick, P. (1986) One-parent families: a social and economic profile. *Family Relations* 35:9–17. **P. 53, L. 38** U.S. Supreme Court (November 28, 1988). **P. 54, L. 16** Furstenberg, F., and Harris, K. (1990, June 10). Huge number of families found with absentee dads. (Report on University of Pennsylvania study of one thousand children from disrupted homes, 1976–87.) *The Santa Rosa Press Democrat.* **P. 54, L. 35** Daroff, L., Marks, S., and Friedman, A. (1986) Adolescent drug use: The parents predicament. In G. Beschner and A. S. Friedman, eds., *Teen Drug Use.* Lexington, MA: D.C. Heath, pp. 185–209 **P. 55, L. 26** Savage, D. (1988, November 15) Court refuses to let man stop wife's abortion. *The Los Angeles Times.* **P. 55, L. 34** New York Times Staff. (1989, January 30) Lots of lesbians having babies. Reprinted in the *San Francisco Chronicle.* **P. 55, L. 39** Skelton, G (1989, March 19) After abortion: guilt, regret (survey: men tend to have more qualms). *Los Angeles Times;* reprinted in *The Santa Rosa Press Democrat.* **P. 56, L. 39** SA, p. 176. Also (1987) U.S. Department of Justice, Federal Bureau of Investigation. *Crime in the United States.* Washington, D.C.: USGPO, 1989, **P. 57, L. 3** Cahill, T. (1990) Prison rape: Torture in the American gulag. In: *Men & Intimacy,* Ed. Franklin Abbot, The Crossing Press. **P. 57, L. 13** Farrell (1986). Freedom, Cal. Also, information provided by: *People organized to stop Rape of Imprisoned Persons.* Fort Bragg, Cal. **P. 57, L. 15** (1989, September 19) *Male Rage: Stop Blaming Us for Everything.* Sally Jessie Raphael television talk show #919–9. **P. 57, L. 25** ASI. U.S. National Center for Health Statistics.

CHAPTER 3

P. 61, L. 3 Rothberg, J. (1986) *Shaking the Pumpkin: Traditional Poetry of the Indian North Americas.* English version of "How Her Teeth Were Pulled" by Jarold Ramsey. New York: Alfred Van Der Marck. **P. 65, L. 6** (1990, April) Poll of three thousand women. Roper Organization. **P. 65, L. 10** Friedan, B. (1974) *The Feminine Mystique.* New York: Dell Publishing. **P. 66, L. 5** Barry, D. (1990) *Dave Barry Turns Forty.* New York: Crown Publishers. **P. 66, L. 11** Daly, M. (1984) *Pure Lust.* Boston: Beacon Press, p. ix. **P. 66, L. 15** Spretnak, C., ed. (1982) *The Politics of Women's Spirituality.* New York: Anchor Books, p. xiii. **P. 66, L. 17** Budapest, Z. (1975) *The Feminist Book of Light and Shadows.* Venice, CA: TK, p. 1 **P. 66, L. 20** Daly (1984), pp. x, 2. **P. 66, L. 27** Brownmiller, S. (1975) *Against Our Will: Men, Women and Rape.* New York: Simon and Schuster. **P. 67, L. 3** Andrews, L. (1988) *Medicine Woman's Journey through the Year.* Engagement calendar. San Francisco: Harper and Row. **P. 67, L. 5** Spretnak (1982), p. xx. **P. 67, L. 11** Caldicott, H. (1987) Book jacket notes from Eisler, R. (1987) *The Chalice and the Blade.* San Francisco: Harper and Row. **P. 67, L. 16** Brothers, J. (1989, February 20) "People" section. *The Santa Rosa Press Democrat.* **P. 67, L. 23** Mead, M. (1949) *Male and Female.* New York: William Morrow. **P. 67, L. 28** Bly, R. (1988, June) Personal communication. **P. 67, L. 30** Adams, C. (1980) Child of the glacier. *American Man Magazine.* **P. 68, L. 12** Hayward, F. (1989, February 21) Men in TV commercials a pretty useless bunch. Quoted in *The Santa Rosa Press Democrat.* **P. 68, L. 21** Horovitz, B. (1989, August 12) Parade of nitwits: men are taking their lumps in ads. *Los Angeles Times.* Reprinted in *The Santa Rosa Press Democrat.* **P. 68, L. 27** Baker, K. (1989, March 17). The women of Brewster Place. *The Santa Rosa Press Democrat.* p. D–3. Also: Carmen, J. (1989, March 17) Men get bashed on "Brewster." *Datebook, San Francisco Chronicle.* **P. 68, L. 34** Douglas, A. (1988) *The Feminization of American Culture.* New York: Doubleday. **P. 69, L. 14** Goldberg (1979), pp. 6,28. **P. 69, L. 32** Miller, A., and Miller, R. (1989, February 15) Readers tackle "superwoman." *San Francisco Chronicle.* Briefing, p. 9. **P. 70, L. 19** (1989, May 15) Sex bias claimed at maritime academy. *San Francisco Chronicle.* **P. 70, L. 37** Associated Press (1990, February) Swearing foreman costs company. *San Francisco Chronicle.* **P. 71, L. 1** (1990, November 28) Three in NFL Fined for Harassing Sportswriter. *San Francisco Chronicle,* p. 1. **P. 71, L. 27** Harte, S. (1989, August 27) Men cautious, cynical about sex bias: men think sex harassment can become a murky concept. *Cox News Service,* reprinted in the *San Francisco Chronicle.* **P. 72, L. 10** Sayles, J. (June, 1990) *Donahue.* Television talk show. **P. 72, L. 25** ASI. U.S. Bureau of Labor Statistics (1989) Washington, D.C.: U.S. Department of Labor. **P. 72, L. 34** Vermeulen, M. (1990, June 17) What people earn. *Parade,* p. 4 **P. 74, L. 24** Kline, K. (1989, May 10) Woman bank robber called a 'soft touch.' *Los Angeles Daily News.* **P. 74, L. 33** U.S. Department of Justice, Bureau of Justice Statistics. *Profile of Felons Convicted in State Courts,* (1986) NCJ-H0021 Washington, D.C.: U.S. Department of Justice (1990, January) P. 6, table 4. See also: Wiilbanks, W. (1986) Are female felons treated more leniently by the criminal justices system? *Justice Quarterly* 3(4): 519. **P. 74, L. 39** U.S. Department of Justice, Bureau of Justice Statistics *Sourcebook of Criminal Justic Statistics.* Washington, D.C.: USGPO. (1990) p. 620. **P. 75, L. 4** Ibid, p. 623. **P. 75, L. 6** U.S. Department of Justice, Federal Bureau of Investigation. *Crime in the United States.* (1987) Washington, D.C.: USGPO. 1989, p. 181. **P. 75, L. 8** Associated Press (1988) Dateline: Placerville. Two Women freed after killing mutual lover. **P. 75, L. 14** UPI (1989, October 28) Battered wife freed in killing [by Governor Booth Gardner]. *San Francisco Chronicle.* **P. 75, L. 18** New York Times staff (1990, December) Clemency granted to 25 women. Reprinted in *The Santa Rosa Press Democrat.* **P. 75, L. 29** Channel 7, 5:00 news report (1990, June 13). Killer: Terry Shapiro; Shelter: Next Door; Shelter counselors: Robin Yeaman and Linda Wilson. **P. 76, L. 16** Curtis, L. (1974) *Criminal Violence: National Patterns and Behavior.* Lexington, MA: TK. Also Steinmetz, S. (1985) Battered husbands: a historical and cross-cultural study. In Baumli (1985), pp. 203–7. **P. 76, L. 37** Roy, M., ed. (1977) *Battered Women.* New York: Van Nostrand Reinhold, pp. 63–72. **P. 77, L. 18** Gelles, R. (1974) *The Violent Home: A Study of Physical Aggression between Husbands and Wives.* Beverly Hills, CA: Sage Publications. **P. 77, L. 19** Archer, J., and Lloyd, B. (1982) *Sex and Gender.* Cambridge: Cambridge University Press. **P. 77, L. 22** Steinmetz, S. (1978) The battered husband syndrome. *Victimology* 2(3/4): 499–509. Also Steinmetz, S. (1980) Women and violence: victims and perpetrators. *American Journal of Psychotherapy* 34(3): 334–50. Adler, E. (1981) The underside of married life: power, influence and violence. In L. H. Bowker, ed., *Women and Crime in America*. New York: Macmillan, pp. 300–19.   **P. 77, L. 26**   Wilson, S. (1989, June 18) Bloodthirsty women. *San Francisco Chronicle, This World*, p. Z–5.   **P. 78, L. 11**   Gutman, D. (1987) *Reclaimed Powers: Toward a Psychology of Men and Women in Later Life*. New York: Basic Books.   **P. 78, L. 15**   Spencer, D., and Phillips, R. (1989, July 27) Vehicles for real men: macho guys now buy their masculinity. *The Washington Post*, reprinted in the *San Francisco Chronicle*.   **P. 79, L. 29**   Bly, R. (1982, May) Interview with Keith Thompson. *New Age*.   **P. 80, L. 15**   Monick, E. (1987) *Phallos: Sacred Image of the Masculine*. Toronto: Inner City Books, p. 9.   **P. 80, L. 28**   Gerzon, M. (1982) *A Choice of Heros*. Boston: Houghton Mifflin.   **P. 81, L. 36**   Lawlor, R. (1989) *Earth Honoring: The New Male Sexuality*. Rochester, VT: Park Street Press, p. 80.

CHAPTER 4

P. 94, L. 30   Dass, R. (1971) *Be Here Now*. New York: Crown Publishers.   **P. 96, L. 19**   Sununu, J. (1990, July 5) *San Francisco Chronicle*, p. A–10. Reprinted from *M* magazine.   **P. 97, L. 16**   Gilmore, D. (1990) *Manhood in the Making: Cultural Concepts of Masculinity*. New Haven: Yale University Press.   **P. 97, L. 23**   Benderly, B. (1990, April 15) The importance of being macho. *New York Times Book Review*.   **P. 97, L. 35**   (1963) *Funk and Wagnalls Standard College Dictionary Text Edition*. New York: Harcourt, Brace and World.

CHAPTER 5

P. 105, L. 16   Moore, R., and Gillette, D. (1990) *King, Warrior, Magician, Lover: Rediscovering the Archetypes of the Mature Masculine*. San Francisco: Harper.   **P. 109, L. 9**   Lovelock, J. (1979) *Gaia: A New Look at Life on Earth*. London and New York: Oxford University Press.   **P. 109, L. 30**   Monick (1987), pp. 44–45.   **P. 110, L. 14**   Downing, C. (1987) *The Goddess: Mythological Images of the Feminine*. New York: Crossroad Ave, Harrison, J. E. (1922) *Prolegomena to the Study of Greek Religion*. Cambridge: Cambridge University Press.   **P. 110, L. 39**   Meade, M. (1989, December) Personal communication.   **P. 111, L. 28**   Hillman, J. (1979) *The Dream and the Underworld*. New York: Harper and Row, p. 70.   **P. 112, L. 26**   Monick (1987), p. 11.   **P. 112, L. 38**   Lee, S. (1964) *A History of Far Eastern Art*. Englewood Cliffs, NJ: Prentice-Hall; New York: Harry N. Abrams, p. 22.   **P. 113, L. 2**   Conrad, J. (1957) *The Horn and the Sword: The History of the Bull as a Symbol of Power and Fertility*. Westport, CT: Greenwood Press.   **P. 113, L. 8**   Vanggaard, T. (1972) *Phallos: A Symbol and Its History in the Male World*. New York: International University Press, pp. 62–84.   **P. 113, L. 12**   Czaja, M. (1974) *Gods of Myth and Stone: Phallicism in Japanese Folk Religion*. New York: Weatherhill, p. 169. (These icons are from the early to middle Jamon period [5,000–2,000 B.C.]   **P. 113, L. 15**   Aston, W. (1905) *Shinto: The Way of the Gods*. London: Longmens, Green, p. 196.   **P. 113, L. 17**   Michell, J. (1963) *The New View over Atlantis*. San Francisco: Harper and Row, pp. 110–11.   **P. 113, L. 23**   Conrad (1957), p. 22.   **P. 113, L. 31**   Piggott, S. (1954) *The Neolithic Cultures of the British Isles*. Cambridge: Cambridge University Press, p. 22.   **P. 113, L. 37**   Sharkey, J. (1975) *Celtic Mysteries: The Ancient Religion*. New York: Avon Books.   **P. 114, L. 24**   Gimbutas, M. (1989) *The Language of the Goddess*. San Francisco: Harper and Row; Eisler, R. (1987) *The Chalice and the Blade*. San Francisco: Harper and Row; Stone, M. (1976) *When God Was a Woman*. New York: Harcourt Brace Jovanovich.   **P. 116, L. 27**   Gimbutas (1989).   **P. 117, L. 13**   Getty, A. (1989) Personal communications. See also Getty, A. (1990) *The Goddess: Mother of Living Nature*. London: Thames and Hudson, p. 15.   **P. 118, L. 9**   Keuls, E. (1985) *The Reign of the Phallus*. New York: Harper and Row, p. 2.   **P. 118, L. 18**   Plutarch (1957) *Moralia*. 15 vols. English trans. Frank Cole Babbit et al. London: W. Heinemann, p. 797.   **P. 119, L. 4**   Wolkstein, D., and Kramer, S. (1983) *Inanna, Queen of Heaven and Earth: Her Stories and Hymns from Sumer*. New York: Harper and Row, pp. 38–44, 75–86.   **P. 122, L. 4**   Hillman, J. (1972) *Pan and the Nightmare*. Dallas: Spring Publications, pp. 8–10.   **P. 123, L. 18**   Fadiman, J. (1988, November) Personal communication.

CHAPTER 6

P. 125, L. 4 Browning, E. (1900) "The Dead Pan." *The Complete Poetical Works of Elizabeth Barrett Browning.* Cambridge ed. New York: Houghton Mifflin. **P. 126, L. 39** Coleman, A., and Coleman, L. (1981) *Earth Father/Sky Father.* Englewood Cliffs, NJ: Prentice Hall. Reprinted (1988) with new preface as *The Father: Mythology and Changing Roles.* Wilmette, IL: Chiron Publications, p. 24. **P. 127, L. 24** Perera, S. (1982) *Descent to the Goddess: A Way of Initiation for Women.* Toronto: Inner City Books, p. 67. **P. 127, L. 29** Teish, L. (1985) *Jambalaya: The Natural Woman's Book.* San Francisco: Harper and Row, pp. 112–27. **P. 129, L. 15** Guirand, F., ed. (1959) *New Larousse Encyclopedia of Mythology.* 1989 ed. New York: Crown Publishers, p. 36. **P. 129, L. 15** Wolkstein and Kramer (1983), p. x. **P. 129, L. 23** Rush, A. (1976) *Moon, Moon.* New York: Random House; Berkeley: Moon Books, pp. 129–201. **P. 131, L. 2** Johnson, R. (1987) "Ecstacy: Understanding the Psychology of Joy" San Francisco: Harper and Row. **P. 132, L. 3** Dass, R. (1976) Personal communication. **P. 133, L. 25** Monick (1987). **P. 137, L. 1** Radin, P. (1956) *The Trickster: A Study in American Indian Mythology.* With commentaries by Karl Kerenyi and C. G. Jung. New York: Philosophical Library, pp. ix–x. **P. 137, L. 12** Campbell, J. (1988) *Mythologies of the Great Hunt,* pt. 2 of *The Way of the Animal Powers,* vol. 1 of *Historical Atlas of World Mythology.* New York: Harper and Row, p. 237. **P. 137, L. 15** Jung, CW, vol. 9, pt. 1, 472. **P. 137, L. 19** Welsch, R. (1981) *Omaha Tribal Myths and Trickster Tales.* Chicago: Swallow Press, pp. 17–20. **P. 137, L. 32** Pelton, R. (1980) *The Trickster in West Africa: A Study of Mythic Irony and Sacred Delight.* Berkeley: University of California Press, pp. 1–9. See also Ricketts, M. (1965) The North American Trickster. *History of Religions* 5:589. Lopez, B. (1977) *Giving Birth to Thunder, Sleeping with His Daughter: Coyote Builds North America.* Kansas City MO: Sheed Andrews and McMeel, p. xi. **P. 138, L. 8** Nisker, W. (1990) *Crazy Widsom.* Berkeley: Ten Speed Press, p. 7. **P. 138, L. 19** Pelton, (1980), p. 230; Jung, C. (1956) On the psychology of the trickster figure. Trans. R. F. Hull, In Radin, *The Trickster: A Study in American Indian Mythology.* New York: Philosophical Library, pp. 200–202. **P. 139, L. 8** Koller, J., Arnerr, C., Nemirow, S., and Cloud, P., eds. (1982) *Coyote's Journal.* Berkeley: Wingbow Press. **P. 139, L. 10** Grinnell, G. (1916) *Blackfoot Lodge Tales.* New York: Charles Schribner's Sons, p. 257. **P. 139, L. 17** CW, vol. 9, pt. 1, 472. **P. 140, L. 1** Jung (1956), pp. 200–202. **P. 140, L. 24** Campbell (1988), pp. 185, 239. **P. 140, L. 24** CW, vol. 14, 637. **P. 141, L. 23** Barclay, R. (1969) Apology to the true Christian divinity. In C. Hyers, *Holy Laughter: Essays on Religion in the Comic Perspective.* New York: Seabury (original publication, 1976). **P. 141, L. 24** Goldstein, J. (1987) Therapeutic effects of laughter. In W. Fry and W. Salameh, eds. *Handbook of Humor and Psychotherapy: Advance in the Clinical Use of Humor.* Sarasota, FL: Professional Resource Exchange, p. 3, 14. **P. 143, L. 8** Campbell (1988), p. 209. **P. 144, L. 3** Van Over, R., ed. (1980) *Sun Songs: Creation Myths from around the World.* New York: New American Library, p. 357. **P. 144, L. 28** Sherpa, L. (1990, February) Personal communication. **P. 145, L. 24** Pettazzoni, R. (1947) The truth of myth. In A. Dundes, ed., *Sacred Narrative: Readings in the Theory of Myth.* Berkeley: University of California Press, 1984, pp. 99–109. **P. 146, L. 28** Tripp, E. (1970) *The Meridian Handbook of Classical Mythology.* (Crowell's handbook of classical mythology) New York: New American Library, p. 443. **P. 147, L. 12** Roscher, W. (1900) *Ephialtes: A Pathological-Mythological Treatise on the Nightmare in Cassical Antiquity.* Trans. B. G. Tuebner, in Hillman, J. (1972) *Pan and the Nightmare.* (An essay on Pan) Dallas: Spring Publications, p. 156. **P. 147, L. 21** Tripp (1970), p. 443. **P. 149, L. 3** Hillman, J. (1972) *Pan and the Nightmare. (An essay on Pan)* Dallas: Spring Publications, p. 32. **P. 149, L. 22** Ibid, p. 62.

CHAPTER 7

P. 155, L. 3 MacArthur, D. (1964, April 5) *New York Times.* **P. 159, L. 24** Diamond, M. (1986) Becoming a father: a psycholanalytic perspective. In R. Friedman and L. Lerner, eds., *Toward a New Psychology of Men: Psycholanalytic and Social Perspectives* (Winter 1986). New York: Guilford Press, pp. 445–68. Reprinted from: *The Psycholanalytic Review* 73. **P. 159, L. 33** Lacan, J. (1978) *The Four Fundamentals of Psychoanalysis.* Ed, J. Miller; trans., A. Sheridan. New York: Norton. Also R. Con Davis, ed. (1981) *The Fictional Father: Lacanian Readings of the Text.* Amherst: University of Massachusetts Press.

P. 160, L. 9 Winnicott, D. (1971) *Therapeutic Consultation in Child Psychiatry.* New York: Basic Books, p. xiv. **P. 160, L. 23** Kohut, H., and Wolf, E. (1978) The disorders of the self and their treatment: an outline. *International Journal of Psychoanalysis* 59: 417–20. **P. 160, L. 42** Bly, R. (1990) *Iron John: A Book about Men.* Reading, MA: Addison-Wesley. **P. 170, L. 20** Shakespeare, W. *Hamlet,* 1.2:22. ed. G. Hubbard (1987) Oxford: Clarendon Press; New York: Oxford University Press. **P. 171, L. 11** Gardner, B. (1989) Presentation of feminist perspectives on *Hamlet.* Carpinteria, CA: Pacifica Graduate Institute. **P. 172, L. 15** Johnson, R. (1991) "Transformation: Understanding the three levels of masculine consciousness" San Francisco: Harper and Row. **P. 172, L. 26** Shakespeare, *Hamlet,* 1.2. 230–32; 3.4 63–64. **P. 173, L. 8** Ibid, 1.2:70. **P. 174, L. 11** Ovid. (1955) *Metamorphosis* Trans. Mary M. Innes. Baltimore: Penguin Books, pp. 496–526. **P. 174, L. 22** Harrison, J. E. (1927) *Themis: A Study of the Social Origins of Greek Religion.* Cleveland; World Publishing Company, pp. 19–20.

CHAPTER 8

P. 183, L. 27 Dowling, C. (1981) *The Cinderella Complex: Women's Hidden Fear of Independence.* New York: Summit Books. **P. 194, L. 13** Yankelovich, D. (1974) The meaning of work. In J. Rosow, ed., *The Worker and the Job.* Englewood Cliffs, NJ: Prentice-Hall.

CHAPTER 9

P. 201, L. 3 Spenser, E. (1596; 1979) *The Oxford Dictionary of Quotations.* 3rd ed. Oxford: Oxford University Press, p. 516:8 **P. 203, L. 1** Kushner, H. (1990) *When All You've Ever Wanted Isn't Enough.* New York: Summit Books. **P. 203, L. 6** Felder, L. (1989) *A Fresh Start: How to Let Go of Emotional Baggage and Enjoy Your Life Again.* New York: New American Library/Signet. **P. 203, L. 32** SA, p 81. **P. 205, L. 19** Sterns, P. (1979) *Be a Man: Males in Modern Society.* New York: Holmes and Meier, pp. 39–58. Also Dubbert, J. (1979) *A Man's Place: Masculinity in Transition.* Englewood Cliffs, NJ: Prentice-Hall. **P. 205, L. 41** Gutman, (1987), p. 49. **P. 212, L. 32** CW, vol. 12, 439. **P. 212, L. 35** Hillman, J. (1975) *Re-visioning Psychology.* New York: Harper and Row, p. 206. **P. 212, L. 42** Tripp (1970). **P. 213, L. 1** Boer (1970), p. 90. **P. 213, L. 2** Bolen, J. (1989) *Gods in Every Man: A New Psychology of Men's Lives and Loves.* San Francisco: Harper and Row, p. 110. **P. 213, L. 25** Castaneda, C. (1971) *A Separate Reality: Further Conversations with Don Juan.* New York: Simon and Schuster, p. 107. **P. 213, L. 37** Walker, B. (1983) *The Woman's Encyclopedia of Myths and Secrets.* San Francisco: Harper and Row, p. 215. **P. 214, L. 7** Hillman, J. (1979) *The Dream and the Underworld.* New York: Harper and Row, pp. 38,35. **P. 215, L. 12** Boer (1970), pp. 91–135. **P. 216, L. 1** Hyde, R. (1977) *Hades and the Soul.* Master's thesis. Rohnert Park, CA: University of California Press, p. 8. **P. 216, L. 29** Ovid (1955), p. 136. **P. 217, L. 10** Levine, S. (1982) *Who Dies?* Garden City, NJ: Anchor Press, p. 205. **P. 218, L. 1** Hyde (1977), p. 16. **P. 219, L. 34** Homer (1974), *The Odyssey.* Trans. A. Murry. Cambridge: Harvard University Press, 11:489–91. **P. 220, L. 3** Bly, R. (1988) Personal communication and audiotape. **P. 222, L. 31** Levine (1982), p. 148.

CHAPTER 10

P. 230, L. 8 Thompson, K. (1986, April/May) A man need a lodge. *Utne Reader.* **P. 230, L. 14** Druck, K. (1985) *Secrets Men Keep.* New York: Doubleday. **P. 230, L. 33** Logan, D. (1985) Some thought about my feelings. In F. Baumli, ed. *Men Freeing Men.* New York: New Atlantic Press, p. 19. **P. 240, L. 14** Hart, M. (1991) *Drumming at the Edge of Magic.* San Francisco: Harper Books. **P. 240, L. 22** Bly, C. (1989, November/December) The danger in men's groups, *Utne Reader* 36: 59. **P. 244, L. 20** "Newsweek" (Jan. 24, 1991) p. 50. **P. 246, L. 17** Eisler, R., and Loye, D. (1990) *The Partnership Way: New Tools for Living and Learning, Healing Our Families, Our Communities, and Our World.* San Francisco: Harper.

CHAPTER 11

P. 249, L. 3 Mead, M. (1949) *Male and Female: A Study of the Sexes in a Changing World.* New York: William Morrow, p. 30. **P. 251, L. 3** Cambell, A., with Converse, P., and Rogers, W. (1975) The American way of mating: marriage si, children only maybe. *Psychology Today.* 8: 37–43; Speitzer, E., Snyder, E., and Larson, D. (1975) Age, marital status, and labor-force participation as related to life satisfaction. *Sex Roles* 1:235–47. **P. 251, L. 8** SA, p. 85 **P. 251, L. 32** Freud, S. (1924–1950) *Collected Papers.* 5 vols., trans. various. London: Hogarth Press. **P. 252, L. 26** Diamond (1986). **P. 252, L. 2** Horney, K. (1967) "The distrust between the sexes." In Harold Kelman (ed) "Feminine Psychology" New York: W. W. Norton and Co. Inc. pp. 107–18. **P. 252, L. 23** Lacan, (1978). **P. 252, L. 33** Bem, S. (1974) The measurement of psychological androgyny. *Journal of Personality and Social Psychology* 42:155–62. **P. 253, L. 3** Monick (1987), pp. 9–10, 53. **P. 253, L. 12** Hillman (1985) *Anima: An Anatomy of a Personified Notion.* Dallas: Spring Publications, p. 61. **P. 253, L. 20** CW, vol. 9, pt. 1, pp. 20–42. **P. 253, L. 28** Neumann, E. (1963) *The Great Mother: Analysis of the Archetype.* trans. Ralph Manheim. Bollingen Series XLVII. Princeton: Princeton University Press, pp. 25–26. **P. 253, L. 38** Hillman (1985), p. 13. **P. 254, L. 15** Berry, P. (1982) *Echo's Subtle Body.* Dallas: Spring Publications. **P. 254, L. 16** Ponce, C. (1988) *Working the Soul: Reflections on Jungian Psychology.* Berkeley: North Atlantic Books, p. 34. **P. 254, L. 22** Moore and Gillette (1990). **P. 254, L. 31** Hoyenga, K. B., and Hoyenga, K. T. (1979) *The Question of Sex Differences: Psychological, Cultural and Biological Issues.* Boston: Little, Brown, p. 358. **P. 256, L. 3** SA, p. 147. **P. 256, L. 8** SA, p. 152. **P. 257, L. 30** Divoky, Dl. (1989, April) Ritalin: education's fix-it drug? *Phi Delta Kappan* 70:599–605. **P. 257, L. 34** Whalen, C., and Henker, B., eds. (1980) *Hyperactive Children: The Social Ecology of Identification and Treatment.* New York: Academic Press, p. 4. Also Ross, M., and Ross, S. (1982) *Hyperactivity: Current Issues, Research, and Theory.* New York: John Wiley and Sons, p. 3. **P. 258, L. 10** Edell, D. (1990, November 28) Newscast. Channel 7. San Francisco. **P. 260, L. 4** Sexton, P. (1969) *The Feminized Male: Classroom, White Collars and the Decline of Manliness.* New York: Random House. **P. 260, L. 36** Montagu (1971). **P. 261, L. 13** Holloway, R., and de Lacoste-Utamsing, C. (1982, June 25) Sexual dimorphism in the human corpus callosum. *Science* 216: 1431. **P. 261, L. 18** Witelson, S. (1989, April 12) Study submitted for publication to *Brain.* Quoted in Goleman, D. Brains of men, woman differ; findings hold great potential. *New York Times.* Reprinted in *San Francisco Chronicle.* **P. 261, L. 23** Geschwind, N. (1979) Specializations of the human brain. *Scientific American* 241 (3): 180–99. **P. 261, L. 28** Goleman (1989, April 12), p. B-5. **P. 265, L. 27** Mehrabian, A. (1971) Verbal and nonverbal interactions of strangers in a waiting station. *Research in Personality* 5: 127–38. **P. 265, L. 31** Jones, S. E. (1971) A comparative proxemics analysis of dyadic interaction in selected subcultures of New York City. *Journal of Social Psychology* 84: 34–44. **P. 265, L. 33** Fisher, J., and Bryne, D. (1975) Too close for comfort: sex differences in response to invasions of personal space. *Journal of Personality and Social Psychology* 32: 15–21; Krail, K., and Leventhal, G. (1976) The sex variable in the intrusion of personal space. *Sociometry* 39: 170–73. **P. 265, L. 39** Guardo, C., and Meisels, M. (1971) Factor structure of children's personal space schemata. *Child Development* 42: 1307–12. **P. 266, L. 1** Sommer, R. (1974) Studies in personal space. *Sociometry* 37: 423–31. **P. 266, L. 9** Exline, R. (1972) Visual interaction: the glances of power and preference. In J. K. Cole, ed., *Nebraska Symposium on Motivation,* 1971, Lincon: University of Nebraska Press, pp. 163–206. **P. 266, L. 12** Kleinke, C., et al. (1973) Effects of self-attributed and other-attributed gaze on interpersonal evaluations between males and females. *Journal of Experimental Social Psychology* 9: 154–63. **P. 266, L. 17** Deaux, K. (1976) *The Behavior of Women and Men.* Belmont, CA: Brooks-Cole; Key, M. (1975) *Male/Female Language.* Metuchen, NJ: Scarecrow Press; Bugental, D., Love, L., and Gianetto, R. (1971) Perfidious feminine faces. *Journal of Personality and Social Psychology* 17: 314–18. **P. 266, L. 23** Argyle, M., Lalljee, J., and Cook, M. (1968) The effects of visibility on interaction in a dyad. *Psychological Record* 26: 3–17. **P. 266, L. 30** Tannen, D. (1990) *You Just Don't Understand: Women and Men in Conversation.* New York: William Morrow, pp. 246,268–69. **P. 267, L. 15** Ibid, p. 121. **P. 267, L. 24** Marino, T. (1979) Resensitizing men: a male perspective. *Personnel and Guidance Journal* 58: 102–5. **P. 267, L. 32** Scher, M. (1979) On counseling men. *Personnel and Guidance Journal* 57: 252–55. **P. 267, L. 39** Cook, E. (1985) *Psychological Androgyny.*

New York: Pergamon Press. **P. 268, L. 13** Downing, N. (1981, March) Counseling men: issues for female counselors. Paper presented at the annual convention of the American College Personnel Association, Cincinnati, OH; Carlson, R. (1981) Male client, female therapist. *Personnel and Guidance Journal* 60: 228–31. **P. 268, L. 19** Hoyenga and Hoyenga (1979), pp. 309–11, 348. **P. 268, L. 22** Scher M. (1981) Men in hiding: a challenge for the counseler. *Personnel and Guidance Journal* 60: 199–202. **P. 269, L. 35** Stein, L., del Gaudio, A., and Ansley, M. (1976) A comparison of female and male neurotic depressives. *Journal of Clinical Psychology* 32: 19–21. **P. 269, L. 37** Winokur, G. (1973) The types of affective disorders. *Journal of Nervous and Mental Disease* 156: 82–96. **P. 269, L. 39** Doherty, E. (1976) Length of hospitalization in a short-term therapeutic community: a multivariate study by sex across time. *Archives of General Psychiatry* 33: 87–92. **P. 269, L. 40** Keskiner, A., et al. (1973) Advantages of being female in psychiatric rehabilitation. *Archives of General Psychiatry* 28: 689–92. **P. 270, L. 3** Distler, L., May, P., Tuma, A (1964) Anxiety and ego strength as predictors of response to treatment in schizophrenic patients. *Journal of Consulting Psychology* 28: 170–77. **P. 270, L. 5** Kesey, K. (1962) *One Flew over the Cuckoo's Nest*. New York: Penguin Books. **P. 270, L. 36** Bear, S., et al. (1979) Even cowboys sing the blues: difficulties experienced by men trying to adopt nontraditional sex roles and how clinicians can be helpful to them. *Sex Roles* 5: 191–98. **P. 271, L. 15** Mitchel, J., ed. (1987) *The Selected Meline Kline*. New York: Freedom Press, p. 210. **P. 271, L. 20** Winnicott, D. (1958) *Collected Papers: Through Pediatrics to Psychoanalysis*. New York: Basic Books, p. 297. **P. 271, L. 37** Kline, M. (1975) *The Psycho-Analysis of Children*. Trans. Alix Strachey. New York: Dell Publishing Company, pp. 136, 243–46, 254. **P. 272, L. 28** Winnicott, D. (1971) *Therapeutic Consultation in Child Psychiatry*. New York: Basic Books, p. 10. **P. 273, L. 39** *Sourcebook of Criminal Justice Statistics* (1988). Washington, D.C.: U.S. Department of Justice, Bureau of Justice Statistics. p. 492. Also SA; California Department of Corrections, Offender Information Services Branch. *Offence groups of felons in California prisons.* 1985–1987. Table N–1. **P. 274, L. 20** Pennebaker, J. (1982) *The Psychology of Physical Symptoms*. New York: Springer-Verlag; Kessler, R., Brown R., and Broman, C. (1981) Sex differences in psychiatric help seeking: evidence from four large surveys. *Journal of Health and Behavior* 22: 49–64. **P. 274, L. 25** Cooperstock, R. (1979) A review of women's psychotropic drug use. *Canadian Journal of Psychiatry* 24: 29–33; Cooperstock, R. (1976) Women and psychotropic drugs. In A. MacLennan, ed. *Women: Their Use of Alcohol and Other Legal Drugs*. Toronto: Alcoholism and Drug Addiction Research Foundation of Ontario, pp. 83–111. **P. 274, L. 27** Brahen, S. (1973). Housewife drug abuse. *Journal of Drug Education* 3: 13–24; Cooperstock, R. (1978) Sex differences in psychotropic drug use. *Social Science and Medicine* 12B: 170–86; Parry, D., et al. (1974) Increasing alcohol intake as a coping mechanism for psychic distress. In R. Cooperstock, ed., *Social Aspects of the Medical Use of Psychotropic Drugs*. Toronto: Alcoholism and Drug Addiction Research Foundation of Ontario. **P. 275, L. 9** *Sourcebook of Criminal Justice Statistics* (1988), p. 492. California Department of Corrections, Offender Information Services Branch. *Offence groups of felons in California prisons.* 1985–1987. Table N–1. **P. 275, L. 23** Cahill, (1990)